A Silent Prayer

A PRAYER SERIES I

Samreen Ahsan

iUniverse

A SILENT PRAYER
A Prayer Series I

This is a work of fiction. All of the characters, names, incidents, organizations, and dialogue in this novel are either the products of the author's imagination or are used fictitiously.

iUniverse books may be ordered through booksellers or by contacting:

iUniverse LLC
1663 Liberty Drive
Bloomington, IN 47403
www.iuniverse.com
1-800-Authors (1-800-288-4677)

Because of the dynamic nature of the Internet, any web addresses or links contained in this book may have changed since publication and may no longer be valid. The views expressed in this work are solely those of the author and do not necessarily reflect the views of the publisher, and the publisher hereby disclaims any responsibility for them.

The cover image has been taken from Shutterstock.com

ISBN: 978-1-4917-2037-0 (sc)
ISBN: 978-1-4917-2039-4 (hc)
ISBN: 978-1-4917-2038-7 (e)

Library of Congress Control Number: 2014900456

Printed in the United States of America.

iUniverse rev. date: 02/03/2014

TABLE OF CONTENTS

PREFACE

Our whole world is an inspiration. God's creativity is marked everywhere, in the colors of the sky, the landscapes, the waters, the humans, the angels, the demons; each element is stamped by the Almighty. The only Divine existence, who knows everything from the beginning till the end. The one who moves the Earth from day to night, and night to day. The one who decides our life and death. The one who has created time.

Each story, every book, motivates me. But in this story, the inspiration has been taken from *Arabian Nights*, City of Toronto, City of Edmonton, Via Rail, Adobe® and the Holy Qur'an. The characters in the book are purely fictional. Any resemblance to real persons, living or dead, is purely coincidental.

AUTHOR'S NOTE:

The book starts with the male character's point of view, symbolized by ♂, and the next chapter is from the female character's point of view, symbolized by ♀. Chapter by chapter, the point of view alternates between the characters, so that the reader has the advantage of learning what both characters are thinking and feeling.

ACKNOWLEDGEMENTS

I sincerely thank all my friends for their tremendous support. This is the first time I have created a book from the fabric of my imagination, but I thoroughly enjoyed writing it. I dedicate my work to my parents, who have given me immeasurable love and lots of room for my wild imagination since childhood. Everything I am is because of them. Special thanks to my friend, Ammara for designing the beautiful cover for the book. Her creativity means a lot to me. I would also like to mention my editor, Lauren Sweet, who has worked really hard to make this book worth reading for all of you. And finally, my husband, without whose support this work would have never been possible. His unconditional love, care and patience is what makes this effort worthwhile.

I hope everyone enjoys the book.

Bonne lecture!

Samreen Ahsan.

AN ENCOUNTER

♂

February 2012

"No deal. I'm sorry, but what you ask is impossible," I say.

I'm having an uncomfortable business dinner in a fancy French restaurant located in an old district of downtown Toronto. The restaurant is filled with people engrossed in each other, talking about their own worlds and their problems. I wonder at the fact that each human has his own story to tell; everyone has a past, a present and a future to look forward to. For me, the past is something I never want to dig into, my present is an open book to the public, and my future—I've never thought about it.

"Come on, Gibson, you've built half of Toronto, and you're saying this hotel project is not possible? Have you suddenly decided you no longer want to make money?" Xavier Groston is a tall man in his late forties, a businessman who knows how to make the best out of the worst situation. That's what makes him a god in the construction business on the American West Coast. To him, everything starts and ends with money and power; his advice to everyone: never give your heart to someone you are expecting something from—the chances are greater for failure.

"Mr. Groston, I understand your situation, but the property you are interested in has been given to the local community center. Every day, needy people go there to eat and sleep, to receive food and clothing donations. Now you want me to kick them out?"

I'm quite frustrated with this meeting. This business tycoon wants me to demolish the community center and its surroundings and build a five-star hotel on it. The man is either much too mercenary, or he's drunk. I understand his aggressiveness; the property is a prime location for a hotel, and it would bring both of us money and more business. But this is not about money. Over the past five years, poor and homeless people have found a safe place at the community center, regardless of any religion, caste or creed. I confess that I'm not a religious person at all but this is something I can't play with; even being an atheist, I still have some fragments of reverence. I gave my word to the mayor of Toronto and the people of the community that the property would be theirs to use. Now Mr. Groston is asking me to destroy my credibility and take back my so-called altruistic donation.

"I can offer you better properties, Mr. Groston, all around Ontario," I say. "My agents know the province really well and I am sure they will come up with the best deal in town, which would be fruitful for both of us." I try to distract this stubborn man, but he fails to acknowledge me.

"So you are refusing my proposition. You cannot relocate this center anywhere else?" Groston doesn't seem to wish to end this meeting.

"Mr. Groston, as much as I intend to do business with you, I protect my own reputation as well. You may own half of the West Coast and millions of dollars' worth of properties, but the Canadian market is quite different. That community center serves hundreds of people every day—not just providing food and shelter, but a venue for community and religious activities. In fact, without it, many poor people and senior citizens in the area would have no place to attend religious services. In America, it may be the almighty dollar that rules, but here in Canada we try to remember that communities are for the people that live in them, not merely for those who make money off them." My empathic values with *O Canada* are finally coming out. "My property agents will call you tomorrow, to show you some of the finest properties in all of Ontario, but I'm afraid this one is not available."

Mr. Xavier Groston finally leaves, agreeing to look at some other properties, though I know he still wants this one. I stand up with him and shake hands at his departure, then sit back down for a while, thinking about his proposal. It would make a lot of money, but sometimes other things are far more valuable. On that Canada Day five years back when some seniors had approached me about land for the center, I had only the huge property that I had purchased to build a five-star hotel. Out of nowhere, a sense of humanitarianism had emerged in me and I had donated the property. That land is still under my name; no one ever got a chance to get it changed. So legally, I could do as I liked with it, including building Groston's hotel project. But people trust me and I don't want to break their trust. I wouldn't say that I'm an unpretentious person, but I am loyal to my work. Anything I do or commit to, I stick to it.

I look around the restaurant. This was one of the earliest construction projects that my company had done. It was an early nineteenth-century building, and I'm proud that we preserved its original beauty. It reminds me of an old restaurant in Marseille where I once had dinner with a client. Like that restaurant, this one features complete French architecture with lights embedded in the brick walls, and accented with antique furniture. The interior centers on the huge Swarovski chandelier, and one can see the perfection in the artwork that covers the ceiling—an early medieval-era handpainted work, displaying deceased kings and queens. The lights fixed on the walls give the impression of a castle's lanterns, but are modern fixtures. The tables and chairs are made of old dark wood, most likely imported from France to provide the feel of a castle's dining area. I look at my wine glass and close my eyes to concentrate on the music—a song of a man declaring his love to a woman.

How could a woman change a man's heart like that?

I finally leave the restaurant, which is on the top floor. The building has six levels, each with a different kind of business, all earning well. *That's the reason they give me their rent on time*, I think, and smile to myself. I look around for the elevator and get a glimpse of a fire door to the stairs. Somehow, my heart tells me to go down that way. But when I open the door, I notice that there are stairs going up to a higher level. *I thought the restaurant was on the top floor.* It has been a long time since I renovated this building—did it have stairway access to the roof? Even though it's crazy to go out on a rooftop in snowy February weather, I go up the stairs anyway. Outside, there is a wonderful view of the Toronto night skyline. I notice that there's a lot of junk piled on the rooftop, looking like no one has moved it for ages. I look out at the lakeshore on one side and the CN tower and more high-rises on the other. The view is worth standing in the cold, and I'm glad I came up.

As I stare out over the city, a sound catches my attention. It's music, but not the music from the restaurant. It's magical-sounding. I try to determine where it's coming from. There is another building connected to this one, sharing the same wall. This is quite common in our city, similar to a semi-detached house. The barrier between my roof and theirs is low, and I climb over and jump down, getting my clothes wet. The music is getting clearer. I see a door and head toward it. It feels like it has not been opened for years; in fact, like no one has ever opened it at all. I struggle with the rusted knob and finally get it to turn and open the door. I am expecting another set of fire stairs, but instead there is a passage. There is nothing to the right or left and I follow the passage; or rather, I follow the magical music.

The sound of the music is so warm and comforting that I realize I am not feeling cold anymore. I take a few more steps and what I see freezes me, just like the weather outside. There are no doors, no stairs in this piece of architecture. It's nothing but a spiral passage leading down to ground level. I look down to the bottom and my heart comes into my throat. A girl is dancing to the music. From here on the sixth level I can't see her face clearly, but the way she moves takes my breath away. I feel as if the dance and the music are casting a spell on me. The girl is lost in her dance, not caring about anyone watching her. I see the shadows of other people dancing with her, but since the light is on her, I am unable to see more than shadowy figures. For the first time in my life, I feel my soul is pulling me . . . toward her.

I start walking down that spiral passage. The music becomes clearer and melts in my ears, in my body, in my soul. I have never heard of anything like this. How can mere humans create such a heartwarming composition? I am on the second-to-last level and able to see her more clearly. She is dancing like an angel, something truly celestial. She seems to be dressed for a masquerade, in an ankle-length pink chiffon dress with a mask over her eyes. It seems like she is not carrying any weight; she is a light dove borne away by the wind. Then, I see one shadow lifting her up in the air and she swirls around with the lights and music. It is impossible to take in. I can still see the shadows dancing with her, but I don't see any physical dancers except her. *Did I drink too much tonight?* I think to myself. *Why can't I see the other people? Surely they must be behind the lights.*

I feel I must see the girl more closely, meet her, let her know how amazing she is when she dances. It is very unlike me, chasing after a girl. From within, my subconscious is yelling not to go against my assuetude. I ignore it and keep moving. *Why can't I take my eyes off her?* This has never happened to me before. Or perhaps, I have never seen anyone like her. The intensity of the music augments my fascination. Under the colorful lights, she moves like a flower in the wind, flying like rainbow colors after a beautiful rain. I realize I've now reached her level, and I see that she is dancing alone.

Where did the other people go, whose shadows I saw from the top?

I look back to her, admiring her body and all her movements. The violins behind me accelerate, and so does her body. She moves round and round with the music, unaware of my presence until all of a sudden, she crashes against me. I hold her by her waist tightly to give her support. The music stops, and so does her dance. She is trying to catch her breath, her breasts moving and touching my chest as the air fills her lungs. Our eyes meet. Under the pink mask, her big eyes, darker than ebony, catch my attention. She looks at me as if she is looking directly through my soul. The madness in her eyes rips my existence and peels off my flesh and bone to search my soul. The darkness in them draws me to let her devour my presence, insanely and willingly.

I haven't been dancing, but my heart is keeping pace with hers. Her lips are rose pink and I deeply feel the urge to kiss them, to find out if they are actually as soft as they look. Her fragrance is diffusing in me like a drug, slowly and venomously. Never have I scented such a perfume, one that could take me to another world where there is no pain, where only pleasure exists.

I want to touch her skin, but its softness and tenderness scares me in a way I have never experienced. Instead of touching her, I raise my hand to take the mask off of her beautiful face, wondering if it is as perfect underneath as it looks. She backs off and releases herself from my grip. The lights grow dimmer. The music fades. It is just me and her, staring at each other in consternation. I watch her stepping back, but cannot follow her; it's as if my feet are frozen to the ground and I cannot move at all.

I see her pick up her bag and look back at me, and then she leaves me in the darkness that she has cast on me with her one last look.

I stand there numb, not sure for how long.

What was that?

Where are the others who were dancing with her? Where was the music coming from, when there is no sound system here? Where was the light coming from, when there is only one light fixture behind me? There is certainly no one else here now. What I saw from above was either my imagination, or a hallucination. I wonder if the girl was real too, or just a part of my wild imaginings.

No, Gibson, you didn't imagine this woman. You are far too practical. Women come to you. You don't go after them and you do not imagine things.

I rush out of the spiral structure to catch my breath. Inside my body, my heart is skipping from one place to another. I feel like I have caught a really high fever. My body is trembling, and I can't even stand properly on my own feet. I lean on one of the bike stands that are fixed at the corner of the walkway. A cold rain is falling, and I realize I will definitely catch a fever if I stand here much longer.

I turn around to look back, and I'm flabbergasted. There is no spiral structure behind me. It twists my mind completely, wondering where I saw that beautiful girl, and where I came out from. All the practical solutions are coming to my mind now. I had a phone with a camera; why didn't I video her while she was dancing?

I had never seen such an alluring woman in my entire life. A refinement that surpasses all levels of beauty and grace. An artistic existence so pure that even the angels would envy it. How could someone make your heart beat so fast, without even touching, without even kissing, without even making love? The urge to see her again is unexplainable.

I haven't hesitated to talk to people my entire life but this woman struck me mute, as by a lightning bolt from above. I have never felt so helpless. Thinking of her as I head toward home, my heart calls out William Wordsworth's poem:

She was a phantom of delight
When first she gleamed upon my sight;
A lovely Apparition, sent
To be a moment's ornament;
Her eyes as stars of Twilight fair;
Like Twilight's, too, her dusky hair;
But all things else about her drawn
From May-time and the cheerful Dawn;
A dancing Shape, an Image gay,
To haunt, to startle, and way-lay.

ONE FINE DAY

♀

November 2012

It's 6:15 a.m. and my phone alarm wakes me up from a deep sleep. I'm tired, and put my alarm to snooze. Then suddenly I remember that today, I'm not going to my office. I have been invited to a breakfast meeting at Gibson Enterprises headquarters on King Street.

Shit.

I forgot to check the subway route last night. The thought of it drives sleep from my head; I get up and head to the washroom. I come out in no time and blow my long hair dry. *I definitely need a haircut in winter.* This drying process takes a long time in the mornings.

I finish my morning prayers in ten minutes and dress for work. I haven't even decided what to wear. I have never attended a breakfast meeting, except those in my office. I wasn't sure why I'd been invited to this one—my boss hadn't told me much. But as a senior Creative Designer for Greenway Advertising, I couldn't skip it, and I had to look professional. I settle on a long navy-blue sweater dress with matching tights.

Born and brought up in Beirut, I have collected all the usual values of Muslim families. Offering my prayers on time. Not exposing my body parts for men's attention. Remaining reserved from strangers. And most importantly, no sexual relationships outside marriage. I am not really a perfect Muslim girl, though. I do not cover my head with a scarf; I believe that modesty lies within your heart and not in your appearance. Although I am

Lebanese, I have inherited all of my mother's Egyptian features: dark eyes, black hair, clear skin. I don't find myself very attractive, so I do not understand why men keep offering me relationships and friendships that I am not interested in. Do I have an "available" sign on my forehead?

Not anymore.

I shift my mind from past to present, as this is not the right time to dig up old memories. I am seven seas away from that old misery. I give myself some final touches and look one last time in the mirror before leaving. Taking my necessary stuff—my bag, phone, umbrella and jacket—I lock my apartment and take the elevator. My apartment is on the sixteenth floor of a high-rise condominium on Yonge Street, very close to the Finch subway station. I simply adore my neighborhood. Everything is very close to my place—the theaters, restaurants, subway station, and the mall. Just outside my building is a bakery where I always buy breakfast. They sell the best pumpkin bread.

It is really cold outside, even without snow. I open my umbrella to avoid the November rain and walk toward the station, listening to music through my earbuds. As usual, the station is overcrowded, though many people take off on Fridays. I check the map to see which route will take me to King Street and pull out the address of Gibson Enterprises headquarters to verify which will be the closest station. I usually enjoy walking, but not in winter.

The train comes in plenty of time, and I find a seat, pull out my Kindle and start reading. The story is interesting—a girl with time travel power. I am enjoying it, even though I don't believe in such a thing. The past always ends. It cannot be reincarnated. Only if God wants it to be. He is the creator of the Universe. If He can create the time, He can also bring it back or take it to the future. There is nothing impossible in His hands.

Can He erase my nightmares? I do not doubt His abilities, but if everything is possible for Him, why doesn't He consider my appeal? I tell myself that everything has its own time. Maybe my time has not come. My mind shifts back to my book and I start reading again.

When I reach my destination, I exit the station and notice that it is not raining anymore. I walk down the entire block and see the Gibson Enterprises sign on the opposite side of the street. It is a

SAMREEN AHSAN

tremendously tall building, fifty stories at least, touching the skies above. Outside the building is an ostentatious stone and marble entry with the company's name etched on it. It makes me smile, wondering how much money has been spent just to carve the marble. As I continue toward the main entrance, my bag gets stuck on one of the decorative bolts sticking out of the wall. Everything spills out of it like spring showers.

Damn! Why do things like this always happen to me? And always in the wrong place? I free the strap on my bag and begin to pick up my belongings.

Thank God it's not raining, otherwise my Kindle would have been soaked by now. I realize someone is gazing down at me intently, and I look up to meet the most beautiful dark green eyes I have ever come across. I look away and continue picking things up, cursing my handbag and the decorative bolts and wondering why the hell he is not helping me pick up the stuff. I look up again and the emerald eyes are still on me, apparently dumbfounded. They are not just eyes; they are like two precious gemstones with all four Cs: Color, which is composing my soul, Cut, which is ripping my clothes off to expose me, Clarity, as if he is looking through me, and Crystal, like he is an open book, with nothing to hide. Each emotion is visible from his eyes. As if he has not seen anyone like me. As if I am the only woman on this planet at this very moment.

Or is he enjoying my misery?

I get up and look at his blank face, then head to the door.

We were told two days ago that since the main office of Greenway Advertising is also located somewhere in this building, we are authorized to go through the turnstile by swiping our badges. I check the time: 8:55 a.m., still five minutes to the start of the meeting. I would have arrived early if not for the bolts. I reach the turnstile and slip my hand in the front pocket of my bag where I always keep my badge.

It's not there. *Damn! Where is it? Did I lose it when I dropped everything?*

I curse myself and turn back so as not to block other people coming through. My body slams into a tall strong masculine form, causing me to lose my balance. He holds me tightly by my waist. I meet those amazing eyes again as he swipes the badge and propels me through the Plexiglas door into the building.

Whoa! What was that?

He releases me and I see a silent smile curving his lips. He has not spoken yet. The security guards are looking at me with 'it's okay' expressions on their faces. *What kind of security do they have here?* I am here for the first time and they let the green-eyed man bring me through the high-security door without any questions. Why didn't they check his ID?

He finally condescends to speak, hiding his smile. "You dropped this when you were struggling with the bolts." He hands me my badge.

So you were enjoying the sight and didn't have the courtesy to give it to me earlier?

"Thank you for picking it up for me." I don't hide the sarcasm in my voice. I leave the doorway, as people are passing through the turnstile and it is not appropriate to stand here and gaze at this alluring man. I move toward the elevator and take out my phone to confirm where the breakfast meeting is actually happening. The invite says "The Maple Room," but not where it is located. I read the email again and again to make sure I am not missing the floor number. *I should ask the management or those guards if they know.*

"You look lost. May I help you?" I look up from my phone and meet those green eyes again. This time he is actually smiling. His bright shiny teeth look like they belong in a toothpaste commercial. For the first time, I notice that he is not only the owner of beautiful emerald eyes but he has a charming physique—the kind of guy who can seduce a girl with his sexy body. Along with a beautiful smile and magical eyes, he has a really charming face with a little bit of stubble, but very neatly trimmed. He is *hot*. Just like a Hollywood celebrity.

Control yourself, Rania.

I put my diva back to sleep again. He is still looking at me for a response.

"You work here?" *What am I asking?* Of course he works here; the guards know him, that's why they let him in without question.

He closes his eyes for a moment and opens them, smirking at me. "Yes, Miss Rania, I . . . work here."

Oh! He knows my name.

"I read your name from the badge you dropped."

I'm glad he told me before I asked how he knew. "Okay, that is good to know. Then you can tell me where the Maple Room is. I am already running late and my meeting invite does not show me the floor number."

"The Maple Room?" he asks, as if hearing it for the first time.

"Yes, Maple Room. You know where it is?" I am not sure if he is sure or not.

He closes his eyes once again for a moment. "Yes, I know where it is. I can take you there." He is looking at me as if searching for something. No man has ever looked at me like that. I feel his gaze traveling down through my heart, unlocking all the doors, straight to my soul.

"Well thanks, Mr . . . . ?" I don't know his name.

"Adam," he says.

"Thank you very much, Mr. Adam, but if you can tell me on which floor it is located, I can go by myself. I am sure you have work to do and you could be late because of me. I don't want your boss to get annoyed at you."

And I am old enough to find the room myself if you just tell me the damn floor.

"No, Rania, I don't have anything particular to do right now. I can take you to your meeting. Consider it my pleasure." He speaks very warmly and scrutinizes me from head to toe. It makes me self-conscious and I shift, taking a half step away. *What's his problem?* But I'm already late and I don't want to start an argument.

"Thanks for your help. I really appreciate it." I have to say something nice, and this is the best I can do at the moment. I put my finger on the elevator call button.

"SHIT." *Shit.*

We both speak together. Our hands meet on the call button, my hand over his, and I feel a sudden spark as if thousands of watts are surging in my neurons. *Why did he say the same thing I did?* Did he feel the same ignition? We both take a step back. *What was I thinking?* If he was supposed to show me the room then it was obvious he should call the elevator.

Embarrassed, I say a silent prayer to either disappear from here, or give him amnesia for a while.

Ting.

The elevator door opens and we both step in, trying not to get electrocuted any further by each other's touch. I had not noticed that there are others standing behind us, waiting for the elevator.

The elevator starts to fill up and he shifts to stand behind me. I can't see him, but I still hear him breathing. His heart is beating like a drum and I can hear it very clearly. *Or is it my heart?* I can't tell. The elevator goes up, stopping at each level, people getting on and off. Every person entering the elevator smiles at the man behind me. *So people do know him here.*

By the time we reach the 45th floor, the elevator is empty except for the two of us. One wall of the elevator is glass, and I can see his reflection. His eyes are closed, as if he is trying to feel something. He is still breathing hard. He opens his eyes and looks up into my eyes through the reflection. I think I broke his concentration.

"We have almost reached the top. You have forgotten to press the button. Which floor is it?" I say very politely, trying not to dominate the situation.

He moves his head closer, behind my neck. "*Pleasures!*" he says in a very low tone. *What? What is he talking about?*

I look at him uncertainly. He closes his eyes again, tilting his face toward the ceiling. "You are wearing *Pleasures.* Right?"

My perfume? *All this time, he was breathing behind me to smell my fragrance?* I ignore his observation skills and finally gather my courage to turn around and voice my frustration.

"Do you really know where we have to go?"

He looks down at the floor. "No, I don't know."

"So you were wasting my time?" I can't believe it; he was entertaining himself all along. First, he was enjoying my misery outside while I fought with the bolts, and then he kept my badge purposely and, without even asking me, grabbed me and pushed me through the security door. He showed off with his manners, offering to act as a guide, and all he could do was sniff behind me to identify my fragrance.

He still looks down with no answer. Without wasting further time, I press the ground level button to go back where we started, so that I can ask the management to help me out or call someone from my team to find out where I have to go. *I shouldn't have trusted him.* He presses the sub-basement button without saying anything. The elevator descends from the 45th floor down to ground level—luckily, without stopping and wasting any more time. His eyes are still reading my face, trying to discover something. The doors at the ground level open and without even looking at him, I move forward. He stops me by holding my elbow and the door closes again within seconds, the elevator descending to the lower level, the sub-basement.

How dare he bully me?

"I told you I will take you to your meeting. Why can't you trust me?" This time, his eyes are more intense.

The doors of the elevator open at the lower level.

He leads me out, still holding me firmly by my elbow. He releases his grip gently and looks at me again.

"I am sorry to delay your arrival, but I was preoccupied. Let's go, it's closer from here." I follow his lead, not sure what to say.

During our short walk, I notice he is wearing a very expensive suit fitted elegantly on his masculine body. It is navy blue with an ice-blue shirt, accented with a matching tie. The outfit looks pricy, very close to my whole month's salary. His movement is very elegant, like that of a high-profile gentleman. His watch, which is just visible on his left wrist, also looks very valuable. He must be spending a lot of his salary just to look good. He stops by another glass door and swipes his badge on it, and heads into the corridor.

The corridor is quiet and I can hear only our footsteps. We don't speak at all. At the end of the long passage, I see a double door entrance to a very large room. The name 'Maple Room' is written outside on a hardwood board, embossed with bronze letters. Both doors are wide open and I see my team in there.

"Here we are . . . finally," he says with pride, as if he has discovered a new country.

"Yes, finally. Thank you." I smile at him. I couldn't agree more.

"So, what is this all about?" He gazes at me again, this time with curiosity, and then peeks inside the room.

"Well . . . frankly speaking . . . I don't know. We were invited to attend a breakfast here. And some other departments plan to show up as well. Other than that, I really do not have any information."

And even if I have, who are you to ask?

"Can I join you? I haven't eaten anything this morning." He takes a gander inside the room again, to check out the food. He looks quite serious.

Is he really hungry?

"I don't know what to say, Mr. Adam. I am not organizing this meeting. And this is actually not my office. I am not sure if I can bring uninvited guests with me. I have no idea about the policies of Gibson Enterprises." I look inside the room, following his gaze, to find out what he is looking for. It is very rude of me to refuse someone breakfast who confessed to being hungry. "I am sorry, Mr. Adam, to refuse you like this. If you had come to my office, I would have invited you for breakfast, but this place is new to me too." I look at him with an apologetic smile. "But . . . umm . . ." I start digging in my handbag and take out my travel mug and my pumpkin bread from the bakery, which I haven't had a chance to eat at all. "You can have this meanwhile; it's tea though, not sure if you take tea or coffee, and this is pumpkin bread, which I am sure you will like. It's the best in town." He looks down at the items I am offering him with amusement. "Oh yes, I took only one sip of the tea," I say. "It is still hot though. You do not need to warm it up. I already have a breakfast invitation, so you can have this."

He takes the food from me without saying a single word. "You don't need to apologize," he says. "I completely understand. And please call me Adam only. No 'Mr.'" He gives me his million-dollar smile. "And thank you for the breakfast. I really appreciate it. I will return your mug soon." He starts digging in the brown paper bag, as if wondering whether I have given him the right food.

"If you don't mind, can I ask you something . . . umm . . . Adam?" The question pops into my mind from nowhere. He nods, but without taking his eyes off of me. "If you knew this place was in the sub-basement, why did you let the elevator go all the way up?"

He searches my face intently again.

"I don't know . . ." He shakes his head. "I really don't know . . . you made me . . . lost . . . I got carried away by your presence . . . by your . . . fragrance."

Lost? Fragrance? That's it?

I look at him with my mouth open. I have nothing to say.

"It was really nice meeting you, Rania. I hope to see you soon. Enjoy your breakfast." He smiles and turns around, and within seconds he is out of my sight.

AT FIRST SIGHT

♂

Shit! Is that really her? Is she the same woman who cast the spell on me?

"Sylvain, get in here immediately," I say to my personal assistant in a very unpleasant manner, without looking at her. She follows me into my office.

"Is something wrong, Mr. Gibson?" she asks in a motherly tone.

Something wrong? I am fucked up, Sylvain!

"There is some breakfast meeting or get-together going on in sub-basement . . . umm . . . in the Maple Room. Find out all the details about it—who is holding it; what it's about. Ask the security department to fetch me the list of all the invitees along with the pictures from their security badges." I have never been so insistent about anything.

Sylvain leaves immediately. I sit down behind my huge dark wooden desk and swivel my leather chair to face the view outside. It has started raining again. My office is on the fifty-fourth floor. It feels powerful to take in the view and own a place so high, yet I felt so weak in front of that girl.

What is in her that I couldn't articulate?

She is undoubtedly the most beautiful woman I have ever seen, and it was quite unsettling to me that the charm that other women usually see in me was completely invisible to her. Is she truly an enchantress from some other world, or is she a part of my fantasy that I have conjured? I am spellbound. A human can't cast a spell. There must be some witchcraft going on.

At the sight of her, my heart had begun beating like a drum. It's the same feeling I had eight months back when I met the woman dancing passionately in that old building. I can never forget how those ebony eyes looked at me from behind the mask, how she was trying to catch her breath, her breasts resting on me.

Is she the same girl?

No, she can't be. Rania is an ordinary girl, doing a regular job. There was magic in that enchantress, in her eyes, in her lips, in her movements, yet the same magic exists in Rania's eyes too. And her fragrance, it was so familiar. The same aroma that intoxicated me that day, when I lost my mind. I lost it today too. The spark that I got when her hand touched mine, did she feel the same sensation?

I look at my hand carefully to check if it has turned blue due to the electrical current. Nothing like this has happened to me before.

Fuck! What is wrong with me?

I have slept with so many women, but never felt anything except fulfilling my body's needs. I wonder how, just with a touch of her hand, she made all my reflexes work together within my body at the same time. What would it be like to be close to her? The explosion would surely kill me. And that death would be so much sweeter than this life.

What must she be thinking about me, a rude self-centered man who didn't have the courtesy to help a lady? I could have called her back and given her the badge. What the hell was I thinking?

A knock at the door brings me back into the world of reality.

"Come in, Sylvain." I know it's her. No one would come to the door unannounced except her and Ali.

"Mr. Gibson, I have all the details. The meeting was organized by Ben Dynham, CEO of Greenway Advertising. Their office is on the thirteenth floor of this building. It is just the regular holiday breakfast for all their creative teams. Their sales and marketing departments work from this campus, whereas the other departments like Creative Graphics and Creative Minds work from the Inwood International head office on Bloor Street. The meeting room is booked till 12:30, under Mr. Dynham's name." Sylvain looks proud of having delivered the information so quickly.

She hands me the list of invitees, which I start scrutinizing immediately. It has their employee and badge numbers, along with the badge pictures.

"Anything else, Mr. Gibson?" she asks gently.

"Yes, send Ali in." I am still going through the list and not looking at her. *There she is. Rania Ahmed.* It is very easy to locate her in the list; she has the most beautiful picture. *How can someone look so fascinating on a security badge?* I could look at this picture for years. The eyes contain the same magic. I get completely lost in her beauty, not realizing when Ali steps into my room. He must have knocked on the door, which I didn't hear at all. I look away from the paper and place it on my desk.

"This girl." I point with my index finger to let Ali know who I mean. He looks intently and reads out her name. "I want her complete background check, where she lives, where she goes, her hobbies and activities, her job description, her weekly schedule, her relationships, her shopping interests. I want to know everything about her."

Ali looks at me, surprised and dubious. He's no doubt wondering when I developed stalking tendencies. Ali bin Moosa has been working with me and my dad for twelve years, almost as long as Sylvain. He was my father's right hand and then, after his death, he started working for me. He is kind of a brother to me, although he's ten years older. An ex-army officer, of Moroccan background with a tall broad physique, he is a trained fighter and knows how to handle the most critical situations. He knows all my habits, my secrets, my interests. I always get my employees' background checks, but I have never been so aggressive about it. Not even about my clients with whom I do million-dollar deals.

"This information will take at least an hour, if you can wait." He knows me very well, and he knows I am anxious to know the details. "And about her weekly schedule, we need to monitor her activities for a week; we cannot really find out about her daily schedule. Are you sure you want to go with this?" He is right. It is not appropriate to stalk her. It would be violating her privacy.

Fuck her privacy.

I want to be her only private concern.

"I can't trust anyone other than you, Ali. You investigate everything about her personally. Make sure this conversation remains between us. Do not ask anyone about it. Be her shadow."

Ali stands here in amusement and swallows each word I have said to him. "I will find out the details and email them to you in an hour. Anything else?"

"Yes, one more thing, Ali. Inform Mr. Dynham that I will be joining the breakfast shortly." Ali leaves my office with more work on his shoulders.

Show time!

STRANGER IN DISGUISE

♀

Still speechless, I enter the meeting room, which is filled with team members from my office. I see Ben, my boss, talking to the marketing guys. Ben is one of my father's closest friends; they studied together thirty years ago at Glasgow University in Scotland. Ben moved to Canada ten years back and started his advertising firm. With many years of hard work, he has achieved the highest-profile corporate clientele in Canada, from large telecoms to winery businesses. I am really proud of him. He has always thought of me as his daughter, since he never had one of his own. Besides my father, he was the first man who held me after I was born.

He has a son, Mike, who is around my age and my only friend here. We grew up together in Beirut. In high school, we promised if we could not find a suitable partner for marriage by the age of twenty-five, we would marry each other. The thought of Mike makes me smile. He is a sweetheart. After high school, Mike took admission in Ryerson University and moved here with his father. When I came to Toronto, Ben and Mike were my emotional support system, and they still are. Ben always wanted Mike to join his business, but he became a cop instead. I love him very much and I would not do anything to jeopardize my friendship with him, although what he wants from me I cannot give to him. On my twenty-fifth birthday, he said: "Rania, it is high time that we should keep the promises we made together." And I asked him to extend the promise five more years. My father is very fond of Mike, but I know he would never want me to marry someone outside my religious boundary. But the real reason I cannot marry him is that I never felt anything romantic for him. He is my friend and will always stay in that same compartment of my heart.

I bring my mind back to the room and head toward where my office friends are sitting, having breakfast. As I sit, Ben comes over to me.

"Good morning, princess, where have you been? You missed my speech." Ben winks at me with his mischievous smile. He reminds me of Dad so much.

"Well . . ." I look around to avoid eye contact. "I got stuck . . . in . . . umm . . . a situation." I am not sure if I should tell him about my accident.

"You didn't take anything to eat? Please, help yourself," Ben says in a very affectionate way, just like my father would have.

"I am not hungry right now. But I will have something in a while. Thanks for asking, Ben." I actually lost my appetite when I heard the words *I got carried away.*

A call on his cell phone distracts Ben.

"Yes? Dynham speaking. Yes . . . uh huh . . . really? Well, the pleasure is all mine . . . he is most welcome. Thank you for letting me know." Ben puts the phone back in his jacket pocket and smiles from his heart.

"Your girlfriend called?" I ask him, while taking a sip of my coffee.

"No, not my girlfriend. Gibson Enterprises. Mr. Gibson will be coming here shortly to join us for breakfast. I am delighted. He is a very reserved man and he doesn't go anywhere if there is no business involved. If he is coming, I am sure he wants to talk to me about our further work with Gibson." Ben shifts his gaze from me to the others around us with an announcement. "And further work means all your jobs are secure."

We all talk about our piled-up deliverables, and Ben asks me if I can join him at a seminar in New York where private business owners and entrepreneurs gather every year to display their work and contributions to the world of advertising. It has always been a big event, and Ben makes lots of contacts for his company. Last year, it was a conference on animation in the media world. This year, they are highlighting graphics in e-magazines and e-catalogs. Ben is doing me a big favor; it is a great opportunity for me and my career.

While we are all engrossed in our futures, I look toward the entrance and see a man holding my travel mug. It's him.

What the hell is he doing here?

I go and meet him at the door.

"What are you doing here? I told you I can't bring people in here," I say to him, annoyed.

"Oh, I'm sorry. I came to return this and say thank you." He hands me the mug, his sweet husky voice melting all my annoyance.

"You didn't have to. It was okay."

"Rania . . ." Ben appears from nowhere and puts his arm around my shoulder. "You know Mr. Gibson?"

I look up at the green-eyed man with open mouth. *Shit.* I want to disappear.

"Adam Gibson." He extends his hand to me for a friendly shake.

God, bury me please.

I give my hand to him without saying a single word.

"Yes, Mr. Dynham, we met recently . . . in a . . . very interesting situation." Adam smiles and winks at me wickedly, still holding my hand in his.

Ben shifts his gaze from Adam to me, his eyes carrying thousands of questions. I retrieve my hand from Adam's firm grip and look at Ben with a foolish smile on my face.

"Well . . . I was a bit lost looking for this place . . ." I am talking to Ben but my eyes are on this overly sexy man. "Mr. Gibson was kind enough to guide me here." I look down at my shoes; I want to avoid all the eyes on me.

"You are very welcome here, Mr. Gibson. It is a great honor for our firm that you joined us for breakfast. Some journalists and photographers are also here. I hope you don't mind if they cover you for this event." Ben looks really nervous. This handsome young man, who was holding my hand a minute ago, is a gold mine to Ben. He wants to make the most of this acquaintance.

Though our firm has an office here in Gibson's building, Ben has never had a chance to even meet Adam Gibson personally. He has been trying to get Gibson's company as a corporate client for years and this seems to be his only chance. I know already from his expression what he will ask me in the future.

"No, Mr. Dynham, I wouldn't mind at all, if your beautiful Creative Designer keeps me company." He continues, "But before any photographs, I would request that she accompany me for the breakfast. She owes me one." He looks at Ben. "I wanted to join her for breakfast, but she refused to entertain a famished person. The policies are very well defined here." He smirks impishly; he is making fun of me in front of my boss.

How rude! Could this be more embarrassing?

Ben looks at me dubiously, as if I have been hiding something from him for years. I am not interested in what is going on in his mind. I just want to vanish from here.

"Of course, Mr. Gibson," Ben says. "It is a privilege for us. Rania, please escort Mr. Gibson to the breakfast buffet." Ben peeks at me and then smiles at Adam. "Mr. Gibson, please enjoy your breakfast. I will see you shortly."

I leave the conversation without bothering to look back. Adam follows me like my shadow. I hand him an empty plate with the cutlery. I can feel him watching me intently.

What does he want from me?

I have nothing to offer him. Every time our eyes meet, I feel he wants to ask me something. "Would you like some pancakes, Mr. Gibson?" I don't look at him.

"Yes, thank you, Rania. I'm not Mr. Gibson. Please call me Adam." He moves up close behind me, whispering in my ear. "Not for you, at least."

Oh my! I need some space.

He is so close that if I dared to turn around, we would end up with skin-to-skin contact. I pretend to ignore his intimate whispers. I don't even have the courage to look around to check if anybody is watching us or not. I know how the media scavenge like vultures, seeking for gossip.

"I thought you ate the pumpkin bread. You still want more?" I finally find the courage to look in his eyes.

"I am always yearning for more, Ms. Ahmed. You have no idea how greedy and voracious I am." He searches my face. I avert my eyes and move a few steps to the side, creating distance between us. He still keeps following me, watching me intently. Those green eyes could kill me. I cannot bear it anymore.

I wish I could escape.

"You are not eating anything?" he asks me in a friendly way, giving up on the sexy whispers. I feel like I can breathe again.

Does he think after all that just happened, my stomach wouldn't have knots?

"No. I have already. But thanks for asking. You want a muffin?" I ask, choosing a blueberry muffin for him.

He looks at the muffin and smiles. "Yes, please. You don't need to ask every time you pick something. Fill me with whatever your heart desires."

Okay! Back to the sexy whispering roller coaster ride.

I try to move faster, filling his plate with breakfast so that I don't have to talk to him anymore. He is suffocating me with his whispers. No one has ever talked to me like that. They can all read the 'not interested' sign on my face. Why is this man different? Why can't he see that sign on my forehead?

I should have realized that he runs this empire. It's his damn building; he can come and go anywhere he wants. No wonder the security guards didn't question him. And I pushed him away when he *got carried away.* I notice that he didn't lie at all. He speaks whatever is on his mind. *Very intriguing!*

"Can I ask you something, if you don't mind?" he asks me in a very sweet manner. I stay quiet, pouring coffee for him. "Please look at me, Rania. I am talking to you." I look up. He is standing close to me, very close. I don't say anything, just let him continue. "Have we met before?" His eyes are searching mine.

"You think so?" I avert my gaze and look for sugar and cream.

"You look so . . . familiar. Your eyes . . . I have seen those eyes before," he says, and rests himself on the corner of the buffet table.

"That's so cheesy, Mr. Gibson," I reply, rolling my eyes at him.

"I'm serious." He scowls at me.

"Mr. Gibson, there are almost seven billion people in this world. You think God will not repeat the eyes? And it is said that there are seven more faces similar to each of ours. Did you know that?" Now, I do look at him.

"I know what you are saying . . . but . . ." He comes closer to read my eyes. The coffee cup starts to shake in my hand.

What is he about to say?

"The eyes holding a thousand secrets . . . they cannot be in a population of seven billion. That maddening darkness doesn't exist anywhere else. Please tell me if we have ever met before." He realizes my hand is shaking and takes the cup from me.

"I didn't even know your name, Mr. Gibson. How can you ask if we have met?" I pick up another cup of tea for myself. He hands me the milk pot, but he doesn't stop looking at me. I add milk and sugar to my tea and turn around.

Ben is looking at us skeptically.

Oh crap!

I am not interested in any more interrogation. Ben walks toward us and Adam shifts two steps back to give us space. I take a deep breath, relieved.

Ben asks me to join him and Adam. I don't have a bloody choice, do I? He leads us to an empty table and we sit down, me facing Adam across the table.

"So, Mr. Dynham, how come your marketing team is here and your creative team is operating from another location?" He looks at me specifically when he says *creative*. Ben watches us to find out if he is missing something.

"Mr. Gibson, I always wanted my company to operate from one location, I mean this one. But the office space is all occupied here. We have half of the thirteenth floor, and the Petersons law firm has the other half. If they ever vacate, we'd snap up that space."

Adam takes a sip of his coffee. His posture is slightly tilted toward Ben, right elbow resting on the table. He rubs his lower lip with his index finger, thinking something. I guess this is his habitual gesture of contemplation. He finally looks up with a slight curve to his lips.

"I want your creative people to work from this location, Mr. Dynham, if you are interested in doing business with us."

He has surprised both Ben and me with his proposition. It seems that if Ben wants Gibson's business, that means we all move in here. Adam and me, working at the same location. His gaze has suffocated me enough. *How can I ... ?*

"So, Mr. Dynham, how soon can you move in here? I can vacate the complete floor for you. We can sign the lease later on. Move in first, and then we will further discuss business prospects and—"

He gets interrupted by a phone call. "Excuse me, please ..." He accepts the call, but looks furious at being interrupted. I twist my ring around my finger and when I look up, he is looking at me and then at my ring, though he is still speaking on the phone. Ben has apparently noticed the way he is staring.

"Yes? . . . uh huh . . . that's good . . . so quick? . . . I am impressed . . . yes, I will come up soon . . . see you . . ." He ends the call. He is smiling. Something pleasant has obviously happened. *His girlfriend called?*

"Please excuse me. I need to go to the ladies' room." I need an excuse to get the hell out of here.

"And please excuse me as well; I have to attend an urgent meeting," Adam says, and stands up with me. Ben follows us to be courteous.

"Mr. Gibson, thank you very much for joining us. It is extremely gratifying for us to have the honor of your company. If you don't mind, can we have a photograph together?" Ben interrupts his exit. It is a perfect time to slip out of here. So I move toward the door.

"Ms. Ahmed, please join us. Honor me with your presence," Adam says from behind me.

I close my eyes for a moment and turn. Both the men are waiting for my answer. I have to smile back; I have no other option, do I? Ben waves over a photographer from some business magazine. I stand between Ben and Adam. The photographer asks us to move closer. Adam shifts slightly toward me, crowding me, and I lose my balance. He grabs me by my waist as if he knew I was falling.

"Hey, you okay?"

How can someone ask like this, so charmingly?

"Yes. Thanks." I stand up straight. His hands are still holding me from the back, and he doesn't seem like he's planning to move them. It is not fair that he can send electricity up my spine with just his touch.

The photographer does his work and leaves.

"Thank you very much, Mr. Gibson. We will not take up any more of your very precious time. We all look forward to working with your prestigious company." Ben is shaking hands with Adam very firmly. He is looking forward to this opportunity, and I know he would never put it at risk for any reason.

"I also look forward to it, Mr. Dynham. More than you." Adam's eyes rake down my body from my head to my shoes, when he says *more than you.* "It would be a great privilege for me if Ms. Ahmed would escort me to the elevator." Adam takes one deeper look.

"Please come," I say to Ben. I have a feeling that Ben will be using me in getting this business, like bait. I don't like that idea. He had always treated me like his daughter.

I start walking quickly to the elevator.

"Rania?" I hear Adam's voice behind me but I don't stop. It is a long corridor and I have to get it over with soon and push him inside the elevator so that he can vanish once and for all.

Just keep moving!

"Rania, please stop. I am talking to you." He grabs me by my elbow and pushes me toward the wall.

"Mr. Gibson, I have been asked to escort you to the elevator. I assume you are late for your urgent meeting." He puts one hand on the wall, over my head, blocking the view from the Maple Room, if anyone should happen to be looking at us.

His eyes bore into me, and when I look at him, he says, *"And now, this is the sweetest and most glorious day that ever my eyes did see."*[1] He smiles at me but I look away, ignoring his appreciation for me. "Why are you doing this to me? What have I done to deserve this?" His plea is melting me like snow on a sunny winter afternoon. Our eyes lock.

"Deserve what? What did I do, Mr. Gibson?" I keep my tone very professional.

"You know what I'm talking about. You ignore me . . . all the time. You don't look at me when you talk. I feel like you're trying to escape from me. Do I intimidate you?" His appeal sounds more like a silent prayer.

I don't realize at first that his other hand is on my face, lifting my chin so that I can look into his eyes. There is no sexual intention. No lust. Just a request. At his touch, my heart starts to beat very loudly.

"I am not comfortable talking to strangers, Mr. Gibson. I hardly know you."

"Then let's get to know each other. I want to know you. Everything about you. How about lunch together today? Let me take you out somewhere."

What? He is asking me out? Say something, Rania, before you start melting in his arms.

[1] *Donald Cargill (1619-1681)*

"We just had breakfast; there is no room for lunch, I don't think." I move away from him, and this time he takes his hands off of me.

"How about coffee . . . umm . . . juice? Ice cream?" He sounds really desperate.

"I have some work, Mr. Gibson. I cannot delay it." I look around the corridor and see Ben standing in the doorway; perhaps he has been watching us all the time. I don't care what he might be thinking.

"How about dinner tonight then?" He is unstoppable. *Why doesn't the day end at lunchtime?* He is making me furious. I have handled many men in this situation. I know how to push men away. I am good at it.

"I have plans." I avoid his gaze. I don't want him to catch my lie. I look down and rotate my ring on my finger.

"What plans?" His tone changes immediately, and he scowls.

"I have my personal life as well, Mr. Gibson. Goodbye."

And I escape from his gaze and run into the ladies room. I don't even care if Ben sees it or not. I am sure Adam wants me. There was desperation in those green eyes. He would ask me out to dinner, and then he would take me back to his place, and eventually he would use me as his fucking toy and toss me aside. By now he should know I am not that girl, one who would drool over his bank balance and kiss the ground he walks on.

Not a chance!

RELEVANCE

♂

Do I intimidate her?

My eyes keep following her as she disappears into the ladies' room. She dazzles me every time. What is in her that I have not seen in any other girl? She doesn't seem to be interested in me at all, and still, I can't keep my eyes off her. I know I made her uncomfortable and nervous, ogling her like I did.

You are fucking screwed, Adam!

There is something in her that keeps pulling me toward her, yet she keeps pushing me away. *I have my personal life as well, Mr. Gibson.* Does she have a boyfriend? It's too frustrating to even imagine someone holding her hand, kissing her, getting close to her. I close my eyes and shake my head. The mere idea makes me feel chafed.

Shit! What am I doing?

I realize she is not like the other girls whom I used merely to satisfy my sexual urges. My heart and soul are swinging between celibacy and desire. I don't know what I want from her but I know I want to keep her, admire her beauty . . . *forever.*

I enter my room and Ali is waiting for me. "We have found some information about the . . . girl. You want me to read it out, or will you have a look for yourself?" Ali realizes instantly that I am not myself. That's why he suggests the idea of reading it out to me.

I stand mutely, facing the Toronto skyline, visible through the large floor-to-ceiling windows behind my chair. "Carry on," I say, speaking low, not sure if he has heard me.

"The girl . . . umm . . . Rania Ahmed; she has worked as a creative graphics designer at Greenway Advertising for three years." I stare out the window, listening intently to what Ali has to share. "She graduated from Ryerson University in Software Engineering and started working with Gibbs and Gills software company as a software developer. She did some courses in digital media and printing, and joined Greenway later on." I see Ali's reflection in the glass as he checks my expression. He continues, "She lives in North York near the Finch station, in Archeries Condominiums. Apartment number 1609. The apartment is owned by Ben Dynham, which means she is renting it." The name catches my attention.

"What did you say? Who owns the apartment?" I turn back to face Ali, whose eyes are fixed on his report.

"Ben Dynham. I suppose he is the same guy, CEO of Greenway. Her rent is deducted from her salary. That's what it shows here." *So this means Ben and Rania have a relationship other than an employee and employer. I need more details on that.* Ali continues. "She is originally from Lebanon. Her father's name is Ahmed Al-Bari. We do not have any record of him right now. She came on a student's visa five years back, graduated, and filed for her immigration. Currently, she does not carry a Canadian passport. She is twenty-five years old and will be turning twenty-six in January." Ali looks to see if I have anything to say. I sit down in my black leather chair and close my eyes, leaning against the headrest. "I am not sure what other information I can provide. Her record shows she doesn't even have a driver's license." *Really? No car, and she is living in Toronto?* Ali sounds surprised too. "I am not sure about her personal interests, Adam, but her credit card transactions show that she likes reading. The major transactions are from Amazon, downloading e-books. Apparently, she doesn't have a Facebook account, but she is on some professional websites. Other than that, she has a membership in a dance school, which runs a dance class every day. She is enrolled in the evening classes." My eyes open wide at that.

"I need the address of the dance school." I take the paper from him and check what he has to share.

"Sure. Anything else you would like to know? I will follow her routine as you asked me, but don't you think this is violating her privacy?" I look up at him, and his eyes show some sympathy for her. "I am sorry, Adam, I have no right to intrude in your personal life, but she doesn't seem like the others that have been in your past. I don't want you to end up disappointed. Her record shows she is single. At the age of twenty-five, she has no boyfriend or husband. This means she is the type who waits for the right person. With a belief of . . . umm . . . some kind of soulmate, perhaps. I am from the same religious background, and I know in our culture, women don't have relationships other than with the man they marry. This is how they are raised." Ali takes a seat opposite me, and I know he wants to say more. I stay quiet. I believe his point is valid. "We belong to a very conservative society. Having a sexual, or any kind of physical relationship outside of marriage, is not permissible in our religion. And if this girl is even a little bit religious or follows the values she was raised by, then you would have to try too hard. She may not be your type, Adam." I rest my elbow on the desk and rub my forehead. I am gazing at the paper, my eyes down, but I am not reading it. "I don't know what is going on in your mind or how you plan to go ahead with this girl, but I can see that she has changed you. I have not seen you like this before. You look lost!" Ali has always been like a brother to me, more than a friend, though his job description says he is just my bodyguard. I can tell he is concerned about me now. I lean back on the headrest and close my eyes again.

"If you don't mind my asking you, where did you meet her? I mean the first time?" *First time? Is she the same woman I saw a few months back? But that place never existed.*

"This morning. Outside the building."

"And?"

"Ah . . . I just kept staring at her." Ali's smile leaves his lips and he becomes more attentive to my words, but he waits for me to continue. "I was completely dazzled. I stood there doing . . . nothing. It felt like I was under some spell. And when she looked up at me, I was . . ." I am at a loss for words.

"Awed?" Ali continues on my behalf. He has found the right word.

"Yes, exactly. Thank you." I open my eyes and look at him with gratitude. His smile comes back. Something is going on in his head, but I cannot figure it out. There is too much going on in my own mind.

"I am speechless, Adam. You sound like a mid-century poet. It looks like a *love-at-first-sight* thing to me." He winks at me with a mischievous smile.

Love? I never thought about it. No, it cannot be love. Women are only for sexual pleasure. How can you give your heart at first sight and surrender everything you have? You are not as imbecilic as that. You run an empire here. You don't approach women and beg them to have mercy on you. You are a ruthless man, Adam. You have broken many hearts. You cannot give your heart to someone.

"Why don't you ask her for a date? Take her out for lunch or dinner and get to know her." Ali's suggestions interrupt my thoughts.

"I did. She seemed to . . ." I avert my eyes and look down at the paper. "Ignore me."

"Ignore you? A girl ignoring Adam Gibson?" His voice is full of amusement.

"Yes, Ali. She ignored me." My eyes widen and my words are very specific.

"*No doubt exists that all women are crazy; it's only a question of degree.*"[2] Ali smirks at me and I look at him, open-mouthed. "Did you ask her in a decent manner? I mean, you have never asked a girl out before. I doubt your experience in this field." Ali has a point. He has more experience than me in terms of approaching women. "You met her today and you asked her out already. Isn't it too soon?" He makes it sound as if I have done something against the laws of dating. "Obviously, it is not an at-first-sight thing from her side. Girls' minds don't work like that, Adam. You need to give 'em some space. At least, normal girls, not the ones you pick up at a club or a party. Does she know who you are? I mean, your social status?" Ali's interrogation seems never-ending. He is concerned about me. And he is the only one with whom I can share my feelings.

"Yes, after I surprised her at breakfast. But even after she learned who I was, she still didn't give a damn." I take a sip of water from the glass that Sylvain keeps filled on my desk. "She is the first girl I've met who has no interest in money. She didn't look rich to me, but there was no greed in her eyes. She was dressed simply and . . ."

---

[2]   *W. C. Fields (1880-1946)*

I am out of words.

"Conservatively?" Ali can read my mind. He always comes up with the right words.

"Yes. Thanks." The dress she was wearing showed all her curves, but she was fully covered, not showing a single inch of her body other than her face and hands. Even so, she was seductive. She was not wearing expensive jewelry, but I noticed that she twisted her ring every time she felt uncomfortable. The fact that the ring is on her index finger calms me. She is not engaged.

Fuck! Where am I going with this?

"So, her ignorance of your status and the fact that she is not covetous about wealth . . . that disintegrated your ego?" Ali doesn't look at me when he speaks, as he knows his words will not provide any comfort. He is firing the truth. This girl has dismembered my self-esteem. "You need to be careful this time, Adam. I can only wish you luck." Ali looks at me once again for my response. I peep at him from the corner of my eye. "Take it easy and move slowly. If she refused to go out with you, chances are that she will push you away next time as well." I stay quiet and watch Ali. "If she is not tempted by your status, then do something different . . . please her." *Please her.* I have never tried to please a woman.

"How do I please her? I don't even know what she likes or dislikes." I'm hoping he has some useful advice.

"Try to get to know her," Ali says. "Offer her your friendship rather than your . . ." Ali looks around the room, as if he is searching for the word from the walls. "Your lasciviousness." He pauses and I look at him with vexation. "I am sorry, I—" He looks nervous, like he has crossed some line.

"That's all right, Ali. You made your point. I know what you are saying and I really appreciate it." My words ease the tension in the air and we smile at each other. "I agree with your point about violating her privacy. I think I have enough information. You don't need to chase her. But . . ." I stand up and start to pace behind my desk. "But what if she is not even interested in my friendship?" My question dismays both of us. "I will have to find some other ways to be around her . . . which reminds me . . ." I stop walking and glance at him. "You need to vacate the half of the thirteenth floor occupied by Peterson Law firm. And this should be done as soon as possible. Sometime in the next week—"

"But this is impossible! They just signed the lease in October, for a year, and you are asking me to abrogate the contract?" Ali is gasping in astonishment.

"I don't care, Ali. Whatever it takes. Just do it." I turn toward the window and glance down at the world outside.

"We would have to pay a penalty and return the rent they paid. But it is not about that—I know you can afford it. It's about the Gibson reputation." Ali's concerns do not even pass close to my ears. I keep looking outside.

"I don't care, Ali. I told you. Whatever it takes. If there is a penalty for breaching the contract, that's fine. Return the rent for the whole year; I don't give a damn. In fact, tell them that we will find a suitable place for their firm on the same street. We will bear the charges for all the arrangements and pay the rent for the other location as well. I am sure they will not refuse." I turn around and smile wickedly. Ali's eyes widen with a shock that clearly says: *you-know-how-to-use-your-wealth-at-the-right-time-you-filthy-rich-bastard.* "I have given my word to Ben Dynham. And I know what you are thinking, Ali. I know I am one affluent sinner." I smirk at Ali maliciously. Poor him. He will have to work very hard to make this happen. I am not keen to know how he will do it.

"I think I should leave now," Ali says. "I will contact the law firm and check all the conditions of the contract. How soon do you want to relocate Greenway?" Ali gathers his papers.

"I'd like them to work with us starting Monday morning. Can you do that?" I rest my butt on the corner of the desk.

"No, Adam, it is not possible. It is already Friday afternoon. Half of the people involved are probably gone already. I will arrange the meeting with Ben Dynham and the other law firm to see the possibilities. But what are the chances that Greenway agrees to move in here? I mean, the rest of the departments?" Ali shifts and leans toward me.

"They have already agreed. I put an offer to Dynham. We will outsource our graphics and media printing work to them. He has been looking forward to this opportunity for a long time and—"

"What? You offered them our business? What about the people who are working in our media department? You are taking work from them." Ali backs off a few steps and sighs in bewilderment.

"I am not asking you to fire the whole department. I know there are two hundred people working in that group, and that means two hundred mortgages. We will find something for them. Let's discuss it later."

I look at Ali, who shakes his head bemusedly. He is also smirking.

"I don't know what to say, Adam. Everything you say surprises me. Within half an hour, you have spent a fortune for someone who is not even aware what is going on behind her back. I am just wondering how you will control yourself if she actually agrees to hang out with you. This is crazy, but trust me, I am enjoying it."

The smile on Ali's face is demonstrating the fact that my situation looks fucking delectable to him. He is right, though. I am already spending a lot, just so I can be around her. But I know relocating an office is not as simple as it sounds. This could take weeks, maybe months. I cannot wait. There has to be some other way to see her.

Think, Adam!

"You have some more news to share?" Ali asks me sarcastically.

My mind is swirling with wild thoughts and suddenly an idea pops.

Ting!

"Arrange a party in honor of Greenway joining hands with Gibson. Tonight. Book the best place in town."

"Tonight? But we have not signed any contract with Greenway. The other media people would be there. Without a contract, we cannot publicize the agreement. It is just verbal." Ali is right. I am losing my mind over her. But I don't see any other way to meet her. She will meet me officially.

"You haven't met Dynham, have you? He is quite a greedy man. My verbal commitment was enough for him. He will not ask for a fucking contract. And the party, with all the media coming in, I don't think he would disagree with that. From his side, the party is securing him the business with us." My eyes make contact with his and he knows exactly what I am talking about.

"I know how Dynham is. The fact that he's wanted business from us for years makes it much easier. I will ask Sylvain to arrange the party and send invitations immediately." Ali turns toward the door, then stops. "You are okay with The Fairmont Royal York?"

"Perfect." I smile and turn around to enjoy the view I am blessed with.

AN INVITATION

♀

I go back to the Maple Room and see Ben waiting for me at the doorway.

"Would you care to tell your uncle what just happened?" He looks dishonored, like I had hurt him.

"There is nothing to say, Ben." I look up at him sincerely.

"You didn't have the courtesy to tell me that he was coming here?" He seems angry with me.

"I didn't know. I thought he only showed up to return my travel mug." I look down at the floor.

"He came all the way here to return your mug? That's it? And how did he get it?" Ben is getting more upset. He is concerned, like my father would be.

"We met in the lobby. I told you, I was searching for the room location in my email and he offered to guide me. When we reached here, he asked me if he could come in. Since he was a stranger, I told him I had to abide by corporate policy, and I could not bring him in without permission. So I offered him my tea and bread, in case he was hungry." I skip the entire embarrassing situation at the turnstile.

"Are you kidding me, Rania? You were trying to feed someone who feeds thousands of starving people daily?" Ben's mouth opens in surprise. "Come and sit. We need to talk." Ben takes my hand and guides me to the corner table, close to the doorway. "I will not ask what happened between you two. I figured out that you were unaware that he is Adam Gibson. I guess your kindness has smitten him." Ben is observing my expressions.

"Smitten? I—"

"You didn't notice how he was looking at you? Open your eyes, girl. His eyes were fixed on you only." I don't like Ben probing, but I cannot deny the fact that Adam was blatantly staring. "Now, listen to me very carefully." Ben scoots forward and speaks in a low tone. I feel a chill down my spine, and I have some intuition what he wants to say. "You know how much I wanted Gibson's name on my profile. This opportunity has come to me on a gold platter. A single mistake by you could ruin everything." His tone is threatening. When it comes to business, Ben is uncle to no one.

"What did I do, Ben?" I snap.

"I saw what you were doing in the corridor. You were pushing him away—"

"What exactly are you expecting from me?" I interrupt, suddenly angry.

"I am not asking anything. Just go with the flow. Don't alienate him." Ben has never looked at me like this. I stay quiet and look down at the table while he continues. "Rania, I have always liked you. I know my son is in love with you, and I have always accepted you as my future daughter-in-law. After all these years, I can see that you don't carry any emotion for my son. He is no more than a friend to you." Ben's eyes are focused on me. "I have seen my son drunk and cursing your name some nights. I don't blame you for breaking his heart, because you never made any promises to him. It was always one-sided." I look up at him, to understand what he is trying to say. "I have been patient with him. But not anymore." I am still trying to grasp his meaning. "This business is my baby, more than my son. Mike has grown up and I know he can take care of himself emotionally. But this baby needs me. I have given my heart and soul to it." He closes his eyes to avoid looking at me. Is he feeling guilty because he eavesdropped on us? "You refused to go out with Gibson. Why?"

Why? He, of all people, is asking me this? Like he doesn't know why I push men away?

He opens his eyes and continues, "He doesn't like to be treated like that, Rania. He is an extremely proud man. He never approaches women. He never had to. If this is his first time pursuing a woman like you, then you should give him the benefit of the doubt." He pauses for a moment. "Keep in mind that he is a very dangerous man. If you provoke him, it could be hazardous to my business. Do you understand me?" I nod silently. "So, if he asks you out again, would you agree? For your Uncle Ben?"

I look down at my lap and realize that Ben is holding my hand. "He will not ask me again, if he is a man of virtues." I look up past Ben, but don't meet his eyes.

"You don't think he would? What if—"

Ring ring!

A phone call on Ben's Blackberry interrupts us. He answers the phone.

"Ben Dynham speaking. Yes . . . really? That sounds great . . . yes, I will check my email . . . sure, I will forward . . . thank you . . ." He ends the call with a smile, and shakes his head with closed eyes. He is looking for words, probably, so I wait for him to speak. "You were right, Rania. He *is* a man of virtues." He looks up and sees my astonished face.

"You spurned him, and he took another route, a very prudent one." Ben is still shaking his head in bewilderment.

"What are you talking about, Ben?" The suspense is killing me.

"I am saying that he has planned a party, in honor of Greenway and Gibson doing business together. Can you believe that?"

What? That was ludicrous, to throw a party just to see me. Why not just ask me out again?

I am dumbstruck. *Is Adam actually a man of virtue?*

"When is the party?" I ask him. My interest brings smile to his face.

"Tonight. Fairmont Royal York. 7p.m." Ben's information is short but complete. "They will be emailing us shortly. I will forward the invitation to all my employees. We are *all* invited." He puts more emphasis on *all,* and I know what he is trying to convey.

Without saying anything further, I push back my chair and stand up. Ben looks at me curiously. I collect my travel mug and my jacket and head for the doorway, Ben following. "Are you going somewhere?"

"I need the rest of the day off, Ben." Without waiting for his response, I leave the room to clear my head.

* * *

I step outside the Gibson building and feel the cold November breeze. After this morning, I need some time on my own. I look around and see Gibson's stones and decorative bolts, where I first glimpsed those green eyes. There were some extraordinary messages emitting from them. I have never felt like that. With his big emerald eyes, dark brown hair, sharp features, and extremely seductive appearance, he was an angel in the guise of a man. There was something pulling me toward him. He was affectionate, so why did I push him away? There is no harm in asking someone out for a date. But his scorching gaze was wrecking all the doors in my heart that I had closed long ago. He did not even knock at the doors. He is trying to batter them down without my permission, and it is very hard for me to let him do such thing. He is like a forbidden fruit, attracting everyone around him into the paradise of pleasure. I know the consequences of trying this fruit, but still, I am tempted to take the risk.

I inhale deeply one more time and head to the Starbucks at the corner of the street. It is about time that I do some research on Adam Gibson. I purchase my hot chocolate, sit down in the corner and open my iPhone. I search his name on my browser and lots of interesting results appear.

One newspaper wrote that he has disparate views about women. He had mentioned in one of his interviews that a woman's body is only meant for a man's pleasure and nothing else. If the hunger could be addressed in simple ways, then why would a man entangle himself in the complexity of a relationship? I close my eyes and remember his gaze on me, and it sends shivers down my spine.

Was he looking at me to satiate his hunger? To charm me with his wealth, and then take me to bed?

The thought fills me with abhorrence. I will never let him seduce me. I promise in my heart.

He is a very dangerous man. Ben's words ring an alarm in my ears. I search for more on the Internet about his sexual life, but I believe it has been kept very private. He has been spotted with some women, leaving after parties, but nothing more than that is mentioned. One of the newspapers mentions that he is the youngest business magnate in Canada, a mogul in construction and development. From houses to high-rise condominiums, from resorts to five-star hotels, schools to community centers, he rules almost all of Ontario.

I am more interested in reading about his personal life. I want to know if he is a self-made man or if he inherited this business. I learn that his father started as a builder of private homes. He wanted his son to be an architect, so that he could expand the business. Adam's father died of a heart attack when Adam was twenty-three, just as he finished his university studies, leaving an immature business to his son. With his creativity and intelligence, Adam rode his father's dream to the highest level and in nine years, he touched the skies. *His father must be proud of him from up there.*

I want to know more about him as a man. One of the articles mentions that he was only six when his mother left his dad and married another man, taking their younger daughter, who was two months old at that time. I feel sorry for Adam. A six-year-old boy, how did he live without a mother? Who would have been there to tuck him into bed? Who would have been there to tell him bedtime stories? Who would have comforted him, when he woke up frightened in the middle of the night? But now, he is Adam Gibson. A man with attitude, power, and unlimited wealth. *Does he still see his mother?* I wonder, and then question why I would be interested in his personal life.

As I slide through my browser, one link catches my attention. *"A man with an altruistic soul."*

I open the link and I am flabbergasted to see that a few years back, he donated fifty acres of land to the municipality of Toronto. He has constructed a huge state-of-the-art community center to provide shelter to the homeless. It is mentioned that more than three hundred people come and eat there daily, at Gibson's expense. Apart from the shelter home, the community center holds all kinds of religious activities, whether it is Christians' prayers, Muslims' Salat, Jews' Siddur, Hindus' worship services—it accommodates all. I put the phone down and rest my back on the seat, thinking about him. He is donating an extreme amount of wealth from his treasure box to the needy and afflicted. It is heartwarming. My perception toward him is beginning to change. He is creating his own space in my heart.

I don't want to read any more. It is too much information for me to absorb in a day. No matter how dangerous he is, I am not afraid of him anymore. He has a heart. He has a soul.

* * *

I leave Starbucks and take a long walk. The flavor of the holiday season is already filling up the city, with beautiful decorations of garlands and Christmas trees. Since I told Ben I was taking the rest of the day to blow off all my agitation, I decide to be a kid once again, and visit Santa's parade. University Avenue is crowded with hundreds of families who are waiting for Santa to arrive. There are groups singing Christmas carols with jingle bells, and giving away candies. I have to agree with the song that is being played from somewhere close by—it is truly the most wonderful time of the year. The whole street is blocked in honor of the parade. People are standing on the sidewalks, kids riding in strollers, couples walking hand in hand, bike riders crossing in between people. I close my eyes, engrossed in the atmosphere. For the time being, I feel completely free of all worries.

I feel something hit me, knocking me to the ground. But I don't land on the pavement—strong arms are holding me tight, and I land on something that cushions my fall.

I was so lost in my other world that for a minute I can't figure out what happened.

My thoughts are interrupted by a very familiar masculine voice. "Watch out. Are you fucking blind?" he is shouting. When I open my eyes, I find I am lying on Adam Gibson.

We are both on the concrete sidewalk; he has his arms around me. *Where the hell did he come from, in my other world?* I look at him, speechless and bemused. He shifts to a sitting position, still holding me tight.

I am still trying to absorb where I am. He brushes my hair away from my cheeks and gently cups my face with his warm hands. There is never enough space for me to breathe when he touches me.

The last thing I remember, I closed my eyes and something pushed me. Now when I open my eyes, I am in his arms.

How the hell did that happen?

"Are you okay? Are you hurt, Rania?" There is pure gentleness in his voice. I am still trying to catch my breath. He tucks my hair behind my ears. "Talk to me, Rania. Are you hurt?"

He is treating me like a six-year-old child who has been lost, and now her father is here to rescue her. I shift away from him and he releases me. He is still concerned, his eyes observing my every expression. He waits patiently for me to speak.

"What are you doing here?" I ask him, annoyed.

Silly me!

I could have said something better, like I am fine. His expression changes from concern to astonishment.

"Didn't you see the biker coming your way? You were standing right in his path. He could have hurt you." His expression changes again, back to concern.

"No, I . . . I didn't see anything . . . I . . ." I look around, trying to avoid him looking at me like that.

"He was calling to you to move. Didn't you hear him?" He stands up and holds my hand to help me up. I don't know what to say, so I let him stand me on my feet. My knees are still feeling weak, and he probably notices it. He holds me by my elbow. "Come, sit here on this bench." He guides me to the bench, where we sit together. Adam angles a bit and faces me. I cover my face and rest my elbows on my knees. I have nothing to say. What was I thinking? Why was I standing in the bikers' lane with my eyes and ears closed?

"You came here to save me?" I remove my hands from my face and turn toward him.

"Yes . . . no . . . I mean . . . I . . . I saw you standing there, as if you were not aware of your surroundings. Then I saw the biker coming your way and heard him warning you to move. But you weren't listening, so I moved you out of the way. I hope you're not hurt." He is checking my elbows and turns his head to check my back for injuries.

"But what are you doing here?" *Oh, Rania, is that all you can say? Have you forgotten to say thank you to the person who saved you?*

"You are very welcome, Rania." He is smiling at me, trying to hide his laughter. He makes me realize that I am a rude and stubborn girl, and instead of having the courtesy to thank him, I am asking a dumb question and scowling at him. After all, it is a free country. He can go to anyplace he wants. It is his damn right. I look around the crowd and realize that there are people staring at us as if we are some celebrity couple.

"Umm . . . I am sorry. Thank you . . . for saving me." I look at him nervously, and he watches me with his intense green eyes. "But really, what are you doing at the Santa parade? I thought you had a meeting." I gaze at him to read his expression.

"I can ask you the same. What are you doing here?" He looks more intense, interrogating me as if he had caught me doing some crime.

"I came here to see the Santa parade, and I—"

"I thought you were still at work. I came to . . . see you, and then Ben told me you took the rest of the day off." He checks my every single expression, like he is trying to read what is going on in my mind.

"You are here for me? Why?" Now it is my turn to fire a question. "And how in the world did you know I was here? Wait! Are you stalking—"

"No, no, please, don't think like that." He shrugs in an apologetic manner. "I came down to the room to talk to you and apologize about my behavior in the corridor. So, I met Ben on my way and I asked him about you. He told me you have taken a day off so I—"

"But I didn't tell Ben where I was going." The conversation is igniting.

Is he actually spying on me? But what does he want?

"Thanks to technology. I tracked your phone, and—"

"RANIA! Hey, look here!"

I hear my name being called from somewhere in the crowd. I look around to see where the familiar voice is coming from. I ignore Adam, as I am seriously pissed. Is this the way to apologize to someone? Tracking them down through their phone? I stand up from the bench and head toward the voice.

"Oh my God! Mike?" I rush into the crowd in excitement. My best friend is standing here, and I haven't seen him in three months. He was gone on some special police training to Calgary. I missed him so much, and the happiness in his eyes tells me he has missed me too. I run to him and hug him tightly.

"Oh, Mike. It is so good to see you. How come you are here?"

"I missed you so much, Rania. I came this morning, and they assigned me to monitor the parade. I saw you sitting with that guy, so—"

"I am so happy to see you, Mike. Does Ben know you are here?" I interrupt Mike before he can ask me about the *guy*. I hope he didn't see me and Adam lying on the ground. That would be embarrassing.

"No, Dad doesn't know yet. I was caught up at work." I see Mike's gaze shifting, and I realize Adam is standing next to me.

Ben's words come to mind—that I should be easy on Adam, or else I would end up spoiling his business with Ben. I look at Adam and smile. He returns it, but with an interrogating look.

"Mike, sorry. This is Mr. Gibson. And Mr. Gibson . . . this is Mike, my friend." The two men look at each other curiously, and shake hands.

"Pleasure meeting you, Mr. Gibson. Are you the one who—"

"Yes, I assume you are talking about the one who builds houses?" Mike looks back to me with a question on his face, *what-the-hell-you-are-doing-with-him-in-public?* "So, Rania, it's surprising to know that you have cops as your friends. I should be more cautious, then." Adam winks at me with a wicked smile. Mike is still holding many questions in his head. He is only waiting for Adam to leave.

"I didn't know Rania had friends other than me." Mike speaks with disappointment.

Friend? He thinks Adam is my friend.

Could this be more embarrassing than the morning accident?

"No, Mike, I guess Rania has given this honor only to you. I don't think I'm that lucky. She is very . . ." He speaks to Mike but then he looks at me to continue. "Very reserved." His gaze moves from my head down my whole body. Every time he looks at me like that, I feel a thousand watts of current running down my spine.

How can he do that, with just a look?

I see a hint of satisfaction on Mike's face. Adam looks and sounds very serious. He looks like a wounded dragon, whom I have stabbed directly in his heart with a big sharp dagger.

Or is it just my poor imagination?

"I know I am the luckiest man on this planet." There is a smile in Mike's words, and he speaks with pride. He has made me feel special all these years. Mike is a good guy, with extremely strong looks and build. Every time I used to hang out with him, I noticed many feminine eyes locked on him in desperation. He always asked me if I were jealous when girls stare at him, and I didn't have any answer, though he has mentioned many times that he is jealous of the way other men look at me.

Today, I see jealousy in Mike's eyes, but what's more interesting is that the same jealousy is in Adam's eyes.

Am I thinking too much?

"So, Rania, let's hang out tonight, baby," Mike says in a very sexy manner. "It's been so long. I missed you so much." He's never used that tone to me before. He puts his arms around me and I see Adam looking at us angrily. I don't know why he should be jealous. He is famous as a womanizer, and there is no way I am letting myself be one of his extra flavors.

I shift away from Mike, taking his hands off of me.

"Actually, Mike . . . tonight would not be possible. I have something official to attend. But tomorrow night? I promise." I look at Mike, who is watching Adam gazing at me.

"Sure, girl. Anything for you. I will call you. I have to get back to my duty now. See you." He places a light kiss on my forehead. I am not heated by Mike's kiss, but Adam's eyes on me are burning me from inside. "Pleasure meeting you, Mr. Gibson."

Adam smiles at him and they shake hands. Mike disappears into the crowd, leaving Adam and me with words hanging in the air.

Before we can say anything to each other, I hear the crowd roaring. I turn around and see many people welcoming Santa. In all this conversation, I missed the whole parade. It is sadly about to end. I join the crowd and take my phone out to make a video, ignoring Adam. What is he still doing here?

What does he want to say or ask?

I put my phone back in my pocket and turn toward him.

"You looked like an innocent child when you were looking at Santa." He gives me a smile and steps closer to me. "You looked at him as if you had a secret wish to tell him."

How does he know? Is he a psychiatrist or a mind reader?

His question makes me nervous and I start to twist my ring on my index finger.

"Santa Claus doesn't exist, Mr. Gibson. It is just our imagination." I look toward the parade to avoid any visual contact with him.

"No, he doesn't exist, but a wish does." He is totally unaware that people passing by are noticing us. I am feeling way too awkward.

I am not going to share any wish with him, though the wish does exist. Not waiting for me to speak, Adam continues. "You seem to like all this?" He glances around the area.

"I enjoy everything about the holiday season. The colors, the décor, the glitter, how the trees and houses light up in the dark." I take a deep breath, but avoid looking at Adam. "The lights at night tell us that no matter how much darkness there is, only the light can dispel it." I look back to Adam, who is listening to me seriously. "Everyone likes it, Mr. Gibson. Can't you see all the people here, already in a festive mood?" Adam's gaze gets stronger. He takes a few steps back from me and closes his eyes for a moment, shaking his head. I wait for him to say something.

"No, Rania, I can't see . . . I can't see people . . ." He shakes his head again, eyes still closed.

What is he saying?

He looks at me again and continues. "When you are around . . . I can't see anything . . . other than you."

He steps back, turns around and disappears into the crowd.

Shit! What was that?

THE PARTY

♂

"The property we purchased last year has made us an enormous profit." My lawyer, Tom McKenzie, clinks his champagne glass with mine.

"Toast to the Abyss resorts," I reply. "The northern Ontario market is booming—higher than our expectations. We should look for more land to build high-end luxury resorts. I want Americans to come and spend money at our properties, rather than roaming around in their own country."

I glance at the doorway and my heart stops beating. I feel that time has halted too, as she enters the room. *She looks so fucking amazing.* She is looking around like an innocent child who has entered a magical kingdom for the first time. But the truth is, all the magic is in her. She looks like a beautiful Christmas present, wrapped in a demure red lace dress, a holiday treat I would want to hold on to forever.

Fuck! How does she know I have a thing for lace?

I watch her heading toward Ben Dynham. He asks her something and looks at his watch. She's almost an hour late. I want to ask what took her so long, but it's better to ask Ali later on. I texted her a few hours ago but got no response, which in itself is an untold message. Men are gazing at her like hawks; I feel like kicking all of them out of this party. A man approaches her, asking for a dance. She refuses. I'm pleased that I am not the only one being turned down.

What am I? A fucking teenager?

A few minutes later, some other prick asks her for a dance. Then another, and a few minutes later another.

I should start counting.

I smile in my head. I actually get interested in finding out how many men she will reject tonight. Among the three hundred guests, no woman is as captivating and enticing as she is. I am too afraid to try my luck. She finally sees me, and excuses herself from the conversation she's in to come over and say hello.

"Hi." She offers a handshake with a charming smile. For the first time, in all those dazzling lights, I notice she has dimples on both cheeks.

I realize I've never seen them before because she's never smiled at me like this. My heart starts beating like a drum. I hope she can't hear it.

"You look . . ." I check her out from head to toe, but fail to find the appropriate words. "You look . . . beautiful . . . very magnetic . . . I—"

"Thank you, Mr. Gibson, for your hospitality. And thank you for sending your special man to pick me up." She looks around nervously at the other guests.

"The pleasure is all mine, Rania. And please remember my name. It's Adam." That seems to make her more nervous. We are interrupted by a butler carrying a champagne tray. "Would you like something to drink, Rania? We have some special—"

"I am sorry, I don't drink," she interrupts, looking at the butler.

"Sure. Any juice? Water?" I pause. "Tea?" She smiles and shakes her head, as she remembers what I wanted her to remember.

"No thank you, Mr. Gibson . . . umm . . . I mean, Adam. I don't feel like having anything. I will certainly ask if I need something later. Thanks for offering, though." She gives me another smile, and then avoids eye contact.

So, she is shy!

The music changes in the background and I see lots of people moving on the dance floor. She admires the couples dancing, unaware that I am admiring her.

"Your fragrance . . ." *will screw me one day.* I close my eyes to breathe and open them to continue, ". . . heavenly." She gives me a bashful smile and looks past my shoulder. "Rania, if you don't mind, can I ask for a dance with you?" I ask her hesitantly and prepare myself for the rejection. *Don't say no, don't say no.* I recite the mantra in my head.

"Sure. My pleasure." She smiles at me, but the smile is not reaching her eyes. She's acting different tonight. She's talking to me with normal eye contact, and her attitude is friendlier than this morning. She puts her gold clutch on one of the tables and follows me to the dance floor.

I put one hand behind her curvy waist and hold her hand with the other. Her other hand rests on my shoulder.

"Mr. Gibson, I should warn you in advance. I don't know how to dance. If I trip—"

"Seriously? Who are you kidding, Rania?" I ask her impishly. She looks away, but doesn't say anything, so I continue. "I won't let you fall." I wish I could tell her that I know she dances well. She has been taking classes every day. She is shy and hesitant, so she looks at my shoulder.

"Thank you for saving me today. I am sorry I was rough on you. I shouldn't—"

"You like sparkles?" I interrupt her, and she looks up at me, not expecting the question.

"Yes . . . how do you—"

"It's obvious. Your jewelry, your watch, your dress, everything has a bit of sparkle. You look very alluring."

"You already mentioned it, Mr. Gibson. Thank you." She glances at me once before averting her eyes.

"Don't you like to be complimented?" I ask her gently.

"Who doesn't?" She smiles at me. "But false acclaim leads nowhere."

"You think I'm lying? You don't realize how beautiful you are?" My question concerns me too. I lean closer to her and whisper Lorenz Hart's phrase into her ear. *"Bewitched, bothered and bewildered am I."*

Is she really unaware of it?

She smiles and shakes her head.

"Seventeen men approached you for a dance, and you doubt your attractiveness?"

"You were counting?" She laughs with an open heart, like an innocent child. The sound fills my heart with contentment.

"Actually . . . yes, I was counting. I saw you rejected the first three, and so I entertained myself by counting the number of heartbroken men."

She keeps laughing, as if I have actually cracked a joke.

"I didn't know you had a sense of humor." She wipes a tear of laughter from her eye.

"You think I'm joking? No, seriously, there were seventeen." She continues chuckling, but this time the smile reaches her eyes. "On a serious note, can I ask you something?"

She purses her lips to stop laughing, and concentrates on my words.

"Yes please, Mr. Gibson. No one has made me laugh like this in a long time. Please ask." I still see the sparkle in her eyes.

"I noticed you keep men at arms' length. I mean, strangers. I am still a stranger to you, so I was wondering why you agreed to dance with me." She looks up at me. The smile is gone from her lips and eyes. "It's okay if you don't want to tell me."

"Oh no, Mr. Gibson. I don't think you would like to hear the truth!" She starts to look nervous and gazes around the room, avoiding my eye.

"What is it, Rania? Are you hiding something?" *What is she trying to say?*

"You really want to know why I accepted your offer?" I nod, and she continues. "Can I trust you with the truth?"

"Please, tell me. I won't say a word. Trust me." I follow her gaze as she looks toward Ben. He's watching us dance.

"Your propositions have seduced my boss . . . leaving no choice for me . . ." She takes a deep breath. "If I dared to refuse you . . . he is afraid you might . . ."

She looks down at the floor, her expression sad.

"I might sever my verbal commitment?" I finish what she left unsaid.

Fucking bastard!

I curse Ben Dynham at this moment. She's still looking miserably at the floor. I feel my heart sinking in a giant ocean of emotions. All the time, she was smiling because of my fucking power. I stop dancing and release her. She looks like her pride has been torn in millions of pieces; I didn't know my wealth could crush someone like that. I don't know what to say.

"I am sorry, Mr. Gibson, I didn't—" She trembles with fear, but still, she manages to innocently reach her hand toward me to continue the dance.

"No, Rania. Please, I'm the one who is sorry. You should have told me earlier." I step back and pull my hands away from her. She looks at her boss nervously, and I see him watching us. *Don't get her in more trouble.*

I take the phone from my pocket and pretend I've received a call. She stands here, looking scared. I fake a smile and make an excuse to leave the dance floor. She stands there for a moment, then goes back to where she left her clutch and leans on the back of a chair, trembling. I want to hold her in my arms and comfort her, but I understand she needs some space. She picks up her clutch and heads toward the doorway.

Is she leaving?

She didn't even eat anything. If I stop her at the doorway, Ben will notice, and I don't want to create any more trouble for her. Instead, I choose wireless technology to communicate with her.

> *I am unable to find the words to apologize. I'm sorry to have put you in this position. I never wanted our first dance to end this way. Yet, I feel honored that you put your trust in me. I will never break it. Thank you, and sorry. Please stay for dinner. Adam.*

I join the people at the bar, who are busy having drinks. My eyes are locked on the main door, hoping she will come back. I shouldn't have backed out of the dance like that. But she was dancing with me against her will. She refused to dance with other men because there was no power involved; she was free to make her own decision. In my case, no one asked her what she wanted. I can't even go and ask Ben why he asked her to do such a thing. That would create more problems in her office. I remember Ali telling me that her apartment belongs to Ben. It means there is more between them than just a boss-employee relationship.

I check my phone again, to see if I have missed a reply from her. Then I see her coming back inside. She looks my way, still holding some sadness in her eyes, but her fear is gone. We gaze at each other silently, sharing unspoken secrets. I see her eyes thanking me for my actions, and my eyes are apologizing for her heartache. I call a server and ask him to go and offer her something to drink. She looks at me again and I clink my glass from a distance. She picks up an orange juice and offers me the same gesture. I watch her taking a seat with some women I don't know.

Ali stands beside me and watches me watching her.

"I have never seen such innocence in my life. And this alarming beauty . . ." I sigh deeply.

"*Beauty is worse than wine, it intoxicates both the holder and beholder.*"[3] I notice he is holding a business document. He follows my eyes, and puts the paper in his pocket. He is intelligent enough not to ask me anything regarding work right now. "Apart from elegance, she carries intelligence as well." Ali faces the bar, asking for a drink. He takes a sip from his glass and continues. "You were right, Adam. She is not like other women you have been . . . umm . . . dealing with in the past. You'll have to work really hard." Ali looks at his glass intently while speaking to me. I turn around completely to face the bar. I'm offered another drink. "I saw you made her laugh. You are going to hit the news tomorrow." Ali smirks behind his glass. "*Toronto's most eligible bachelor is finally captivated.*" I shake my head and continue with the drink. "By the way, I found out who her boyfriend is. I mean the young cop." He puts his glass down and looks at me seriously. I wait for him to continue. "He is Mike Dynham. Son of Ben Dynham."

Apart from being her boss, Ben is her boyfriend's father? The way Mike was watching Rania, there was a *marry-me* request in his eyes. She is living under his roof. But if Mike intends to marry her in the future, then why is Ben pushing Rania toward me? Is he nothing but a beast, a person who can't see his son's emotions? Then how would I expect him to consider Rania? *Fucking bastard.*

I still wonder if Rania and Mike are in a live-in relationship. But if that were the case, then why would Rania be the one paying rent? Ali's limited information is enough for me to understand Rania's position. She's doing Ben a favor because of Mike. I turn around and cock my head to glance toward her. She's busy talking to some people. I put my glass on the table and look at Ali.

"I have to make an announcement. Excuse me." I leave the bar and head to the stage, picking up the microphone.

"Ladies and gentlemen! May I have your attention please?" The conversation dies down and everyone looks at me, including Rania. "I thank everyone who honored us by your presence here tonight. I hope you are all having a good time. Dinner will be served shortly. But before that, I would like to surprise all of you with a special performance. I recently learned that most of

---

3   *Aldous Huxley (1894-1963)*

the people around us are already in a *festive* mood." I look toward Rania. Her mouth is open in surprise. "But there is something I would like to mention before the entertainment starts." I pause for a moment. "We light our homes and our surroundings at night during this season, yet we forget to light our hearts, which remain in the darkness. Someone told me a very nice thing, which I will remember always. The lights at night tell us that no matter how much darkness there is, only the light can dispel it. Thank you all. Please enjoy the evening." I put the microphone down and hear people clapping all around the ballroom. I watch Rania's expression, and she looks completely baffled. I decide not to approach her right now, so I take another route and stand beside Ali to wait for the surprise.

Black curtains drop behind the stage, providing a backdrop. As soon as the music starts, twelve young girls appear, dressed in light pink dresses with pink masks over their eyes, and begin to dance. The black background curtains are covered in stars and sparkles, providing a magical experience for the audience. The lights in the ballroom dim, to enhance the shine of the stars onstage. The sparkles remind me to look at Rania instead of watching the performance. She is engrossed in it, tapping her feet to the music. It warms my heart to see how much she loves the dancing. I'd arrange the whole performance just to see that look on her face. I'm glad she decided not to leave, even though she didn't answer my text.

I walk toward her just as the music is about to end. I want to ask her if she liked it. I want to hear her words, see if the dance brought some joy to her sad eyes. When I get close enough to read her eyes, I see tears streaming from them. I stand frozen, unable to take another step. Her tears draw a boundary all around her, an unapproachable territory. If I dared to cross that boundary, I would likely get burned. She looks down for a moment and wipes her tears with her napkin, then looks around to see if anyone noticed. She doesn't know I'm the only one who can't see anything except her. She glances once again at the crowd, and heads for the main door to escape.

What the fuck just happened?

Everyone else is busy applauding the mesmerizing performance, but my eyes keep following her. She cuts through the crowd and exits. I follow her blindly, ignoring the people trying to talk to me about the performance. I desperately want to know what made her cry. I wanted to see joy in her eyes, yet I've made another blunder and grieved her once again. Luckily, I catch her in the lobby.

"Rania, I won't ask what made you cry, as I believe it would be too personal, but I am extremely sorry if I've done anything wrong, anything disrespectful."

"No, please." She looks at me strangely. "Please, don't apologize again and again, when you haven't done anything. It is very embarrassing."

"I didn't mean to embarrass you," I whisper politely.

"I should be the one to say sorry." She shakes her head and closes her eyes in despair.

"Why are you sorry? About our dance? Trust me, it's okay! In fact, I'm delighted that you trusted me." I pause for a moment and then continue. "But about that performance, I saw you crying. I thought that you enjoy watching and doing dance. I thought it would please you."

"How do you know?" She looks up at me. "How do you know I dance, or that I like dance?" She keeps looking in my eyes, and it's my turn to avoid her gaze.

"Remember . . . you called me a stalker this afternoon and . . ." I look up at her with a smile. Our eyes meet and we burst into laughter together. I still see tears in her eyes, but she is better than a few minutes ago.

"I would like to know someday how your secret spying agency works."

I would like to tell you, someday, how I feel about you. I speak in my head but can't let her know what I'm thinking.

"Adam, I want to go home now." She requests it so gently that it almost melts my heart.

"The dinner is being served. You haven't eaten anything. You can't leave without dinner."

"Thanks for asking, but I don't think I feel like eating anything right now. Please allow me to go home." Her humble plea makes me speechless for a moment. I have no right to keep her here, but I want to be close to her. I want to take away her tears, make her laugh like she did when she was dancing with me.

"If that's what you want, then I won't force you," I say, looking into her eyes. She's left me no choice. "Come, I will drop you home." I guide her toward the exit.

"No, thanks. You are the host of the party. Please don't bother. I will get a cab."

"No, Rania. You are not going in a cab, and I would appreciate it if you don't argue anymore about this." My tone is a bit harsh and she looks fearful again.

"Thanks for your concern, but you should join your party. Ben must be looking for you."

"If that's the case, then I must go." I know the greedy bastard is waiting for me. "But I will ask Ali to give you a ride. It's almost ten, and too late for you to use public transport." She stays quiet, but nods in agreement. I call Ali and ask him to join us in the lobby. "I still owe you dinner, by the way," I murmur, as if I'm talking to myself. She hears me and peeks at me with surprise. "You're leaving without eating anything." I look up and discover a beautiful smile waiting for me.

"You are a good host, Adam." Her praise affects me like a warm breeze in the harsh snow.

"Thanks for the compliment, but I would really like to take you out for dinner. Perhaps tomorrow night?"

"Tomorrow?" I realize it's still too soon to ask her. "I have some plans tomorrow, but—"

"Oh yes, I forgot. With Mike, of course." I glance around to distract myself from the discomforting idea of Mike sitting beside her, having a romantic dinner.

We both remain silent until Ali appears to break the ice. "Ali, please give Miss Rania a ride and make sure she reaches home safely." Ali looks at us both quizzically.

"Certainly, Mr. Gibson." I give him a secret *we-will-talk-about-it-later* look. I glance back to her.

"Where did you put your jacket?"

"I gave it to the coat check lady." She opens her clutch and takes out the claim check.

"I will bring it." Ali excuses himself and leaves to get her jacket.

Before we get a chance to say anything, Ali comes back. I take the jacket from him and help her into it. Her jacket is ash-gray, and the style complements her body. It has her fragrance, too. She hands me her clutch while she buttons it. Ali wisely stands at a distance, to give us a chance to exchange good-byes.

"Thanks for the wonderful evening, Adam."

"Wonderful?" *Really!* I give a wicked smile. She understands it very well. She looks down shyly.

Damn me! I embarrassed her again.

"I should leave now. Thank you. Good night." She steps back and waits for my response. *Say something, you fucking dimwit, before she leaves!*

"Good night, Rania." I also step away from her, and watch her leaving the lobby with Ali. *You are such a dumb ass, Gibson.*

I join the party again. There are many people waiting for me, from business associates to paparazzi. They all talk to me with interest and take pictures of me, but my mind is somewhere else. I respond to everyone with yes and no answers. No one has the slightest idea what's on my mind.

You threw the party for her and she left without eating anything. How could you eat now?

I realize that she'll be going home with an empty stomach. I text Ali, asking him to get something for her to eat, with her permission, before dropping her off. The party is supposed to end at midnight, and I'm disappointed she left so soon. I wanted to be with her, but she reminded me of my damn position, which forces me to be here with a bunch of brainless people.

I divert my mind to the business conversation, as thinking about her is not profitable. I can still feel her in my arms, see the way she cried and opened up to me; it was far more exhilarating than any million-dollar deal. After so much trouble, I was able to give her comfort, though it was just for a moment. I want to know so much about her that even if I spent my whole fortune trying to dig out information, I wouldn't be able to find it all. Everything is in her heart, and my power fails there.

What had happened to her that brought tears to her eyes? Whom did she remember when she saw the dance? People are still talking to me, and I am lost in thoughts of her.

"Hey, Mr. Gibson. I was looking for you." I turn around and find myself facing Ben Dynham.

"Good evening, Mr. Dynham. Thank you for coming." I fake a smile, and curse him in my heart. *It's all because of you, you prick.*

"It's a wonderful party, Mr. Gibson. We all want to thank you for the lovely welcome dinner. I look forward to our prosperous business relationship." The bastard can't talk about anything besides business. He doesn't care if his son's girlfriend was crying in my arms a while ago. "I was looking for you to personally thank you for your hospitality, but I guess you got busy with something." *I know what you want to ask, you greedy monster.* He's waiting for me to say something, but he doesn't have the balls to ask where Rania is.

"Oh yes, I went to see off Miss Ahmed. She wasn't feeling well."

"She left? So soon?" he asks me with surprise, pretending he doesn't know.

"Yes, she asked my pardon for leaving early, and I sent her home safely in my car." *Don't be hard on her, you moron.* He reads my expression, but he's lucky he can't read my mind. I swear to myself, if he even thinks of pushing her at me one more time against her will, I will take his balls off. Ben Dynham smiles back at me with an expression that says he has found out everything he wants to know from me.

I don't notice when Ben leaves. I'm too busy wondering if Ali has asked her about the dinner. Ali knows how to deal with women, but this time, it is my woman and it would be hard on his nerves too.

Yes, my woman.

I close my eyes for a moment to picture her in my head, and my phone distracts me with a text message.

> *I have no doubts about mentioning once again that you are a good host. Thank you for the dinner. Your special man was kind enough to let me know that you wanted me to eat something. I appreciate your concern. I am enjoying my chocolate shake right now, but I would like to let you know that I have reached home safely. Thank you for what you did and for everything you tried.*
> *Rania*

I stand frozen, reading her message again and again. So she did realize that I was trying something. She did get my hidden messages, which I couldn't say due to her innocence. Ali is right. She is intelligent, besides having the beauty of a goddess.

Suddenly, I feel lighthearted. I see people noticing that I'm smiling to myself.

What am I? Fourteen?

I take the corner seat at the bar and start typing.

> *Your praise has actually made me believe that the light exists. I am able to see it now. But a chocolate shake is not a dinner. I still owe you one.*

I wait for her message eagerly, like a child waiting for candies. I don't even notice when the bartender hands me a drink. My phone vibrates again with her text.

> *What if I say, I owe you a dinner?*

I look at her message dubiously. People around me are talking to me; I have no fucking clue what I'm saying. My mind is on the wireless ride. I can't understand her last message.

> *What do you mean you owe me?*

I wait for her reply. It takes forever. After ten minutes, I receive her response.

> *You were very kind today . . . and understanding. I want to thank you. Would you give me the honor of being your host? I will try to be a good one.*

What? Is she inviting me for dinner?

I can't believe my luck. I jump from my seat in excitement, which startles everyone around me. Is she joking? Or playing games with me?

Calm down, Gibson! You are not a fucking adolescent.

I decide to cut the crap of sending messages and waiting for them endlessly, so I call her.

"Excuse me, gentlemen. I need to make an urgent call." There's too much noise in the party hall, so I escape to the lobby. I dial her number with my heart pumping frantically.

After three rings, I hear her beautiful voice. "Hello."

"Hi. This is . . . umm . . . this is me." *You don't have a name, moron?* "I hope I didn't disturb you." I can hear the hesitation in my voice. *The oh-so Mr. Confidant is finally shaky and nervous.*

"No, you didn't. But you surprised me. Your party is over?" I can hear her sipping her chocolate shake. She can do magic with her voice too.

"No, the party is still going on. Listen! Are you playing some game with me?" I'm trying really hard to conceal my nervousness.

"Game? What game?" She sounds surprised. *Oh no! Please don't hang up the phone.*

"Your last text. I couldn't understand it. That's why I called—"

"Oh, really? I thought you were intelligent enough to decode messages." She interrupts me, and from her tone I can sense she's smiling too. She's in a lighthearted mood.

So, she is playing games.

I remain silent, as I don't know what she has in mind.

She continues, "Adam, you have been really kind to me today. I have been thinking about . . ." She pauses for a moment and then continues hesitantly, ". . . us and I found myself at fault. You proved to be a perfect host tonight, and I escaped from there like a fool."

"That's all right, Rania. It was your wish not to stay. I had no right to ask you—"

"No, please, Adam. Let me finish what I have to say." Her voice warms me through the phone. "I don't want you to think that I am some rude, self-centered girl. It's just that I am not comfortable with strangers. This morning when you asked me out, I didn't know what to say, as I never expected that. I didn't know how to deal with you, so I escaped. I am still surprised that you wanted to see me again after my rude behavior. Yet, you found another way to meet me and arranged a party." She pauses for a moment. I hear her breathing. *So, she knows I threw the party for her.* "I am not blind, Adam. I can see your kindness and . . . feel it too. But what I don't get is that even when I was not good to you, you were there when I needed a shoulder to cry on. I never thought I could cry in front of a stranger . . . I—"

"You still consider me a stranger?" *We are not strangers, Rania. We were never meant to be.*

"I don't know. I just want to say I am very sorry about my rudeness. And I want to make it up to you. I know you went to a great deal of trouble for me and I left the party in the middle, without saying why. You were kind enough to understand me. I have no words to thank you."

"You don't need to thank me, please." *It is not me who is kind; it is you, who has a tender loving heart.*

"No, Adam. Please let me thank you. Let me be a good host. I know it is not enough to reciprocate, but I really want to invite you for dinner. If you can take some time out of your busy schedule . . . on Sunday evening?"

What? Is she serious? Is she inviting me?

Of course, it's just a dinner, but at least I can hope for more. *You don't need to ask.* I smile from the other side of the phone.

"Rania . . . I really don't know what to say. I am . . . awed. I feel honored that you're asking me. But please, let's make it the other way around. I would like to take you to dinner."

We both pause for a moment. As soon as I think of saying something, she interrupts me.

"But I want to thank you."

"You don't have to thank me for anything, Rania, but if that's what you wish, we will meet at the place of your choice. You can offer me your hospitality there." I can't stop smiling, and I feel she is too.

"Please, Adam. Don't complicate it. It would be on me. And you need to choose the place. I don't know what kind of food you like."

"I will eat anything you want me to. Whatever pleases you, pleases me." I imagine her cuddled up in bed, wearing her nightdress. I wish I could have seen her when I made her smile.

"Thank you, Adam. I will text you the address tomorrow. We will meet there at seven in the evening." I don't want this conversation to end so soon.

"If you don't mind, can I pick you up from your place?" I feel the nervousness in my voice, and I am sure she hears me too.

"I can come by myself. Please don't bother."

"If you are not comfortable with the idea, I will send Ali to give you a ride. But please, no cabs or subways. Consider it a way of thanking me, if you really want to." I am literally bargaining with her. *Is this some kind of a business deal?*

She pauses for a moment, thinking. "But then, how would you get there?"

"Rania, I own more than one car," I murmur. I hear her giggling on the other end.

"Of course, I almost forgot. I am talking to Mr. Gibson." Her innocent giggles gladden my heart too. I see people passing by giving me strange looks. No one has ever seen me smiling over a phone call. She continues with a hint of humor in her voice. "All right then, I will see Ali at seven on Sunday. If not tomorrow, then I will text you the address on Sunday afternoon." She is still sipping her chocolate shake.

"I'll wait for your message, Rania." *And you don't know how desperately I'm waiting to see you again.* How will I pass these forty-eight hours? *Rania, you're sending me to an endless journey of time.*

"Good night, Adam." *Say something, you moron.*

"Good night, Rania." *Fuck me!*

She disconnects the line, leaving me with hope. A hope of a journey to a magical kingdom with my enchantress.

THE DREAM

"Please don't hurt me. Please don't hurt me. No . . . stay away from me." She was crying in pain but he was all over her, touching her everywhere, hurting her everywhere, torturing her everywhere.

"You frigid girl. You are as cold as ice. You are nothing but a wasted piece of dead meat. When will you learn to warm your husband's bed?" He was drunk, pouring dirty words in her ears.

She tried to push him away. *"I am your wife. Please have some mercy. I am having your baby."*

"My baby? A whore carrying my baby? I saw you talking to someone in my bedroom and you say you are the mother of my child, you hooker. Come here, you bitch, I want to fuck you so hard that you will forget everything other than your husband." He pulled her by her hair over to the bed. *"You fuck other men behind my back, and you defy your own husband. Where is that asshole, you whore?"*

"Please don't call me that. Show some respect. I swear there was no one in the room. I swear on my baby. If you think you made a mistake by marrying me, then free me." She was trying hard to breathe.

"Free you? You think I will leave you so soon? I married a fool. I thought you'd bring wealth to me. You betrayed me. All you brought with you is this shit dead body with no heart."

He slapped her hard in the face. She was crying in pain, trying to catch her breath.

"I will not give you my money for your drugs and other women—" She twisted away from him and tried to get to the door.

He grabbed her. *"Where the fuck do you think you are going? You dead shit—"*

"No, let me go. You are hurting me . . . ah . . ." She cried out, but there was no one to hear her. No one to come to her rescue. A man was fucking her hard, bruising her body, crushing her soul. She had no escape. She cried from her eyes and from her heart.

She didn't complain, as she knew she was cursed.

THE CITY NEWS

♀

It is a beautiful Saturday morning. I wake up with a smile on my face; my conversation with Adam last night was quite interesting. I feel better that I made him realize that my leaving was not because he was a poor host.

The street outside my apartment is crowded with people going about their usual Saturday morning activities. Since the sun is out, I decide to go for a run.

There are many people in the main lobby. They are all smiling at me. *That's strange!*

I ignore all the smirks and head outside. I turn on some music on my iPhone, put in the earbuds, and start running. A number of people stare at me as I pass. I glance down at my clothes, but nothing is out of the ordinary that I can see.

So many people are staring at me that I start to feel uncomfortable, and I finally quit my run and head back to my apartment. I am hungry, since my only dinner last night was the chocolate shake. As I eat a bowl of cereal I think about the coming weekend. It will be challenging, but I'm looking forward to it, especially spending time with Mike. Before he went away to his training, we saw each other almost every weekend, and I got really bored while he was away. He was always there to bring laughter to my life, cracking jokes and telling me about the people he encountered working as a cop. He'd even tell me about the criminals he interrogated. I love hearing his real-life stories.

And yes, there is Sunday evening to look forward to. I am giving Adam a chance. In one day, he has shown me so much kindness. I've never met a man like him. With everything the media has said about him, being a womanizer and all, he never treated me like that. I am surprised that he didn't overreact when I told him that Ben pushed me into dancing with him. I hadn't expected him to be so understanding.

I remember I promised to text him the location where we should meet. I haven't decided on the restaurant yet. It's hard for me to afford the kind of fancy restaurant a rich man like him is used to, and I don't know what kind of food he prefers. *Whatever pleases you, pleases me.* What does that mean? Is he trying to say that he trusts my choice, or is he trying to tell me something else?

After breakfast, I decide to walk down the lane to Indigo Bookstore to check out the latest books. Meanwhile, I open my phone to send Adam the address of the restaurant. I'm nervous, though I shouldn't be. It is not a date. Opening my phone, I am surprised to find a text message from him.

> *Time seems to be at a standstill. I am wondering if you*
> *know how to maneuver it. I look forward to seeing you.*
> *Thank you for putting your trust in me. Adam.*

The message was sent around three in the morning. *He was awake at that hour? Thinking about me?* I smile to myself. Adam is very unpredictable. Within a single day, he has showered me with so much emotion, it is getting hard for me to endure.

I decide it's better not to think about it anymore, so I search for the restaurant and text him the address.

> *Time waits for no one, you have to catch it, rather than*
> *waiting for it to pass by. I will see you tomorrow.*

I head out to the bookstore. A cold rain has started falling, so I'm glad the store is only a ten-minute walk away. As I walk, I encounter the same gazes and whispers as earlier.

I know there's nothing strange about my looks; I checked myself before leaving. But something is going on. I walk faster.

The bookstore is quiet and peaceful, not at all crowded. I pass the newsstand and I see a familiar picture in the paper.

SHIT!

The front page is filled with pictures of Adam and me. The headline reads: ***TORONTO'S BACHELOR CAPTIVATED.*** One of the pictures is from the meeting yesterday morning. I certainly remember that. But there is another picture of us sitting on the bench at the parade, Adam holding me by my elbow, looking at me with his intense eyes. There is a caption under the picture.

Adam Gibson spotted on Friday afternoon near Santa's parade with his newest conquest.

How the hell did they get this one? It must have been taken right after my near-accident. I hadn't noticed anyone taking our picture.

There is one more picture of us with a surprising caption. **Toronto's most elite bachelor is bewitched, and in an utterly festive mood.**

Shit. It was taken during our dance, when he cracked the joke about my seventeen refusals. I am laughing heartily in the photograph and he is smiling at me with indulgence. I can't believe I didn't notice people taking our picture. I should have realized that it was a huge event and with a man like him, the presence of paparazzi was a given. I now realize why people have been staring at me all morning. They thought I was Adam's girlfriend.

Oh my God, this is so embarrassing.

I quickly buy the paper and hurry home to see what the article says.

It is disappointing for all the young women in Toronto that our city's sexiest and most eligible bachelor seems to have been taken off the market. Though Adam Gibson has always insisted that he doesn't believe in relationships, a picture says a thousand words. If this isn't a relationship, then what do we call it? The lucky lady, Rania Ahmed, is a graphic designer with Greenway Advertising. Although this is the first time Adam and Rania have been seen together publicly, the pictures make it clear that they are more than just acquaintances. Can it be that this girl is taming Adam Gibson, bringing him out of his high-rises and down to earth? Should we all keep our fingers crossed and hope to hear good news from the couple?"

Oh God! How could this happen? I'll have to refuse Mike for tonight. I just can't go out like this when people are staring at me all the time and when I know I am part of the headlines. Just as I think about texting Mike, my phone buzzes with a text message from Adam.

Are you okay?

I'm pretty sure I know what he's talking about, but I text back:

Why? Your spying services are off today?

I smile over my message. I am sure he does too. Within seconds, he texts me back.

I was curious if you've been out, and if you noticed anything unusual.

I answer:

Yes. Unusual and unexpected. Now I know what you are talking about. How about you?

How about you? What kind of silly question is that to ask him? Why can't I think before typing? He has always been a head-turning charmer. There is nothing new about it. I wait impatiently for his message.

I'm not talking about myself. Just wanted to know if you are upset about all the gossip.

He knows how to show concern, even in a text.

It is more shocking than upsetting. You come with the paparazzi package. I should have known.

Within a few seconds, my phone starts ringing.

"Hi," I say, closing the paper.

"Hi, how are you doing?" He sounds concerned and hesitant.

"I am good, thanks, and—"

"Are you upset?" he raises his voice a bit.

"I told you. It was more shocking than upsetting."

"But upsetting too?" He sounds really nervous. *Why is he nervous?* I am not biting him.

"Of course, it is upsetting. I was not expecting all this. I don't know how I will face people on Monday at work." I close my eyes and sit on the corner of the couch.

"I won't keep you much longer. You need to go and get ready for your plans with . . . umm . . . your friend." He doesn't seem to want to say Mike's name.

"I am not going anywhere. I changed my plans. We can still talk—"

"So, can we meet tonight? I want to talk about it." I sense he is hiding something. There is awkwardness in his tone. I want to talk about it too, so I decide to go with his offer. I remain silent for a while and he waits for me to speak.

"Yes, I want to talk about it too. I will call the restaurant and change it for today. That's fine with you?"

"Sounds great to me, but let me call them and arrange it. I have the information. I will send Ali to pick you up. Will you be ready by six-thirty?" He is calm, his voice gentle.

"Thanks. Yes, I will be. I will see you there, bye."

"Bye."

After hanging up the phone, I call Mike and apologize to him for not seeing him today.

In the evening, I hunt through my closet, not sure what to wear for the dinner. *So many outfits, but I still can't decide. Damn it!* After some digging, I choose to wear a long-sleeved light pink knitted blouse, accented with copper beads on the neckline. I take out a matching scarf, and decide to wear a deep brown corduroy skirt. I change my clothes and give final touches to my makeup. Still, I'm not as attractive as he is.

Who cares! It is not a date!

I put my boots on, take my bag, and head out the door.

THE VERY FIRST DATE

♂

Rania has invited me to a Persian restaurant on Bay Street. Ali has gone to pick her up, and they should be here any minute. The restaurant is a low-profile one, but the atmosphere is warm and welcoming. Soothing Persian music blends perfectly with the ambience. Surprisingly, all the tables in the restaurant are private, each encircled with a wooden gazebo. I'm relieved, because we need to talk, and we don't want to be bothered by strangers. All the patrons are seated on floor cushions, relaxing in the cozy environment, and the tables are at knee height.

I like her choice. I don't care if the food is up to the mark or not, as the place is more than I expected. The walls are deep red, and the only lights seem to be on the individual tables. I'm pleased that she agreed to meet me today. Time seemed to stop when she left the party.

I am furious at the gossip columnists. I don't know how Rania will react to all this media exposure. She didn't sound angry over the phone, though. Or is she too kind to express her grudge against me? If I were to put myself in her shoes, I can't imagine facing people at work, either. I will have to do something to protect her from this bizarre situation. I look at the pictures again on my phone.

She is something extraordinary.

I decide to enlarge our dance picture and place it somewhere in my apartment, so that it will greet me when I come home. I would also like to keep the picture at my bedside, so when I wake up in the morning, I will see her charming smile.

Fuck! What am I? Eighteen?

Even though I'm upset with the paparazzi, I am delighted that our precious moment was captured, when she was laughing delightedly. I can only adore her through pictures; she would never let me tell her how I feel. Her reserve is one of the things that attracted me most.

I've had sex with so many women, but none of them made me feel as good as I felt when I looked into her eyes, when she laughed innocently at my silly jokes, when she put her trust in me and let me see her cry. I will never do anything to damage that trust.

I am engrossed in my phone, gazing at her pictures one by one, when I suddenly hear her sweet familiar voice.

"Hi, I hope I am not late," she says, putting her bag down on the floor. I stand up from my cushion and welcome her with a handshake.

"No, you're on time. I arrived a couple of minutes ago." I'm lying; I've been here much longer. How can I tell her that each second waiting for her felt like eternity? We both sit, on opposite sides of the table. She looks incredibly beautiful in her skirt and pink top. "You look . . ." *So fucking hot!* I pause and gaze at her intensely, looking for the right word: "magnificent." She looks down, blushing. "Your blouse matches your skin." She raises her eyes to mine, an unusual shyness in them.

"Thanks, but I guess I look famished. We need to order fast, or else I will die." She changes the topic, avoiding my eyes completely. "Let's order an appetizer first. What would you like to have?"

"Anything you like. I'm your guest and I'm here to be entertained by your hospitality." I wink at her, relaxing back on the cozy cushions. She glances at me once and hides her face behind the menu. My humor makes her feel awkward. After a few minutes of hide and seek, she puts the menu down and calls the waiter. She orders bruschetta made on Persian flat bread with their blended yogurt, and fresh lime juice for both of us.

We sit quiet for a moment, each waiting for the other to break the ice. I had no idea how fucking difficult it could be, to talk to a girl when she's the one to whom I want to tell everything I feel about her. She starts looking for something in her bag to keep herself busy. Finally, she takes out the newspaper and hands it to me.

"This is insane, Adam. How can they print pictures like that? There is no such thing as privacy? And who the bloody hell took this picture?" She points to the one of us on the bench.

I never knew my name could sound so good, until she said it. I smile at her annoyance and keep my arms crossed over my chest. *Man, she looks so innocent when she's angry.* "Will you stop looking at me and say something, please?" She slaps the paper down and slides back with her arms crossed as well. I take my eyes off her to look at the paper.

"How you manage to look beautiful in this, I just don't know. You—"

"Are you trying to tease me, or make fun of this situation?" She gives me one of her sharp looks.

"Neither. I'm just stating a fact. I can't lie to you, Rania. Your eyes make me speak the truth only." My eyes are as serious as my tone. She feels uncomfortable and shifts a bit on her cushion.

"You are not angry at the way they spoiled your reputation?" She unfolds her arms and rests one elbow on the table, her head on her hand.

"I don't care what they wrote about me. What concerned me was how you would feel. Please tell me the truth." She fixes her eyes on the table, her delicate fingers toying with the napkin.

Yeah, baby, there is a lot more you can do with those pretty fucking fingers.

"I don't know how I will face people at work on Monday. This is all so embarrassing." She puts her head down on her folded arms, hiding her face.

"Are you embarrassed about being spotted with me, and assumed to be in a relationship, or you are embarrassed because you had been turning down other men, and according to the media, finally ended up with me?" She keeps her head down, not saying anything. "Rania, please, look at me, and tell me how you feel."

"What makes you say I push men away?" She finally manages to look at me.

"I was keeping count at the party, remember? I'm sure I can extrapolate from that. You turned me down too, so—"

"What else do you know about me?" She gives me a shrewd look, and rests her back on the cushion.

We are interrupted by the waiter, who brings our appetizer. She takes a sip of her lime juice, and says, "You keep telling me you can't lie to me. Now tell me what you know about me. I want to know how your secret agency works and how deep it goes. We will talk about this paper thing later on."

She is damn serious.

"Is this how you treat your guests, Rania?" I grin at her, trying to ease the tension in the air. But she stays silent, waiting for my response. "Okay, you want to know? I will tell you the truth. Obviously, I know where you live . . ." I pause for a moment and she rolls her eyes at me. "I also know where you work and other official details. I know you don't drive, as you don't have a driver's license on your record. I know you graduated from Ryerson University as a software engineer, and later on changed your field to graphics and joined Ben's company." I pause again. "Nothing more than that, except that your . . . umm . . . boyfriend happens to be Ben's son."

"Mike is not my boyfriend." Her eyes are burning. That is the best news I've had all day.

"He isn't? But I thought . . . I mean, you acted like you're very close to him. You don't treat other men that way."

"Well, it's not what you think. Mike and I are childhood friends. He has always been there for me and I am grateful to God that He has blessed me with one sincere friend at least." I am trying my best to conceal my happiness and excitement, so I start talking to her about Mike. It is much easier for me to tolerate that fucking hunky cop when I know this girl has no feelings for him.

"But the way he looked at you, it didn't look like friendship," I point out.

"When we were at school, we promised each other that if neither of us had found a suitable partner by age twenty-five, we'd get married." She smiles as if thinking about the past. "He is still holding his promise for me."

Holy shit! I was right. The guy is in love with her.

"Do you feel the same for him?" I say a silent prayer in my head. *Oh Lord in heaven, please show some mercy.* She is quiet for a moment, playing with her straw, then continues without looking at me.

"No, I don't feel like that about him or anyone. There will be no one." Suddenly her declaration reflects in her eyes and I see a tragic past through the tears. For the first time I realize she has suffered a broken heart. Her past is not letting her go, so she can't step into the future. I don't want her to cry, so I change the subject.

"Umm . . . there's one more thing I didn't tell you. My intelligence service also mentioned that you attend a dance school." I continue with my appetizer. We both get interrupted again by the waiter, who shows up to take the main course order.

"Please have a look at the menu; I am not sure what to order for you."

"Anything you want. Order the same as you're ordering for yourself. I've liked your choices so far."

"You should not trust a stranger like that. What if I poison you?" She peeks one eye out from behind the menu to look at me. I lean back and relax, closing my eyes, and reveal the truth.

"I am already intoxicated with your divine beauty, Rania. How much more can you do to me?" I keep my eyes closed, so I don't see her expression. All I hear is that she ignores my confession, and orders chicken kobideh for both of us. After the waiter excuses himself, I open my eyes, and I see her fixing her scarf, looking agitated. I have embarrassed her again.

Why am I behaving like a shit?

"You don't like when someone compliments you?" I look at her keenly, waiting for her answer.

"I don't trust those types of comments from men." She busies herself with her lime juice and continues. "They all send the same message." She pauses, then looks at me. "It's like an I-want-to-fuck-you sign on their heads." And she looks down, her fingers once again toying with a straw.

Her words jar me. I wasn't expecting this kind of remark from her. I adjust myself to different position, but nothing changes the tension in the air.

"But that's not always the case, is it?" I cock my head toward her to get her attention.

"It always has been. What else do men want, other than a sleeping partner? All men these days think the same, but certainly not from the head." She looks at me in a skeptical way. *Is she treating me like those other men?* But I have never told her what I wanted from her. Is she intelligent enough to figure it out? She can see my soul through her ebony eyes.

"You think Mike is the same? When he looks at you or compliments you? I'm sure he does." I busy myself with my drink.

"Mike is different. Yes, he does compliment me, but I have never seen lust in his eyes. It has always been pure love. Though

I'm not sure I believe in love." She looks down again and starts eating her bread with yogurt. There are so many messages in everything she's saying today. She knows Mike loves her, but she has nothing to offer in return? *Why not?* What is holding her back? What happened to her?

"You read books. I assume you must have read love stories too. You still don't believe in it?" My eyes are locked on her, and she looks at me without blinking.

"How do you know I read books? Your secret spying agency informed you of that as well?" She grins at me, and takes a sip of her juice.

"I saw you picking up your Kindle when you were collecting your stuff outside my head office."

"I appreciate your powers of observation, Mr. Gibson, but you were not courteous enough to help me, and—"

"I was shocked," I interrupt her. She gives me a suspect look, and waits for me to say more. "I was shocked . . . umm . . . I never thought I would be smitten."

Shit! I am actually saying this to her.

I look deeply into her eyes, and she averts her gaze and shifts her body in confusion. She is not at all comfortable when someone says something nice to her. What makes her feel so uneasy?

Why the fuck I am acting like a prick?

I have a strong gut feeling that someone has messed with her emotions really bad. I don't dare ask her about it so soon. I want to know everything about her, all the things only she can tell me, but I will have to become friends with her first. Making sexy remarks will only push her away from me. She is close to Mike because he doesn't wear a fuck-me look. I can never dare to ask her for any sexual commitment, unless I gain her trust. But that's not the only thing I want from her.

I close my eyes and shake my head.

"Mr. Gibson, I don't want to give you any false messages. You should be very clear by now that I am not the person you are looking for . . ." *Is she a fucking mind reader?* She pauses for a moment, waiting for me to look at her, and continues when I meet her eyes, open-mouthed. "I mean . . . I have read about you, and you should know that—"

"You are not a one-night stand for me, Rania." I close my eyes again. "Please, don't ever think that I see you that way." *You are the one to hold and cherish forever.*

I open my eyes, finding her looking shocked. Her expression is asking so many questions, like *how-do-you-see-me?* Have I scared her with the truth? Is it too much information to dump on her? I have to change the subject, so I distract her.

"So, what else do you know about me? Shall I say you have been stalking me?"

"I only read what is on the Internet," she snaps out in an instant. "You don't believe in God? I mean, I read you deny His existence."

"Yes, I do. He doesn't exist for me. You can say I am an atheist." Our eyes are locked.

"You don't see His existence in all the things around you?" She tilts her head toward me to get more into this topic. I remain quiet and let her continue. "You don't see changing weather, colors of the land, and shades in the water? You think no one is behind their individuality? He gave you fame, money, power, honor and instead of being thankful, you deny His existence?" She obviously wants to talk about this, talk about God.

"Thankful for what I've done myself? I have all this because I worked hard for it."

"But, what about the blessings you got without even working hard? Don't you think you are obliged to be thankful for those?"

"Like what?" She has succeeded in getting me interested.

"Like the senses He gave you, your vision, so that you can see His beautiful creations, your ears, so that you can listen to all the good things in life, your speech, through which you succeeded in taking over this city, your sense of touch, through which you can feel. He gave you all this and much more, without you asking Him. There are many people in this world who are deprived even of these blessings. Don't you think these bounties are enough for you to be thankful?"

We look at each other keenly. I don't know how to react. I drop my gaze. She is trying to make me believe that God has always existed. She understands that I have nothing to say, so she continues with suppositions.

"Don't you recognize Him from the failure of your intentions?"[4]
I look at her blankly. She has made me speechless . . . again.
She is so right; my intentions did fail in the face of His decisions.
Regardless of the fact that I desire to kiss her, fuck her, claim her
entirely, her constrained attitude guarded her from my ferocious
plan, and that makes me realize that I did fail here. In a single
question, she guides me to all the enlightened paths that I have
never come across. I keep looking at her blankly, so she diverts her
attention to the waiter, asking how long it will take for our order.

"You seem to carry a strong faith within you." I chuckle at her.

"I wouldn't have survived, if I didn't have faith." She looks
down again, playing with her ring.

"So, you are thankful to Him for everything?"

"Yes, I try to be, at least!"

"And how do *you* thank Him?" I lean forward to hear her
properly.

"There is a protocol defined in every religion. All religions
have the same belief, yet, the medium of communication with Him
is different. I follow what has been taught in my religion. I pray.
But it doesn't mean that He doesn't listen, if you approach Him in
any other way. He does!"

"And what about the things you are not blessed with? Is there
any protocol to complain as well?" The conversation between us
heats up, and I feel like I'm sitting in a classroom, firing questions
at my teacher.

"If you ask me, I have no complaints. Everyone is responsible
for his own deeds. We do wrong things without believing in Him,
and then we complain. Though, it should have been the other way
around, we should believe in Him first, so there would no mishaps
in life. People who are most ungrateful, are the ones abandoned.
When you are thankful, you are contented."

"And what about the people who have everything and are still
not grateful? Yet, they are showered with bounty. Why do they get
all these things in life?"

"You are one of them, Mr. Gibson. What are you complaining
for? Your ungratefulness for your bounties?" She has a smart
mouth, and intelligence. No one has ever shown me a mirror that
can reflect me inside. She has a wide vision when it comes to

---
[4]   *Ali ibn Abi Talib (607-661)*

her faith. Through her, I am able to see the light, which has been cloaked due to my ignorance. I am able to believe in His existence.

What is going on?

"I respect your faith, Rania. It is very strong. Always hold onto it. You are very lucky that you have been guided."

"Yes, I know. Do you know God says that when you take one step toward Him, He will take ten steps toward you? I was lucky that I took that step. And He guided me all the way."

"Then, how can I become sure that He will show me the light someday?"

"You have already seen the light, Mr. Gibson. You are a good soul. Do you know how much goodness and grace you are getting from your generous donations?"

"You still didn't tell me why you reject men." I change the subject completely. I really don't feel comfortable when people praise me for my donations. She doesn't say anything. She keeps looking around, totally ignoring my question. "I have an offer for you," I say. "I see that you don't like men asking you for dates. What if we affirm what's written in the papers and, going forward, we act publicly like we are in a relationship. Then you can avoid all the shit men give you every day." She looks at me blankly. *She is definitely not buying this.* "Consider our relationship, as defined by the media, as an excuse to avoid all the sleaze balls oozing at you. No one will bother you if your name is linked with me. Think about it!"

We are distracted by the arrival of our main course. It looks very delicious and healthy. All her choices are perfect so far, like her. We start our meal quietly. I give her time to think about my proposal. *What the fuck am I thinking?* Why would she agree to be my girlfriend? And this is not an appropriate way to ask a girl if she is interested. *Damn me!* I curse myself in my head. I have messed up everything. I have to say something to take it back, but I don't know what to say.

"Rania, I won't lie to you. I am bloody attracted to you, but I will never push you against your will. I know you don't see me the same way. In fact, I don't see anything in your eyes, except the pain." She has taken her first bite from her meal, but as soon as I mention the word *pain*, she coughs as if she's choking. I offer her water but she's coughing too hard. I crawl toward her and rub her back.

Sitting next to her is the ultimate feeling. Without any sexual encounter, this girl can give me so much pleasure; what will I do if she agrees to my offer? *I would definitely be on cloud nine.* I continue rubbing her back until she is able to speak.

"I am sorry. I guess something got stuck in my throat." She takes a drink of water. She is breathing hard, and I see her breasts moving with her heartbeat.

Oh hell!

I crawl back to my seat so that she won't notice my masculinity getting harder.

"Can I ask you something?" she says hesitantly. She gets my attention as soon she speaks, but I continue my meal.

"Anything, Rania. We are here to talk openly."

"If you know I have nothing to offer you, that I cannot fulfill your expectations, then why are you offering me this? You are not getting anything in return." I notice she's not eating. She's only playing with her rice.

Did I destroy her appetite as well?

I'm not doing anything to put her at ease, I realize. I am only making things difficult for her. I put my fork down and lean back again, arms folded over my chest. I watch her carefully, wondering what to say in return. She doesn't look at me at all, still playing with her food.

"You're not eating anything, Rania. Please, eat first and then we'll talk." I take my fork in my hand to continue with my food. She still doesn't take a bite. "Eat, Rania! Please, finish your meal." My tone is a bit harsh with concern.

"I want my answer first, Adam. Why would you offer, if you are not getting anything in return? What do you want from me?" she asks furiously, and I see her eyes getting wet with tears.

"I want only you. Nothing else." I almost whisper.

She tries hard to avoid the pain coming out of her eyes. *Oh no! What did I do now?*

"Want me for what, Adam? I know bloody well what your eyes tell me, which you don't say from your mouth. Please accept that I cannot give you anything. No pleasure. Nothing. So stop chasing a shadow." She puts her fork down with a clatter and wipes her eyes with a napkin. "I am a piece of dead meat, Adam. You get me? There is nothing in me. Stop wasting your time . . . and mine as well." Her voice quivers and she hides her face in her napkin.

I crawl once again to her side, hoping that I can bring her some comfort.

"No, Rania. Please, I'm sorry. I didn't mean to make you cry, but if you want to, it's okay." I put my arm around her. She doesn't push me away. Surprisingly, she snuggles herself into my embrace, but she holds back her tears. There is no lust between us. Just two people opening their truths. I cannot describe the feelings that are gushing through me right now. Even though she has Mike as her best friend, I feel she lacks a shoulder to cry on, someone to share all her sorrows.

For the first time in my life, I feel a divine power giving me a message. A command to hold and protect her. A message that He wants someone to mend the broken pieces of her heart. She is a lonely tormented soul, and I can see the pain in her silence. I have never gotten this message from any woman, even if they cried out my name when I fucked them hard. Yet this girl, not saying anything, says so many things to me that my heart is not able to decipher them.

I never believed in God, but I can relate this feeling to that divine power.

Does He truly exist?

I sit quietly holding her. She is crying now—not like she did at the party, but her silent tears say so much.

"I am sorry . . . I don't know what happens to me when you . . ." She wipes her tears from her face. My face is just an inch away from hers. I want to kiss away her tears and make her feel better, but I don't dare to. Instead, I wipe her face with my hand and continue where she left off.

"When I put my arms around you?" I look into her eyes, trying to read everything she wants to say. She looks down, but doesn't say anything. "I will only say I am thankful that you trust me enough, so that you can let your inner sorrows come out. I don't know what it is between us. When I said I'm attracted to you, I was not lying. But it's not lust. When I see you, I see something celestial and pure standing in front of me. I never believed God existed, until now, when I felt that He might be directing us to put our trust together. When I look into your eyes, I cannot lie, and I say everything that comes into my mind, whether you like it or not. Maybe this is the path He wants us to take. Trusting each other."

She moves away from me and looks down, but I'm sure she's listening. "You asked me why I'm offering for you to be my girlfriend, and trust me, I didn't know how to answer. And I still don't know. I wanted to take you out of the awkward situation that you are afraid of at work. People might talk about us, but at least, men will leave you alone. You captured my attention when I saw you crossing the street, heading to my building. I have been chasing you ever since. But there is no reason, or if there is, I don't know it. I only wanted to make your life easy. I want to clean up the mess I created."

I take a deep breath. "You asked me what I would get in return. I am a businessman, and I don't do anything unless it profits me. I will gain your trust. I will gain your affection. I will always be there to wipe your tears, but I also want to be a part of that laughter you share with your friends. This is all new to me too, Rania. I have no idea how to communicate with a girl, when I want everything other than sleeping with her. My way of asking might be offensive to you, but trust me, I didn't intend it. I didn't intend to make you feel like I'm a stalker. And I don't know myself what happens to me when you're with me. I can't explain it."

My eyes are locked on her, but she keeps looking down, playing with her ring.

"Why do you want to protect me? Why are you being so generous?" She looks into my eyes with seriousness, as if she is looking through my soul.

"I don't know." I close my eyes and shake my head. "I'm feeling charged to do all this. I can't say anything more." I open my eyes and find her eyes fixed on me with amazement.

"Charged by whom?"

"Maybe . . . God?"

"But you said you never believed in His existence."

I shrug. "You leave me no choice, other than acknowledging this fact."

"That's a very lame reason for believing in Him, Mr. Gibson."

We both remain in silence for a few minutes, trying to understand what just happened with us. Within a day, I feel like we have walked so far together. We have not shared any secrets, but I still feel a strong connection. To avoid the awkward situation, I hand her a fork. "Please finish your food. We will talk later." And on that, I crawl back to my seat.

We both finish our meals in silence. The food is not warm anymore, but it still tastes scrumptious. Does she understand my taste buds, or do we share the same tastes? We finish our food almost at the same time.

"The food is really good. I like your choice." I give her a friendly smile to release the pressure in the atmosphere.

"Thanks. It is one of my favorites too. Would you like to have some dessert?" She is trying to prove her hospitality. I nod at her with a smile. The waiter comes back, asking us about dessert, and she orders a hot fudge sundae for both of us to share. We share a few moments of silence until our dessert arrives.

We both look at the dessert and crack up at the size. It's huge; we will never finish it.

"Oh my! I love it." She takes a big spoonful of ice cream from the bowl, with all the nuts and chocolate, and starts to lick the spoon slowly. *Oh fuck! Is she tempting me on purpose?* No, she seems completely ignorant of my feelings.

"For the love of God, stop licking your spoon like that. It's making me wild." She is stunned for a moment, spoon in her mouth. Then, slowly, she takes the spoon out of her mouth, caressing it with her tongue, and giggles sinfully.

"What's with you and licking, huh?" She takes more ice cream and repeats the process, teasingly. This time, she also licks her upper lip.

Fuck! Stop it, girl, or else I will suck your chocolate-coated lip, right here.

"Don't provoke me, Rania. There is an animal inside every man, so you—"

"Who knows that better than me, Mr. Gibson? Some men I can't even refer to as humans. They are only animals." With that grave statement, she puts her spoon down and closes her eyes, hiding her fear. I want to ask her what animal has eaten her up. But I have to gain her trust first. I put my hand on hers, to provide her some comfort. She doesn't recoil, but her eyes are still closed.

"I'm sorry. I was just teasing you." She looks at me with distress.

"No, I'm sorry. I shouldn't have said anything to you. Please forgive me."

"That's okay." She grins slightly.

"Like it or not, it was very erotic, you playing with the spoon," I confess again, and start digging into my side of the ice cream. She giggles with pleasure, taking it as a joke. To lift her mood, I argue with her like a child. "Hey, you ate all the nuts from the top. That's not fair." She checks the ice cream innocently, to see if I'm telling the truth. I wave to the waiter to bring extra nuts for us.

"They must be thinking we will stay here forever." She giggles at me again. And our nuts come within an instant. I start sprinkling them all over the ice cream, which is about to melt like my heart.

"Hey, you are putting more nuts in your territory. That's not fair, either." She starts pulling nuts from the spoon to her side.

"Okay, let me put the rest on your side." We both chuckle like four-year-old kids who accidentally have to share one ice cream. She is busy savoring the dessert. It has done wonders. She likes ice cream; it changes her mood. I want to say something, but somehow, the power of her innocence has silenced me. Perhaps I should take her for dessert more often, if she agrees to go.

"Can I ask you something, if you don't mind?" She nods, enjoying her fudge. "You told me you pray when you are grateful. What do you do when you know you did something wrong and you seek forgiveness?" I look at her seriously. She looks at me with bright eyes.

"It depends whom you are seeking forgiveness from. If you have hurt a person, you need to ask pardon from him first, and only then will God forgive you. If you have hurt His creatures, you have hurt Him, as well. But if you have done something wrong which you think only He knows about, then you ask Him."

"And how do you ask Him? I mean what do *you* do?"

"I pray." She shrugs her shoulder.

"So, when you are thankful, you pray and when you are sorry, you pray? What do you do when you want something from Him?"

"Same! Prayer is the gateway for everything. You want to thank Him. You want to repent for your sins. You want to communicate. He understands what you intend. He lives in your heart. You don't need to mention to Him that you are doing this for a certain reason. He knows it, before you know."

"I like your way of believing in Him, Rania. I have never heard anything like that from anyone. Not even from my mother." The

SAMREEN AHSAN

thought of my mother hurts me, always. There is a void in my heart that no one can ever fill.

"Where is your mother now?" She puts her spoon down and looks at me. "Only if you want to tell me."

"There is nothing much to say. She left my dad when I was six. Before that, I had only seen my parents fighting. The only good thing in my childhood was my baby sister, Eva." I smile at the thought of her. "Eva was two months old when they left. I missed her more than my mom. You say God exists, but where was He when I was calling Him to help me? Why didn't He hear a child's cry?"

"I can't tell you, Mr. Gibson, why He didn't answer your prayer that time, but please remember that prayers are never abandoned. Sooner or later, they are always answered, and in so much better ways than you could have imagined." Her words are comforting, but they do not hit my heart. We have different beliefs based on our pasts. She continues with her dessert and I follow her. "So, does your secret spying company hire people?" She winks at me mischievously. I know she wants to change the subject. "I have read many mystery books. I want to know how this all works, not to mention that I am still annoyed about being stalked."

"Please don't say that. I'm not a stalker. I just wanted to find out about you, before I could talk to you."

"You could have asked me. God has given me the ability to speak."

"But you were ignoring me. I thought you would never talk. And trust me, I still don't believe my luck that I'm sitting across from you, sharing a dessert." I look deeply into her eyes and she gets my message.

"And you won't tell me why you wanted to talk to me?" She starts moving her spoon in the bowl.

"Someday, I will. But not today." I sigh and wait for her to look at me. She doesn't ask me any more. I want to tell her everything, my one night experience with an enchantress, but I fear she would never believe me.

"So, what kind of books do you read apart from mysteries?" I change the subject.

"All kinds of fiction."

"Why fiction only?"

"Because it takes you to the world of imagination, where reality doesn't exist. It's like a journey to some other world, far from cruel reality. Do you read too?"

"No, Rania. I don't. I don't have the time or, in fact, the patience to read fiction. I live in the real world."

"Then your reality is more colorful than your imagination." She looks at me dreamily—and enviously. She is silent for a moment, then continues. "Anyhow, I read you have dated quite a few women. I am sure it must be colorful. You don't need to imagine, when you can have it in the real world."

I laugh at her remarks, and show her the newspaper that she has kept at the corner of the table.

"You see this, Rania? It says I have been spotted only with you. They say you are my girlfriend." My tone is serious and I don't take my eyes off of her. "The women you are talking about, they were only bed partners. I never had anyone to date, to talk to and share our views." She looks at me, open-mouthed. "I didn't use them or take advantage of them. I didn't force anyone. They all needed money and I was looking for pleasure. That's it."

She is still in shock. "So you keep . . . I mean . . . umm . . . do you have something like . . . umm . . . submissives?" she asks hesitantly.

"No, Rania. I don't keep submissives. And I don't see any point in keeping one woman for a long time, when you are spending money for them. You don't wear a single dress every day, when you can afford a variety." My comments shock her. It's too much information. She's going to run away screaming.

I'm afraid she'll think I look at her the same way. I have to do or say something to make this better.

I take a small box out of the inner pocket of my jacket and place it on the table.

"I have something for you, Rania." She leans toward the box, dark blue with Tiffany & Co embossed on it, but doesn't touch it. Her expression says loudly that she is not expecting this.

"I can't take it, but thank you." She leans back again, pushing the box to my side of the table.

"Please don't refuse it. At least open it and see if you like it or not." I push the box back toward her.

"I am sorry, Adam. I can't take it. I am not used to these kinds of gestures. So please—"

"Then get used to it. You are my girlfriend."

"I am not your girlfriend. I haven't agreed to your proposition." She pushes the box back to me and leans back. She looks angry, and she won't meet my eyes.

Damn!

"Don't act like a child. You knew this would go in your favor, so please accept this gift. I have not been rejected ever—"

"Then get used to it." She throws my words back to me, but in a more irascible way.

We both sit in silence for a long time. I am offended by her rejecting my gift. She is resentful of my dominance. She is one difficult woman. What woman won't accept a Tiffany's gift? She hasn't even bothered to open it and see what it is. Even though I feel rejected, she makes one more inroad into my heart. She is not like other women, running after money. This is all my fault. I am pushing too hard for her to accept it. I should have gained her trust first, before giving her gifts. It is our first date, and she hasn't agreed to accept me as her boyfriend. That's a first for me too.

A girl rejecting me!

Our dessert is finished and the waiter brings the bill, placing it on the table. I realize that we have been in the restaurant for almost three hours. How has the time passed so quickly? She lays her hand on the bill to grab it, but I stop her by holding her wrist.

"Now, at least don't argue on this one." I keep holding her hand possessively, but she struggles hard to get it out of my grasp.

"Adam, please. We decided that this dinner is on me, so stop acting like a male chauvinist." She is a wildcat this time. I grip her hand tighter and keep looking at it.

Yeah, baby, I am gonna tie your pretty hands someday, if you give me a hard time.

"If you pay for this, then you accept my offer and my gift." I have no intention of letting her go, unless I make her agree to my terms. I'm just afraid she will return the bill and walk out. This is the biggest gamble of my life.

"What kind of bargaining is that?" She looks around the restaurant and back to me, with wide eyes. "Let go of my hand, Adam. You are creating a scene. People are looking at us." She is hissing through her teeth. I keep looking at her, steamily.

"I know there is no one here except us. The restaurant is almost closed. If you are worried about the damn waiter, I don't give a shit. Be a good girl and give me the bill. This is beyond my tolerance." I don't even bother to look around the restaurant, to see if people are there. She is firing right at my ego. "You will let me pay for this dinner and you will accept my offer, along with the damn gift." She looks at me, stunned and intimidated. She takes it as a threat, so she lets the bill go. I release her hand and she leans back, creating distance between us. *Shit! I lost her.* She let me win this battle, but I achieved nothing. I take my credit card out and wave the waiter over to collect the bill. We both sit silent during the payment. As soon as the waiter leaves, thanking me, she gathers her bag and stands up.

"Where are you going?" I grip her arm tightly.

"The restaurant is almost closed. You plan to stay here forever?" *I wish I could.* I have to be more cautious when speaking. She's constantly firing my words back at me. She is still raging. I have to calm her down, but there's nothing coming to mind. I stand up with her, but don't let her go. "You are forgetting something," she reminds me, looking at the box we left on the table.

"That's for you. I won't pick it up. You are dumping it, so why do you care?" She takes her arm out of my grip and picks up the box. Then she grabs my hand and places the box on my palm.

"If you have money to waste, then give it to someone who needs it and appreciates it. I am neither needy nor greedy." She turns away from me and I stop her again.

"But you never bothered to open it. At least show some courtesy—"

"Adam, I am not from medieval times. I know what Tiffany sells."

"Rania, please! Stop being so hard on me." My tone is more like a request than a command. She closes her eyes and calms down her anger.

"You don't need to do all this. You are making me feel cheap." She shrugs in frustration, but she keeps her eyes closed. I move closer to her and take her face in my hands. She still manages to keep her eyes closed, but doesn't push me away.

"Hey, please, don't say that. I would never want to make you feel cheap." I whisper, but she can still hear me. "Every other girl likes to get gifts. I thought it would make you happy."

"I am not like *every* girl. I told you that. I don't deserve these precious things." She opens her eyes as she speaks. All I see is agony. "I don't know why you are wasting your time."

"You don't even know what you deserve. This gift is not even worthy of you. It is just my way of apologizing for the trouble I caused. If you don't want it, that's okay, but please don't think like that." I put the box back inside my jacket. *What kind of woman is she? Rejecting a twenty-five-thousand-dollar necklace?* I promise myself that this personalized piece of art will only adorn her beautiful neckline.

"It is late," she says. "I want to go home now." She turns around and heads to the closet beside the door. I follow her blindly and help her with her jacket. We go outside, where cold hard wind awaits us. She takes out her phone and makes a call.

"Yeah, hi. Can you please send a cab to . . ."

What? I'm standing next to her and she's calling a fucking cab at this hour?

I take the phone from her and end the call.

"What the hell do you think you're doing?" I ask her angrily.

"Calling a cab?" she responds innocently, as if she is totally unaware of what she just did.

"Can't you find a better way to insult someone?" I grit my teeth to control my anger. She shrugs in bewilderment.

"What's with you and public transportation?" she inquires curiously. But when I open the passenger door, she slips inside.

We stay quiet all the way to her apartment. I turn on the radio, to break the silence. The radio starts playing a happy Christmas song, and I see her smiling. She enjoys the song innocently, closing her eyes, tapping her hands on her knees. I feel like she's somewhere else, lost in the music. I want to ask her what she's thinking about, but I don't want to break the moment. When the song ends, she opens her eyes and looks at me. I have never seen that look in her eyes, but I can't decipher the message. I concentrate on the road until I stop the car in front of her building. I step out and open the door for her. She gets out and wraps her arms around herself, to avoid the cold wind. It's never been as hard to say something as in this moment, but I gather all my courage. Our date has finally ended and I don't know how to say good-bye to her.

"Thank you for the wonderful evening. I can never forget it." I smile at her.

"Thank you? You paid. I should say thank you."

Oh! She is still annoyed.

"Thank you for selecting the restaurant. I really enjoyed the food and your company. But if it bothers you, you can pay next time. I won't argue. I promise." I grin at her. She is still expressionless.

"There will be no next time, Mr. Gibson. Good night!" She turns around and disappears inside without listening to my farewell words, taking all my hopes with her.

I know I have to try really really hard.

A BEAUTIFUL JOURNEY

♀

It is Monday morning. I am en route to Edmonton on Via Rail, thinking about the phone call I received from Ben yesterday. My father was being questioned at his workplace, about the daughter of the UN Secretariat dating a rich Canadian Casanova. Ben told me Baba sounded really deranged.

There was another picture of us in the paper today, from the restaurant on Saturday night. I just don't understand why the media can't give us space to breathe. Maybe with Adam, this is just part of the package. He's always in the limelight, and that meant I would be in it too. I had no clue what it's like to date the most influential man in Toronto. He is an open book, and staying close to him means people will turn my pages too. Ben warned me that I was giving Adam hope, and my father is not happy about it. I know how hard he has worked to attain his position in the Arab world, and my stupid actions are bringing shame to him.

Ben also told me that there is an Adobe® Summit for graphic designers and illustrators in Edmonton he wanted to send me to. I'm traveling by train because I wanted time to think about myself, and space from Adam.

After what happened to me in the past, I never had a single day to look forward to in my life. I am just living my life and waiting for it to end, whenever God decides. I would never take my life myself, because that would send me to Hell for eternity. But I have been living in Hell for five years, and will be there for many more years to come. Everything is mortal, and everything has to come to an end, one day. I hope one fine day this will come to an end too.

On Saturday night, after Adam dropped me at my place, I rushed into my apartment without saying goodbye to him. I was crying, missing my mother, when all of a sudden he knocked at my door. I was so scared, seeing him standing at my doorstep, that I fell down on my knees and couldn't stop crying. He held me in his arms to comfort me, and then put me to bed without any questions, caressing me gently until I fell asleep. I don't know if he slept next to me or not, but when I woke up I found flowers at my bedside with a note saying that I looked pure and innocent while I slept. For the first time, after five years of misery, I hadn't had any nightmares. I had planned to call and thank him for the lovely flowers, but after Ben's call, the idea of giving Adam hope made me reconsider. I pretended to ignore his flowers and the deep message, and move on. My life is locked in a gilded cage of belief and culture. We are from two different worlds, and neither of us can be a part of the other's.

And here I am, escaping from my forbidden fruit, traveling to a new city.

When the train starts to cruise, I open my cell phone and am surprised to find a voicemail from Adam.

"Hi, Rania. This is Adam. I just called to see if you're doing okay. I wish I could do something to make you feel better, but thanks for letting me in. I hope you received the flowers." He pauses, with a deep breath. *"You look very pure and innocent when you sleep."* He pauses again, as if he is failing to find words. *"I don't know if I should say this or not, but I miss you. I'm in Montreal on business and will be back tonight. I was hoping you'd call, but I'm sure you must be busy. I just wanted to know if you are doing okay. I look forward to seeing you tomorrow. Thanks again. Take care."*

Even after my rudeness, not calling him and thanking him for his kindness, he is still worried about me. After so many years, someone is worried about me. No one would believe that I've seen another side of Adam, which no one knows. *One who is not thankful to a person, is not thankful to God.* The Prophet's quote buzzes in my mind and I decide I will call him to say thanks during my journey.

A beautiful young lady comes by to offer me coffee or tea. I am hungry; last night I had no appetite because I spent the whole evening thinking about Adam. I ask her if she can get me something to eat, and hot tea. I wonder if he was thinking about me or not. But he said he was out of town on business. *Who works on Sundays?*

By the time he tries to get in touch with me, I will be gone. Ben is right, this will give me a chance to think about what I want to do. I don't want to put my father's job at risk. It is the only good thing left in his life, after my mother's death, and I'm proud of his success. It has been five years since I've seen him. He has always contacted me through Ben. I don't blame him, as what I did was unforgivable.

I am distracted by the young lady again, bringing tea and biscuits to brighten my morning. I plan to sleep and read throughout my journey, as I have to stay in my compartment— not much space to roam around. I hear some babies crying at the corner of the passage, which makes me smile. I have always adored babies, and I wonder if I will ever have one of my own.

By the time the train crosses the borders of GTA, I've finished my breakfast. The next main stop is Winnipeg, two days from now. I watch the view for almost an hour and read my book, but eventually I fall asleep. I wake to the sound of hustle and bustle, and realize that I have slept throughout the journey. The train has stopped at some station, densely covered with snow. *I can't have been sleeping for two days.*

I peek outside to see which station it is, but I can't figure it out. I am sure it is not Winnipeg. I enjoy watching people getting on and off the train. It reminds me that no matter how tough life is, it must go on.

A Chinese woman distracts me, arriving to inform me that they are shifting passengers bound for Edmonton to another compartment. I tell her that my seat has been reserved for the journey, but she convinces me that seats can be changed without notice. She assures me that my luggage will be moved. The other coach is much more modern than my previous one. It looks like first class or business class. I ask the lady again if she is sure that I have to move, and she nods with a smile. The lady informs me I can have a look around, but that I must sit down once the train starts. I see beautiful, relaxing couches with high definition flat-screens. There is a small bar and a dance floor, for the rich people who want to party in the train.

The sleeper cabins are tastefully designed with comfortable beds and attached mini washrooms. *Who would want to stay in a hotel, when you could travel in business class?* I am surprised at my luck and check my tickets, but I am definitely booked in the economy class, and this is not it. I head back to my seat, and the lady appears again to ask me if I would like something to drink. The orange juice is delightfully served with fresh fruit, chilled to the perfect temperature.

The train starts again and I notice that there is no one else in the coach. *What's going on?* I feel strange and scared, but I am excited too, about this mistake. I take out my Kindle and start reading my book. I am on a fictional joy ride, and I don't at first realize that it has started to get dark, even though my watch shows it's only two in the afternoon. My eyes are strained from hours of reading, so I rub them to clear my vision.

"Reading is good, but you shouldn't overstrain your eyes." It is a familiar voice. I open my eyes and look up to find Adam sitting opposite me. I rub my eyes again, wondering if I am daydreaming, and he smiles at me. His gaze is, as usual, very intense, and he keeps stroking his lower lip with his index finger. I look around the compartment to make sure where I am, wondering if I'm imagining this. "It's just the two of us, Rania. There is no one else." He still smirks at my expression. *Where am I? What is he doing here?*

I give him a frightened and shocked look, expecting him to read my eyes, which he does. He answers my question without me having to ask. "You are still on Via Rail and you are still heading to Edmonton." I stand up, gaping at him. "Don't worry," he says. "You're not kidnapped. Sit down, Rania." I take my seat.

There is no one whom I could call for help. But what would I call for? He is not harassing me. I don't own the sleeper. He watches me, noticing my every action. My hands and my body tremble, but I try hard to control it. I don't want him to see me like that. He leans closer to me and holds my trembling hands firmly, his focus getting more intense.

"Are you running from me?" I see a dark shadow in his eyes. How can I tell him I am not running, but I needed some time to think? I never expected to see him here. I have no freaking idea where we even are, geographically.

I keep my head down, looking at our entwined hands. I don't have the courage to look in his intense eyes and tell the truth. He is already hurt; I don't want to hurt him more. I have never been as rude and cold-hearted as I always pretend to be in front of him.

"Is there anything I have done to frighten you?" He gently caresses my hand with his thumbs, to ease my tension. His touch creates strong reactions in me, but I just sit here, pretending to be numb. I want to shake my head to let him know that he didn't do anything wrong, but instead I grab his hands tighter and close my eyes with fear. He moves closer and kneels down in front of me to catch my gaze.

"Please say something, Rania. You didn't say anything to me, and you ran away. I was expecting . . ." He pauses for a moment to find the words. "I was hoping for a call from you. You didn't say anything yesterday." He struggles hard to get me to look at him, but I am too afraid to make eye contact. I know I will collapse and will not be able to control myself. It is very dumb of me, sitting like that, so I gather all my courage to speak.

"Thank you for the flowers." I look up at him. His shoulders relax as soon as I speak.

"I thought you didn't notice. I—"

"It was the first thing I saw in the morning. Thank you. But I guess you didn't realize what you wrote." I glance outside the window. "I am neither pure, nor innocent." I know he is looking at me. He moves and sits next to me, very close, reading my every expression. Everything that Ben told me about my father's job and Adam's nature; it all comes to mind at once. I look at him with confidence. "I am not running. It is an official trip. I have to attend a summit." I move closer to the window, creating distance between us. He is intelligent enough to understand my hesitation, so without saying anything, he moves back to his seat, facing me.

We sit in silence for a long time; the only sound we hear is the movement of the train. I feel his eyes on me, but I keep looking out the window. There is nothing other than white landscape. Finally, I decide to break the ice.

"Did Ben tell you where I was?"

"I went to see you at work. Ben wasn't there. They told me that you were asked to attend some summit in Edmonton, and you would be coming back at the end of the week." He pauses for a moment to take a deep breath and leans forward to catch my attention. "For me, it's impossible to be away from you for a week. Since you weren't on any flights, the train was the only other option." He pauses. "By the time I found out where you were, your train was almost outside the border of Ontario." He waits for me to say something, but when I don't, he continues. "I would have had to wait three days to see you in Edmonton, which was impossible for me. I don't have much patience, Rania." He leans back, but keeps watching me seriously.

"How did you get here?" My voice is full of curiosity, but I try to control it.

The corners of his lips lift in a smile. "You know, Rania, that I can track you down. Why do you always ask?"

"No, of course, with your stalking habits, you would know where I was, but how did you reach here?" I interrogate him like a child.

"My friend is in control and operations for Via Rail. I asked him to stop the train for a while at the nearest station. You were in Sudbury when you were asked to move in here." *What? It was him, who arranged for me to move from economy class to this lavish coach? I thought they made a mistake.*

"But how did you reach Sudbury? It is almost an eight-hour drive. Were you using some kind of speed jet or something?" I sound very sarcastic, but the fact is, I am amazed.

He compresses his lips, as if he is trying to hide his laughter. "Yes, but you can call it a helicopter." *This man knows how to use his fucking money.* "You are a very pathetic liar, Rania. You should not lie. It shows on your face." He gives me a mischievous smile. I look at him in surprise. What is he talking about? "I know you are escaping from me. I don't know why I scare you. I don't know if it was yesterday's news or my flowers or my voicemail, but I am dead sure you're escaping." He leans forward, killing the distance between us, and holds my hands again. "This whole coach is booked for us, all the way through Edmonton. We will be together for almost three days. There is no media, no waiter, no one to take our pictures and post them on the Internet. It is just us."

Three days with him alone? In this coach? I can't breathe properly when he is around, and he is expecting me to stay with him for three days.

"This train will stop at Winnipeg. If you are not comfortable by that time, I will head off. But for these two days, I want you to tell me everything that you are holding back in your mind. What is it that scares you about me? Have I been too hard on you or harassed you? Because every time I look in your eyes, I see only fear of me." He pauses for a second and continues. "I thought you were reserved with all men, but when I saw you with Mike, there was no fear, no pain in your eyes. I want the same thing, Rania. I want to be the one to whom you can talk freely and open yourself. I don't expect you to be friendly to everyone, frankly speaking. When I can't endure you being friendly with Mike, how would I expect it with other men? I like you being restrained, but I want to be the one with whom you can laugh, share your sorrows, and open up your cocoon where you have hidden all your secrets." He stops for a moment. "I'm not asking you to sleep with me. I know you're judging me from my past habits, but trust me, that is not it this time." I see sincerity in his eyes. All his declarations diffuse in my blood like a drug, but I have only one question in my mind.

"Why me, Adam?" I finally get the courage to look at him.

"I don't know . . ." He shakes his head. "I feel I had been living in the dark, and you're the only one who could bring me into the light. I know it's crazy for me to follow you down the train tracks. But I'm living the life of a moth that wants to stay close to light, yet it knows it will burn soon. I know you have nothing to give me, and I will end up burning, but I can't help it."

Adam's sudden confessions bring tears to my eyes. He doesn't admit that he is in love with me, but what I see in his eyes is beyond the feeling of love. I can't name it. How can I enlighten him, when my soul is lost in darkness? His truth is melting me inside. I try to remain calm, as it is time for me to comfort him. I never imagined a man like Adam Gibson would ask me for nothing but my trust.

"Adam, please . . ."

"I will not go anywhere, Rania, until you tell me why you are running from me."

"Ben called me in the morning." It is time to reveal the truth. It is pointless hiding from him, as he will find out himself, and that will provoke him to make things more troublesome for me. "He was not happy with the media attention."

"What's his fucking problem?" he snaps.

"He is sort of my guardian here. My father has given him responsibility for me. Baba is not happy about the news." I pause for a moment. "He works as a UN Secretariat in the Middle East region. He has a very respectable job and people are gossiping about his daughter." I avert my gaze to look outside. It is dark, and I have no idea how much time has passed.

Adam says, "People should mind their own business."

"Adam, you and I belong to different cultures. In our culture and religion, girls don't have relationships with boys before marriage. You were never a part of that culture, so I can't make you understand, but all I can say is that this is creating trouble for my father at his work." My tone is sharp and clear.

"He can let you hang around with Mike since childhood, but this news is creating issues at his work. That's bigotry." Adam's statement is filled with sarcasm. "Where is culture and religion in Mike's case?"

"Stop comparing yourself with Mike. He is my friend. You are . . . nothing." It is true, whether he likes it or not. He looks at me with shock. "Ben tried to convince Baba that there is nothing between us. He said he is not so stupid that he can't see what was in your eyes, when you were dancing with me." As soon as I say it, Adam closes his eyes, hiding his feelings from me.

"But why don't you tell him we are just friends? Like you and Mike are. We will start with a friendship. I won't ask you to move ahead until you have complete trust in me. Can't you have two friends? Does Mike have all the copyrights?" Adam sounds very frustrated.

"It's not about Mike. With him, I don't end up on the front page of the newspapers every day. It's you who brings a spotlight on me." I snap at him in my distress.

"So, if I were some ordinary guy, you would have accepted my friendship?" I am quiet, not sure what to say in response. I never thought about it that way.

What if he was just Adam, with no wealthy and notable baggage attached to him, would I consider making him my friend? Of course, I would have. My father would never have known about it. I look at him intently, and then nod in silence. He scratches his forehead, thinking. "So basically, my wealth is a problem for you. You won't accept me with this?"

"It is not about wealth, Adam. People know you; anything you do becomes news. Please, keep me out of it. The media is always digging into your life. I don't want . . ." I go mute, realizing what I am saying.

"You don't want them to dig into your past?" He watches me cynically. I turn my face to view the darkness outside. "What is it that you're hiding? Maybe I can protect you." I turn at his statement. *He will protect me?*

"It's not what you think, Adam." I shake my head dejectedly and close my eyes.

"Then I want to know what it is." I hear him moving from his seat and sitting next to me. He puts his arms around me, realizing I need his comfort. *How does he know me so well?* How does he know when to hold my hand, when to say kind words, when to wrap his arms around me? He is entering through the darkest passage of my heart, without even knocking at the door. A tree of forbidden fruit, walking down close to tempt me. "I will not ask you what happened in your past," he says. "Your tears said everything that night. But if you think that being with me will bring your past into your present, then I take all the responsibility to protect you from it. But please, don't ask me to stay away from you. I can't do that." He takes a deep breath. "If you think the fame is creating trouble, we can keep our relationship private. I will use all my power to protect you, Rania. All I want is your trust. That's it." He keeps rubbing his hand gently on my arm, comforting me. I never want to leave here. I already feel protected. I look up at him.

"Why do you want to protect me?"

"I don't know. I feel like doing it. Maybe God has appointed me for that. You know everyone is sent with a purpose. I guess this is my purpose."

"But when you don't believe He exists, then how can you say He is charging you with something?"

He looks deeply into my eyes for a moment.

"I told you earlier, you leave me no choice other than believing in Him." He smiles at me very lovingly and beautifully. I can never forget his smile. He stands up and offers a hand to me.

"Come, dance with me." His sweet smile makes me follow his steps. He takes me to the dance floor. The music starts playing itself. I don't know how he is doing it, but it certainly impresses me. My mood gets lighter in his arms, hearing the music. We dance slowly for a long time. I see the lights changing above us, and wonder if someone else is there. He interrupts my thoughts.

"There is no one here, Rania. I have promised to protect your privacy, and I will keep my promise." His eyes hold a bold promise.

"So, you booked the whole coach, just to—"

"I can keep this train moving for the rest of my life, if you keep on dancing with me."

I avert my eyes, but I know his are deeply locked on me. His words are creating a blaze around us. "You always surprise me." I look up at him and smile. He closes his eyes for a moment.

"I can't even express what you do to me." His words are almost a whisper in the air, but their warmth fills the room with affection. He pretends I didn't hear, so I keep it like that, pretending to be unaware of it.

"This is very lavish. You shouldn't have spent so much."

"It's nothing compared with this, our dance." We keep dancing, lost in our thoughts. Finally, he breaks the silence. "So, what did you do yesterday, apart from meeting your *guardian*?" His tone is sarcastic when he talks about Ben.

"I was babysitting all day." I smile, and he looks at me quizzically. "One of my neighbors has twin girls, around nine months old. They are adorable. I guess they are the best things in my life. I look forward to every Sunday afternoon." I smile.

"You babysit every Sunday?"

"Almost. I give the parents some time out; meanwhile, I play with the babies. But they are going on vacation for a few weeks, so I am going to miss the little angels. Their innocence makes me forget everything. I'm always surprised when the day is over."

"I can see that on your face. I'm sure they must be charmed with you too." We continue with our slow dance, and I don't object when he envelops me in his arms. I rest my head on his chest, feeling his warm body. His intoxicating cologne fills my senses. *What is happening to me?* I am freeing myself with his flow. He said he is drawn toward me, but he doesn't know that the feeling is mutual. I don't know if I will ever be able to express my feelings to him. But I have to tell him that I am grateful for his comfort.

"Adam?" I pause for a moment, waiting for his response.

"Mmm?" he says softly, to acknowledge me. So I continue.

"Thank you for everything." The music still plays behind us, tracks keep changing, and I don't listen to any of it. I am enjoying my peace. "In case I didn't mention it earlier . . . I trust you." He eases his embrace and our eyes meet. His expression says how contented he is to hear this from me. "I hope we never break this trust."

"That will never happen. I won't let it break . . . ever. If I promise to protect you, I will protect you, till my last breath."

"But you don't know what you are getting into, Adam. You don't know me."

"It's enough for me that you trust me. I would like to know you better, but I want to give us time, till our bond gets stronger and we trust each other completely. When you don't have to think before talking to me. You just say whatever is in your heart." He hugs me and I rest my head on his chest again. We keep dancing, till I am distracted by the background song: *Every breath you take.* The song's lyrics make me smile, and I sense he is smiling too. We look at each other, laughing heartily.

After our blissful, magical moment, I excuse myself to go to the washroom. He guides me and I keep following him. The whole compartment is ours, though. We can go anywhere we want to. I just wonder what we will do in here for two more days. I am hungry, also. I look up through the panoramic windows and it is deep dark outside. I check the time and it is almost seven in the evening. I realize I had only breakfast and then a little fruit. I slept all the way, till he surprised me.

"I will arrange dinner for us. You can freshen up." *Is he a mind reader?* I don't say anything, and escape into the washroom.

At the end of our dinner, I say, "Do you mind if I ask you something personal?" I have his complete attention, so I go on. "The article in the paper, with the picture of us dancing, said that was the first time you've been spotted dancing with someone. But I also read that you pick up women at parties."

He laughs at my question, though I am serious. I don't think it was funny.

"Do you want to know whether I bother to dance with women before shagging them?" He tries to control his laughter. I nod. "About the dancing, it's not that I haven't ever danced with anyone. I do dance, but it's usually very formal, like dancing with a business associate. Nothing like I was with you. That's what surprised the media. We didn't have a business relationship, but still, I . . ." He stops. He knows I understood, so he doesn't bother finishing his sentence.

After a pause, my interrogation starts again. "So, the ladies you . . . I mean . . . slept with. Were they your business colleagues or . . ." I'm not sure how to continue, so I start playing with the glass.

"No, Rania. I don't fuck with my business at all. Some of the encounters were arranged for me by my business associates, as a gift or a gesture; some by my people. I don't pick them. I use them for my pleasure and they get well paid for it. It is pure business." He takes a sip of his drink, but his eyes are locked on me.

"So, you call fucking a business, and you say you don't fuck with your business. How very smart!" I try to suppress my smile, but he sees me smirking because of my dimples.

We remain in silence and finish our meals. It is an odd topic to discuss. I realize I shouldn't have asked about it. It is too personal. But since he told me we should put our trust in each other, it is important for me to hear everything from his mouth and not judge him from the media.

"And what if you don't like a lady that you are given? How do you ask her to go?"

He looks at me sharply, as if he didn't get my question. "It's never happened. I never saw their faces, really. Even if I did, I don't remember. Their job was to fulfill my sexual needs." His statement is so abrupt and open that I choke on my juice and drop my glass, coughing. Luckily, the glass lands on the bar and not on the floor, but my clothes are ruined. He stands up from the bar stool instantly, drying the juice, which flows down from the table toward me. He then puts a hand on my back and rubs it.

"Are you okay?" I nod in silence, wiping the juice from my clothes. He puts the glass away and wipes up all the liquid. "Please, go and change, you will catch cold. Your luggage is in your room." He leads me to a small, but very cozy cabin. I stay silent and lock my door to change my shirt. I check the time and decide it is better to change into my night T-shirt and pajamas, rather than changing just the shirt. Within no time, I come out of the room and find him seated on the lounger, with a flat screen TV facing him. I sit on another couch, and he watches me fetch a plush throw from the side table.

After an awkward silence, he says, "Say whatever is on your mind. You may ask anything. Don't hold it here." He points toward his head. "I know what you want to ask me, things about my lifestyle." He keeps observing me keenly, watching my every move. I cuddle myself in the throw, hiding my nightclothes from him.

"I don't know what to ask. Umm . . . did you like anyone, in all those women?"

"I told you. I don't remember any. They were paid to please me. That's it."

"Have you ever tried pleasing any one of them?" My question catches his attention strongly. He shakes his head. "I mean, I have read that when a man provides pleasure to a woman, and when a woman makes sounds when she is pleased, and indulges herself in his pleasure, that's what takes a man to ecstasy. A man enjoys watching a pleased woman more than being pleased." I pause for a moment. "Have you ever thought of pleasing anyone?"

His gaze gets deeper and more intense. His mind is arrested, thinking, and I notice him stroking his lips with his index finger. *Is he wondering what to say, or is he getting the wrong idea about me?*

"You read a lot." *That's it? That's all you have to say?* "I get what you're saying," he says, "but I never thought about it. It was always just an exchange of money. None of them ever demanded any pleasure from me." He pauses for a moment and continues. "I am a very private man, Rania. You've read about my lifestyle, but have you seen any photographs of me linked with any woman?" He adjusts himself on the couch. "Other than you, of course. But when I was twenty-six, I got involved in a D/s relationship. She was my submissive for two years, but then she became demanding, assuming I was her boyfriend rather than her master." He relaxes by taking off his shoes and socks, and places his feet on the ottoman. "After that experience, I decided it wasn't really a good idea. There was a lot of paperwork and confidentiality involved, and I was starting to get bored with her expectations. So I changed my lifestyle."

"You mean, to this . . . umm . . . pay-as-you-go mechanism?"

"Exactly! You are very smart, Rania. I am impressed." He smirks and winks at the same time.

"So . . . in all those years, you didn't have any girlfriends?"

He looks at me blankly, probably thinking of an answer. *Is it too personal?*

"No, I never liked anyone. And even if I did, I couldn't afford to keep a woman."

"Afford in what sense?"

"Afford in the sense that women demand gifts, dates, hangouts and time. I didn't have time and money for all that."

Really? He notices my baffled expression.

"I told you, I haven't been rich all my life. I have seen what poverty is. I know what hunger is. When my mother left us, my father was in a very bad financial state. He could hardly afford meals for us. He used to drop me at the community center after school, and then went back to work. I used to eat whatever the donators provided. You can't understand what hunger is unless you have experienced it. I was homeless for three years." His confession stuns me. Is this the reason for him providing shelter and food to the needy—because he has experienced such need in his childhood? I truly feel sorry for him. We both get lost in our own thoughts for a while, before he breaks the silent bars between us.

"So, are you an only child, or do you have siblings?" He changes the subject.

"I am the only one. I had a very colorful childhood. I was born and brought up in Beirut. When I was fifteen, my father got his UN job and moved to Dubai. I did my high school and college there. I moved here when I was twenty. You know the rest."

"How did your mother die?" Adam's question has fired directly at my heart. I go pale and freeze.

"I am tired. I would like to sleep. Good night, Adam." I stand up, not answering this personal question. He grabs my hand as I pass by.

"I'm sorry. I didn't know I was crossing a line." He pulls me closer to him and pushes me down on the couch. "You don't need to tell me everything today, if you don't trust me enough," he says, caressing my hands. "We need to let our friendship grow before I can ask about your past." My eyes are still down on our hands. "Do you like watching movies?" He changes the subject to cheer me up. He picks up the remote control and starts playing with it. "Let's see what we have."

I shift and relax as he browses the list, asking me what I would like to watch. We agree on watching all the *Home Alone* movies in succession.

I stand up, and he grabs my hand again. "You aren't going to watch?"

"How can we watch a movie without hot chocolate?" I wink at him and he releases his grip. I head toward the kitchen.

THE MOMENT

♂

I gaze at her, making hot chocolate for us. I pause the movie to wait for her. Watching her doing something for me is more stimulating than a glass of whiskey. No one has offered me hot chocolate since I was a child. She comes back holding two mugs. "Be careful, Adam. It's very hot." She hands me the mug, then sits beside me, warming her hands with her own mug.

"Thanks, Rania. I haven't had this since . . . my mom left." I take a sip, and it takes me back in time. Without saying anything, she starts the movie, and we both relax on the couch.

At one point, she hands me her mug and grabs the plush throw, which she wraps around both of us. She's completely lost in the movie and doesn't realize how close she is sitting to me. I feel her warmth next to me and it's driving me crazy.

Control yourself, Adam!

She laughs like a child when the boy in the movie causes trouble for everyone. All I do is admire her beauty and innocence, watching a children's movie. After we finish our hot chocolate, she cuddles back in the throw, folding her arms. I feel her getting cold, so I wrap my arm around her and surprisingly, she doesn't object. She snuggles into my arm very chastely, and keeps enjoying the movie. Her laughter close to my heart makes me want to hold her tight, but I try to keep my hands to myself.

When the next movie starts, I feel she has stopped responding to it. I turn my head and find her sleeping on my arm. She is tired from all the surprises I've given her since this morning. I want to know what she has gone through in her past. I have seen her crying for her mother when I visited her home after our first date, but she doesn't want to talk about her. *Why?*

I wonder if she thought about everything I confessed to her. *Will she help me see the light?* As I spend more time with her, she is becoming a folded mystery, wrapped in a hard shell, which can only be broken with trust and time. If she feels comfortable sleeping in my arms, then I'm sure one day I will find the passage to that mysterious door, which she called a hideous past. I feel the warmth of her body and, sometime later, I fall asleep too.

* * *

I don't know how long I have slept, but I wake up with the urge to go to the washroom. Just as I finish, I hear a loud scream, and I rush back to find Rania on the floor, whimpering. She's moaning in her sleep: *it-hurts-please-have-mercy-on-me* over and over. I kneel down with her on the floor and shake her hard to wake her up.

"Rania, wake up. It's okay, dear. It's just a dream. I'm here. Wake up." I shake her again, to bring her out of her dream. She opens her eyes, filled with tears, and tries to catch her breath. I cup her face in my hands, wiping her tears. "It was only a dream. You're safe." Even after I speak, she keeps looking at me like I'm a ghost. I move the hair out of her face to see her clearly. The movie is still playing on repeat mode, so I assume we have slept for more than two hours. She still looks at me through ghostly wide eyes.

"Are you okay? Talk to me." Obviously she was dreaming about someone hurting her, but I don't know who.

She hugs me tightly, crying, as if I have rescued her from a prison camp.

She is trembling badly, and all I can do is hug her back and let her know that I will be at her side. She cries for a long time, until she is out of tears and the pain is released from her body.

When she finally settles down, I pull her away and wipe her face with my hands. She still sobs, so I give her time.

"Are you okay? Let me get you some water." I release her to fetch the water, but she grabs my arm tightly.

"No, please, don't leave me. What if he comes here and hurts me?" She looks around in fear. *Who is she talking about?* It's not appropriate to ask right now, as she doesn't look mentally stable to me. She is still terrified.

"No, Rania. He cannot come here. You're safe with me. We're on a train right now. He doesn't know where you are, okay?" I tuck her hair back, and hold her up. "You had a bad dream. No one is here. Let me put you to bed now. It's very late and you need to sleep." I pull her up, but her knees are still weak from fear, so I support her to her cabin. She's still looking around like she expects to be attacked, but she doesn't say anything. I tuck her under the blanket and rest her head on the pillow.

"Let me get water for you. And no one else is here, so be calm." I rush back to the bar and get her water. When I come back, I find her sitting on the bed, holding some pills. She takes water from me and gulps the medication with it. I look at the bottle next to her pillow carefully, to see what it is.

"I can't sleep if I don't take my pills."

"You take pills in order to sleep?" I ask her, surprised, and she nods silently. "Daily?" She nods again, head down. "But that night when I came to your apartment, you slept without them."

"I don't know what happened that night. It was my first night without a pill."

"In how long?"

"Around five years."

Shit! "That's a pretty long time, Rania. Don't you think it's harmful for your health? These will damage your brain cells." I put the bottle under her pillow.

"The doctor keeps changing it; otherwise, I will get immune to one formula and it won't work."

"But still, it's not good for you."

"I don't desire a long life, either." She shocks me with her confession. Her eyes are blank, with no hope or desire for anything. Who has taken the dreams from her eyes? *Who did she dream of?* I wish I could ask her, but I guess if she's not going to tell me right now, it's better not to push. I hope that one day, when she trusts me completely, she will reveal all her secrets. She lies back down and I tuck her under the blanket again. I turn off the light beside her bed and turn to leave. Surprised, she grabs my hand.

"Thank you, Adam . . . for everything." Her sincere words travel down through my soul. I feel appreciated and gratified that my presence means something to her.

I kiss her forehead without even thinking. "The pleasure is all mine. Good night, my dear." She closes her eyes and says good night.

I step out of her room and make a glass of whiskey for myself. Since I already took a nap, I am not in the mood to sleep. It's three in the morning, Toronto time. We're somewhere in Manitoba and will be stopping at Winnipeg tomorrow evening. I never dreamt I would spend time with someone on a train for two days, and never want to end it. She is still a stranger to me, with her hidden secrets, but the connection between us is beyond what words can explain. For the first time in my life, I realize I have no friend with whom to share my feelings about her. I have no one to tell what an emotional ride I am on. *What if I share my feelings with her?* She is too vulnerable to emotion. I want her to be my friend, but she has already set her boundaries. I know if I ever dare to cross them, she will run away.

She has kept herself in a capsule for so long. Will she ever allow anyone to break it? Will I ever be able to find a passage to her heart? But why do I need to sneak into her heart? Am I looking for a long-term relationship with her, when she has clearly stated that she has nothing to offer me, not emotionally, nor physically? Why do I keep chasing her, though she has never encouraged me? Why do I ask her to help me find the light, when she has kept herself in darkness for so long? Who has done this to her? *Was she in an abusive relationship?* The thought of someone touching her and then hurting her infuriates me. I can't imagine anyone would ruin her purity and innocence. I am lost in thought, eyes closed, when I feel her sit on the other end of the couch. I open my eyes and see her wrapped in the blanket, holding a jar of body butter.

"I couldn't sleep, and I noticed you are not sleeping, either. My pill hasn't taken effect yet." She opens the jar. "And I can't sleep with dry feet, either." Her smile affects me like a drug diffusing in my blood, anesthetizing me slowly. *I don't know if it's the whiskey or her presence, but I'm getting drunk and sleepy.*

I hold my glass tightly to control my body's reaction. If I don't stop myself, I will lose her forever. She gently scoops some body butter out of the jar and starts rubbing her feet. I put the glass down and watch her intently.

"Do you want to try me? I can give you a foot massage." I feel dizzy watching her. She smiles back at me and hands me the jar.

"I always avail myself of the opportunity for a foot massage." Without any hesitation, she adjusts herself on the couch and places her feet on my lap. "You will be a very good friend if you massage me well, Mr. Gibson." She winks at me cheerfully. *So she is fond of foot massages.* I take out the butter and apply it to her feet gently, massaging every part.

"Your feet are cold. You want me to get you socks?"

"No, they will be fine after the massage." She closes her eyes, concentrating on my touch. Her feet start to get warm.

"Did anyone ever tell you, you have beautiful feet?"

"Have you seen any woman's feet, other than mine?" she asks with a wicked smile. I purse my lips. She has a point.

I rub her heels, and she makes small sounds.

"Am I hurting you, Rania? If I am, please tell me." I pause the massage for a moment. She opens her eyes instantly.

"No, not at all. I am enjoying the blessedness." And she closes her eyes again. So, the sounds are of pleasure, not pain. *I have read when a man provides pleasure to a woman, and when a woman makes sounds, when she is pleased, and indulges herself in pleasure, that's what takes man to ecstasy.* She is right. Her sounds are turning me on like anything. I feel her body warming up on my touch. Are her feet a starting point for turning her on?

Control yourself, Adam. If sounds can drive you crazy, what would you do when you make . . . fuck it off!

I shake my head to blow out all the dirty thoughts that are clouding my mind. I notice she has fallen asleep. *The pill worked.* She looks innocent and untouchable while sleeping. I shift her feet and adjust them on the couch, covering them with her blanket. I crawl on the floor, close to her head, and brush away a few strands of hair from her face. I know I will never get another chance to examine her so closely. As I immerse my soul in her beauty, I recall William Wordsworth's phrases:

I saw her upon nearer view,
A Spirit, yet a Woman too!
Her household motions light and free,
And steps of virgin liberty;
A countenance in which did meet
Sweet records, promises as sweet;
A creature not too bright or good
For human nature's daily food;
For transient sorrows, simple wiles,
Praise, blame, love, kisses, tears, and smiles.

I kiss her forehead lightly, not wanting to wake her up, and whisper in her ear. "You are the most beautiful woman I have ever seen." I kiss her forehead again, and leave the room to let her sleep.

CLAIM

♀

"Yes, the property is worth five million. We need to get all the details about the area to see if it is worth buying or not. And yes, arrange the meeting with local hydro." I hear Adam's voice in my sleep. I get up from the couch with a clear mind. He is sitting on the bar stool with his laptop open, talking on the phone.

"Yes, send me the details. I will be checking my emails on and off . . . uh huh . . . no, I won't be able to attend today. You guys carry on . . . no, not on Thursday either . . . I have some commitments already . . . yes . . . that's better . . . and please, don't schedule any meetings for the whole week . . . I am not available . . . bye for now." I keep gazing at him, admiring the sight.

I realize why girls are crazy over him. He is very hot, charming, and a sin magnet. He is wearing light gray pajamas and a white t-shirt, which fit his body perfectly. He has beautiful strong arms and shoulders, which make me want to dissolve in him. If I were a normal girl, with no past, and if he had asked me out, I would have said yes. I wish I could tell him what he is getting into with me. I have started to trust him, though. I remember how he held me after my nightmare last night. How he promised he would be there to protect me. What if I tell him the truth? Would he still keep his promise? Till now, I have been enjoying the blessings God has bestowed on me.

Yes, Adam is a blessing to me.

He is engrossed in his office work, and I in him. While writing an email, he looks up and catches me staring at him. I avert my eyes instantly, not wanting him to know that I was admiring him.

"Hey, good morning, beautiful. I didn't know you were awake." He gives me his million-dollar smile and closes his laptop lid.

"Yeah, I woke up when you were talking on the phone."

"Oh, I'm sorry I disturbed you." He comes over and sits next to me. "You look beautiful in the morning." His eyes watch me deeply.

"Thanks . . . I guess I overslept . . ." I check the time and it is noon. "I haven't slept so long in ages. I guess your foot massage did wonders. Thank you." I smile at him shyly.

"Hmm, I know. You fell asleep while I was massaging you. And you didn't wake up after that?" I shake my head. "So, what would you like to have for breakfast? Other than tea and pumpkin bread." He winks at me.

"You remember, huh?" I ask him, surprised.

"Of course I remember. The first time you ever fed me. You think I'd forget that? I couldn't get the same bread, but we have other kinds here. Come, join me. I'm famished." He holds my hand and leads me to the bar.

"I need to go to the washroom. I will join you in a minute." He releases my hand and I escape.

After a few minutes, I rejoin Adam at the bar. The countertop is spread lavishly with breads, muffins and assorted breakfast food. "There is so much food. Why did you order this much?"

"I didn't know what you like, so you have a choice now."

"Thank you, Adam, but I intend to eat a normal breakfast. For me, a slice of bread with tea is enough. Please don't waste the food."

"Okay, we will not waste it. Now, start your breakfast." He hands me a cup of tea and bread.

"How do you know I drink this tea?" I am surprised to see a Tetley teabag.

"I saw it in your kitchen, before leaving on Sunday morning." *Oh, so he stayed whole night.* He takes a sip of his coffee, watching me. *How much has he noticed?*

We remain quiet, concentrating on our breakfast. After a few minutes, his phone chimes. Since his hands are busy with food, he puts the call on speaker. "Yes, Sylvain. Any news?"

"Mr. Gibson, I have sent all the details to Mr. Fraser and they said they are interested in meeting you personally. I told them you are busy this week, but they—"

"Tell them I am out of town for a week. If they want to meet with me, I am available on Monday, but this week is not possible. I am booked already." He looks at me when he says booked.

"Yes, Mr. Gibson. I will schedule it for Monday. Thank you. Good day."

Is he postponing all his business meetings because of me? I feel special all of a sudden. I wonder how long this feeling is going to last. His phone rings again. He checks the caller ID and his expression changes. He puts the phone on speaker again.

"Yes, Mrs. Moore."

"Hi, Adam. How are you?" The woman calls him by his first name, which means this is not an official call.

"I am good. Why did you call?" I feel tension in his voice.

"I read the news. I am happy for you. The girl is pretty."

"Yes, she is." Adam speaks low, looking at me. *Oh, they are talking about me.* "Is that the only reason you called?" I notice he has stopped eating. He keeps his eyes closed and rubs his forehead.

"It's nice that you finally found someone. Even in the picture, it's obvious from the way you look at her."

"Oh! So you can read my eyes, huh?" Adam sounds very sarcastic.

"Adam, I am your mother. Of course I can read my son." *What? It's his mother?*

"Did you want anything else, Mrs. Moore?" Adam asks annoyingly. *How can he talk to his mother like that?*

"I called to invite you for a family holiday dinner on Saturday."

"We are not family, Mrs. Moore. You have your own family, and I suppose they will show up." He keeps his eyes closed, but I feel how stressed he is.

"You are my family too, Adam. I was wondering if you could bring Rania with you—"

"We have already accepted an invitation somewhere else. I'm afraid we won't be able to come." *When did that happen?*

"You do this every year, Adam—"

"And you still call me every year. I will talk to you later, bye." And he hangs up the phone. He remains quiet for a moment. I stand up from my stool and place my hand on his shoulder.

"Adam, were you talking to your mother?" He nods in silence. "Do you realize how you were acting? She was—"

"You don't know anything, Rania."

"No, I don't know, but right now I can see that you spoke to her very rudely, and this is not the way to talk to her," I scold him.

"What? You think I'm at fault?" He looks at me in surprise.

"I don't know who has done what, but right now you are at fault. She called to invite you for the holidays, and you—"

"I haven't seen her in ages, Rania. I can't accept it now."

"Call her and apologize," I order him, crossing my hands over my chest.

"What? You expect me to call her and say sorry? For what?"

"For your behavior, Adam. This is not the right way."

He stands up from his stool and shakes his head in frustration. "I can't believe you are asking me this."

"Yes, you will do it. We have accepted each other as friends, so in friendship you will listen to me."

"What? Are you threatening me?" His eyes deepen on me.

"I am not threatening you, Adam, but you are wasting all your good deeds, when you are not good to your mother. God will not like it."

"I had only one relative, and that was my father. Then God took my father from me, left me with nothing. And you say I should be grateful to Him?"

"But He gave you a good heart, Adam. You feed and provide shelter to so many people. He is watching you. You have a very powerful soul. Nothing will be wasted. You will be rewarded in life, maybe in a form of a stronger relationship. Or a more prosperous life."

"I don't want wealth and prosperity anymore. I have more than enough."

"But don't abandon the relatives that are left to you. Time doesn't wait for anyone. I can't believe you reject her every year, but see, she still calls you. It is only because her love is unconditional."

"Oh yeah? Where was her love, when I was only six and she left me? She married a rich man, leaving my father and me in hard times. Where was love then?" He holds back his anger and I realize he is restraining his tears also. I put my arm around his shoulders and sit him back on the stool.

"Say everything you are keeping in your head. I am here to listen."

He stays quiet for a moment, then finally speaks. "I haven't seen her in so many years, except occasionally at parties, but it has been a long time. She calls me every year, but I always refuse. It's very hard for me to confront her now, after so long. I can't do it. I don't know how I would react. I don't know if I would be able to talk to her or not. That frustration comes out in the form of rudeness, every time I talk to her. I can never forget what she did to me, Rania. I needed her so much. We had no home, and when I used to sleep in shelters with strangers . . ." He doesn't speak after that. I see pain in his eyes. He suffered so much in his childhood and there is nothing I can do to change it.

"I can understand your pain, Adam, but it's over now. You cannot go back and fix it, but you can make the most of what you have now. Did you ever try asking her why she left you? You have heard only your father's side of the story."

"I don't want to listen to her. What would she say? What reason could there be to leave a child?"

"At least try to talk to her. She wants you in her life, Adam, and I know, deep inside, you want her in yours too. You are prolonging your pain and hers as well, behaving like that. Life is too long to hate someone, but it is too short to love." I pause for a moment, then pick up his phone from the counter. "Now, you will call her and apologize and tell her that you will be joining her for dinner."

"But she has asked you to come also."

"I will come with you, Adam. Now that I have promised to be your friend, I will make sure you talk to your mother and sort out all your differences." I smile at him, giving him his phone. "Call her now."

"I can't believe you're making me do this. I didn't know you could dominate . . . me." He shakes his head with surprise.

"I am not dominating. I want to end this pain of yours, once and for all. It's gonna hurt for a while, but then you will be free. Now be a good guy and call her."

He picks up the phone and dials the number. She answers on the second ring. "Adam, you called back?" I hear astonishment in her voice.

"I called to say . . . umm . . . I'm sorry for my behavior . . ." He looks at me in confusion.

"Oh, Brian, my son has called me . . ." She is talking to someone, but I don't know who. "That's all right, my dear. You've called me; for the first time, that's what matters most." *All mothers are the same.* I smile to myself.

"I also called to say that we will join you for the holiday dinner after all."

"You will?" Mrs. Moore's voice is filled with happiness.

"Yes, we both will come." He looks at me with tenderness.

"Oh, Brian, he said he would come for dinner. I am so happy, Adam. I love you so much." He is extremely quiet, so I move my lips for him to say, *i-love-you-too-mother.* He rolls his eyes at me and I give him one more warning look.

"I love you too . . . Mom." He averts his eyes from me. *Whom is he hiding from?*

"Oh, Brian! He said he loves me too." I feel a sense of achievement in her voice. It is a joy to hear.

"I will see you on Saturday. Bye." He hangs up the phone without listening to any goodbye from her side.

I immediately ask him, "Who is Brian?"

"Her husband. Brian Moore," he says blankly. He stands up from the bar stool and I follow him.

"Thank you for listening, Adam," I say to his back.

"I need some time alone." He doesn't look back at me, and disappears into his cabin.

I know I made him do something against his will. I never really expected that he would listen to me and talk to his mother, when he has not talked to her in so many years. I decide when I go to dinner with him, I will make sure all grudges get resolved between mother and son. Adam has suffered so much, all those years, and it is painful to see him like that. In only a couple of days, since we have met, we have got so much closer. He has revealed so much to me about his past, his habits, his grudges, but soon he will expect me to do the same. Will I ever be able to tell him about my past? Will I ever get the courage to go back in time, along with him, and open all the doors that I have shut down for five years? He is giving me plenty of time and patience to build a bridge of trust between us, but one day he will expect me to walk down that bridge to him. If he asks for more than friendship, will I ever be able to give it to him?

He has told me he wanted some time alone. It is better to leave him in solitude for the time being, and not bother him. I settle by the window. The land is all white outside, but the sight is still breathtaking. I am blissfully enjoying the view and Adam's company. Traveling in business class is something I never expected in my life. He has brought surprises to me every time we have met—from the dance performance and the Tiffany box to this travel upgrade. Was it asking too much to make him call his mother? Did he really want time for himself, or was he escaping me? I put all my crazy thoughts aside and open my ebook reader.

After a while, I hear Adam's phone ringing on the counter. I ignore it at first, but when it rings multiple times, I decide I should take it to him. I look into his cabin and see him sleeping peacefully. His phone rings again, with an "unknown" caller ID. I put the phone on silent and tiptoe out of his cabin so as not to disturb him.

I wonder what it is about Adam that attracts me so much. He is the first man, after so many years, whom I don't mind holding my hands or embracing me with tenderness. I don't feel uncomfortable dancing with him; in fact, I can never refuse if he asks for a dance. Why did I feel so protected, when he held me after my nightmare? Why do I believe him when he says he will always be there for me? Why do I even want to believe him?

After reading for three hours, I start to feel hungry. I check the time and it is almost five in the evening. I realize I am still in my nightclothes, so I head to my cabin and take a relaxing shower and change. I pick a black velvet long skirt with a pale blue blouse to wear. I look at myself in the mirror and wonder what Adam sees in me. *Why does he think I am pretty?* Is it because I resemble my mother, and I know she was very beautiful? But Adam has never met my mother.

Adam is still sleeping, so I sit at the corner of his bed, watching him. He looks much younger in sleep—not even thirty. He keeps himself in good shape, and I wonder how many girls have enjoyed his bed. I am completely engrossed in his beauty when he shifts and drops his hand in my lap. As soon as he touches my body, he opens his eyes.

INTEREST

♂

I move in my sleep and drop my hand on her. A current passes through my body and I open my eyes immediately.

"Hi." She welcomes me with her gorgeous smile.

"You look so beautiful." I pause and take a deep breath, looking at her lovingly. "Am I dreaming, or is it really you?" I touch her face to confirm it's her. My action makes her smile again.

"It is me. I don't think you have issues with nightmares." She winks at me mischievously.

"If this is a dream, then I would like to stay in it forever." My hand is still on her face and I start to caress her lips with my thumb. I want to kiss her passionately and let her know how precious she is to me, but I know I don't dare to push the limits she has set on us. "Your fragrance will kill me someday. I can't even explain the effect it has on me." My tone is filled with passion, and I assume she is able to read my intentions. She shifts and looks away.

"You were drinking before sleeping?" She looks toward my glass of whiskey. I close my eyes, agreeing with her.

"I'm sorry. I know you don't like it."

"It is not about like or dislike. I have seen people turn brutish after this." She still looks at my glass.

"I am not an alcoholic."

"I trust you." It is better to change the subject, so I look at my watch.

"Shit, I slept for so long. We should get something for lunch," I say. She stands up from the bed immediately. "Please feel free to order anything from the menu," I tell her. "I will join you in a few minutes."

"When you were sleeping, your phone rang many times. I checked, but you were sound asleep, so I didn't bother you." She hands me the phone. I find twelve missed calls from . . . . Rania notices my expression changing. "Is everything okay?" she asks innocently. I nod in silence and head toward the washroom.

After a quick shower, I hear music. From the corner of the passage, I see her dancing in front of the flat screen. She doesn't know I'm watching her, and enjoying the sight. There is a music video of *Thriller Night* on TV and she copies all the steps exactly, as if she has been practicing it for a long time. Her body sways like a flame in a wind, stunningly beautiful in a black skirt.

During one of the moves, she turns her head and sees me. She stops instantly, as if I caught her stealing something precious.

"Please, carry on. You dance really amazingly." I walk toward her and she steps back nervously.

"I'm sorry, I didn't know you were . . ."

"If I told you I was here, then you would have stopped earlier. I would have missed it." I look at her from head to toe and she skips her eyes away from me. "You look dazzling when you dance." She blushes with shyness. *Oh, that blush pink shade.* She moves away from me and heads toward the bar.

"I am sorry, I couldn't decide on anything for lunch." She changes the subject. "I can't have a proper meal at this hour."

"No worries. We will have snacks, and then dinner at Winnipeg tonight. We have two hours' stopover there." I sit next to her. "How about a shake or a smoothie? And some fruits?" I check the drinks menu and then look at her. She smiles and relaxes, and we agree on smoothies and fresh fruits. I use my phone to place the order, and continue talking to her. "So, you know all the dance moves in this video?"

"I have been dancing to it since I was a child. This was the first video that started me dancing. My mother used to enjoy watching me." I see painful and pleasant memories mingled in her eyes, though she smiles sweetly. It's obvious that her mother meant a lot to her, but whenever the topic comes up, she becomes so vulnerable.

"What was your mother's name?"

"Sarah." She doesn't say anything after that. I realize she doesn't want to talk about it. Ali interrupts us with our snacks, and his presence surprises Rania. She doesn't speak to him, but just gives him a smile. After Ali has left, I lift the smoothie glass in my hand.

"Toast to our friendship." She smiles at me and accepts my gesture. The smoothie is really good. I don't know how to break our silence, and luckily her phone chimes. She puts it on the speaker.

"Hi, Ben. Good evening."

"Hey, Rania, how is your train trip going so far?"

"Never better." She smiles and looks at me.

"Listen, do you know where Gibson is?"

"Why do you ask?"

"Oh yeah, how would you know. You are traveling. I was just wondering if he called you. I spoke to his assistant and she told me Mr. Gibson is out of town for the whole week. I was just wondering if he would meet you in Edmonton. But obviously, why would he do that? He is not your lover." *So if I am chasing her, is it because of love?*

"Ben, please, don't be so concerned. I am fine. How is the moving going?"

"Ah yes, we will be able to work from the new location next Monday. You carry on and enjoy the summit. I heard there are some fresh graduates attending as well. Try to meet them and see if any are a good fit for us. I trust you."

"Thanks, Ben. I will keep that in mind."

"I have emailed your hotel bookings and summit tickets. Just show them your phone. And one more thing." He pauses for a moment. "Stay safe. He is a dangerous man, Rania. Keep your eyes and ears open. Your father is very concerned." *Me? Dangerous?*

"I know he is concerned about his name. Don't worry, tell him I won't ruin it."

"But Gibson is a man with power. He possesses what he wants. I don't want you to end up being one of his possessions—" *Hmm . . . Really?*

"That will not happen, Ben. I will be fine. Take care. Bye." And she hangs up the phone.

"Dangerous, huh?" I smirk at her. She stays quiet, focusing on her smoothie. "What's his fucking problem? He's not your dad." I'm really annoyed now.

"There are many reasons. He wanted me to marry his son, that's the first reason. Secondly, I believe he sees my mother in me. That's what makes him more protective of me." I look at her quizzically. "Ben and my parents graduated from the same university. They all met in Scotland. Ben was the first guy who proposed to my mother." She continues with her smoothie.

"Seriously? He was your mom's boyfriend?"

"Not a boyfriend. He was in love with her, but it was one-sided. My father joined a semester later and he also put his heart in front of my mother. Belonging to the same culture and religion, my father had the privilege of marrying the beautiful maiden, right after their graduation." She pauses for a moment, thinking. "I think he doesn't treat me as Ahmed's daughter, but he treats me as Sarah's daughter and feels a responsibility to take care of me."

"That is very surprising. And an interesting story. So, your mom and dad had a love marriage?"

"Yes, they did. My grandfather was not happy with the idea, though, because my mother was Egyptian and Father was from Lebanon. So, my grandfather wanted her to marry an Egyptian and stay in the same country."

"Your parents told you their love story?"

"I was sixteen when my mother told me. Whenever she talked about Ben, I always saw sparkles in her eyes. It was a very strange affection."

"So, you think your mom was in love with Ben too?"

"I don't know—she never confessed that. All I know is my father had the advantage of being a Muslim. But he loved her. All my childhood, I never saw them arguing or fighting. My father is still in love with my mother. He never married again." She looks down at her glass, toying with the straw. "Whenever I saw them together, I believed that fairytales do exist. Love exists. We just need to find the right person." She takes a pause. "Mom had a very hard labor during my birth. My father wanted a son too, but he couldn't see my mother in pain again. So he never demanded another child. I guess that's what love is." She smiles to herself, her eyes carrying a dream. I also see pain in her eyes, so I decide to change the subject.

"And what makes him think I am dangerous? I mean Ben." I take a sip of my smoothie, looking at her.

"With all due respect, Mr. Gibson, your lifestyle says everything." She laughs heartily and I join her.

"Do you see danger?" I ask on a serious note. She keeps looking at me with sharp eyes, not sure what to say, but her gaze tells me that there is something.

"I see danger. I won't lie. But not for me." She drops her gaze to the table. "You are risking your reputation, Adam." She is back on the same topic, *us*. It's time to change it again.

"You go to the dance school daily?" I ask her abruptly, and she looks at me with surprise.

"Yes, I do."

"Don't you get tired?"

"Why do you think I need a foot massage before I sleep?" She winks at me impishly.

"Then, why do you dance if it hurts that much?"

"I am not a gym fan. It is something I can't do. So I dance to burn my calories. And it also makes me feel good. No matter how tired my feet get." Our snack is almost finished, so we move to the couch. "You work out too?" she asks, giving me a strange look.

"What makes you think that?"

"Your body is in good shape. I'm sure you do." She checks me out from head to toe, like I always do to her. I smile and nod in silence. It surprises me that she has even noticed my appearance. It makes me feel very special. She picks up the Edmonton weekly guide and buries herself in it. I sit close to her, to see what she is engrossed in. She reads the details about some opera show, and then checks her train schedule.

"You like live performances?" I look from the magazine to her.

"I have never attended one, but they fascinate me. Anyhow, it is tomorrow evening. It is not possible." She closes the magazine and is about to put it aside. I grab the magazine from her and read it carefully.

"Don't worry, I will take you." I'm serious, but she laughs at me.

"It is tomorrow evening, Adam, and we don't have tickets. By the time we get there, it will be over. So never mind." She stands up from the couch, looking for something. I grab her hand tightly.

"You don't trust me? If I say I will take you there, I will." She looks at me with surprise.

"You have got to be kidding me. I was just reading it. Nothing serious." She sits down next to me, watching me with astonishment. "Adam, I know you can make anything possible with your wealth, but please don't make it so awkward. Even if you could make it possible, I don't want you to spend a rubbish amount of money to do it."

"I just want to see you happy. If I don't spend it now, I will spend it some other day. The money and me are a package. You might as well get used to it." I gaze at her deeply and tuck her hair behind her ears. She shakes her head in bewilderment.

"I have always liked your surprises, Adam, but this is—"

"Done, we're going then." I check my watch and say, "You need to go now and pack your stuff, and get ready for the surprises." I stand up and lead her to her room. She is still in shock. "Do you trust me, Rania?" I block her way and whisper closely in her ear. She looks up at me with dazzled eyes.

"Yes, I do." And she escapes into her room.

THE FLIGHT

♀

I enter my cabin, still surprised at Adam's remarkable offer. *Is he serious?*

I don't have much to pack, except for my medication, basic makeup and nightclothes. I am still lost in what Adam just told me. After a few minutes, I hear another voice coming from the bar area. I poke my head out of the room, and find Ali and Adam talking. As soon as I come in, Ali waves to me and leaves.

"You don't have to do all this. Please don't spend a hideous amount of money on the show. We can see it some other time."

"It's all done. And it is not much. So relax." He smiles and continues, "But I like this sparkle in your eyes when you are surprised. You look very innocent and charming." He watches me very lovingly, which makes me feel special.

"Thank you for all your surprises, Adam, but this is making me feel bad. I feel I am using you, and I can't even do anything in return."

"Don't ever say that again." He gets angry instantly. "You are not using me. I'm doing all this because I want to." He takes my hand in his and continues. "You don't know what you do to me. Your presence is what matters to me most. You trust me . . . that's all I want from you. So, we are, in fact, in a give and take relationship." I just don't get it, what he sees in me. There is no point in arguing with Adam, though, because he always wins. I should have been more cautious before looking into the magazine. Adam starts working on his laptop, so I get up and decide to check my email. I settle myself by the window and start reading my office emails on my phone.

An hour later, an announcement is made for Winnipeg Station. Adam has disappeared, so I go look for him and surprisingly, I find him in my room. He carries my trolley bag and guides me toward the exit. The city is densely covered with snow, with a temperature of minus seventeen degrees, but it's decorated with holiday lights and Christmas trees, which makes it more welcoming. Adam hands our luggage to someone, then grabs me tightly by the shoulder as if I am a child who might get lost in a crowd. There is a BMW waiting for us outside the station. It is very warm and cozy inside the car. Adam dusts off the snow from my face and hair.

"God, your face is freezing." He cups my face with both hands. "Let's get you a coffee or a tea to warm you up." He asks the driver to stop at any of the coffee shops on our way to *somewhere*. I start to enjoy the royal treatment Adam is giving me. His little concerns and worries about me are making a special place in my heart. No one has ever made me feel so much appreciated since my mother. Since the day we met, Adam has given me the feeling that I am playing a substantial role in his life, though the truth is, he is the one to be treasured.

He takes care of me with a hot chocolate.

Adam is busy with his phone calls and I am sitting next to him, enjoying the warmth. I have spent two days with him, alone in a train compartment, but not even once was I fearful; in fact, I felt very protected. Being in his arms gives me the feeling that I am invincible, and no one can harm me. He told me I was having an effect on him, but should I tell him that the feeling is mutual? I could never have imagined sleeping in a man's arms like that, even with Mike, though he is my best friend. Adam told me he wanted to attain Mike's place in my heart, but should I tell him that his place is more valuable and treasured? He is the very first man in my life who has made me feel so special. If my little desire to go to the opera is so significant to him, then what will he do if I really ask him for something? I am starting to feel like a woman once more, only because Adam is igniting all the flames in my heart that I extinguished years back.

I close my eyes once again, afraid of what will happen when Adam learns the truth about me. He has always taken me to be a pure and innocent person who has some painful past. I wish I could tell him that along with all my nightmares, I have encountered demons in my life. I wish I could tell him how tormented my soul is, and now that he is in my life, he is secretly picking up all the burned and broken pieces. I want him to be in my life, but I know if he gets to know more about me, he will torture himself and spoil his reputation in society. My burned pieces will burn him too. I wish I could tell him I am not the girl he always sees.

Our car stops in front of the Winnipeg Airport.

"We are taking a flight to Edmonton," he says. "It's going to take an hour. That way we can attend the show tomorrow." He speaks generously, while adjusting my scarf around my neck. The wind is hard and cold, so we rush inside the boarding lounge. After all the clearance and check-ins, we are asked to wait in the business class lounge.

"We already had bookings for the train. Are you in the habit of wasting money, just like that?"

"It is called spending money at the right time. If it will bring a smile to your face, I can spend more than that." Adam always makes me speechless. There is no point in arguing with him. I will have to be more cautious in the future; as now I know, he watches my every move. I don't want him to spend so much money on me. I have no right to his treasure. "Would you like to have dinner here?" he asks me, as we seat ourselves in the luxurious lounge. "We have some time before we go."

"After a smoothie and then hot chocolate, you think I would have room? But I must say you feed me well, Adam." I smile at him with all my heart.

"I like feeding people. And feeding you is a different experience. It is very sexy!" His gaze on me deepens.

Oh!

I avert my eyes from him, to avoid his intensity. His green eyes have the power to sneak directly into my soul, and that is not fair. Every time he looks at me like that, without even touching me, he is able to pass a thousand watts of current through every inch of my body. "I would like to feed you with my hands one day." His voice gets more serious and passionate, as do his eyes, and it gives me different signals that I have ever received from him before. I huddle into the corner of the couch, keeping a safe distance from him. There is no one else in the lounge.

Is it the privacy, or the coziness of the area that is making him more intense?

"You are very beautiful, Rania. I would like to paint you on canvas one day." He still keeps a safe distance, but his eyes don't.

"You paint as well? I didn't know that."

"No one does. I do it at home, in my spare time. I haven't ever painted a real person. It's either landscapes or objects. But I wonder if I would be able to capture your beauty." He pauses for a moment and continues. "Only God can create such divine beauty. Humans are far from this talent, I believe."

"But I thought you didn't believe in Him."

"I told you earlier, you left me no choice. You are making me believe in Him. So, whoever has created you is a perfectionist." His way of complimenting me is so different from other men. It is very sexy, yet also respectful and gracious. We look at each other quietly, until we get interrupted by a very handsome young Frenchman.

"Bonjour, Mademoiselle." He greets me with a warm gesture and a kiss on the back of my hand.

"My name is Eugene. As a part of our business class service, we would like to offer you a massage in our spa. Hot stone, aromatherapy, acupuncture—"

"I would be interested in a foot massage." I stand up with excitement.

"Of course, ma'am. I am a reflexologist by profession and I can—"

"Do you have a masseuse here?" Adam interrupts.

"Not at the moment, sir." Eugene seems to hesitate.

"Eugene is here to give me a foot massage, Adam." I look back and forth from Adam to Eugene.

"Thank you for your offer, Mr. Eugene. We are not interested," Adam says very rudely to the masseur. He grabs my hand and heads to the other side. The masseur is astonished at Adam's behavior and leaves, giving strange looks to both of us.

"That was very rude of you, Adam." I look at him furiously, crossing my arms over my chest.

"And what were you doing? Taking a massage from a Frenchman?" He is angrier than me. *What's wrong with him?*

"Oh, come on, Adam. He is a reflexologist. I know he is good-looking, but I don't mind if he—"

"But I do mind. Do you get me? I *do* mind if some other man gives you a massage." His eyes become more intense and he leans closer to me. I look at him quizzically. *Is he serious?* "Do you know what kind of sounds you make when you are given a foot massage? Extremely pleasurable and highly erotic! You want to indulge that man, so that he can fuck himself from your sounds and take all the pleasures?" His words shock me. I look at him with my mouth open in surprise. Do I really make sounds during a massage?

Oh my God! This is so embarrassing.

I sit back on the sofa, still shocked by his attitude. Is he getting possessive about me? If not, then what should I call it? All my life, I have been escaping from this feeling, from a possessive man. The feeling which swallows all other feelings like love, trust, and companionship. I start to shiver and feel like my past is holding up a mirror to me once again. Adam notices my sudden mood change and sits beside me.

"I'm sorry for my behavior." So, he finally admits his mistake. "Last night, when I gave you a massage, you were making sounds which only a man can understand. The feeling that I got at that moment—I don't want another man to experience it." He looks down at his fingers, entwined on his lap. "I don't know what you call it, Rania, possessiveness or jealousy. But I can't share that feeling with anyone." He stands up without even looking at me, picks up the newspaper, and sits on the other side of the room. I sit here quietly, not sure what to say. Being jealous or possessive, is it one of Adam's normal traits? What other traits are there in his personality that I have not seen or experienced? *He possesses what he wants. I don't want you to end up being one of his possessions.* Ben's words churn in my mind with all the mixed feelings that I have for Adam.

He has shown me care and kindness; he has surprised me in various ways that I have never dreamt about. Yet, his sudden change in attitude has created an alarm in my head. I guess Ben is right; I should be more cautious. It was just a foot massage by a stranger, and he is frenzied about it. What if I tell him about my past? How deranged would he act? Where is the trust that he has been asking for? I want to ask him about it, but his frozen attitude shows that it is not the right time. I will ask him when he has control over his emotions.

An announcement is made to board the plane, and I pick up my bag and head toward the door without looking at him. He follows me without saying a word. Our seats are together, obviously, so I have no other choice but to sit next to him. The airhostess asks us if we want champagne, and Adam orders orange juice for both of us. I look at him in surprise that he didn't order champagne for himself. He reads my eyes and breaks the silence between us.

"We need to talk with a clear mind. The alcohol won't let me talk properly." *Is he a mind reader?*

"What do you want to talk about? Your stubbornness?" I ask him sarcastically, cocking my head. The airhostess shows up again with our juice. He turns toward me and holds my hand tightly.

"I'm sorry, Rania. If I've upset you, I am ready to apologize to that *good looking* masseur also, but please don't be so distant with me." His expression is as serious as his tone, but somehow, his way of calling the masseur good looking makes me laugh and banishes all my anger and fear. With one apology, he eases all the tensions between us.

"Oh, Adam, you are very cute." I put my other hand on his. "So, I can get a massage now?"

"No, I didn't say that. I will ask them if they have a masseuse here on board." He leans away from me, back to his jealous mode.

"What's the problem with—"

"I don't want any man to touch you, Rania. It's as simple as that. Or do you want to be touched by another man?" He looks at me in vexation.

I look at him, wondering what has happened to him. "And why do you think I want to be touched by some stranger?"

"Exactly! I am doing what you want. I am protecting you from the ferocious eyes."

"Oh my God! I can't believe it." I put my hands on my mouth, trying to hide my laughter. He is acting like a kid who is not willing to share his toys. "He was a professional masseur. I was not dating him."

"Don't you even dare think about dating another man." His look ravages the entire comfort zone between us. *What is wrong with him?*

"*Another* man? What do you mean by that? Who am I dating?"

"What do you call this, then?"

"Excuse me, Mr. Gibson, we are just friends. I am not dating. You are not my boyfriend." My tone is a bit harsh, and loud enough that the people around us look at us with curiosity. Our argument is getting us nowhere.

I realize it is better to be quiet than to argue during the flight and create a scene. He is not in his regular mood, so to avoid bickering, I take out my ebook reader and continue with my reading. I know he is looking at me, trying to say something, but my cold behavior and unresponsiveness give him the message. He is treating me like a possession that he can claim whenever he wants. If an encounter with a professional masseur is so difficult for him, then will he also get enraged over my friendship with Mike? *No, I can't let him dominate me like that.* I won't jeopardize my years of friendship with Mike over his stupid, arrogant, jealous attitude.

"I know you're not reading." He interrupts my wild thoughts. *How does he know that?* "You can't be reading a single page for ten minutes. Tell me what you're thinking." He leans his head toward me, whispering very low, so that no one can hear us.

"Why don't you tell me, Mr. Mind Reader, what I am thinking?" I ask him crisply. He smiles at my question and shakes his head, running his fingers through his hair.

"I don't know what I shall do to you. You are an impossible girl." He takes a sip of his juice and glances at me. "You think I'm a control freak? That's what you were thinking?" I shift away from him and huddle toward the window. *He is a freaking mind reader.* "Your face shows everything, whatever is going on in your head. You can't lie . . . not to me at least!" He takes another sip, and relaxes with grace. We don't speak for a while, until he finally breaks the silence. "Don't get me wrong, Rania, but I was not raised with any relationships in my life—no siblings, no parents, no childhood friends. Yes, a father, who never had time for me. I don't know what should I call this, friendship or a date, but it is the first for me in either case. I never had a female friend in my life. No girlfriends. But this, whatever it is, I want to keep it. It's the most precious possession I have . . . and the most sacred feeling, which I can't imagine losing." Adam's disclosure sends shivers deep down in me. *Am I really so important to him?*

I look at him with a totally awed expression, dumfounded. I have nothing to say to him that is as comforting as his epiphany, but I hold his hand firmly and reassure him with my smile. We don't speak for the rest of the flight. I don't know where Adam is taking me or what he has planned, but I trust him unconditionally. When we leave the plane, he seems to be shielding me from the eyes of others. I also hope no one will recognize him in this new city. If he is recognized throughout the nation, it could create a lot of trouble for me.

Being business class passengers, we are out of the airport in no time. I have never traveled so luxuriously in my life—first the lavish train and then massage options in the boarding lounge, which I was not able to use. Everything looks like a fairytale to me, and I wish to stay in this magical kingdom for a long time, to enjoy all the bliss. Adam appears to be God's gift to me, and I wonder what good deed have I done to attain such blessings of care, kindness and friendship from one person.

I am soon seated in a deep blue Lexus with Adam. I have no idea where he is taking me, but it's almost ten, so he will definitely take me somewhere to sleep. Adam is busy on the phone with someone, giving instructions about office work, so I entertain myself watching all the city glitz and glamour. Christmas is around the corner, so the downtown streets are decorated with holiday lights and trees. This is my first visit to Edmonton, but I never imagined it being so opulent.

Our car stops in front of The Fairmont Hotel MacDonald, at the grand entrance. It is a huge gray building, looking like it was built early in the last century. Adam is still on the phone, but his eyes and attention are on me. He holds my hand and helps me out of the car, and we enter the lobby. *Why is nobody taking care of the luggage?* We head toward the reception desk, where we are greeted by a graceful lady in her forties, dressed in a black suit. Adam offers his credit card and Fairmont President Club member card. The lady looks at the card and smiles at both of us.

"Good evening, Mr. Gibson. Thank you for choosing our hotel. As a President Club member, we are upgrading you to our special Queen Elizabeth Suite on the eighth floor. I am sure you will enjoy your three-day stay with us." She hands us two room cards with her pretty smile. *Three days? But I already have a booking somewhere else.*

I follow Adam blindly to the room. When he opens the door, I am speechless for a moment. We enter a large dining area that easily seats eight, with light gray walls and elegant lighting. Beyond that is a lavish, yet cozy living area, with deep gray velvet sofas and a big flat screen television. What surprises me most is the staircase behind the living room, which reminds me the room lacks a bed. *Holy shit! It is a two-story suite.*

I am busy absorbing the beauty and elegance of the room when Adam interrupts me.

"You like it?"

"I have no words. But it is too much for . . . I mean, a whole family could stay here." I head toward the window and see the beautiful city view, engulfed in darkness and snow.

"For now, it is just two of us." Adam speaks with tenderness, taking off his jacket. *Two of us? Does he plan for us to sleep in one room?* I ignore his statement and look at the view again.

"Don't you want to see the bedroom upstairs?"

I follow him up the stairs, where a double door opens into the master suite. At the entrance there is a beautiful white chaise, perfect for reading, with a stunning city-view window. The room has light brown wallpaper, and is elegantly decorated. There is a large king-size bed, with luxurious bedding and deep red velvet cushions—almost too beautiful to sleep on. There is an en-suite washroom, which has a double sink vanity and a jetted bathtub decorated with ivory candles. It looks like a honeymoon suite.

Oh no!

What if someone leaks the news that Adam and I checked into a hotel together?

"Where is my room, Adam?"

"This is your room." He gives me a generous smile.

"It is too big for me." I look around the bedroom.

"Not if you let me sleep here somewhere. This poor guy doesn't have a room tonight." *Poor guy? I'd like to be as poor as you!* He sits down on the chaise. "I can sleep here."

"Adam, you're kidding me, right?" I cross my arms over my chest. "You expect us to sleep in one room?"

"Yes, because the hotel is overbooked. This is the only room available. Also, my beautiful friend has a problem with nightmares, and I have promised to be there for her." He copies me and folds his arms over his chest, but he smiles mischievously. *So, you are in a playful mood!* He observes my tension intently, then stands up and walks over to me. His gaze is dark and deep, which makes me step back, creating a distance between us. I know his desire is to destroy all the boundaries. "You don't trust me? You think I would do anything against your will?" He reads my face with his intense, serious gaze. He takes something out of his pocket. "I want you to sleep without this poison from now on." He shows me my sleeping pills. *Where the hell did he get those from?* "I stole this from your luggage and I'm not going to give it to you." His tone is extremely serious. "You did sleep well, the whole night without waking up, when I stayed with you in your apartment. I want to see if my presence keeps you away from all this shit or not."

"You can't do this to me. I've been taking these pills for years. I can't sleep without them."

"Yes, you will, and I will make sure you don't take this shit from now on. I want to experiment and see how you will sleep without this, with me."

"Then what will happen, Adam? What if your experiment is successful? You can't be guarding my sleep every night."

"Yes, I can. You don't know me, Rania. I am extremely good at keeping promises."

"Oh my God! I can't believe it." I rake my fingers through my hair and shake my head in distress. Adam is impossible to deal with. He expects me to allow him to sleep in the same room with me, so that I don't get any nightmares. What kind of theory is this?

"You still get nightmares with these pills. So what's the purpose of taking them, other than damaging your brain cells?"

"Yes, I do, but at least my sleep is not broken. If I don't take them, and I get the nightmares and wake up, I can't get back to sleep, no matter how hard I try."

"You will try, Rania. And I will make it happen. Now that I've seen you doing this rubbish, I just can't let you rely on them. And I will expect you to be a good girl and cooperate with me." He puts the pills back in his trouser pocket.

"You promised to guard my privacy, and you bring me to a hotel and want to share a room with me. Do you think no one will find out?" I ask him furiously.

"No, no one will. I've given them special instructions and they will be accountable if the news leaks out. Believe me, I won't let it happen. Please don't make a fuss about sharing a room. We were alone on the train for two days and you still think I'm going to attack you like an animal?"

"It is not about trust, Adam. I am not saying you will harm me. But it doesn't look good, socially or ethically, that we are sharing a room. Anyone from outside would think we have more than a friendship. What if my father hears about this?"

"Your father will never hear about it, and why do you give a shit what other people think? You won't end up in the news, I promise you, so please have some faith in me."

There is no point in arguing with him—at least, not for tonight. An attendant rings the room bell downstairs, so we both head down. He has our luggage, and Adam instructs him to leave it on the upper level. He is rewarded with a hundred dollar bill, as a tip, just to bring our bags. *Why does Adam waste so much money?* I turn on the television, pretending I didn't notice his generous act. After a while, there is another attendant with the dinner trolley. I am surprised to see the selection of food Adam has chosen.

How did he know I wanted a regular sandwich? He is truly a mind reader.

We both dive into the food immediately, eating without talking to each other.

After dinner, Adam makes a few calls and disappears upstairs. I become engrossed in an animated movie, which I thoroughly enjoy. After almost half an hour, I notice Adam sitting on the other couch watching me intently, rubbing his index finger on his lips, which he usually does when he's thinking. I glance at him for a second. He has showered and changed into a white T-shirt and navy blue pajamas, which look extremely sexy and masculine on him. I return to the movie, trying to pretend I'm not drooling at his beauty, though I am. *You are a pathetic liar . . . anything you think comes to your face.* His words tingle in my mind and I am afraid of him seeing the truth on my stupid face.

"You like watching children's movies?" He interrupts my wild thoughts. *I was not watching the movie; I was lost in you.*

"It is not for kids. This movie has made more money this year than any other."

"It's an animation. Kids watch it, I guess." He looks back and forth from me to the movie.

"You will like it, once you start watching it. It has nothing to do with kids. But I watch romantic movies too. Although I don't believe in that bullshit."

"You think romance is bullshit?"

"A guy meets a girl, starts dating with a kiss and ends with wild sex in the bedroom. That's what all romantic movies are about. You can't call them love stories. It's pure lust, one of the deadly sins." His expression says he is not convinced. "Do you believe in romance?" I ask.

"I haven't experienced it, but yes, I do believe in it. And if you call it lust, then definitely I believe in it, but I think it's another form of love."

"I believe lust exists in love, but love is not necessarily present when lust is involved. Love is not a sin; lust is. It is up to the person, if they want to put romance in the lust or the love category. I see it as lust." My eyes are still on the TV.

"So, all the people who fall in love and surprise their lovers with hearts and flowers, you don't think it's romantic? You think it's lust?" Adam gives me his complete attention.

"I don't know. I told you earlier. I am not that kind of a girl, so I can't really comment on it. But then, what happens at the end? If a guy offers hearts and flowers to a girl, he expects the girl's naked body in his bed. It is cruel to say, but that's the truth. So where is love then? It all starts with lust, doesn't it?"

"But sex is another form of sharing and expressing love."

"So, when you had sex with all the females in your past, you were in love with all of them?" My question has rendered Adam speechless. He keeps rubbing his finger on his lower lip, trying to figure out what to say in return.

"I am not saying sex is equivalent to love, but at the end, when two people are passionate about each other, they would certainly opt for sex. It's how our human bodies are made, since the very beginning of time." He pauses for a moment and continues. "I agree sex is a part of lust, but it is also a part of sharing each other, physically and emotionally."

"If you are emotionally attached to someone, you would want to physically attach to her too?"

"Of course, I would want to. I would want to make her feel, through my body, how I feel about her."

Really?

I hear seriousness in his voice. Our conversation is warming up the room.

"That happens only once or twice. Then men get used to the same body, and there is no passion, no surprise." I look back toward the movie, to avoid his gaze. I don't want him to read my eyes and sneak into my past once again. It is too painful to share with anyone.

"Are you afraid of sex, or are you afraid to fall in love?" Adam's sudden interrogation surprises me. *What kind of question is that?*

I ignore him and walk away.

PARADOXICAL

♂

I grab her hand as she passes by me, ignoring my question.

"I'm asking you something, Rania. Which scares you more? Love or sex?" I stand up and move her back to the couch. She pretends to look toward the movie, when I know she is not. I read every single expression on her face. She closes her eyes for a moment, and finally speaks with trembling words.

"Both! Love breaks the heart and tortures the soul, whereas, sex bruises the body. It's painful both ways." She doesn't look at me, but I have her attention. I tuck a few strands of hair behind her ears, to see her more clearly. She is indeed hiding pain, and I can't stop asking her this time.

"Who has done this to you, Rania? Who has made you so . . . bitter?" I fix my eyes on her, but she locks her gaze on the movie. I pick up the remote and turn off the television, so that I can get her complete attention. I put my hands on her shoulders and realize she's trembling. "What happened to you in the past? You can trust me."

I see tears forming in her eyes, but she doesn't blink. She keeps staring at the blank television screen as if she's frozen. The only movement is her breathing. I want to comfort her, but my question has troubled her.

"I want to remove all the scars and bruises from your soul and body, if only you ever give me a chance."

Without even looking at me, she turns to go.

"I need to change and take a shower. I am tired." She rushes upstairs. I don't know what to do now. Should I follow her, make her tell me everything once and for all? Every time I try to dig out her past, she pushes me away. If I drag it out of her, she may try to run from me. I want our friendship and trust to blossom, but the more I try, the more distant we become.

Dealing with an emotional female is a first for me, and a very overwhelming experience. One minute she is talking to me openly, and within seconds, she cuts off everything and walks away just because she felt I was over the line. It surprises me that she didn't argue with me like she usually does, when I stole her pills from her bag. Will I be able to keep my promise? Will she allow me to guard her sleep at night? She's afraid she will ruin her father's reputation, but what that man is doing is completely unjustified. How could he leave his daughter alone in a strange country, and expect her not to get involved in a relationship? Does he know his daughter is suffering from a painful past? Does he know about her nightmares?

I want to ask her everything, about her relationship with her father, about her mother's death, about the man in her past. I can't believe anyone would hurt her, emotionally or physically. But someone was responsible for taking all the emotions out of her.

After about thirty minutes, I realize she hasn't returned from the shower. I go upstairs to check on her. There is light underneath the washroom door, but no sound. I knock gently. "Rania, are you okay?" I knock again, but I don't hear anything from inside. Since there is no lock on the door, I open it an inch. I don't want to invade her privacy, but I want to make sure she's all right. She's standing in front of the vanity mirror in her night clothes, with a towel over her shoulder. She looks completely blank; she doesn't even notice my reflection in the mirror. She is lost somewhere, water dripping off her hair, wetting the floor mat. I look around the washroom and feel the presence of something else, besides us. It's something that I can't explain. It feels heavy—very heavy. I tap on her shoulder gently. She flinches at my touch, as if I scare the hell out of her.

"Hey, are you okay?" She looks at me blankly, and then at the door. I am sure she's wondering how I got in, so I explain. "I knocked several times. You weren't responding. I was worried." She still looks blankly at me, not convinced by my assertions. "By the way, if you don't know, the door doesn't have a lock. I'm not a ghost who can sneak through locked doors." I wink at her, trying my best to cheer her up. She looks at me with wide eyes.

"Who are you, then?" Her question shocks me. "You show up everywhere I go, like *they* do. If you are not a ghost, then who are you?" *What is she talking about?* "You are not my shadow. You are not one of *them*. Then, who are you?"

"What are you talking about, Rania? Who follows you, besides me?" She doesn't say a word, just walks out of the washroom like a ghost. I want to bring her back to this moment, so I grab her by the arm. "Your hair is completely wet. Let me dry it. Otherwise, you will catch cold." I pull her back in front of the vanity and open up the hair dryer.

I start drying her hair, parting the strands with my fingers. She stands completely frozen, but her eyes are locked on me through the reflection. I have never seen this look, this blankness in her eyes. There is something definitely wrong.

She is scaring me.

I concentrate on her hair, drying a few strands at a time, but every time I look at her in the mirror she has same empty expression. She has beautiful hair and it is a great pleasure to touch it. I never knew a woman's hair could be so soft, like silk threads. I only remember my mother's hair, when I used to ask her if she would let me brush it. But drying a woman's hair, a woman who is a charmer, a seductress, a beautiful goddess—I never imagined a moment like this.

When I pick her hair up I notice a burn scar just below her neck, on the back of her right shoulder. It looks like a cigarette burn. *Sex bruises the body.* Is she talking about this scar? Are there more like this? I move her T-shirt a little, and see more scars from cuts and burns on her back. She is still frozen and doesn't notice me looking at her scars.

"What is this, Rania? Who has done this to you?" I stop the hair dryer and repeat my question, so that she can hear me loud and clear. I turn her to face me. "I want to know the name of the bastard who has tortured you, Rania. Talk to me." I shake her hard and shout at her in my distress.

Rania gives a wild scream and falls on her knees, her head bowed down to the floor mat. Her whole body is trembling. I sit down on the floor and lift her head gently. *What is going on?*

She continues screaming, and I let her, despite the fact that other hotel guests might hear. I want her to let out all her fears. She shivers hard and all I can do is wrap my arms around her in a tight embrace. She cries and screams in pain for more than ten minutes, until she has no energy left to shed any more tears. Finally, she gathers her breath to speak.

"Please don't ask me about my past, Adam. It is very painful to go back in time. I want to forget everything." She rests in my arms and whispers into my body. I shift back and hold her face in my hands.

"If that's what you want, then I will not ask you ever again. Your screams said everything. If it's painful for you to go back, then I'm sorry." I wipe her tears with my thumb and kiss her forehead to soothe her. I lift her from the floor mat and lead her toward the bed to tuck her in. She is completely exhausted. I settle her under the comforter and turn off the bedside lamp. I'm about to go lie down on the chaise when she grabs my hand.

"Please don't go."

"I'm not going anywhere. I'll stay here in the room with you. You can go to sleep." I sit beside her and rub her forehead gently.

"I trust you, Adam. Please lie down with me. I am afraid of nightmares." Her sudden appeal surprises me; she must be feeling very vulnerable and afraid. She rolls herself toward the other pillow to make space for me.

We both rest our heads on the pillow, facing each other. She smiles sadly, but she still manages to talk to me.

"Thank you. Thank you for everything." She holds my hand tightly and tucks it under her head. "Who are you, Adam?" I look at her with wide eyes, not sure what she's asking. "Are you an angel or a fine spirit? You can't be a genie, I mean Jinni, are you?" Her questions startle me. "Please, tell me who you are."

"I am a normal human being, Rania. What made you think I'm an angel?" I caress her hair with my fingers and she closes her eyes at my touch.

"Humans don't possess angelic qualities. Neither do Jinn. I haven't seen anyone like you." Her voice is almost a whisper. She melts me with her words and I want to kiss her passionately, to do something only humans can do, but I control my feelings for the time being.

"I don't possess any angelic qualities. I have broken many hearts, I was not a good son, and I have been through almost all levels of sin. I'm a human version of Satan. Don't think of me so highly."

"No, you cannot be Satan. He was created from the smokeless fire. The difference between Satan and a human is the flesh and fire. You don't possess any fiery quality."

I look at her strangely. "What would you know about Satan?"

"I thought you said you don't believe in God's existence. Why would you believe in Satan?" she asks.

"Honestly speaking, God has not done much to me in the past to justify His existence, but yes, I know for sure Satan exists. I guess all humans are half demon." I pause for a moment. "What do you know about Satan?"

"Not much. When God created Adam in heaven, He asked all His angels and other creatures to bow to the newly created flesh. All creatures obeyed God, except Satan. He was gifted with will, unlike angels, and he possessed all the characteristics which we humans possess—envy, disbelief, arrogance, stubbornness, and false pride."

"He wasn't an angel?"

"No, Satan is a Jinni, a demon. Before God created mankind, Satan dwelled on the earth, along with the angels, and imitated the angels' actions and behaviors. At that time, he was one of the most devout worshippers of God. Satan was also very knowledgeable, and that caused him to be very proud and consider himself one of the best of God's creations."

"Why did he refuse to bow to Adam?" I ask her intensely.

"Pride. Pride took everything from him. He thought he was more divine and powerful than Adam, so he refused to obey God, though it was His command. God never wanted the angels to worship humans. But since Satan was a proud Jinni and disobeyed God, he was thrown out of heaven and got designated as the King of Hell." She pauses for a moment, looking intensely into my eyes. "You are certainly not a Satan."

"I'm not an angel, either. I do possess will. That makes me either human or Satan."

"But you are not obeying your will, Adam. You are doing everything against it. It was not your will to be there with me all the time, to protect me. You are obeying God. That is very unlike a human or even a demon." Her knowledge about the entire Satan and angel concept is captivating. I want to learn more from her, though I don't believe in all this. It is like a bedtime story; the more she tells me, the more I want to hear.

"How do you know all this?"

"It is all in the Holy Quran. Even the Holy Bible contains this information, how Satan disobeyed God. Haven't you read it?"

"What makes you think I'm a Christian?"

"I thought so . . ."

"I haven't read any word of God. I told you I never believed in Him."

"You still don't, do you," she says, as a statement. I take a deep breath and look back into her eyes.

"I don't know. Sometimes I do and sometimes . . ." I pause for a moment. *This is such a strange topic.* "So, are there any differences between Jinn and humans, other than their appearance?"

"Humans are made of clay. God collected seven different kinds of clay from the earth to create Adam. Clay supports and gives life, whereas, fire destroys and burns." She pauses for a moment and continues. "But like Satan, humans also carry pride, envy and arrogance, which sometimes work as a fire. There is a very thin line between humans and Jinn. Though they are invisible to humans, they do exist."

"So, there is only one Jinni, I mean Satan?"

"No. There are many, more than the human population. They have a world within our world, but we can't see them unless they want to be seen. There are males and females. There are good and bad ones, as well. You know what the interesting part is? Each human has been assigned a Jinni, a demon. We don't see it but it is always there. We recognize it when our soul is not strong enough to protect our body and our demon takes it over, which makes us do all the possible sins."

"That's very interesting. I thought it's us who commit sins. I thought our souls were demonic."

"No and yes. We are physically involved in a sin. God created humans with goodness. If our soul is not strong enough to believe in Him, our demon overtakes our body, by manipulating our soul. It is our duty to protect ourselves from our demon."

"So what happened to Satan, when he was thrown out of heaven?" I ask her with more interest. *Do I really have to believe all this?*

"He did not ask for forgiveness, due to his pride. He only asked for respite from his punishment, till the Day of Resurrection. So God delayed his punishment till that day." She continues sharing her story. "Once Satan knew he was safe from destruction, he rebelled and declared war on Adam and his descendants. He is determined to make disobedience attractive to humans and to tempt them to commit immoral acts and go against everything that is pleasing to God, so that they will share his fate on the Day of Judgment. He created sinful acts that are more attractive to humans than the acts that are counted as good deeds. God, on the other hand, gave him all his powers, knowing that the humans He created have the ability to love, forgive and repent. He has faith in His creation, that no matter how much Satan tries to magnetize a human to commit a sin, a person always has an open door for repentance."

"So you are saying that no matter how sinful you are, if you ask for forgiveness, you will be forgiven?"

"Yes, that's what God's nature is. You just need to seek the light and find the right path."

She explains to me everything about sins and rewards in such a simple way. I never imagined I would listen to all this from her. At this moment, I feel she is holding a light for me, to guide me to the right path. I was right about her. She has something magnetic that is pulling me toward her. Perhaps it's the light in her that I am attracted to. She looks tired and sleepy to me, so we don't talk any more.

As far as what she just said about Jinn or demons, my theory is, if I don't see something with my own eyes, I don't believe it. But the way she explained everything, it's hard not to believe it. I would never have found the light in my life, I would never have asked for forgiveness from my mother, I would never have thought about repentance, if she were not in my life. For the very first time, I thank God for the blessing that He has bestowed on me. I feel as if I've been rewarded in exchange for an unknown deed. What good have I done in my life, to get Rania's faith and companionship? She is a friend, a listener, a companion, a savior, a guide. How easily she brought all my childhood memories back with her simple act of making hot chocolate. How effortlessly she made me agree to see my mother, even after so many years. She is making me face my own demons that haunted me for years.

I see her sleeping peacefully next to me, holding my hand under her face. Her scars are creating millions of questions in my mind. When I investigated her background, I didn't find out if she was visiting a psychiatrist. If she can't share her past with me, she can at least discuss it with a doctor. How will she take it if I ask her to do that? She doesn't want to rehash her past for anyone. I watch her face, collecting all her beauty in my eyes.

Who could harm such an innocent girl?

I will do anything to make her happy and protect her from her demons, even if I have to pass through hell for her. I have no idea what kind of feeling is developing inside me, but it is far from lust and greed. The feeling is sacred and pure, just like her. I am not denying the fact that I am physically attracted to her and want to claim her body, but more than that, I want to conquer her heart and soul, and keep them safe with me forever. With her divine beauty and enchantment before me, I close my eyes and fall into a deep sleep.

FLOWERS

♀

A ray of sunlight hits me in the eyes and I awaken. The first thing I notice: Adam, sleeping next to me. I held his hand under my face the whole night and he didn't complain, even for a single moment. I wonder how two people, emotionally so close to each other, can have a chaste relationship, sacred and based on trust and friendship. I always thought Mike was my best friend, but when I look at Adam, I see a man who is sincere and loyal to me. Our relationship is free of lust and carnality, which is helping us to flourish and grow together in a circle of hope and belief. I never thought I would find a man who would promise to protect me even in my sleep, without harming me physically and emotionally.

I gaze at his charming face. I cannot deny that I am attracted and captivated by his physical appearance. Is it too soon to fall for him? If he ever tries to become physically close to me, will I refuse, or is this something I am also craving? Is it okay to flow with his emotions, or is he just forbidden fruit for me? I close my eyes, take a deep breath, and slip out of bed smoothly, not disturbing his sleep.

After my regular washroom trip, I decide to explore the hotel until Adam wakes up. I put on some jeans and go down to the main level. It is a beautiful morning in Edmonton; the room looks even brighter and more welcoming in daylight. I take my room card and handbag, and head for the lobby. It is warm, paneled in beautiful dark wood, with lots of people from business and political backgrounds. I check out a few stores beside the lavish lobby, which give me the idea of buying something for Adam. He deserves a show of gratitude, though no words, no gift, could repay what he has done for me.

I have no idea what to purchase for him, as he has everything. After an hour of searching, I end up in a jewelry and gift shop and decide to buy a silver photo frame. They offer engraving, so I order a message to be etched onto the frame. I hope Adam likes it. I also buy cufflinks for him and get his initials engraved on them.

When they hand me my finished photo frame, it looks empty, so I ask them if they have printing facilities so I can add a picture to highlight the frame and my feelings for him. The store people are generous enough to offer all kinds of services, without hassle. I check the time on the giant wall clock and realize Adam will be looking for me, if he wakes up to find me gone. I thank the store manager and head toward the elevator.

When I enter the room, Adam has his phone in one hand, and the other hand tangled in his hair.

"Here she is. I will talk to you later." He snaps the phone shut as soon as I step in. "Where the hell were you?" He looks tense and worn out.

"Is everything okay?"

"I woke up and couldn't find you. I searched everywhere in the hotel, asked people at the reception desk, but no one knew where you were." He's breathing hard from distress.

"You could have called me." I try to calm the tension between us.

"You left your damn phone on the table. There was no way I could find you. Where were you, Rania?" His tone is harsh, but I sense worry in his voice.

"I went out for a walk—"

"Why didn't you wake me up?"

"You were sleeping, Adam. Why would I wake you?"

"I thought you ran away." He shakes his head in misery and sits on the couch. I put my bag down and sit next to him.

"Why would I run away?"

"I don't know. I thought I might have done something wrong. You acted so strange last night." He is still agitated and his words are acting like a strong heat, melting my frozen heart. I want to tell him I went to buy something for him to express my feelings, but I also wanted to surprise him with my gift before we leave for our musical evening.

"You don't need to worry about me anymore, Adam. I am not going to run away from you. What you did last night—I can't even express it. I don't know how you did it. I had no nightmares, I took no pill, yet I slept peacefully the whole night. You think I would run away after that? No, I am very selfish and I want to sleep without nightmares."

"Please don't leave again without telling me. I was so worried." His appeal is almost a whisper.

"I am sorry. I will take care next time." I pause for a moment. "Whom were you talking to, when I came in?"

"Reception. I called everywhere. No one saw you leaving the hotel."

"That's because I never left. I wonder how come they didn't see me in the lobby? Anyways . . ." I stand up from the couch. "Please, order something for breakfast. I am famished. I checked the bakery; they have French bread. Please, ask them if we could get it, or if we could go down and have breakfast there." I wink at him to cheer him up. I don't know why he gets so worried about me all the time. I was only gone for an hour or so. He smiles at my voracious demand.

"I would love to feed you. Let me ask them." He heads toward the desk to call reception.

"I will change, in the meantime." I smile back to him and head upstairs.

I check myself in the mirror and find out I look hideous—still in the t-shirt I wore to bed, with my hair a mess and no makeup. No wonder the hotel management didn't recognize me. I open my luggage and take out my favorite deep green top. I put on some makeup, and glance at the hair dryer. I remember taking a shower last night, but I don't remember taking the hair dryer out from the wall. My brush is also on the vanity, though I clearly remember I didn't take it out of my cosmetics bag. The towel I used last night is lying on the floor. I never leave my towel on the floor. I pick it up and hang it on the rack beside the shower column. *Why didn't I notice all this, when I came in earlier?*

Maybe my mind was crowded with thoughts of Adam. I remember lying down with him and talking to him about Satan and sins, but I don't remember coming out of the shower, dropping my towel on the floor or drying my hair. As I try to recall what happened, I hear a knock at the washroom door.

"Come in, please." I start brushing my hair. I look into the vanity mirror and see Adam standing behind me, his mouth open in shock. I jerk my head to ask him what is the matter.

"You look . . . beautiful. I have never seen you wearing jeans."

"Thanks."

"And that color looks stunning on you."

"It's my favorite color." I look into his eyes. *How I love the color of your eyes.* We gaze at each other through the reflection, and then he averts his eyes.

"The breakfast is here, by the way." He is about to leave, when I turn around and call him back.

"Adam, I need to ask one thing." He stops and gives me his complete attention. I step toward him, but avoid his gaze. "Did anything strange happen last night?"

"Why do you ask that?" He sounds concerned.

"It sounds crazy, but I remember taking a shower last night, but I just noticed my towel on the floor this morning and I don't remember leaving it there. The hair dryer was out and I don't remember using it. I don't even remember coming out of the washroom and lying down on the bed."

Adam draws his eyebrows together. The look on his face tells me that there is something I should know.

"You don't remember what happened in the washroom last night?" He takes a few steps closer to me. I shake my head in agitation, then close my eyes and concentrate, seeing if I can remember anything.

"You don't remember me drying your hair?" He gazes at me intently. I shake my head again, astonished.

"What is wrong with me, Adam? What else happened? Please, tell me." Adam's silence is scaring me.

"Nothing is wrong," he says very gently, and tucks my hair behind my ear. "You took a long time in the shower. When I came up here to check on you, you didn't hear me knock, so I opened the door. You were standing here and I came in and helped you dry your hair and . . ." He doesn't speak for a while, so I start to panic again.

"And? What happened then?" I say. He puts his hand on my cheek and looks at me with a strange expression. *Is he hiding something from me?*

"Nothing happened. You were very tired. I tucked you into bed. You said you trusted me and I could sleep next to you—"

"Yes, I remember that. But why don't I remember you coming in the washroom?" I look down in distress and try my level best to remember. "If I was so tired, then how come I remember our conversation?"

Speak up, Adam!

"Come downstairs. Don't think so much. Let's have breakfast." He takes my hand and pulls me through the bedroom, down to the main level dining area. He has succeeded in ordering the French bread and cheese for me from the bakery. I smile when I see it. Adam sits at the head of the table and I sit beside him. He offers me tea from the pretty china teapot. Adam starts on his Spanish omelet, but he is still smiling.

"Have you ever been to Paris?" he says, as he takes a bite. I shake my head and fix my eyes on my breakfast, so he continues. "Paris is the home of cheese and bread. Beautiful bakeries around every corner. When you go out for a morning walk in the old town, all you can smell is the fresh bread."

"I am sure it must be tempting."

"Yes, it is. I will take you there someday." He sounds serious. We finish our breakfast without talking any further.

Afterwards, we move to the living area and sit on the couch.

"If you don't mind, can I ask you something, Adam?" Adam is busy with his phone, probably checking emails, but my question turns his attention toward me.

"You don't need to ask. Just say it."

"Umm . . . I was wondering . . . the opera is around eight in the evening. I wanted to visit the Muttart Conservatory. It is not that far. I can take a cab. I just wanted to tell you, so that you don't end up calling half of the city to look for me."

"You don't want me to come with you?" His tone is disappointed. *Is he hurt I didn't ask him to join me?*

"It's a work day for you. I don't want to interrupt your schedule."

"I have no work when I'm with you. I'm completely yours." His pensive looks give me an electric charge. "But only if you want me to come."

"Of course, I want you to come. I just thought you might be busy. I didn't mean to hurt you."

"I'm not hurt, Rania. I'm glad you told me what you want. Let's leave in half an hour. I have to make some calls and answer some emails first." His warm gesture brings a smile to my face. Adam picks up his laptop and heads to the desk.

I get absorbed in a morning television show, and am surprised to see Adam standing next to me, dressed in his casual attire. He is wearing black jeans with a sweater T-shirt, the same color as my top. I have never seen him wearing deep green before, and I can't help smiling.

"You look very nice. That color suits you. It matches your eyes." I stand up and check him out lustfully from top to bottom.

"It is a great privilege to receive a compliment from such a beautiful girl."

I giggle at him and we head down to the lobby, where the same deep blue Lexus is waiting for us. As we drive, Adam is busy over his phone calls and emails, but he tries his best to give his attention to me as well. I feel really bad that I am disturbing his work for no reason, but he has assured me he wants my company. He tells me during our ride that he would worry about me, wandering a strange city alone, and his worry would still not let him concentrate on his work. I feel as though I should have kept my mouth shut about the Conservatory and stayed in the hotel.

After a thirty-minute drive, we reach the Conservatory and are greeted by an Italian man in his early twenties, who gives us tickets and badges. The Conservatory is built of multiple glass pyramid structures, so all the plants can obtain natural light. I enjoy reading about the rare plants, and Adam follows me quietly. He doesn't seem interested in plants, so I don't know why he wanted to come. It is warm inside, so we ask the Italian boy if we can hang our jackets somewhere. When I take off my woolen hat, my hair clip catches Adam's eye.

"Where did you get that?"

"It was my mother's. It's pretty, isn't it?" I touch the clip with pride.

"Yes, and it looks fascinating on you. Your clip reminds me of . . ." He is out of words after that, but his eyes are fixed on the clip. I wait for him to continue. "My mother. She used to wear something similar to it." He looks sad. It is obvious how he has missed his mother all these years. I am glad I pushed him to talk to her and break the ice between them. He is at least talking to me about her, and not avoiding the subject.

I smile at him with pleasure. "That is so sweet, Adam. You still remember?" He nods his head.

"Yes, I remember brushing her hair one day and dressing it up with this kind of stuff. I was not even five at the time." He shifts his gaze from my hair to my eyes. "You know, it's her birthday on Saturday, not a holiday dinner. She always uses the holidays as an excuse to invite me."

"That's wonderful, Adam. We should get something for her then."

"I don't know what I should give her. She must have everything. She married a rich man." He sounds bitter.

"Money doesn't buy everything. Why don't you give her a hair accessory similar to the one she used to have? It would let her know you still remember fixing her hair." My suggestion makes him smile through his eyes and his heart, as if I have resolved a long-standing riddle for him.

"Will you help me choose it?"

"Of course I will. What are friends for?" I smile back at him and we continue our tour of the plants.

The entire morning, I learn about exotic plants and Adam amuses himself by taking my picture with his phone. I don't know how many he has taken, but he seems to be enjoying the morning with the plants and me.

"I am surprised there is no one here today. People these days don't spend time with plants, I suppose." I look around the area, disillusioned.

"That's because the place is booked for the two of us." Adam speaks from behind me, and I turn to him with bewilderment. He smiles at my shocked expression and takes another picture with his phone. "Don't be so surprised. It's part of our pact, remember . . . protecting your privacy." He winks mischievously. "I like this bewildered Rania." He looks at his phone. I am speechless for a moment. *How can he manage to reserve the damn place on such a short notice?*

"How can they do you such a big favor? Do people always do what you ask them to do?"

"It's not a favor. My theory is, if money can buy anything, you should never ask for favors. It is very easy to return the money, but too hard to return favors. You can never justify them."

Yeah, easy for you maybe.

"You paid to book this whole place? Why?"

"You didn't want us to be seen in public together. I promised you I would take care of it."

"I thought it would be different here. You should have told me; we wouldn't have come here at all." It is disgraceful of me to have made him spend so much money, again. Of course he will never tell me how he managed to book this place in such a short time. "I don't feel good about this."

"Hey, come on. Relax and enjoy yourself. By the way, I didn't know spending the day with plants could be fun." He puts his arm around my shoulder and gives me a friendly hug.

"Come on, we haven't seen the roses yet."

"What fun are you having?" I ask him. "You are not even reading the details. You have only taken pictures."

"That's fun for me. I'm having the best time. Just you and me, and the poor speechless plants. At least, they won't publicize our presence." Adam's face and voice are filled with amusement. It seems he is actually having fun. "You might not know it, but I haven't ever been to a place like this, except for school field trips or official events. Nothing like this, having time on my own." He turns me, so I can face him properly. "Thanks for bringing an ordinary activity into my life, in an extraordinary way."

I didn't know he found pleasure in doing little things, like a common man. Adam lacked all those fun activities in his life, which he had deserved to do in his youth. He spent all his teenage life lonely, or struggling with his father. In his early twenties, he lost his father, and then he threw himself into raising his father's business to the heights. I can't imagine how hard he has worked to achieve his current social status. He is seeking joy in small trips and hot chocolates. He is no different than other men, yet, his way of expressing his feelings to me is exceptional.

"If these moments can be bought, I am ready to spend all my wealth on them. But this is all possible because of you, Rania. You are my only friend; you are the only person in the whole world with whom I would want to share all these little pleasures." He closes his eyes and continues. "And there will be no one else."

"Thank you, Adam. I feel very special and . . . blessed." I smile, placing my hand on his shoulder, and he opens his eyes at my touch. We enter a hallway that is filled with roses of all colors. It is a heavenly view. Adam takes my picture with almost every variety, as I read their details. His eyes get stuck on a lavender rose's description.

"Commonly used for the expression of love at first sight." His comment catches my attention and I walk toward him. "That's quite a piece of information!" His eyes are fixed on the lavender roses and he is lost in thought, rubbing his index finger on his lower lip.

"They are beautiful, aren't they?" I say, breaking into his thought. He looks at me with a strange and unreadable expression, and I continue talking. "God has amazed humans with all the beautiful colors and fragrances of flowers. Humans have chosen a different message for each flower, but I see them as pure and angelic beauty. Any color rose, for me, represents divinity and perfection. A human cannot achieve perfection. It is God's individuality which is perfect."

"I have never seen flowers the way you do. I always thought they were just for weddings, funerals and parties. You have a very different way of looking at nature."

"That's because I appreciate everything in nature. God has created beauty for our eyes, everywhere. It's up to us to acknowledge it or not. Have you ever been to a tulip festival?" Adam shakes his head. "In the spring, we will go to one together." I give him an exhilarated smile, which makes him elated.

"I can't wait for the spring, then. If you're going to be there, then I'm sure it must be breathtaking."

We finish our tour, stopping at the souvenir shop on our way out. I pick up some magnets and brooches with different flower designs, and then my attention is diverted by masquerade masks that are displayed in the corner of the store. I pick up one bronze-colored mask and tie it around my eyes. I check myself in the mirror and am astounded to see that I look completely different in it—unrecognizable. Suddenly Adam is standing behind me, and his reflection in the mirror is flabbergasted.

"Excuse me! Have we met before? Are you—" His question surprises me. *Didn't he recognize me?* Well, how could he? Even I am not able to recognize myself. I take off the mask and smile at his frozen face.

"Hey, it's me. And yes, we have met." I wink at him. He is still frozen and startled. "What happened, Adam? Why are you acting so weird?" He is utterly quiet for some time, and then he finally speaks.

"You dazzled me."

"You didn't recognize me?" I look at the other masks while talking to him.

"You reminded me of . . ." He is silent after that.

"Who?" I give him all my attention.

"Never mind. Shall we go?" He shakes his head in disbelief and changes the subject, but I know there is something stuck in his mind.

"Yes, sure." I reach the counter and the young blonde cashier gives me my total. Her eyes are glued on Adam. *I know he is handsome, but take your damn eyes off of him.* I don't know if it is jealousy or what, but I don't like the way she's staring at him. I take my wallet out of my bag, but Adam has already given his credit card to the girl.

"Adam, please, let me pay." I grab his hand and push it aside. "This is my stuff, so please, don't try to act like my boyfriend."

"He isn't your boyfriend?" asks the blonde girl, her eyes sparkling. She is totally drooling over Adam.

"Yes, I am. But my beautiful girlfriend keeps forgetting about it." Adam gives the blonde an impersonal smile.

"Adam, don't create a scene here. Let me pay, please," I murmur.

"I can't let you pay in front of me. For God's sake! Why do you make things so difficult sometimes?" His generous look is changing to anger.

"You are a big time mid-century sexist." I deliberately speak loudly, so the girl can hear. He looks at me confusedly, and then to the girl, who is staring at us open-mouthed. "I am not buying anything." I put all the stuff on the counter. "Sorry for the trouble." And I leave the store without even looking at Adam.

I wait outside near the exit of the conservatory, where I ask the guy to bring my jacket so we can leave as soon as possible. Adam joins me ten minutes later, and I wonder what took him so long. *That blonde would be trying her best to seduce him, for sure.*

I put my jealous thoughts aside and see he has the store bag in his hand. The Italian boy brings our jackets and other accessories and we dress ourselves for the harsh weather outside. Adam reads my annoyed expression, so he doesn't say anything until we settle ourselves in the car.

As we drive, I look out the window and pretend he doesn't exist. *What does he think, I can't afford to buy souvenirs for myself?* He doesn't have to pay for everything I want to buy. He has already spent an enormous amount of money in less than a week. If he keeps spending at that rate, he'll be a beggar in a month. He has earned all this wealth with struggle and devotion. I can't let him spend it so wildly. And the fact that he thinks I can't afford such a small amount makes me feel insignificant.

"You're not going to talk?" I hear Adam's voice from the other side of the car. I don't respond. He says something to the driver in French, which I totally ignore, but after a few minutes the car stops at a corner and the driver steps outside. I look at Adam. "He is not going to drive the car unless you talk to me," Adam says seriously.

"Are you kidding me? The poor man will freeze to death." I try to open the door from my side, but it is locked.

"He's a local. He's used to these temperatures. If you pity him so much, then talk to me. I'll call him back." He comes a little closer to me and places the package on my lap. "You left this at the store." I push the package away and ignore him.

"It's not mine. You paid for it, so it's yours." I cross my arms over my chest and look outside to the poor driver. "Please call him inside."

"You have pity for everyone. Why are you so merciless to me?" he whispers in my ear. I realize he is only an inch away from me. I shift closer to the window and look at him curiously.

"Merciless? That's what you think of me?"

"You won't take this package. You always refuse me whenever I—"

"Adam, I can't accept presents from you."

"But this is yours. You forgot it on the counter."

"You paid for it, Adam. It's not mine." I frown over his argument. *He is too much.*

"But what difference does it make?"

"It makes a difference to me. Please, stop spending so much money on me. I feel disgraced." I hide my face in my hands and rest my elbows on my knees. *Why is he so difficult at times?*

"Don't talk about yourself like that in front of me. If that's the case . . ." He pauses, so I open my eyes to see what he is doing. He takes the receipt out of his pocket. "Pay me for it. Or let's go back to the store and I'll return it, and then, you pay yourself." He opens my palm and places the receipt on it. "Please don't feel so low about yourself. I never wanted to crush your self-esteem." His sudden change in attitude, having all the sweetness in the world, melts my heart. We are arguing over only fifty-two dollars. "The poor man is freezing outside," he says. "Have some mercy on him. Do you want to pay me now, or go back to that blonde?"

His sudden mention of the girl in a comic way makes me laugh, and it flushes out all the anger inside me. He waves to the driver, who returns and starts the car, and we are back on the road. I take out the exact amount of money and place it on his palm. He takes a pen from his pocket and hands it to me.

"Write something on it. You are giving me something for the first time. I want to keep it forever." His sincerity matches his eyes. I don't argue, as it is his money, so I write on the fifty-dollar bill:

For our arguments.

I sign my name and add the date. He takes the bill and grins from ear to ear, and puts the money in his wallet.

"Happy now?" he confirms, with his tender heart. I nod and smile back at him.

Our car stops on an old town street and I follow Adam to a local Italian restaurant. It is a main street, with lots of local businesses, though not crowded because it is a weekday. The aroma of food makes me realize that I am starving. We sit at a window table, so we can enjoy the view of the snow-covered street. Our server brings warm garlic bread right away and asks us if we would like to start with drinks and appetizers. Adam orders fresh orange juice for me and red wine for himself, with roasted peppers and mozzarella bites as an appetizer for us to share. I look around the restaurant and figure out that the absence of other people is once more due to his enormous spending.

"How do you manage to book places all to yourself, so quickly?" I finally ask the question which has been buzzing in my mind since the day he showed up on the train. He smiles and shakes his head humorously.

"It's not just for me. It's for us." He leans back in the chair. "You are very innocent, Rania. You have no idea how money works in this world. Let's not talk about it. Enjoy your lunch." I put my juice glass down and look at him.

"I want to know about the opera. You can't be—"

"No, I haven't booked the whole theater. I'm not brainless. The artists can't perform if there are only two people in the audience." He has a good point. "Anyhow, we will have a private box, so you don't need to worry."

On that, a blonde waitress steps in to take the orders for our main course. She keeps staring at Adam in the same way the store blonde did, and I feel like I don't exist at this table. *All blondes like him.* She is wearing a very short black skirt over her long slender legs, with a white blouse, which is open at the top to show the perfect amount of cleavage. I hide my face behind the menu, as I can't stop laughing at the blonde ogling Adam. I order chicken cacciatore and Adam orders baked shrimp scampi. He is aware of the girl's wild sexy looks and the inviting messages she is sending through her body. I have to return the menu card back to this hottie, so I purse my lips to hide my laugh. As soon as she leaves, I chuckle and put my hands over my mouth. Adam looks at me intently.

"What's so funny?" His innocent question makes me laugh more.

"You don't know what just happened?" He shakes his head, as if he is actually unaware of it. "Oh, come on, Adam. That blonde was completely checking you out. What do you say?" I wink at him. He blushes at my remarks, but doesn't say anything. "Didn't you notice the way she stood, displaying the right parts of her body, as if she was begging for wall-banging sex?" And I start laughing again. Adam tries to laugh too, but he presses his lips together in embarrassment. "Oh my God! You look so cute when you blush. Let me call that hottie and see your expression again." I look toward the kitchen area.

"Are you crazy? You're making fun of an awkward situation." He moves my face to look at him.

"I just can't believe Adam Gibson can blush over a blonde checking him out. I should take a picture of that." I can't stop laughing. Adam leans back and folds his arms over his chest. He wonders at my laughter, but I know he is enjoying the moment also. I wipe my watery eyes on the napkin and continue on my fun excursion. "So, what did that store blonde say to you, when I left?"

"That little girl?" he asks with surprise.

"Yes, but I am sure she was not that little. She must be past puberty." My abrupt remarks make him laugh.

"Yes, I agree. You want to know what she said?" I nod with a smile. "She said 'your girlfriend is very egoistic.'"

"What? Just that? And you took more than ten minutes to listen to that?"

"You were keeping track of my time with her?" Adam raises one of his eyebrows in surprise. He wants to know if I was jealous or curious. I was both, in fact, but I don't let him know. "She said I should have let you pay, and said you are very hot and beautiful and I am lucky to have you."

"She was checking *you* out and you are saying she was admiring me? You think I will believe that?" I busy myself with the appetizer, as I realize he might not tell me what they said. He is undoubtedly handsome and intelligent; any girl can ask him out. It is his personal life. I shouldn't question him about every girl.

"She was checking *you* out, Rania. She was homosexual." He chuckles behind his wine glass. *What? Is he serious?* "She wanted to know if I could help her find a girl like you, the way I did for myself, so I told her that God has made only one piece like that and that it is fortunately just for me." I look at him, startled, but the way he speaks tells me he is not lying. "She also told me that she was watching you when you entered the store and how you tied the mask over your eyes, which blew her away. She fell in love with you." I put my hands on my mouth to hide my astonishment. "She told me I should not argue with a beauty like you." He takes a sip of his wine, but his eyes are locked on me. "You are very innocent, Rania. You can't read people's eyes. You don't know what the other person is feeling for you. It's good sometimes, as it is easier to ignore the assholes, but it's dangerous as well. You can't tell the other person's intentions." I avert my eyes and look down at my glass. All the humor and laughs are gone. "Anyhow, she gave me her number to give to you, in case you need a friend someday, but I assured her that would not happen. Over my dead body!"

He hands me a piece of paper and smirks at me devilishly. His sincerity makes me smile again. I take her name and number.

"I can't believe it."

"She's lucky she was a girl. I can't imagine how I would have reacted if she were male." His expression gets serious suddenly.

"Why? What would you have done?" *Oh please, Adam. Don't tell me you would get jealous.*

"Don't ask me, and don't ever provoke me, either." There is an awkwardness between us. I am glad when the blonde waitress returns with our main course, and we finish our meals without talking to each other.

By the time we reach our room after our late lunch, the sun has already set. We relax on separate couches, and Adam breaks the silence.

"Have you decided what to wear tonight?" I look at him, surprised, so he continues. "Women mostly wear evening dresses to the opera."

"Does it matter? I thought I could wear anything."

"Yes, you can, but I hope you don't feel underdressed."

"But I don't have an evening dress with me. I just came with a couple of casuals and two dresses for official events."

"I know that." Adam speaks reluctantly, while taking off his socks. We still have a few hours before we go, so I decide to take a hot shower and hit the nearest store to shop, but I have promised myself I will not take him with me. Otherwise, he will dominate me once again, and will never let me pay for my own clothes.

When I reach the bedroom, I see some boxes and bags from Holt Renfrew on the bed. Since I haven't ordered anything from there, I assume they are Adam's, so I don't bother to open them. Adam follows me and sees the boxes as well.

"Oh, they delivered already. That was quick," he says, sitting at the corner of the bed. "Won't you open them, Rania?"

"What is this?" I ask him, taking out a top from my luggage.

"It's for you. Let me know if you like it." *For me? Is he crazy?* There are four packages.

"I didn't order anything, Adam." I ignore the parcels and continue digging in my luggage.

"You don't take care of yourself much, so I thought I would take the responsibility." He stands up and hands me one of the bags. I open it up and find an elegant full-length lace dress, with the label of Burberry Prorsum on it.

"I can't accept this, Adam." I put the dress down on the bed and he comes over to me.

"Why? Don't you like it?"

"Who wouldn't? But this is too much. Why do you keep on—"

"It's a dress for this evening. It's not a big deal." He shrugs his shoulders innocently. "Please, try it on and if you don't like it, we'll go and get something else."

"It couldn't be better, Adam. Is this your choice?" I look at the pink dress and then back to him.

"No, the fashion advisor at the store picked it up. I told her what I wanted, and that's it."

"Thanks for all the effort, Adam, but . . ."

"Please, don't make it such a big deal. Now, try it on and let me know if it's okay." He picks up the dress and hands it to me.

"It looks perfect. I have never worn anything like it. It's precious." I caress the soft lace.

"Not more than you. Why don't you check out the other stuff?"

"This is all for me?" I look at the other boxes in surprise. He nods with a smile and goes into the washroom. I sit on the corner of the bed, gaping at the boxes, and deciding which one to open first. I hear the sound of the shower from the washroom, which means he will be in there for a while. I start with the shoebox and am dazzled to find sparkling Jimmy Choo sandals. They fit me perfectly. How did the fashion advisor know my size? *Did Adam tell her everything?* My feet look prettier in the designer shoes. The dress itself is extraordinary. I have never desired anything like that; it is more than I deserve in life.

Adam is making everything like a fairytale. I open the third box and find a Chanel scarf that matches the dress. The silk of the scarf is extremely soft, and I touch it to my cheek. There is also a pair of stockings. He has thought of every detail. He has made me feel like a woman—a very special woman. I open the last box and find a silver Fendi evening clutch that matches the dress and shoes perfectly. The box also has matching earrings and hair accessories. I can't wait to try everything on for tonight. I look at the dress again. It is full length, with no body exposure, to preserve my femininity.

He does care.

All the items have the prices removed from their tags, but I know it is more than five thousand dollars. *So much to spend on a single evening!* It is almost my month's salary. I take the tags off everything so I can put them on after Adam is done taking his shower. The door of the washroom opens and Adam steps out, with just a towel wrapped around his waist.

Oh my!

He looks absolutely sexy and stunning, like a Greek god. He walks toward the closet with his wet, half-naked body, in a very provocative manner, ignoring my existence completely.

He is so fucking sexy!

I bite my lower lip; this is titillating. I have never seen his body like this and my mouth is open so far I feel like it will hit the floor. Droplets of water fall from his broad shoulders, down to his lean cut waist. I want to lick all those droplets and my hands itch badly to touch his bare chest. In a relationship between a man and a woman, there is a very fine line which divides friendship from intimacy. I am standing on that line. I know if I move a bit, I will fall on the other side. I have never felt so seductively attracted to any man, and somewhere down in my body, it tickles . . . pleasurably.

Control the fucking woman inside you, Rania. He is a bloody mind reader.

He picks up his clothes from the closet and heads back to the washroom. After a few minutes, he appears in black trousers and a white button-down dress shirt, showered in a very sexy fragrance.

Oh, Gibson! You look so much better without clothes.

I'm still staring at him and realize I look awful next to him. No matter how hard I try, I can never match his charm and grace. He finally manages to look at me.

"Everything is perfect, Adam. Thank you."

"I'm glad you liked it. I will thank Olivia personally. She picked all the stuff." He goes back to the washroom, still speaking, leaving the door open.

"How did she know my size?" I ask him from the bed, raising my voice.

"I told her." He steps out of the washroom and sits at the other corner of the bed. "I saw your shoe size from your boots and when I stole your pills from your luggage, I checked the size of your top."

"It was a perfect guess. I tried the sandals. They are perfect. Thank you." He smiles with relief that I haven't made an issue over his presents this time. "I am not used to all this, Adam." His smile vanishes instantly.

"Then get used to it." He stands up from the bed and starts digging in his bag for something. "We have to leave in an hour. You should get ready now."

I smile back at him and gather my belongings, heading to the washroom without saying anything further.

OPERA

♂

I'm relieved Rania accepted all the things I asked Olivia to buy for her. I call her and thank for all she did in such a short time. I wait eagerly to see Rania in the pink dress. I remember how much pink suited her, when we had dinner last Saturday at the Persian restaurant. The color matches her skin when she blushes. I make some official calls and check the time again. I wonder if she's taking too long, or if it's me who is impatient to see her. I have never felt so bonded with anyone, and it's been less than a week. *What is she doing to you, Gibson?* I've revived all the fun things that I missed in my childhood and adolescence. She is showing me a new life, a life which could be as simple as the blinking of an eye, and as pleasing as a bed of roses.

I never knew spending a day with plants could be so much fun. I adored taking her picture, and I'm grateful she allowed me to. How she laughed at me over the waitress's flirting; my heart almost melted at the sight. She has an infectious smile. No one could help smiling back.

I can never forget how she looked when she put the mask on. What if I tell her she looked exactly like that woman I met nine months ago, who was dancing with invisible people? More like shadows. Would she believe me if I told her my spiritual experience? She has a good knowledge of ghosts and genies, and I will ask her when we come back from the show. But it's hard to believe. That place never existed. I have been there many times since, and there is no spiral structure there. I put my thoughts aside and put on my socks and shoes. Then I hear her coming down the stairs.

I glance at her as she emerges into the living room. I close my eyes instantly, unable to handle the beauty that is standing in front of me. "Shall we leave?" she says. I open my eyes and stand up to look at her divine beauty. She doesn't realize she has taken my breath away, snatched the rug from under my feet. *Why the fuck am I getting hard?* It pisses me off so much that I lose control of my body. I close my eyes once again.

"I can't take you out anywhere. You can't go like that." I shake my head in passion and open my eyes. She looks confused and checks herself from feet to waist.

"Is something wrong with the dress? The fit seems to be good."

"You have already killed me with your refinement. How many men do you plan to wound tonight?" I gaze at her seductive body from head to toe. *And the fucking lace. I just want to rip it off of you.* If it's this hard for me to control myself in front of her, how will I control the hungry eyes of other men? She shakes her head with a giggle. "I feel sorry for other men. Have some mercy on them."

"Oh, come on, Adam. Don't praise me so high. Yes, I feel great in this dress. It's lovely. I feel like a princess in it." She touches her dress with her beautiful hands.

"You are a princess, at least for me. Thanks for accepting it." *Oh yes, you are no doubt.*

"Thank you for making me a princess. I know I am worth ten thousand dollars all together right now." She winks at me with her infectious smile.

"You have no idea how much you are worth." I drink in her beauty with my eyes. "Pink is your color. You blossom under it." She moves away and heads toward the dining area, but I see her blushing.

"By the way, you look really handsome yourself, Mr. Gibson. The hot blonde waitress would faint if she could see you right now." She looks at me from head to toe, seductively. *Is she as attracted to me as I am to her? Does she feel the same magnetism?*

I step closer to her, so many wild questions in my head. The look on her face tells me that she's read what's going in my mind. She backs up until her back is against the wall. There is no one to stop us now. My body craves her touch, and I'm getting the same signals from her also. Her breathing speeds up, and I move to within an inch of her, so close that I can feel the heat from her body. She closes her eyes. Suddenly, I feel heaviness around me, the same heavy atmosphere that I felt in the washroom last night when she was staring blankly at the mirror. At this moment, I don't see any seduction or magnetism in her face; I only see fear and trepidation. *I can't kiss you, if you get so scared.* I look at her cold face and kiss her forehead, then back away. Her stiff body relaxes and she opens her eyes when she feels the distance between us. Distance which needs more time and trust to end.

"Let's go," I whisper to her, acting as if nothing happened. As I pick up my jacket, she disappears into the living room. She comes back with a paper bag in her hand.

"This is for you, Adam." She hands me the package with her lovely smile.

"For me? It's not my birthday." I take the bag from her and glance inside it.

"You've showered all these gifts on me. It was not my birthday, either." She looks hurt. I hold her hand and make her sit on the dining chair next to me. "I can't reciprocate the favors you have done for me," she says, "but I hope you like this."

"I was not doing you any favors, Rania. I told you, I am a very selfish man. I was only doing it for myself." I take out the small package from the bag. "But thank you. Can I open it now?" She smiles and nods silently. I open the package neatly, feeling like a little boy eager to open his Christmas present. There is a box with sterling silver cufflinks, with my initials engraved on them.

"They're lovely. Thank you, but when did you buy them?"

"This morning. When you were busy calling the whole city looking for me." There is another box inside the paper bag, so I open it eagerly. It is a beautiful silver tabletop photo frame, with crystals on the sides, and two engraved messages on the top and bottom of the frame.

For our good time
I am lucky to have found you

What surprises me is the picture of our first dance together, looking into each other's eyes with a passionate smile. The picture and the message on it melt my heart and bring tears to my eyes. I turn my head away, so that she can't see me being so emotional. I close my eyes for a second to calm myself, then look back at her.

"Thank you so much, Rania. This is wonderful. I don't have words to express it." I take a deep breath. "No one has given me a present, just for me, since my sixth birthday." She places her hand on my shoulder. "My mother used to bring gifts for me on birthdays. My father was never the present type. After Mom left, Dad used to take me to McDonalds for the Happy Meal and I used to get the free toy, which was my birthday gift. At that time, a good meal was a better present than a toy." I put my hand over hers. "You are giving me all the childhood treasures that I missed all those years. Thank you." My eyes are still watery, and she notices it. She stands up and kisses my forehead with her warm lips, then hugs me. I want to stay like this forever, enfolded in her presence, and I will never desire anything ever again. We stay here motionless for a few minutes, without speaking.

Our privacy is disturbed by a text message alert from her phone. She takes the phone out of her clutch and reads the message, which brings a worried expression to her face. I stand up to see what is troubling her. She hands me the phone silently. The message is from her boss.

> *I got a call from the hotel that you haven't checked in yet. Is your train delayed? Let me know.*

What's his fucking problem? I look at her tense face and respond to the message on her behalf.

> *Yes, the train got delayed. I will be checking in in half an hour. Thanks for your concern.*

I give the phone back to her. She reads it and looks at me in confusion.

"Don't worry. I will take care of it. Shall we leave?"

On our way to the opera, I ask Rania to forward me the hotel confirmation. I make a couple of calls to resolve this issue, and she looks out the window, obviously thinking about something. *Is she thinking about my attempt to kiss her?* Did she get frightened because she read everything through my eyes? I decide not to say anything. I have no idea what happened to me in that moment; was it a demon pushing me to commit a sin, or was it an angel that stopped me when I saw her frightened face? Whatever it was, I can't describe the heavy feeling I had at that moment. It was as if I felt someone else there.

We reach the theater fifteen minutes before the performance starts. We mingle with the crowd, and Rania seems fairly comfortable, even though we are in public. We meet a senator and his wife and they compliment her on how beautiful she is. I see lots of men gazing at her like animals, but I keep my arm around her waist to let all the fuckers know that she is beyond their reach. As long as I have blood in my body, I will not let anybody destroy her.

We settle in our box and look at our programs. The opera is Othello, and Rania reads everything carefully before concentrating deeply on the performance. She is completely engrossed in the show for two hours, and I am engrossed in her. I see tears on her face when Othello confronts his wife Desdemona and accuses her of adultery with Cassio. Desdemona tries to convince her husband that she is innocent, but he doesn't listen to her, and kills her. Rania gasps and covers her mouth with her hands, then jumps up and leaves the box.

I rush after her. After searching for a few minutes, I find her behind a red curtain, trying to control her emotional cyclone. She leans against the wall, breathing hard. As soon as she sees me, she tries to wipe her tears away.

"Take me back, please." Her voice breaks.

"What happened, Rania? Are you okay?" I come closer to her, wanting to support her.

"Why couldn't he trust his wife? She loved him. She left her father, her wealth, everything for that man and what did he do to her? Accused her of adultery and killed her." She wipes her tears again. "Why can't a man trust a woman's love? Why does a woman have to pay so much for the love of a man?"

"Relax!" I hug her tightly, but she is still sobbing. "It's just a play, Rania. Why are you taking it so seriously?" I speak into her hair. She pushes me away and shrugs her shoulders in vexation.

I don't understand why she is taking the opera so seriously. Is it something related to her past? *It couldn't be. No one could accuse you, Rania. You are too naive to do anything like that.* I don't know how to react to the situation, and she is too vulnerable to talk about it. I hold her hand, and in no time we are out of the theater, before the show has even ended.

She doesn't speak to me, her body still trembling with distress. As soon as we enter our suite, she takes off her jacket and rushes upstairs to the bedroom. I go after her; she looks pretty bad, emotionally and physically. When I get there, the bedroom is empty and the washroom door is closed. Without even knocking, I open the door and find her throwing up into the sink. *Shit. She is sick.* I rush toward her and hold her hair back, so she can get rid of everything. Was it something she ate at lunch, or is it her emotional cyclone that's making her so sick?

When she is completely drained, I wipe her face with a wet towel and take her out of the washroom. She is completely exhausted, and seems only half-conscious. I lay her down on the bed and call for a doctor immediately. I hate seeing her like this. I sit by her pillow and rub her hands. She is cold and frozen and not responding to anything. I take off her sandals and rub her feet gently. I have no training in first aid, and I don't know what to do. After about ten minutes, I hear the doorbell from the main level, and I rush quickly to open the door.

"Doctor Lucas." The doctor offers his hand. He is accompanied by his assistant.

"Adam Gibson. Please, come in."

The doctor checks Rania's pulse and tries to open her eyes, and then asks his assistant to check her blood pressure.

"If you don't mind, can I ask what relationship you have with her?" the doctor asks, worriedly.

"She is my girlfriend. Anything serious, Doctor?"

"She is experiencing orthostatic hypotension." The doctor is still holding her wrist. He looks at me and continues. "A kind of low blood pressure, that often happens when a person stays idle in one position for a long time." The doctor takes some medicine from his bag, and an IV injection. "Do you know if she is allergic to anything?" I shake my head. "Is she pregnant?"

"No, Doctor. Not a chance."

"Do you know if she is on any medication? An anti-depressant or anti-anxiety?" I open the bedside drawer and take out her medicine, and hand it over to him.

"She has been taking this?" The doctor looks at the bottle dubiously, and then to me. "Any idea for how long?"

"She told me she has been taking them for four or five years. But she has not been taking them the last couple of nights."

"Did she consult a doctor before discontinuing them?"

"No, Doctor. What's wrong?"

"Nothing to worry about. Her blood pressure dropped suddenly from anxiety or a shock. Anything happen recently?"

"Not much. We went to watch an opera and she got emotional about it. When we came back here, she threw up everything she had at lunch, and then passed out. But why isn't she waking up, Doctor?"

"She will, in a little while. She is just drained. When she wakes up, make sure you feed her properly. I have given her medicine to regulate her blood pressure, but I would advise you to take her to consult a physician before quitting this medicine." He rotates the bottle and hands it back to me. "Has she been sleeping well without it?"

"Yes, she slept well." Am I supposed to inform the doctor about her nightmare, or is it too personal to share? "She had trouble sleeping before, so she told me she was given this medicine."

"Indeed. That's what this medicine used for. But are you sure she slept well last night?"

"Definitely, Doctor. I was with her all night. She didn't wake up and she went to sleep before I did."

"That's interesting. It's good she doesn't need it anymore. Anyhow, these are not good on a long-term basis and I would not recommend them at such a young age, especially to women. It can affect their ability to bear children."

"Any precautions, Doctor?"

"Not really. Just feed her well, especially with fresh juices. And make sure she doesn't experience any shock. Her body is too weak to respond to traumas." He stands up and pauses for a second. "And no pregnancy in the meantime, Mr. Gibson. It would not be good for the baby or for her. Make sure she has blood tests before opting for pregnancy. Let her body heal in its own way first." He starts to leave, then pauses at the door. "And please, take care of her. She is vulnerable. Good night." He shakes hands with me and leaves.

After the doctor has left, I tuck Rania under the warm comforter and lie down on the chaise. I don't remember when I fall asleep, but before long Rania's voice wakes me up.

"No—please don't hurt me . . . you said you loved me . . . how can you not trust me . . . no please . . . no . . ."

She rises up to a sitting position, panicking and sweating hard. I run to her, embracing her tightly to make her feel secure.

She looks around the semi-darkened room in fear, and then looks at me with her ghostly eyes. She is completely worn out with her dreadful nightmare.

Who is the bastard who keeps haunting her, even in her sleep?

I want to ask her every detail, but every time I try to talk to her, she gets so emotional I don't want to push her. I turn on the rest of the lamps, to reassure her that she is not lost in the darkness, and hand her a glass of water. Her hands shake in fear, so I help her drink it.

"You don't need to be frightened, Rania." I tuck her hair gently behind her ears. "I am with you."

She gives me a dreary look. "What will happen when you're not there?"

"That won't happen. I will not let it happen. Trust me!"

"What happened to me, Adam? How did I get here?" She looks at me sadly. "Am I sick?"

"Your blood pressure was very low. I called the emergency service to treat you. They gave you some medicine while you were sleeping. But the doctor said you are very weak due to improper diet, and he has asked me to make sure you get proper nutrition."

"When did the doctor come?

"Half an hour ago. You were unconscious." She checks her wrist, probably wanting to know the time, then she touches her other wrist and her ears. "I took your jewelry off. It was bothering you."

With that, I call room service and ask for dinner and fresh juice. There is still a horrified look on her face, but she manages to get up and makes her way to the washroom.

After ten minutes, she comes out in her pajamas and T-shirt. She sits at the corner of the bed, thinking about something, so I join her.

"I am a mess. I am troubling you for no reason. You did so much to take me to the play and I . . ." With that, she loses her voice and hides her face in her hands. "I messed up everything." I wrap my arm around her and rub her shoulder gently.

"You don't take care of yourself properly. Someone has to . . . and I want to be that lucky person."

She takes her hands off of her face and looks at me. I see hope and pain mingled in her tear-filled eyes. As soon as I hold her face, she closes her eyes. I can't resist kissing her innocent face.

I want to tell her so much—what I feel, and how much I long for her, but her vulnerability stops me every time. I give her a deep kiss on her forehead and then move my lips slowly to her eyes. I feel her breath getting stronger with the touch of my lips, but I don't see the fear on her face that I saw before we left for the play. I give soft baby kisses to both of her eyes and feel her body heating up for me. All the feelings thrashing inside are entirely new to me. I never knew my heart could beat so fast for a woman. I have fucked so many women in my life, but this is something else, something far from haste, greed and lust. I take my time on my journey to discover her beautiful face through my lips, from eyes to cheeks, and then to her nose, but I constantly check her expression. Her fragrance is driving me crazy. She has her eyes closed all this time; I only feel the warmth coming from her body. I keep exploring her face with my lips, kissing every corner of her skin gently, but she doesn't pull back from me at all. I touch her warm lips with my thumb and she gasps at my touch. As soon as I decide to kiss her lips, I see a teardrop coming from her right eye. At that very instant, her body suddenly feels cold. Very cold. I feel the same heaviness in the air again, as if there is something around us, something hollow. And something pushing me away.

Has she realized I am about to kiss her on the lips?

Is her fear of kissing me coming from her eyes? Her body temperature falls right after the tear. Suddenly, room service rings the doorbell, and she opens her eyes. There is no passion, no affection in her eyes. They are empty. I pull myself away and get up from the bed.

"Our food is here. Please, join me for dinner." And with that, I head to the main level to open the door.

Rania joins me after a couple of minutes, while the server sets up the table. There is a sudden wave of awkwardness between us. In all these passionate moments, I didn't realize I was putting our friendship and trust at stake. If she doesn't want me as her partner, I will also lose a friend. I will lose her trust if I keep trying to kiss her; she might run away and never look back. Right now, she trusts me enough to allow me to sleep by her side, as she knows I would never hurt her. If I keep on showing my feelings through my body, I am afraid I might lose her one day. I should have known from my first trial that she is not ready to take a step further in our relationship.

She joins me at the dinner table, looking at the food blankly. The table is filled with fruits, fresh juices, sandwiches and snacks. I know she will not eat much, since it is nearly midnight, and neither can I, so I ordered light snacks. She is noticeably quiet, maybe avoiding what just happened. She eats her grilled cheese sandwich without talking to me or looking at me at all. With all the tension in the air, I don't even have the courage to talk. She finishes her meal before I do and waits till I finish mine. Her eyes are cold and her body is as unresponsive as a stone. She stands up from the table, still not looking at me. I ask where she is going.

"I am tired, Adam," she says with no expression. "I want to sleep. Good night." And she walks out of the room.

THE SUMMIT

♀

I wake up in the morning with a sudden jerk and realize I didn't set my alarm. The summit is supposed to start around nine. It is still dark, so I step down from the bed on tiptoes. The other side is empty, which means Adam didn't sleep next to me. I check the time on the bedside clock and it is half past seven. I still have almost an hour and a half to get ready. Before going to the washroom, I glance at the chaise and find Adam sleeping peacefully.

This man can afford the best beds in the world, yet he is sleeping on a chaise, because of me.

I feel despicable. I offer him nothing, and he accommodates me in every situation. He understands every movement of my body. I know he wanted to kiss me last night, but I don't know how he found the fear inside me. He never questioned, he never demanded, but he was always there. But what amazes me more is that my body did not refuse him when he started exploring my face with his sensuous lips. I have never allowed anyone to be that close to me in the last five years, yet when he touched me, there was a current passing inside me, tearing all my nerves into bits and pieces and forcing me to surrender to him.

Who are you, Adam? An angel? A guardian? What should I call you?

When we started our friendship, I thought he would take advantage of our solitude and might seduce me, but he proved me wrong every time. Whenever I had a sudden wave of skepticism about him, he proved that all men are not the same. He proved I can trust him with anything—my nightmares, my past, my demons. After all the time I've spent with him, I realize it is me who is taking advantage of him, benefiting from his trust and loyalty. It is me who is getting everything, and this man lying on the chaise is getting nothing.

Sometimes life puts us in a situation where we get two right paths. The two sides of the coin are displayed together. My life stands at a crossroad. One path is the ordinary life that I had, with nightmares, but it is also safeguarding my father's reputation. The other path leads me to Adam, revealing me to the light, but the intensity of that light is burning everything around it, except me. I'm getting all the benefits and warmth from that light. Should I be selfish, or should I spend my whole life asking for an apology from my father?

I push all these thoughts from my mind and head quietly to the washroom. I don't even bother to take a shower, as the noise may wake Adam. I get ready in no time. I take out all the summit information from my bag. It is fifteen minutes' drive from where I am. I hear Adam's phone ringing somewhere, so I follow the sound and see *'unknown'* calling once again. Since he is sleeping, I put his phone on silent and lay it at his side. He is still sleeping peacefully and from the depth of his sleep, I can see he was up late. I look at him lovingly one last time and then leave for my work.

On my way, I decide to send him a text message, so that he doesn't end up being worried about me once again.

Thank you for understanding—in every way.
I send one more message.

I have left to attend the summit. I will hopefully see you in the evening.

When I reach the Westin hotel, where the summit is, I check my cell, but there is no message from him. *Still sleeping!* I am a bit disappointed and send him another message.

The summit is about to start. In case you are worried, I behaved like a good girl and had my breakfast. I will also make sure I take my lunch on time. Please don't worry about me. I am fine. Take care.

I was not expecting so many people to attend the summit. It is a global event, beyond my imagination. I am glad I have dressed extremely formally and professionally. At the entrance, everyone is asked to show their invitations, so that the security can provide badges with the proper names for each individual. There are people from social media companies, telecoms, and other technology-oriented businesses. There is hands-on-training in new technologies in Adobe® and other creative products used for digital marketing and publishing. I hope to learn a great deal about the latest publishing products, which will be extremely helpful to incorporate at Greenway. The summit starts with a small speech from the digital media head. The guy's name is Ethan Murray. He is an Englishman, tall and handsome, in his late thirties, very high-profile in the technology world. Everyone knows him. I am very lucky to get a seat at one of the front tables. It is a breakthrough in my career to attend this summit, and I feel obliged to Ben for making it happen.

"Good morning, ladies and gentlemen. I welcome you all to Adobe® Digital Marketing Summit 2012. The Summit offers an unmatched networking opportunity with your industry peers, to learn how others are tracking current digital marketing challenges." Mr. Murray sips his coffee. He is dressed perfectly in a black suit and a light gray shirt, and three hundred faces are turned to him. "The summit offers more than seventy breakout sessions, featuring many real-world customer success stories, based on solutions from the Adobe® Digital Marketing Suite. Many sessions will feature in-depth case studies, highlighting best practices from technology experts. Each session will have an emphasis on specific takeaways for attendees to implement immediately. It includes seven different tracks: Digital Analytics, Targeting and Optimization, Web Experience Management, Digital Advertising, Social Marketing, Marketing Innovations, and Tech Labs." As Mr. Murray continues with his speech, he focuses on each person in turn. He is looking at me when my phone chimes. I completely forgot to put it on 'silent,' and since it is ringing loudly, Mr. Murray has to halt his speech for a moment.

Oh shit, this is so embarrassing.

It is Adam on my phone. I had forgotten him for the moment. I put my phone on silent and let it ring. Mr. Murray continues his speech. I'm not paying attention anymore, due to the silent calls coming from Adam. I end his call deliberately and type a text message.

*I am at the summit. Your phone call came in the middle of a
serious speech by the media head. Sorry for not taking your
call. I will see you in the evening.*

Within a few seconds, I receive his message.

*Sorry to bother you. I am glad you are doing well. I was just
worried when I woke up and you were gone. Thanks for
leaving the messages on my phone. I look forward to seeing
you this evening. Not sure how I will spend my day. I still
miss yesterday's tour.*

His message puts a smile on my face.

*You are a busy man, Mr. Gibson. I am sure you will have lots
of official work to do. There were lots of pretty ladies by the
poolside, though. If you get bored, you have plenty of sexy
options there.*

I send the message, with a winked smile. He replies back
instantly.

*When did you get a chance to visit the pool? Anyhow, I
have an interview with CBC Edmonton within an hour. Is it
possible to meet for lunch?*

Interview with CBC? Everyone knows he is here? It is useless
to ask all the details at the moment, so I decide to keep this
discussion for dinner.

*I am sorry. I have training the whole day. I don't think I
would be able to come out. See you later. Take care.*

"You seem to be distracted this morning." I hear a familiar
voice coming from the next seat. I didn't realize that in all these
exchanges of text messages, the speech has ended and Murray
is seated next to me. Some other men from the social media
companies are making short speeches after him. "Ethan Murray."
He holds out his hand and I shake hands with him, smiling.

"Rania Ahmed."

"Rania . . . that's a pretty name. Where are you from?"

"I am from Toronto. I work for Greenway Advertising." I am a
bit intrigued.

He speaks with grace and charisma, with a typical British
accent. "So, what training do you plan to take today?"

"I plan to take Creative Suite® training. And I am very glad to be part of it. Your speech was very informative."

"You hardly heard it. Your phone kept you busy." He cocks one eyebrow. I purse my lips in embarrassment and curse my phone. He observes my expression and continues. "What exactly is your job?"

"I work with the digital media and printing department. Basically, catalog designing and publishing. They are mostly e-catalogs, designed for different operating systems and smart phones."

"That sounds interesting. So, where did you graduate from?"

"Ryerson University. But digital media was not my field. I studied software engineering, but playing with color was always my passion, so I took some courses and chose this field." I smile genuinely, feeling good about my choice.

"That's impressive. You look quite young to have all those talents. Have you planned further study in this field?"

"Yes, Mr. Murray. I'm planning to do a Masters in digital media and graphics, but probably not until next year."

"Please, call me Ethan. I don't like to be addressed so formally by a beautiful woman like you." Murray's gaze gets deeper as he speaks. I smile back at him, not sure what to say. Luckily, Murray gets distracted by other high-profile people and he excuses himself from his seat to join in their discussion. I head to the training area, where the session has already started. I stay there until lunchtime, learning many new things about the latest tools.

There are many people from Toronto, which makes it much simpler to communicate and learn things, as we share similar interests. In between presentations, we discuss our favorite places in the city. By the time we break for lunch, I'm starving. As soon as I step out of the training area, Murray greets me.

"Good to find you here. I was looking for you." He blocks my way. I glance at the other people from my training session waiting for me to join them. Murray says, "You guys carry on, if you are going for lunch. Miss Ahmed will join you back for training in an hour." The two girls look at me dubiously, and everyone leaves. "Please join me for lunch, Miss Ahmed," Ethan says. "I want you to meet some people. Come." I follow him silently. The people he wants me to meet may also be well-known in the field, like him. Meeting them could be a great opportunity. We exit the summit hall and enter an exquisite restaurant within the hotel. Murray introduces me to his two colleagues, who work in the same department, and they all launch into a technology-oriented discussion, regarding Creative Cloud™ and its advanced features. I listen to their discussion quietly, while sipping orange juice. I have no idea why Murray has invited me to the lunch, where my presence is not even noticed. After a short discussion, the other men excuse themselves and I am left alone with Murray at a table for four.

"So, what would you like to have, Rania?" He glances at me over his menu.

"I will have Caesar salad and minestrone soup, please." I look at the waiter, who is ready to take our order.

"That's it? That is your lunch?" Mr. Murray asks me curiously, and puts the menu card down on the table.

"Yes, please."

"I will have mustard salmon with cobb salad, please." Murray hands both the menu cards to the waiter and he departs instantly. "Thank you for joining me for lunch," he says, adjusting his thick black glasses over his deep gray eyes. "I always enjoy feeding beautiful women."

"Thank you for inviting me, Mr. Murray. I was not expecting, umm—"

"*Expect the unexpected,*" he interrupts me. "Where are you originally from?"

"I am from Lebanon." I try to speak to the point. Where is this conversation going? *Why am I here?* I start to feel uncomfortable about the way Murray is studying my face. We remain silent for a moment, until the waiter appears with my soup and salad and meal for Murray.

"You don't talk much?"

"I do. It's not like that."

"So, is it me, who is making you talk less?"

"No, Mr. Murray. I do talk, but we hardly know each other."

"Yes, that's a good point, Rania. That's why I invited you for lunch. We should get to know each other." He speaks with confidence, aware of his every word. Luckily, just then I hear my phone vibrating in my handbag.

"Excuse me." I avert my eyes and take the phone from my bag. I have never been so elated to receive a call from Adam. "Hi," I say. "It's so good to hear your voice." That's certainly the truth.

"Really?" He sounds pleased. "Then I'm glad I called. How is your training going?"

"It's good. I am enjoying it and learning a lot. It is an exceptional experience." Murray's gaze is still probing me through his thick-rimmed glasses. "How about you? How was your interview?"

"It went well. Boring at the start though . . . you know, general business questions. They were interested in us also."

"Really? What did they ask?"

"I will tell you when we meet. You had lunch?"

"I am having it right now." I put a forkful of salad in my mouth.

"Please, carry on. I was wondering if we could hang out and see a movie tonight?"

"That sounds interesting. I will call you when I'm free." I smile over the phone.

"Take care." And he hangs up the phone.

I put the phone back in my purse. "Sorry about that."

"Boyfriend?" He adjusts his glasses, interrogating me.

"Yeah. How did you know?"

"You were blushing like a rose. It was obvious." I look out the window, to deflect his remarks, but his eyes are still on me. "You are very beautiful, Miss Ahmed. Has your boyfriend told you that?" I look back at him in shock.

I adjust my scarf and look into the salad plate. "Yes, he keeps reminding me."

"*Never lose an opportunity of seeing anything beautiful, for beauty is God's handwriting.*"[5] His eyes bore into me as he speaks. What a sleaze. I look away.

"Have you ever been to San Francisco?" He changes the subject quickly, which makes me look at him. I shake my head. "It's a beautiful city, with amazing weather all year round. You should visit there. Be my guest." He takes a bite from his plate.

"Well, thank you, Mr. Murray. I will, hopefully."

"There is another summit in New York, around New Year's. Do you have an invitation for that?" I look at him quizzically,

---

5   *Charles Kingsley (1819-1875)*

wondering exactly where this is going. "You are a bright young woman. These kinds of summits and conferences will accelerate your career. May I have your email, so that I can send you an invite? I will send you two invitations; you can bring your department head or whoever is interested in coming."

"That is very kind of you, Mr. Murray. But I guess I already have an invitation for that. My boss has mentioned it, but in case it's not the same one . . ." I take out a pen and write my email address on a paper napkin. "I would love to attend another summit like this. Thank you very much." Now we are talking like professionals.

"Have you ever thought about living in California?"

"No. Why?"

"I would like to offer you a job in my department. We take good care of our employees, Miss Ahmed. I saw your work today, and I must say I am very impressed. You are very skillful and technical, and your choice of colors and perception in digital publishing is unique. The two people you just met, I wanted them to meet you so we could discuss things further." He takes a sip from his glass and continues. "Consider yourself very lucky, Miss Ahmed. This kind of career opportunity comes once in a lifetime." I look at him in astonishment, with no idea how to react. Ethan Murray is offering me a job at Adobe®. It is certainly a big boost on my career path; I have never imagined working in Silicon Valley. People dream about this kind of job, that I am being offered with my soup and salad in a fancy restaurant.

"I am surprised and delighted, Mr. Murray. I—"

"Think about it. I'm not asking for an answer now. We can discuss it tomorrow, or perhaps over the phone one day next week."

"Sure, Mr. Murray. I feel very privileged to have an offer from you, but—"

"I have good experience in digging out gems." He pauses for a moment, then continues. "So . . . what does your boyfriend do?"

"He is a businessman."

"That's interesting. What kind of business?"

"Umm . . . he builds . . . houses . . . communities and . . ." I'm not sure what else to add.

"Rich man. What's his name?" I don't know if I am supposed to disclose his name or not, but since I have already said so much, there is no escape.

"Adam Gibson."

"The man behind Gibson Enterprises?" He takes his glasses off and stares at me.

"You know him?" I ask curiously.

"Who doesn't know the most eligible bachelor in Toronto? I am originally from there, by the way. Though it has been ten years since I moved to Silicon Valley, I keep track of my city's news. He is the talk of the town every time he makes move." He takes a sip and continues. "In fact, I read last week about his recent affair and . . ." He puts his glasses back on. "Are you the same girl who hit the news last week?" I nod in silence. The world seems so small right now. I want to hide somewhere, to avoid all the questions.

"I must say he is a lucky man."

"I am lucky to have him."

After a minimal pause, he continues. "Please, let me know soon about your decision."

"Do you want my resume, Mr. Murray? Or any letters of recommendation?"

He smiles for a moment and tilts his head to look at me from his gray eyes, his glasses resting on his nose. "Do you know *personal beauty is a greater recommendation than any letter of reference? I* don't say it, Aristotle did." He indulges himself pleasurably in his drink, while looking at me. *What the hell is he talking about?* "What are your plans for tonight? Are you coming skiing? Everyone is going."

"No, I have plans with Adam."

"He is here in Edmonton?"

"Yes, Mr. Murray."

"I would like to meet him, then." He smiles with a hint of sharpness in his eyes.

"Sure." I look down to check the time on my watch. "Thank you for the lunch, Mr. Murray, and for your offer. I will let you know soon. My training is starting in ten minutes, so I need to go . . ." I stand up and he joins me.

"Bring your man for skiing tonight. It's going to be fun."

"I am not sure, Mr. Murray. Let me ask him, and I will let you know. Thanks for the invitation, though. Good day."

"Take care." He fixes his glasses and follows me.

I don't know why, but I feel like he is walking deliberately close to me. "Your fragrance is very charming, Miss Ahmed. I like floral perfumes on beautiful ladies. It is a great blend of feminism with flowers." He speaks behind my ear. I feel a wave of danger in his message, so without looking back at him, I speed up to enter the main hallway. Our badges are checked again and we head in.

Fortunately, our ways part and I feel myself breathing normally as I join the others at the training session. I still can't believe my luck that I have been offered such a huge opportunity. Though I have not decided about it, I am dying to share my excitement with Adam. We all get involved in the hands-on training on the recent versions of Creative Suite®, which engrosses me so much that I don't realize how much time has passed. After two hours, Mr. Murray peeks in with an announcement. "We are serving tea and coffee outside. Please, join us, everyone."

We all halt our work and head out, along with our trainer, Mr. Richard, who is a pure Californian in his early forties. Ethan Murray and Richard Godfrey are busy talking to each other, and some of my teammates join the conversation. I see some of the girls getting a little too close to Murray, responding to his magnetic charm and enigmatic looks, which seem to always draw a crowd. I distract myself with pouring myself some tea. As soon as I touch the milk pot, a masculine hand covers mine.

"Allow me." I look behind me to see Ethan Murray. His smile is charming, which makes me smile back at him. I release the milk pot and he adds the milk to my tea.

"Thank you." I pick up the sugar.

"One tea for me, please," he adds.

Without saying anything, I pick up another empty cup and make tea for him. He guides me to sit at a round table, away from everyone else. I see girls from my training session watching me and talking to each other, as if they are gossiping. I ignore them.

"How is your training so far?" he asks.

"It is very informative. There is a lot to play around with, with the tools."

"All the trainees will get the latest versions, so that you can learn more on your own machines."

"That's better still." I take a sip of my tea. "So, you were involved in the development and enhancement of the latest version?"

"Yes, in bits and pieces. But primarily in documenting it in the web world. Most of my time is spent on integration research and writing tutorials about the products."

"I have seen your books."

"You have a chance to read them?"

"Frankly speaking, Mr. Murray, technology books don't attract me."

"Then what kind of books do you read?"

"Fiction, mostly."

"Interesting. You like unreal things?"

"They are less torturous than reality." I speak behind my cup of tea.

"Very astute, Miss Ahmed." We don't speak any more for the entire tea session.

After my tea, I excuse myself and join my training session. I concentrate completely for the next three hours, until Adam calls, reminding me the day is over. Adam informs me that he is waiting outside in the lobby for me, so I pick up my bag and hurry to the washroom to check if I am presentable for my newly created fake boyfriend. When I come out of the washroom, Ethan Murray is waiting for me.

"Are you leaving?"

"Yes, I have to go. Someone is waiting for me."

"Your *rich* boyfriend?" He says "rich" in a sarcastic tone. I know he wants to meet Adam, and he follows me without saying anything further. I see Adam sitting on a black leather sofa, dressed gracefully in his casual clothes. He stands up when he sees me coming toward him. I don't know why, but I have never been so delighted to see him waiting for me. I put my bag down and hug him tightly. He pauses for a moment and I am sure he must be wondering what I'm doing, since I've never acted this way before. He holds me closer in his warm scented embrace.

"I am so tired. I missed you." I speak over his shoulder. I feel like smiling, and he rubs my back gently.

"I missed you too . . ." He pauses for a moment, and continues. "Is everything okay, Rania? You seem upset."

How does he know my body so well, what I think, what I feel? Why is he so damn right, every time?

He knows, though I have told him I missed him, it is not the truth. I pull myself away and he checks my expression.

"I am just stressed out. Take me away." I feel really good in his arms; I feel protected. I hug him again to feel the blessing that is holding me warmly.

"Ahem, ahem." I hear someone clearing his throat. I turn and see Ethan Murray waiting for us. Adam's expression changes as soon as they make eye contact.

"Good to see you, Mr. Gibson. Your girlfriend is very fond of you." Murray looks at me, and then to Adam, with sharp eyes. "You have successfully charmed this beautiful lady."

"How are you, Ethan Murray. It has been a long time." Adam shakes hands with him stiffly. *Do they know each other?* Why didn't Murray mention that to me earlier? They glare each other.

"Do you guys know each other?" I look back and forth between them.

"I told you, Miss Ahmed. Who doesn't know Mr. Gibson?" He gazes at me deeply and I notice the fire in Adam's eyes.

"Let's go, Rania." He grabs me by my shoulders and drags me away.

"Won't you introduce your girlfriend to me, Mr. Gibson?" Murray says behind us, which makes Adam freeze in his tracks.

"You have already introduced yourself, Murray." He leaves my side and gets in Murray's face. "Stay away from her." His voice is low, but I still hear him. I break in between them and pull Adam away.

"Will someone tell me what is going on?" I look at Adam, who seems furious. "Adam? Tell me!"

Ethan Murray adjusts his glasses and looks at me with a jagged smile. Adam grabs my hand and drags me out of the lobby. Our car is waiting outside; I slip inside and Adam joins me. His face and body are stiff and tense, and I also want to know what was behind his exchange with Murray. Obviously there is some history there. I remain quiet all the way back to our hotel.

Ten minutes later, we are seated on the couch. Adam is rubbing his lower lip, thinking really hard about something. He goes to the bar and makes himself a drink, still angry, but putting up a front of calmness for me. He comes back with his glass of whiskey and sits next to me on the couch. "How do you know Ethan Murray?" he asks.

"I should ask you that, Adam." I cross my legs and face him. His eyes are fixed to the wall.

"Answer me first, Rania. How do you know him?"

"I don't know him. I met him this morning. He is a digital media head with Adobe®. He opened the summit with a speech, and afterwards he sat down beside me and introduced himself."

"There were three hundred people there, Rania. What made him sit beside you and introduce himself?" Adam's sudden question shocks me.

"I . . . umm . . . I don't know." I shrug my shoulders.

"What else did he talk about?" He's still staring at the wall. *Why isn't he looking at me?*

"He invited me for . . . lunch . . ." I speak with hesitation, twisting my ring on my finger. He cocks his head toward me with disappointed look.

"You lied to me?"

"I didn't lie to you, Adam. He introduced me to other colleagues and we had lunch. He offered me a job in Silicon Valley."

"And you accepted it?" He rises from the couch. "After all . . . who can refuse the charming Ethan Murray?"

"I just don't understand what you are talking about."

He turns and moves closer to me, squatting down before me, still holding the glass of whiskey. "What else did he say, Rania?" He leans closer, placing one hand under my ear and caressing my cheek with his thumb. "Did he tell you how beautiful you are? Did he tell you that you entranced him? Tell me, Rania. Did you like him complimenting you?"

"What are you talking about, Adam?" I jerk his hand off my face and move away from him. He is not in his right mind—something is bothering him terribly. If I tell Adam it is all true, what he just said, then I have no idea how he will react, so I lie deliberately.

"No, Adam, it was strictly professional. He didn't say anything like that to me." I take the glass and pull him up next to me. "What is it that you are holding back? Please, tell me."

"Did you accept his job offer?" He still doesn't look at me.

"No, I haven't said anything."

"Are you going to accept it?"

"I don't know. He offered me a great deal and—"

"And you will think about it. Right?" He looks down at the floor. "After all, it would be a big boost in your career."

"I haven't decided anything. I have to finish my time in Canada, till I get my citizenship, and—"

"Is that the only reason for you staying here?" He looks straight into my eyes. I am totally confused. "If you had citizenship, would you have considered his offer?"

"Adam! Stop talking in riddles and tell me what this is about!"

"I am sure he must have invited you to the next conference in New York." He looks toward his shoes.

"Yes, he did. How did you know?"

"He intends to fuck you, Rania, that's why." He looks up and faces me. "He wants to use your body, so that he can torture my soul. Will you let that happen?"

"Of course not, Adam. Don't you know me by now?"

"I know you, but I know him also. He is a fucking charmer. How he lures women with his sweet talk, so that before you know it you will be in bed with him."

"Please, stop it, Adam. How can you say something like that?"

"Because I know, Rania." He raises his voice. "He fucked my sister, when she was only sixteen. I didn't see Eva my whole life. One night, she called me from the hospital and told me that she was all alone there after an abortion, because some fucker made her pregnant and left her by herself in the hospital. It took her three months to recover from the trauma. She was only sixteen, damn it. She hadn't even started college yet. I passed the message to the Moore family that she was on a summer break, but the fact was I used to take her to psychiatric treatment and after three months of therapy, she was able to face her family." He pauses for a moment. "Mother still doesn't know about it. It's a secret between Eva and me." He looks at me with tears in his eyes. "You are the only person I've ever told. I am telling you because I see the same danger coming to you. The way he looked at you . . . he was fucking you with his eyes, Rania. He is the true version of Satan, and the worst part is, I *can* see him." I put my hands on my mouth, shocked at his revelations.

He continues bombarding me with the rest. "Eva finally got settled in college and started her academic career. Mom still doesn't know that we ever met. Once I knew she was fine, I didn't see her anymore. Meanwhile, I registered a complaint against Murray; he was doing his doctoral program at the University of Toronto. The university suspended him for six months and he flew to California, where he started his career once again. He tried contacting Eva and blackmailed her. The fucking prick had videos of them having sex. I had to pay him a handsome amount to hand over everything to me, but I know he still has the originals. Who could sexually use and abuse a sixteen-year old girl and then blackmail her with the videos? Isn't he a walking Satan?" I still have my hands over my mouth, riveted to every word. "Have you wondered how you got a seat at the front of the summit, when there were giants of technology attending? You think Ben did that?" He looks straight into my eyes. I am dumbfounded. "He wanted you to sit in front of him. He has been chasing you since he found out I have someone in my life. His luck is fucking awesome that you are in the same field. He sent an invitation through Ben, and asked if you could attend this summit, so he could meet you in a new city and cast a spell on you."

"How do you know all this?"

"I have assigned someone to look after you. You can call it stalking or whatever you want, but since the first time I saw you, I feel like I'm supposed to protect you." He is looking blankly at the wall. "Don't ask me why I'm doing it. It's not in my hands." He looks at me. "Anyway, that person told me about Ethan's intentions Monday morning, when you boarded the train. He informed me that Murray has been watching your every move." *Oh, that unknown number?* "I had to rush after you, to protect you from his filthy hands. If I had told you right away, you wouldn't have believed me because there was no trust relationship between us then. You didn't even know him. I had to spend time with you in the train, to gain your trust." He inhales deeply. "I brought you here with me because it was Murray who arranged your hotel, in the room next to his." He inhales again and continues. "I have already seen my sister traumatized. I can't see you like that."

"Do you trust me, Adam?" I place my hands over his.

"More than anyone."

"Then, do you think I will get seduced by his words?"

"I know he cannot charm you, but he possesses certain magnetic powers, Rania. He knows how to play. He *fucks* with his words."

"He is only playing a mind game with you, Adam. Let him do it. You know I don't get easily carried away by men."

"Yes, that's one of the things I love most about you. Even though you pushed me away, I knew that at least it meant you would not let him play with you." I am finally able to put a smile on his face. I stand up, holding his hand.

"Let's go. You were taking me to a movie, remember?" I wink at him, smiling. He smiles back with sparkling eyes.

I want to cheer him up. I had no idea what he had gone through all those years ago, and how suddenly seeing me with Murray would torture him. I know he cares about me greatly, and I will make sure that the trust remains between us. I will never let Murray cast his spell on me, with his filthy mind. Adam has given me enough insight into his personality to deal with him tomorrow.

Meanwhile, while Adam relaxes, I excuse myself so I can dress casually for our movie night. I don't care if someone catches us in the theater or posts a picture on any social media website; I just want Adam to have a good time. The man who saved his sister without telling his mother and taking no credit for himself, the man who made all this effort to follow me so he can protect me from Murray, totally deserves a happy memory. I want to make him forget about our discussion. My heart has raised him to the highest level of respect and trust. I can never feel about anyone the way I do for this man.

A TRUE COMPANIONSHIP

♂

I wait for her, relaxing on the couch, while finishing the last of my whiskey. How easily she has dealt with such a dramatic situation, pulling out all the knots. She is right, I should trust her. She is a woman of strong mind, and she will not let Murray get to her. A sun of my universe, which only emits light and energy, and doesn't absorb anything because she is too powerful to be influenced by any negativity. Is it her past that has made her so protective of herself, or has she always been unlike other women? Her burn scars showed me a hint of her past, but I will never bring it up until she trusts me completely and tells me everything, like I did with her today. I have nothing to hide her from now, and my soul feels light and free, like it has been released from a death trap.

She comes downstairs, wearing jeans and a white sequined top.

"Is there anything that doesn't look nice on you?" I stand up, meeting her at the staircase. She blushes and smiles shyly. *Ah! What do I do with this pink blush shade?*

"You need to get your eyes tested, Mister." She laughs at me, and heads toward the door. I follow her, smiling. When we get in the car, she checks her phone, and her expression changes. She turns it off and puts it in her jacket pocket.

"So, which movie are we seeing?"

"What do you think of going to Cineplex?"

"Anywhere you want, Adam. Don't worry about the crowd. I don't think anyone will even notice us." She speaks delightfully, warmth emanating from her.

We reach the Cineplex within ten minutes, and find ourselves in line to buy tickets. Rania suggests we should go for a lighthearted animated movie to ease our minds, and I agree to her choice. A few couples notice us in line for popcorn, but we ignore everyone and stay in our own capsule. Two hours later we come out laughing like idiots, repeating lines of dialogue. Rania poses like Dracula, whose daughter has fallen in love with a human, when he wants to protect her from humans. We both laugh heartily, not caring who might be around, and head for the street. The theater is located in the main downtown area, so we leave the car and risk walking in the snow and -15-degree temperature. Rania stops at a few souvenir stores and buys some items to remember our evening. This is the first time I've been to a movie theater in ten years, and I haven't realized what fun I've been missing. Watching a movie with a friend, with whom you can share all your worries, is a blessing, and I am enjoying it to the fullest. Rania is switched onto fun mode tonight. I wonder if she is doing it for me, or if she is really enjoying herself. Anyhow, I'm getting bewitched by her charms. She stops at some crazy hat store and tries on different types of funny hats, entertaining me and the crowd across the street. She puts some hats on my head and takes pictures from my phone, both of us proving that we're complete idiots.

We take a break at a pizza and wings take-out restaurant, where there are only four bar stools in the corner. We are actually dating like a typical teenage couple who can't afford a fancy restaurant, but would rather spend the money on a movie. I follow her blindly, wherever she is taking me. I have the worst pizza of my entire life, but having Rania by my side, cracking jokes and making me laugh, is priceless. She tells me childhood stories— that she was the most destructive kid in her class during middle school. Even the boys were scared of her, but since she was at the top of her class, the teachers and school management ignored her playfulness. I also share some of my teenage stories with her, and tell her how the boys would talk behind the girls' backs, about which girls ignore them and which ones come on to them. She enjoys my typical guy's nonsense and laughs until her eyes water.

After our extremely unhealthy, but blissfully crappy dinner, we walk through the streets again and she asks me for an ice cream. We head to the ice cream parlor and she takes around fifteen minutes trying different flavors. She savors each flavor, eyes closed, before trying the next. After quite some time, I whisper in her ear.

"You are taking a lot more than the expected time to decide. The salesman is getting annoyed. Are you actually going to select a flavor or not?" To my surprise, she orders the largest choco-vanilla cone I have ever seen, and doesn't pick any of the flavors she tried. "What was the point of trying all the flavors, when you were going to pick this?"

She laughs at my question. "You are quite innocent, Mr. Gibson, when it comes to ice cream. That's how it is done. You taste them all, even though you already know what you want. That's the fun part." She winks at me.

"Are you sure you can eat all this? There are three scoops. You will get cold, girl."

"Aren't you going to share with me?" she asks me, and I can't help accepting her offer.

She sits on a couch and I sit in an armchair opposite her, watching her lick the cone. I glance around the ice cream parlor and notice some boys staring at her hungrily. She ignores the atmosphere and continues licking her cone, as if she is on a treasure hunt. I gape at her; it's the most erotic thing I've ever seen. I can't blame these pricks for staring; I am on the same ride with them. *Fuck! I can't resist.* She finally manages to look at me and gets up from her seat to sit on the arm rest of my chair.

"Try it, Gibson. It's heavenly." She hands me the cone, putting one arm over my shoulder to support herself. I can't tell her I haven't licked an ice cream cone since childhood. I manage okay, though I see the boys are still drooling over her or the ice cream, whichever. Rania is unconcerned. All she cares about is her ice cream.

"You know, Mr. Gibson, females have a special relationship with chocolate and ice cream." She takes the cone from me and starts licking the chocolate side of it. "They activate the hormones of happiness. Usually girls crave chocolate and ice creams during their menstrual cycle, to combat the depression that comes with it." *What? Is she serious?* I never thought she would talk to me so openly about something like that. I give her a bewildered look. "Yes, in case you are wondering why I asked for three scoops, I wanted to come out of this shit hole too." She smiles innocently, displaying her beautiful dimples behind the cone. *Is she menstruating right now?*

I look at her from head to toe and she laughs openly. "What are you looking at? You haven't seen a girl on her cycle?" She jerks me from the shoulders to avert my gaze from her. *Is she drunk?*

Does this ice cream have liquor in it? She's never talked to me like that. She hands me the cone and forces me to repeat the licking process. The boys are seated very close to us, and I wonder if they heard us or not. She looks up at the guys, while I fulfill her demand of licking the cone.

"Hey! What are you looking at, you suckers? Haven't seen a hot sexy guy licking a cone?" she calls out toward the boys. I'm startled and drop the cone. I really wasn't expecting that. The guy behind the cash counter laughs hysterically. Rania gets up and walks up to the boys. "Now see what you've done. Stop drooling over him. He is not licking your popsicle, you sleaze balls. He is not one of you." With that, she heads toward the counter to get napkins and comes back to me. She starts cleaning my shoes and the floor, picking up the broken pieces of the cone. I am totally shocked and speechless by her boldness.

The boys are embarrassed at the attention she's drawn to them, and they leave hastily. I am still in a state of shock. Rania is on her knees, wiping my shoes, so I grab her hand to stop her.

"Let me clean it; it will melt inside your shoes," she says. "You will have to learn how to do justice to an ice cream, Mr. Gibson." She looks up with a childlike smile. "Did the boys scare you?" I still look at her, blown away. "They were gay. They were staring at you lustfully when you started licking the cone." She purses her lips, trying to control her laughter.

"What? No, they were looking at you."

"Are you kidding me, Mr. Gibson?" She finishes her task and gets up, the dirty napkins in her hand. "You really think a bunch of boys would come by themselves to an ice cream parlor, having strawberry cones? Did you check out their outfits? Their pink hats? It was so gay. Guys usually hang out at the bar at this hour. What were they doing here?" She laughs and throws away the napkins. "They were *so* into you. I noticed them when we came in. They followed you. You knocked them out with your sexiness." She ruffles my hair gently and heads toward the exit. I look at the guy behind the counter, who winks at me with a smile.

Oh no! Not another one.

I hear Rania's voice behind me, holding the door open. "Are you going to sit there the whole night, seducing that poor guy?" The ice cream man looks at me, embarrassed. *Is she doing all this on purpose?* The ice cream seems to have put her on a roller coaster ride and there is no stopping her. I shake my head and follow her toward the exit.

"You are so unpredictable, Rania."

"Well, Mr. Gibson, you have no idea what you have got yourself into." She nudges me slightly, winking at me. "You have a lot to see. Just wait and watch." With that, she starts walking ahead of me, leaving me amazed. Her mischief has already surprised and shocked me; I can imagine how she would have been at school, when she told me she was the naughtiest among them all.

"Let me call the driver." I take out my phone. She takes the phone from me and puts it in her jacket.

"Are you crazy? I can see the hotel from here. Let's walk." She offers me her arm.

"It is shit cold, Rania, and the hotel is almost two kilometers from here. It will take us more than twenty minutes to walk."

"So what? Don't worry. I won't let you freeze to death. We will run." She grabs my hand and pulls me onto the sidewalk. "Loosen up, Gibson. You are not on an official trip. Stop relying on cars. Normal people walk, regardless if it's raining or snowing." She starts walking briskly, pulling me along by the hand. I fall into step beside her, still holding her hand. She's right; I won't freeze to death. Her touch is keeping me warm, even in this harsh weather. The sun always emits warmth, no matter how cold it is.

We almost slip a couple of times on black ice, but manage to support each other, laughing crazily like high school kids.

I am on a magical journey, learning how normal people live, free from worries about meetings and business deals. This walk with her, hand in hand in the falling snow, is priceless, more valuable than a ride in any luxury car or my helicopter. She stops for a minute to look up at the snow-filled sky and feel the snowflakes falling over her face. She doesn't blink, even for a single second, though some of the flakes dissolve in her eyes. I see tears dripping from the corners of her eyes, but she keeps looking at the sky. The moment is frozen within us. I wonder wildly what she is thinking, but she doesn't say anything. She glances back at me, giving me a very strange look, and hugs me tightly. I am taken completely off-guard. I pull her closer to me, feeling her warmth and passion, and we stand in the midst of this white magical land. It is the best snowfall of my life. She pulls away all of a sudden and starts to jog, dragging me down the street.

Whoa! What was that?

We finally reach the hotel lobby around midnight, two snowmen in woolen coats. Some people stare at us, as if asking how this hotel can rent rooms to idiots. We continue running until we reach the elevator, where we meet a young couple with their five-year-old daughter, holding a doll. She hides behind her parents when she sees two snow creatures running toward her. Rania tilts her head to greet the child.

"What's your name?" She kneels down to talk to the girl.

"Sandra." The girl speaks from behind her father's knees.

"What a pretty name. You like your Rapunzel doll? Can you show it to me?" She knows how to communicate with kids. The girl steps out from behind her father and shows her doll to Rania. "You know, Sandra, I have a Rapunzel like this, with a huge tower. You wanna play with me someday?" She caresses the girl's hair lovingly and stands up. Her parents watch Rania with delight.

"She doesn't talk to anyone. You made her smile." The child's mother breaks in.

"You have a lovely child. God bless her." Rania looks at the child affectionately.

The elevator stops on our floor and we step out. The mother calls out, "Enjoy your honeymoon." The door closes behind us, and Rania laughs.

"Let's get into the room, my new husband, and enjoy the honeymoon." She runs toward the door. I know she isn't serious, but I enjoy hearing it anyway.

The room is warm; Rania flings off her jacket and burrows into the couch.

"Oh my God, I am so tired." She checks her watch. "And I have training tomorrow." She closes her eyes. I bend down beside her and take off her shoes. She opens her eyes and winces.

"Your boots are filled with snow. You will catch cold."

She stops me. "I can do it myself. Please!"

"It doesn't make any difference."

"It does to me. Please, sit down." She pulls my hands away from her shoes and takes them off. Her demeanor has changed suddenly, as if I'm a stranger. She takes off her socks and stands up. "I am going to change. I have to get up early in the morning." She heads to the bedroom without waiting for a reply. I take off my accessories and remember she put my phone inside her jacket. Since we both have the same color iPhones, I mistakenly check her phone and find an unread message.

> *No matter what wonders my eyes have seen, nothing*
> *amazes me more than when I look at you.*
> *Ethan.*
> *(P.S. looking forward to seeing you tomorrow)*

Pervert! I wonder if he picked up the words from a greeting card, hoping he would get into her panties. I notice the message was sent around seven, when we left for the movie. That was when she checked her phone in the car and her expression darkened. She was displeased with this message, not impressed, since I'd already warned her about Murray. I control my temper. She has assured me that she will handle him by herself, so I'll trust her judgment. She probably hid the message so our evening wouldn't be spoiled. I take both phones into the bedroom. She is still in the washroom with the door closed, so I decide to change in the room instead of waiting for her to come out. I put on my pajama trousers, and have just taken off my shirt when she steps out of the washroom. After a quick glance at my half-naked body, she crawls into the bed, avoiding looking at me. I quickly put on my T-shirt so as not to embarrass her, shut off the lamps and slip into bed. She picks up her phone, which I placed on her pillow, and begins setting the alarm. I shift to face her, resting my head on my hand, my elbow on the pillow.

"Thanks for the wonderful evening," I say sincerely. She looks up at me from the phone. "Every time we do something together, I think it's the best time I've ever had, and then the next time is even better."

"I had fun too, though the pizza sucked big time." She puts her eyes back on her phone.

"But I haven't had the most erotic dessert of my life before."

"Erotic?" She giggles. "Sure, it was erotic for those boys." She glances at me for a moment. I watch her face and contemplate such an enchanting creation by God. Yes, only He can create such perfection. "Do you have something to say, Adam?" *How does she know I have something on my mind?*

I am looking at her, completely dazzled. "You are very beautiful." That's all I can say.

"Besides that. There is something else on your mind." She glances at me again.

"If you know, why are you asking?"

"I want you to say it." She is still busy with the phone.

"I read the message on your phone. I picked it up by mistake."

"I know. I saw that. Never mind." She turns off her phone and puts it away on the nightstand.

"Will you still go tomorrow?"

"Why shouldn't I? He can't make me do anything against my will. The position he is in, I doubt he will mess with his career." She snuggles down under the covers and continues. "One complaint is enough, Adam." She smiles with confidence.

"I trust you. You certainly know how to handle assholes." She giggles and shifts her body to face me, resting her head on her arm.

"Are all men like that? I mean assholes?" She questions me with sleepy eyes.

"Most of them are, me included."

"No, I never thought of you like that. You are . . . different." She speaks in a dreamy voice.

"Different in what sense?"

"You know the meaning of respect and abide by it. You treasure trust. I haven't seen this characteristic in most men. They don't trust, especially women." I can see the resentment in her eyes.

It is time to change the subject.

"Tell me one thing. Does Satan create descendants like humans do?" She looks confused at my sudden change in topic.

"Yes, he does. It is not mentioned anywhere in detail how they are created, or maybe I haven't read it, but since they are created from a smokeless fire, I believe they must need a medium to spread the fire." She goes silent for a moment. "The medium could be humans, also."

"How?"

"The Satan dwells in us. Each individual has a demon inside himself. It is up to that person to suppress that demon, or not. I believe Satan takes humans as its medium to create its descendants." She watches me uncertainly. "What makes you so interested in Satan?"

"You made me curious. That night when you asked me who I am—an angel or a ghost in disguise. I had no knowledge of either of them, so I wanted to know all about it."

"I don't know everything."

"But you know enough to explain it to me." I look at her intently and continue. "So, do you really think they exist? I mean, the Jinn?"

"Of course they do. What makes you believe they don't?" She blinks a couple of times, to focus on me.

"I believe what I see. If I haven't seen them, how do you expect me to believe in their existence? That's why I don't even believe in gossip, if I don't hear it with my own ears."

"You don't see heat but you still know it exists, don't you?"

"But I feel heat. I don't feel these creatures exist." I look deeply into her eyes.

She takes a deep breath and straightens herself. "You will feel it, Adam . . . one day you will."

We don't speak after that, but I keep watching her until she closes her eyes and falls into sleep.

*   *   *

In the middle of the night, around 3 a.m., I wake up to get water and find Rania missing. I decide she must have gone downstairs, but I can't find her anywhere. Her shoes and jacket are still there, and the room is locked from the inside, so she must be here. I go back to the bedroom to get my phone and call her, but her phone is still on the bedside table. I sneak into the washroom, though it is dark, to see if she's in there.

No sign of her.

I'm starting to get worried. I sit at the corner of the bed, wondering where she could be, when I see the curtains across the balcony door are parted. I rush over and open the curtains, to see

Rania standing outside in the freezing cold. I open the door and a cold gust of wind hits my body.

"What the hell are you doing outside?" I yell, and pull her inside the room, shutting the door after us. She stands like a stone, not responding to me at all. "How long were you out there? Are you fucking crazy? You'll get frostbite." I rub her arms quickly to warm her, but her eyes are wide and empty. It is the same emptiness as when I dried her hair the other night. What astonishes me, though, is that when I touch her hands, her body temperature is normal, warmer than me. I touch her face, and that's warm as well. It's like she hasn't been outside at all.

Am I dreaming? But this is too real for a dream. I touch her bare feet and they are also not cold. This temperature can freeze a person within seconds, and it took me over ten minutes to search the suite. She looks toward the blank wall and I follow her gaze, but am unable to work out what she's looking at. She walks mutely toward the bed, and I follow. "Rania, will you please tell me what were you doing outside?" She doesn't respond at all. She reaches the bed, crawls under the comforter and closes her eyes.

What was that?

I lie back down on my side of the bed and look at her. She's sleeping peacefully, as if she never woke up at all. She is becoming more of a mystery to me, day by day. There is something she's hiding from me. I have no choice but to wait for her to reveal all her secrets to me. With all these wild thoughts running through my head, I close the lamp and try to sleep again.

AN UNINVITED GUEST

♀

My phone alarm wakes me up at 6:30 a.m. Adam is already awake; I can hear the shower running. I sit up, wondering about Murray's message last night. I am glad Adam has placed his trust in me and will let me deal with Ethan Murray on my own. He has tortured Adam enough, I will not let him do it anymore. *Such a prick!*

Adam has protected me; it is my turn to protect him from the demons. He steps out of the washroom with just the towel wrapped around his wet body, his hair dripping water seductively over his broad shoulders. I watch the strong muscles of his arms and wonder how many women have touched his nude body. I see his chest move as he breathes, and wonder how many women have laid their heads on it. I imagine crossing that line—a thin, fine line between friendship and intimacy. The forbidden fruit is waiting for me. I crave him as much as he craves me. In my despair, I don't realize he is watching me watching him. As he takes his clothes out of his bag, he says, "You want to stay in the room?" *Ah, yes, I want to savor this sweet, forbidden fruit.*

"No . . . umm, I am getting up. I was waiting for you to come out." *Yes, he is forbidden.*

"You could still stay. I'm not hiding anything from you." He sounds sarcastic. He walks over and sits next to me. He has a perfect physique, like a model. "Stop hiding things from me, Rania." He holds my face in his hands. I tilt my eyebrows, not sure what he is asking. "Don't you think we have traveled enough together to share ourselves?" He looks at me seductively. I feel suddenly uncomfortable and move my face a bit away from his touch. "Please, tell me what happened last night," he almost whispers.

"Last night?"

"What were you doing out on the balcony in this weather?"

I look at him curiously. "Adam, I have to get ready. I don't have time to listen to your jokes." I stand up from the bed, but he grabs me firmly by my arm.

"Answer me, Rania. What were you doing outside?"

I laugh at Adam's question and shake my head. "You must be dreaming, Adam. Who would stand outside in this weather?"

"No, Rania. I was not dreaming. I woke up in the middle of the night and couldn't find you. Then, I saw those curtains were partly open, and you were standing outside, watching the sky blankly. I pulled you in right away because it was fucking cold out there."

"You mean there? Those curtains?" I point to the golden drapes. He nods in agreement. "You were dreaming, my dear. There is no balcony in this room."

"Of course there is," he says, going to the window and drawing the curtains. He stops in shock. There is only a window behind them. He looks outside to make sure, and shakes his head in distress. "There was a door here. I am damn sure about it." He looks completely worn out. "I swear, Rania, there was a fucking door. It was too real for a dream."

"I would have believed you, Adam, but there's no balcony." I stand up from the bed and head toward the washroom, leaving him perplexed.

When I come out ten minutes later, I find breakfast waiting. I decide to go with the pancakes, the same as Adam.

"How was your television interview? You only told me a little on the phone."

"It was good. They were more interested in my personal life. I guess Ethan Murray has leaked the news—on my end, no one but Ali knows I'm here."

"Why would he do that?"

"I need to find out. I am just concerned that he knows too much about our relationship." He pauses for a moment. "I mean . . . that we are hiding it from the media, because of your father." Adam's news has disturbed me. He might be right. If Murray finds out we are trying to hide anything, he will make it public and spoil everything. Adam reads my expression and tries to comfort me. "I don't think he knows much, unless he has a personal contact with Ben. I'll find out if he knows Ben, other than professionally. But I highly doubt it. Ben would have called you by now, to confirm if I'm with you."

"So, what exactly did they ask you?"

"They wanted to know what brought me to Edmonton. I told them I'm interested in expanding my business outside Ontario, so they wanted to know if my girlfriend is also here." He mentions it casually, as if it isn't worth talking about. "I didn't tell them anything." He puts a bite of pancake in his mouth. "Money does wonders, my dear. The reporter got enough money to keep his mouth shut. I didn't let them record anything."

"So, the interview will never appear on television?" He smiles with an assurance that I have nothing to worry about.

"But be careful with Ethan Murray," Adam warns. "He is venomous. You won't see him coming until he's already hurt you."

"Then, he doesn't know me." I smile with confidence. "You know, Adam, some people have a lust of being talked about all the time, either good or bad. They enjoy being gossiped about. Ethan Murray is one of them—his actions yesterday prove it. He wanted us to argue about him, even when he wasn't here." I look deeply into Adam's eyes, as he focuses on my words. "I will not give him that satisfaction. I will make him believe that we never talked about him, and yesterday's confrontation didn't bother us." I put my hands over his to reassure him. "Stop worrying about him. You can trust me on that."

"You are so unpredictable, Rania." He looks at me in surprise. With that, I continue my breakfast, but Adam keeps watching me for the rest of the meal.

* * *

We don't speak again until he drops me outside the hotel. "Will you be okay?"

"Yes, I will. Don't worry. I will see you this evening."

"Let me know if that sleazeball tries to get cozy with you." Adam smirks at me. I giggle back at him, wondering when he will grow up.

I go through the grand lobby and head toward the big conference hall. After getting my ID checked, I proceed to the training area and sit down, waiting for our trainer to come. I am surprised to find out that Ethan Murray will be conducting today's session. *Oh crap! Adam will definitely freak out.* Ethan waves *hi* from a distance, to maintain his professionalism in front of the rest of the trainees. Our session starts with his noting that our previous trainer is ill, and he will be conducting today's sessions. During the entire session, he visits each trainee one by one, very professionally, but when he gets to me, he deliberately stands too close to me. I try to act cool and pretend it doesn't bother me. After three hours, one of the guys mentions that we need a lunch break. Immediately, Ethan Murray is at my side.

"You will do lunch with me. I need to talk to you," he whispers in my ear, but his invitation sounds more like a command. I don't say anything in return, as I want to hear what he has to say.

We don't speak until we're seated in the same restaurant as yesterday.

"You didn't reply to my text message." He looks at me through his glasses.

"You didn't ask anything. It was a statement." I pause for a moment and then add, "But thank you. It was quite flattering." I fake a smile.

"You should be used to it by now. Doesn't your boyfriend compliment you?"

"He has very unique ways of complimenting me, Mr. Murray." I adjust my scarf. "That's what makes him different from all other men." Murray's gaze gets deeper, a hint of jealousy in his eyes. I already see defeat in him. *Bring it on, you moron!* "You said you wanted to talk, Mr. Murray? Is it about the job? I haven't decided yet. It will be mine and Adam's mutual decision."

"Did you discuss it with him?"

"Yes, of course. He told me it's totally my decision, but I'm leaving it up to him to decide. After all, he means everything to me." I sound like a teenage girl who is madly in love with her boyfriend, but I have to act like this to make him believe that his shitty actions cannot harm Adam and it was a stupid idea for him to come after me with his pervert mind.

"You guys plan to get married?"

"I am sorry, Mr. Murray. That's a very personal question, and I would rather not answer it." *Buzz off, you prick.*

"You are a very special girl, Rania. I have no grudge against Adam, but he is not going to marry you. He uses women for his pleasure." His tone is serious. *So, the pervert can act well too.* "You need a person who can give you love, respect and trust. Adam is not your type."

"And what makes you different from him?" I tilt one of my eyebrows and ask sarcastically. His face goes pale, as if I have caught him red-handed. "Mr. Murray, I appreciate your concern, but I am still getting the love, respect and trust, even if he is getting the pleasure." *Oh my God! I sound like a whore.*

Murray starts to get really uncomfortable. He must have gotten the hint that I know something unpleasant about him.

"I am just warning you. Adam is not what he seems to be. He is very dangerous, Rania." Murray's eyes burn like fire. "I don't know what he has told you about me and I really don't care. I want you to stay safe and watch your step."

"I have always been attracted to danger. And just for your information, we don't discuss other people when we are together. When it is us, it is just us." I take a sip of water. "So, if you think that we discussed you, it never happened."

"He doesn't love you, Rania. You deserve better."

"As I said, Mr. Murray, I appreciate your concern, but trust me, I will not ask anyone if he loves me or not. I will decide for myself."

"Do you think he loves you?" He looks at me directly in the eyes, over his glasses.

"Love is a very personal feeling, Mr. Murray. I would rather not discuss it with a person who has no experience in it." I leave my seat, but he stops me.

"We haven't ordered lunch yet." He looks around to call a waiter.

"Thanks for inviting me, but I am not hungry today. Have a nice day, Mr. Murray."

I terminate our conversation, tired of his idiotic questions. As I walk out of the restaurant, I feel his eyes on me, all the way to the door.

PARANORMAL

♂

Finally, the long day has ended and it's time for me to pick up Rania. I knew she would be busy the whole day, so I didn't bother texting her, but I am curious whether she talked to Ethan Murray. I kept myself busy visiting some promising properties in the province of Alberta to figure out the business aspect with local builders. I didn't realize I would miss her company so badly. She is making me addicted to her, and I'm enjoying this addiction more than anything else in the world. I have never wanted anything so much as I want to see her smiling, sitting next to me and doing silly things like she did yesterday at the ice cream parlor. She is unpredictable, yet mesmerizing in her own way. Her personality changes startle me. On one hand, she is a fun-loving girl who enjoys all the little pleasures of life, and on the other hand I have seen her crying and screaming from her nightmares. I look up at the sky, wondering if God actually exists and if He is watching me. I pass a message to Him. *Please take away all her pain. She deserves better than nightmares.*

I reach the hotel lobby, where people are coming out of the conference hall. I wait for ten minutes, then try to call her. I get no response, so I head over to security.

"Hello. I'm here to pick up Miss Rania Ahmed. I can't reach her on her phone. I would appreciate it if you could send someone inside to see if she's still in a training session."

The security officer checks her name in his system and looks at me. "She left around 1 p.m."

"Are you sure?"

"Yes, definitely. We have her security badge. She didn't come back after returning her badge." This troubles me. *Why didn't she tell me she was leaving early?*

I call her again, but she still doesn't respond. I call our hotel and they inform me that she already came in. I rush back to the hotel. When I reach the room, the main level is empty. I see her jacket and handbag on one of the chairs. I sneak into her handbag and see her phone, along with the room access card, and her phone is turned off. I head upstairs to look for her, but to my surprise, she isn't there. I have a feeling of *déjà vu*, so I head for the golden drapes, hoping to find a balcony, but there is only a window there. I sit on the chaise and wonder what's going on with me lately.

In all the silence surrounding me, I hear a strange noise, like people whispering behind the washroom door. The light is off, but the voices are definitely coming from there. I go over and try to listen, but the whispers are so soft I can barely hear them. I open the door hesitantly. It's pitch dark, though I think I see a shadow moving. I switch on the light and find Rania standing in front of the mirror.

She's wearing only a towel, covering her from her breasts to halfway down her thighs. *What was she doing in the dark?* She doesn't move when I come in. She stands with wide eyes, frozen like a stone, facing the mirror. Her eyes have the same emptiness that I've seen in them during the other strange incidents. There is no sound now, no whispers. She stands mutely, as if time has stopped for her. I step behind her and look into her eyes through the mirror, but it's like she can't see me. The air feels like a vacuum, making it hard for me to breathe. It feels too heavy, yet too hollow—the same feeling I had yesterday when I tried to kiss her. Like there's a hidden presence in the room. The look in her eyes sends a shiver down my spine. Her hair is wet and tangled from her shower. I move it gently from her shoulders to see the marks on her back and shoulders. There are more than I realized.

I wave my hand in front of her eyes, but she doesn't blink. It doesn't even seem like she's breathing, but if she wasn't, she wouldn't be standing here. I cup her face in my hands and call her name. She doesn't respond, and her body is as cold as ice. I try to give her warmth with my touch. As soon as I touch her forehead with my lips, I hear her breathing against me. I look into her eyes, but they are like two deep dark stones. I repeat what I did the other night, touching her lips with my thumb. That time, her body was warm, but when I explored her face through my lips, it started to get cold. This time it's the opposite. She's cold, but when I touch her, I hear her breathing and her body begins to warm. She doesn't move, but her breath says everything. *She wants my touch, her body wants my touch, and I want it too.*

I move my lips over her face and inhale her fragrance. Her skin feels soft, like a rose petal, velvety under my lips. The sun is close to me and I want to burn in the light and be engulfed in her warmth. Just as I reach her lips, I hear a loud noise from the bedroom, as if someone turned on the television. I rush out there, thinking that someone is in the room, and will see her half-naked through the door. But in the bedroom, the television is off and there is no one there. All is quiet. I rush back to the washroom, but the door is closed. I open it without knocking, and find Rania dressed in her jeans and navy blue top, brushing her hair. *What the fuck?*

"You should knock before coming in," she says angrily. "We still have some boundaries, Adam. Don't try to cross them." She glares at me warningly through her reflection. I stand, dumbfounded. *How can she change clothes in less than a minute?* My heart starts beating out of control, my mind frantically trying to make sense of what's going on. I lean against the doorframe, feeling disoriented.

She turns around and leans toward me. "Are you all right, Adam?" She looks at me tenderly, touching my face. "You look pale." I look into her eyes. The frigid stare is gone, as is the anger. "Were you running?" She grabs my hand and pulls me out of the doorway, sitting me on the bed. "Your heart is beating very loudly. Even I can hear it." She picks up a water bottle from the bedside table and hands it to me. When I reach for it, I realize my hands are shaking. She notices my trembling fingers and holds them tightly. "Adam? Talk to me. Do you want me to call the doctor? Why are you shaking?" I look at her dubiously. How could she be standing frozen, wearing nothing but a towel, and seconds later she is completely dressed and turning my mind upside down? I gather all my courage to speak.

"Where were you?"

"I was in the washroom. You just saw me there."

"I went to pick you up at the summit. You weren't answering your phone. The security guard told me you left early."

"Oh, yeah. I was feeling low and my phone battery ran out. I came back to the room and went to sleep. I woke up half an hour ago and took a shower. I was coming out when you opened the door, without knocking."

"When did you dry your hair?" I touch her hair in puzzlement. She doesn't understand my question at all.

"Ten minutes ago. Why do you ask?"

"When I came in . . ." My voice breaks off. "Your hair was wet and now . . ." I run my fingers through her hair. "Did you dry your hair before I came?"

"Why are you asking all these weird questions?" She giggles at me, making me feel stupid. "Yes, I dried it before you came in. But why do you ask? What's with my hair?"

I scrutinize her face wordlessly, but her attitude is normal, as if nothing happened at all.

"When I came into the washroom, you were in a towel, with water dripping from your hair. And you were standing like . . ."

"Stop daydreaming, Adam. You think I would stand there and let you look at me half-naked in a towel?"

"I wasn't dreaming. I saw your body. You have burn marks on your back and shoulders, don't you?" When I ask that, her face pales, and she looks down at the floor in shock.

"How do you know, Adam?" She looks back at me with wide eyes.

"Because I saw them. I saw them the other night, too, before we had the Satan discussion. But I didn't say anything; you were too vulnerable."

She looks at me fiercely. "I don't know what you are talking about, Adam."

"I came in tonight and found you in the washroom, standing in darkness. I heard whispering and saw shadows, but when I turned on the light, it was only you, wrapped in a towel, staring." I take a deep breath to collect myself. "You were cold as ice, not even breathing, but when I kissed you on the forehead, I heard you start to breathe. And suddenly, I heard noises coming from in here, but no one was there. When I came back to you, you were all dressed and talking to me." I close my eyes after that, but I feel her hand touching my forehead, as if she is checking for a fever.

"Adam, I have no idea what are you talking about. You have been dreaming lately. This morning, you said there is a balcony outside, and now . . ." She places her palm on my forehead again. "Are you okay?"

"Do you have scars or not?" My sudden question scares her. She nods, but doesn't say anything. "If I had not seen your body, how would I know?"

"How come I don't remember you noticing my scars? Could it be your sixth sense? A state of premonition?" she asks confusedly.

"I don't believe in all that, Rania. It was real. You asked me about the other night, when you didn't remember how you got from the washroom into bed. That was real, and so is this."

She places a hand on my shoulder, hesitantly. "Adam, do you think I need to see the doctor? Is it a memory loss issue?" I stare at the blank wall in front of me.

"I don't know who needs to see the doctor, you or me. We have different stories of the same events." I check my watch and then look at her.

"Let's put it out of our minds. Pretend nothing happened. As long as we trust each other, nothing else matters to me." I get up from the bed and Rania looks at me blankly. "We have a flight to catch, back to Toronto. Time to pack up and go home."

During my packing, I get a chance to examine the gifts she gave me the other day. It is exciting, knowing she treasures our moments as much as I do. As we leave the room, she stops at the door and glances back.

"Have you forgotten something?" I ask her curiously.

"Nothing. Just looking at it. We created a memory here." She steps out of the room, leaving me speechless. *How can she say complex things so easily?*

I look back at the room, just the way she did. It is a strange feeling, hard to leave.

* * *

On our flight to Toronto, I hand her a Tiffany's box. She looks at me strangely.

"I bought this yesterday for Mother. Tell me what you think." Her expression changes instantly, brightening with a smile. She opens the box, looking dazzled.

"It's beautiful, Adam. You've made a lovely choice."

"Do you think she will like it? Or shall we get something else?" I ask her, looking at the hair clip.

"It's perfect. This will make her cry with happiness. But you know, Adam? It's not the gift; your presence is what matters to her. Even if you go empty-handed, she will shower you with love just the same." Her statements boost my spirits, and I keep her busy with conversation as we travel.

We reach her apartment building around midnight. I get out of the car with her. Either it's not as cold as Edmonton, or our bodies acclimated in the last few days.

"Thank you for a wonderful time, Rania. I will never forget it, ever," I say, holding both her hands as if I am taking a vow. She smiles shyly and looks down at the concrete.

"I should thank you for everything—the train, the flight, the hotel, the opera and saving me from Murray. I had no idea he was staying next to the room I was supposed to have."

"You never told me if you saw him today." I almost forgot to ask her. When I'm with her, time passes so quickly, and I don't realize it until it's over.

"Not much! We hardly spoke. He was curious about us. I made him believe . . ." She pauses and looks down shyly, smiling and blushing. I wait for her to continue. "I made him believe that we are in a relationship. And he kept warning me about you." We look at each other and then laugh hysterically at the same time. "I wish I could have made a video and showed you how he reacted."

"I believe you."

We stand here for a while, me holding her hands, wondering who will be the first to say good-bye. *Why is it so hard to say it?*

Are we addicted to each other? I am sure about myself, but I can't work out how she feels about me. She has always been so secretive and reserved. She pulls her hands from mine and looks toward the entrance door.

"I shall go now." I stay quiet. *Does she want to say something? Does she want me to come with her, to protect her from nightmares?*

Twice at the hotel suite I tried to kiss her, taking advantage of her weakness. I know if I come inside tonight, I will never be able to control the demon inside me.

"Good night," she says without looking at me, and turns toward the entrance. I watch her leaving me. *Why is it so hard to say good-bye tonight?*

I plan to meet her the next day for dinner, but that seems an eternity from now. She stops and turns around to look at me. I see something new in her eyes; she's never looked at me like this before. She comes running back to me and hugs me tightly. At her heated embrace, I feel my body crumbling into thousands of pieces.

What is this girl doing to me?

She burrows her mouth into my neck and whispers, "Thank you for everything, Adam." The warmth coming from her lips touches my neck and burns my whole body in a fraction of a second. She pulls away and, without meeting my eyes, turns and disappears behind the tinted glass doors.

And I crave more of my sun.

SOMETHING NEW

♀

I wake up around eleven in the morning. I've never slept so late in my life. I remember waking from a dream in the middle of the night, but it was not a nightmare. It was the first time in five years I'd slept alone without a nightmare, when Adam was not around. I'd been lost in the dark woods, and Adam had rescued me from the darkness.

Is it a message from God? Is He sending Adam to protect me?

I know Adam is not a guy to believe in relationships. He hardly believes in God. But still, I am spellbound and captivated by his presence. I slip out of bed and plug in my phone, which has been switched off since I left the training session after lunch. There are a few unread messages.

The first one is from Ethan Murray. I roll my eyes in frustration as I read it.

> *You have cast a spell on this poor man with your angelic beauty. You left without saying a word. Is that one of the characteristics of an enchantress?*

I delete his cheesy message without even thinking. The second message is from Mike, which brings a smile to my face.

> *Hey, girl! Still in Edmonton? Dad told me you would be back on Saturday. Can we dine out together? A movie or bowling? I am off duty on Saturday evening and all yours. Love ya!*

Mike will never stop showering his love on me—his messages are always like this. And I guess I am used to it. There is a message from Adam also, sent around 4 a.m. That was the same time I woke up from my dream.

> *Sorry I couldn't be there for you. Somehow, tonight, I felt if I'd stay with you, I would let my demon win. I was trying to protect you from it.*
> *He was awake at 4 a.m.? Thinking about me?*

Tons of questions juggle in my mind. I decide it's better to respond to the message, than create more questions in my brain. I plan to call Mike after breakfast and as for Adam, I think hard what to write.

> *Your soul defeated your demon last night. I didn't have any nightmares. It was your soul, who met mine in the dream.*
> *Thank you.*

I put my phone down and head to the washroom. Five minutes later, I hear my phone ringing. I rush out and check the ID to find Adam's name.

"Hi, good morning." His sweet voice comes as soon as I accept the call.

"Good morning or afternoon, whatever." I giggle. "How are you?"

"Never been so good. You dreamt about me, last night?" His voice is heavy from sleep, and I sense he is still in bed. My text must have woken him.

"Yes. No nightmares, surprisingly."

"What did you dream?"

"I was lost in the dark woods and you came from nowhere and led me out of them." Adam doesn't say anything. I hear him breathing.

"Adam? Are you there?"

"Yes, I am."

"What is it, then?"

"I dreamed the same thing, and woke up in the middle of the night and texted you without thinking."

We both are silent. I don't remember who hung up first, but neither of us said anything, not even good-bye.

After my breakfast, I call Mike to return his message.

"Somebody has got her memory back?" He sounds excited to hear from me.

"How are you, Mike?"

"I am good. On a duty, though," he says dryly. "We have a lot to talk about, Rania. I was wondering if we could meet. It's been a while." He's right. It has been a while. He was in Calgary for three months, and the day he came back was the day I met Adam for the first time. With Adam around all the time, I never got a chance to talk to my best friend properly. But he is asking about tonight. I know if I don't go with Adam, then he won't see his mother.

"I am sorry, Mike. Tonight is not possible. I am already—"

"Dating Gibson?" he interrupts me. I remain silent, so he continues. "Do you like him, Rania?"

His question totally surprises me. I am still quiet, not sure what to say, or am I too afraid to spill the beans? "Shall I take this silence as a 'yes?'"

"It's not what you think, Mike. We are just friends."

"So *just-a-friend* would chase you all the way to Edmonton?" *Shit. How does he know?* "Just because I stay quiet, doesn't mean I don't know anything." He takes a deep breath. "You remember Kevin? We took photography lessons together?"

"Yes, I remember. The Russian guy with nerd glasses?"

"Yes. Apparently, he was at the summit you attended. He was covering the shoot." *Oh, he told Mike.* "He saw you hugging a guy passionately coming out of the conference hall . . ." I listen to him quietly. *Hugging passionately? Is it true?* "He obviously knew it was Gibson, but then he also told me there was another man, some mature guy, who had eyes on you all the time and followed you when you were meeting Gibson. Did you complain about that weirdo to Gibson? Kevin told me they had an argument."

"The guy is Ethan Murray. He has a very high-profile job, but he's a sleaze and uses it to hit on girls. Unfortunately, he doesn't know he's trying to hit on the wrong girl this time." We both laugh. I ask, "Does Ben know . . ."

"You are my best friend, Rania. As well as I know you, I know my dad too. He is a blabber. I didn't tell him—I knew he would tell your father."

"Thank you, Mike. You are a true friend."

"Yes, and I love you too." His spontaneous remark makes me giggle. "So, he met you in Edmonton? I mean your new Richie rich boyfriend? Or you left from here together?"

"Stop calling him my boyfriend. We are just friends." I raise my voice. I hear Mike inhaling and I am sure he is probably rolling his eyes too.

"Then what should I call him? A stalker? A secret agent? What was he doing there?"

I take a deep breath. "It's a long story, Mike. He came to rescue me from Ethan Murray's plotting."

"What does Murray have to do with you?"

"Not with me, with Adam."

"So what about your date tonight with Mr. Richie rich?" He sounds sarcastic.

"His name is Adam." I roll my eyes again.

"I know, but Richie rich suits him more. After all, he knows how to use his money at the right time." He sounds hurt.

"It's not what you think. It is not a date, Mike. He is taking me to his parents' house." I skip my side of the story. How can I tell Mike that we were alone in a business class coach of Via Rail, all by ourselves for two days? *He certainly knows how to use his damn money.*

"What? Are you serious? You're going to meet his family?" It is his turn to raise his voice to me, but I remain quiet. "Isn't it too soon, Rania? You hardly know him."

"It's hard to explain, Mike. Can we talk about it some other time?"

"No, baby! We need to talk about it right now. He chased you to the other side of the country and now he's taking you to meet his parents. Has he proposed or what?"

"Oh my God, Mike! How could you think that? And why do you think, of all the women in the world, he would propose to me?"

"Because, among all the women in the world, he has chosen you to meet his parents." He spits his words in annoyance. "And of all the men in the world, I am the last one to know."

"Don't be sarcastic, Mike. You are the first one to know. And the last one too." I snap at him.

"Then why is he taking you there?"

"It's not him. It is me who is taking him there. He has some issues with them. I am just accompanying him, to make sure he behaves well."

"Ha!" He laughs hideously. "Since when have you started teaching manners?"

"Don't be ridiculous. He is a good guy. Sometimes he loses his patience. That's all."

"Okay, I trust you, girl. But, what if the news leaks out? You know how the paparazzi chase him like vultures. He is one bloody ticking time bomb." Mike's statement makes me speechless. He is right. What if someone spreads the news that I am going to his family home? This will definitely reach my father. Should I ask Adam to keep it private? But how can he? Anyone could see us there. "I hope that doesn't happen," Mike says. "Good luck teaching him manners. Take care."

He hangs up the phone without waiting for me to say good-bye. He sounds grouchy, but I know he's right. I should have thought about it, before committing to Adam, and now it's too late to back out. I will mess up everything. He has done so much for me, which I can never repay, but at least I can be by his side when he most needs a friend. I have complete faith in Mike, that he will be my secret keeper. Although Ben has always tried to dig out the words from his heart, he has always stood by me.

Time feels like it's passing too slowly. I want to see Adam soon, but I don't want to give him the wrong signals, when I don't know what I am feeling right now. I change my clothes and decide to hit the mall to get something for Adam's mother, since it's her birthday. I end up buying a beautiful flower-shaped brooch for her. It is a generic gift, perhaps, but appropriate for someone I don't know well.

AN UNSPOKEN TRUTH

♂

What time are we going for dinner?
I receive her text message around 6:15 p.m., while I'm driving.
Shit! I forgot to tell her what time. I reply to her immediately.

I'm on my way already. Sorry I didn't inform you earlier.
After thirty seconds, my phone beeps again.

*Then you will have to come up and wait for me. I am just
starting to get ready. I am not locking my front door, so
make yourself at home.*
I smile when I read her message. She's starting to trust me
a bit. When I reach her front door, I let myself in silently and
look around the living area. *She's still not ready.* There's a large
picture hanging on the wall over the couch—a black and white
photo of Rania blowing a dandelion head. Her image has been
captured beautifully, as if she was not aware that it was being
taken. Her black eyes are smiling innocently, her beautiful lips
pursing to blow, her skin so soft and fragile, creating a blaze
around her even in the still image. I lean closer to the picture to
see the photographer's name embossed on the bottom right. *Mike
Dynham.*

If he took this picture, that means he has the original. *Can
I ask him for a copy?* I wonder why didn't I notice it when I was
here last week. Was I too lost in her? I look around the living area
and see another photo of shooting stars in the starry night, over
a desert. It looks really magical. The picture says it was purchased
from a museum gift shop, with the title, "Inspired by Arabian

Nights." *So she likes sparkles in the sky also.* I smile and sit on a dining chair, waiting for her. She steps out of her room without even noticing me, and checks herself in the full-length mirror by the entrance closet. She is fixing her makeup, putting lipstick on her smooth lips, adjusting her top. She is humming, very low, and has no idea I'm watching her like a famished beast. She looks dazzling in a white lace skirt with a matching top; there is no way I can keep my eyes off her tonight. *Someone help me with the fucking lace!*

I can't resist. "Sing louder, beautiful. I can't hear you," I call out from the dining area. She looks at me in shock, as if she weren't expecting me at all.

"When did you come?"

I step toward her, not losing eye contact. When I come close enough, she steps back, but I still move closer to her. She steps back again, till her back is against the mirror. I place my hand on the mirror, right above her head, and touch her face with my other hand. She closes her eyes and breathes heavily. *Do I intimidate her?* Her divine beauty will absolutely drive me crazy someday. I smell her intoxicating fragrance, which drives me crazy all the time, but now isn't the right time to lose my senses. A few strands of hair are stuck behind her pearl earring, and.I untangle them and tuck them behind her ear. She opens her eyes, relief on her face. I gaze at her face, riveted, drinking in each and every feature. *She is so beautiful.*

At least this time she knows I'm here. "Do you know, *in every man's heart, there is a secret nerve that answers to the vibrations of beauty?*"[6] I whisper softly. Her body actually vibrates as I speak. *So I have the same effect on her that she does on me.* "You look like an angel fallen from the sky." She giggles, shakes her head and pushes me away, as if I cracked a joke. *When will she ever take my compliments seriously? Why doesn't she believe how beautiful she is?*

"I have to get my clutch. I am almost ready." She runs into her room, avoiding my intense gaze. *Stop being lustful toward her, Adam. She'll run away from you. This isn't part of a trust pact.*

My conscience argues my demon to sleep again, and I wait for her patiently. We don't speak through the whole hour-long drive to Burlington. She is lost in the music from the radio, and I am lost in

---

6   *Christopher Morley (1890-1957)*

her. She looks confident about meeting my family; in fact, I'm more hesitant and nervous than she is, facing them for the first time. The situation I have avoided for so many years is in front of me, and Rania has pushed me there in such a way that I didn't really realize it until now.

It's a mild evening tonight, very unexpected in December in Toronto, and neither of us are wearing winter jackets. I park the car in front of Moores' estate. It seems like a quiet family dinner, as I don't see any other cars, or else we're early. It's almost seven when we get to the front door. She waits for me to hit the bell, and I have no idea what is stopping me.

"I don't know what to say, Rania. It seems so unreal. I don't know how to handle it."

She places her hands firmly over mine. "Don't worry. I am with you." Her smile brings out my confidence. I ring the doorbell and it is opened by Mrs. Moore.

We step inside together. Mrs. Moore looks at me with wet eyes, covering her mouth with her hands. I have no idea what to do, so I look toward Rania. She gives me a look that says to hug Mrs. Moore. I do, and it's like a dam opening. She cries, holding my shirt tightly, not concerned about anyone else. I look up at Rania in confusion, and she has tears in her eyes too. Do all women react the same way when they're emotional? Rania says something mutely, just moving her lips, and I repeat after her.

"Happy Birthday . . ." I look toward Rania again. ". . . Mom."

Mrs. Moore stops crying and looks at me. "What did you just say?"

I look at her and then to Rania, who mouths the word again. "Mom," I say. Mrs. Moore smiles in the midst of her tears and starts kissing me on my cheeks, as if I'm a kid.

"Oh, my baby, I love you so much. I've missed you so much." She won't stop kissing me. I manage to get a glimpse of Rania and she passes a smile to me. *So, this is natural.* I feel really awkward right now, standing like this, my mother kissing me like a crazy woman. Finally, she stops and manages to look at me. She looks old, after so many years. I see Rania mouthing words to me again, so I repeat after her. "Happy Birthday." I hand over the gift. "Umm . . . this is for you." *Could this be more awkward?*

"For me? You remembered, Adam?" She looks at me and then to the gift bag. "Can I open it?" I nod in silence. She takes the box out of the bag and opens it. She starts crying again. "Adam, you still remember?" She hugs me tightly and cries again.

"Okay. Enough being so emotional." I hear a man's voice behind her, and he takes my mother in his arms. "You're making my wife cry and smile at the same time." He hugs her tightly and caresses her arms lovingly.

"Hello, Mr. Moore." I offer my hand for a handshake.

"Welcome home. It is really good to see you here, Adam. And who is this beautiful lady?" Mr. Moore looks at Rania.

Rania offers her hand. "Rania. Nice meeting you, Mr. Moore."

"Call me Brian, please." He holds Rania's hand firmly. "Hey love, you don't notice anyone besides your son?" Mr. Moore asks his wife.

"I'm sorry, Rania. How are you?" My mother hugs Rania tightly. "Thank you so much for bringing him. It would never have been possible without you. You have completed my family. I owe you for life."

Rania slides back and smiles at my mother. "Please don't mention it. I didn't do anything special, but I will make sure he behaves like a good boy tonight." She winks at Mom, which makes her laugh. "And yes, Happy Birthday, Mrs. Moore. That's for you." Rania hands my mother a small box. *That was very thoughtful of her.*

"Oh, thank you, beautiful. This is the best birthday of my life." She hugs Rania again and kisses her on her forehead. "Please call me Grace."

"Are we going to stand here in the foyer forever, or will you invite your son and his girlfriend to come in?" Mr. Moore eyes mother mischievously. We all step into the grand house and I see Eva in the hallway. She stands there silently, tears coming from her eyes. *Oh no! Not again.*

"Eva?" She stands frozen against the wall, unable to move. I look at Rania once again. I don't know why I keep looking to her for guidance. *Am I relying on her too much?* She pushes me toward Eva, and I go over and hug my sister. "How are you, Eva?" She cries in my arms. I'm not sure if her tears are from happiness or what. *I will never understand women.*

Brian again comes to the rescue. "Come on, Eva, don't get started like your mother. It's time to be happy that your brother is home. I can't handle two crying ladies in a row." He looks at Rania.

"I'm glad you're not next." He winks at Rania, who giggles back. Eva looks at Rania and without saying anything to me, she hugs Rania tightly, like they are two old friends who have met after a long separation.

"I'm so happy, Adam finally found a girl. I don't know what you've done, that he is here with you, but whatever you're doing, please don't stop it." She looks at Rania lovingly and I see Rania is totally confused. "Please keep on loving him like this. You two are perfect for each other." Rania looks at me quizzically, not sure what to say, so I speak on her behalf.

"Eva? Will you let us in and allow us to sit somewhere?"

"I'm sorry, Rania. Please, come in," she says apologetically. I sense Rania is getting uncomfortable with this entire tear-jerking situation. Everyone thinks we're in a romantic relationship and right now, we both are in such a state that we can't say anything to defend ourselves.

"I'll ask Mary to get us drinks. It's time to celebrate." With that, Mom disappears into the kitchen, leaving the four of us in the formal sitting area.

"So, Rania . . . where did you meet my brother? How did he ask you out? I am damn sure it was love at first sight for him. I wanna know everything." Eva sits next to Rania, bombarding her with questions like a kid. Rania looks at me in confusion, but as soon as I decide to speak, Mom comes in.

"Eva, stop making her nervous. Don't ask so many questions." Eva totally ignores her.

"Please, tell me, Rania. I want to know everything. And tell me, how is he in bed? I hope he shows some patience there." She glares at me and then smiles back to Rania. I roll my eyes in frustration, not sure how to shut my sister off. *She is too much.* Rania is silent, but she blushes deeply from shyness. *Why do I get hard from her blush?* She remains quiet and looks at me to answer the questions.

"Quiet, Eva. Don't start." I break in to rescue Rania. "If you want to know, I'll tell you. I met her outside my office, a week ago, okay?" I'm a little annoyed with my sister.

"So what did you feel, the first time you saw her?" she asks spontaneously.

"I was charmed. She is beautiful, so . . ."

"Aww . . . that is so so so romantic. And how did you ask her out for a date?" My mother and her husband look at us, smiling for some reason. Rania breaks in unexpectedly.

"We are just friends, Eva," she says, looking down at her hands. Eva looks at me and then at Rania, perplexed. Rania continues, "I am not his girlfriend."

"What? You think I'm gonna buy this? Why did the newspaper . . . ?"

"The media wants spice to fill up their pages," I interrupt.

"So, no sex?" she asks annoyingly, as if it's a sin not to do it.

"Enough, Eva. Help me in the kitchen, please." Mom takes her out of the room.

Eva keeps on talking. "I can't believe she's not his girlfriend. Why are they hiding? It's so damn obvious . . ." Her voice fades as they walk away. We're silent for a moment, and then Brian starts a conversation.

"Rania, what do you do?"

"I work for an advertising company, designing and publishing electronic catalogues." She smiles at him.

"That's pretty impressive." He acknowledges Rania and looks at me.

"Toast for the family." Mom and Eva step into the room with a tray full of champagne glasses. Eva places the tray on the glass table at the center of the room and offers everyone the toast. Rania looks at me anxiously, her eyes wanting me to say something.

"Eva, can you please bring some juice or soda for Rania? She is not a fan of champagne."

"Sure. Will apple juice be okay for you, Rania?" Rania nods with a smile. Mom watches me and Rania in speculation, back and forth. I don't know what's cooking in her mind, but I'm pretty sure there is something.

"Rania, your family lives in Toronto also?" She looks toward Rania with a smile. Meanwhile, Eva returns with a glass of apple juice.

"No. My dad is in Dubai. I don't have any siblings," Rania responds nervously. If they ask her about her mother, she'll be more nervous than she is now. I change the subject quickly.

"How are your studies going, Eva?" I switch the focus to my sister.

"Oh, very well. My post-graduate program is finishing this year. I plan to apply for PhD, once my thesis is approved."

"Where are you studying?" Rania asks, curious.

"I'm at the University of Toronto. Medieval Studies," Eva says, looking toward her. I see Rania hiding a smile or laughter, I'm not sure which, but she purses her lips and hides them with her clutch bag. I can see her dimples, and am curious to know what she's thinking.

"What's going on? Why are you smiling?"

She shakes her head and smiles noticeably. Eva and I both look at her quizzically. "Nothing! She reminds me of someone." She puts her hand over her mouth again.

"Who?" I ask her seriously. Eva also looks at her intently.

Rania doesn't look at me, but she looks at Eva and responds, "You remind me of a professor I read about recently, from the same university, in Italian Studies." She looks down at her glass, still smiling.

"Oh my God! Are you talking about that Dante specialist?" Eva asks her. Both the girls look at each other for a second, and then laugh out loud. The rest of us look at them, confused. Rania gets control of herself.

"You know, Eva, I actually went to that department to look for him." Rania sounds very passionate.

"Are you kidding me?" Eva says excitedly. "I'm actually studying there because of him. I seriously want that professor in my life." Both of them burst into laughter once again.

"Who are you talking about? You girls know the same person?" They both look at me and laugh again. Eva moves to sit on the glass table in front of us.

"Okay, Adam, I have a question for you." Her eyes sparkle. "Imagine your sister and your girlfriend, in love with the same man. A man who is very charismatic and alarmingly sexy, who has a very powerful personality. But you know he is a terrible sinner. Whom would you protect? Me or her?" She asks jokingly, but she has taken me off-guard. I gape at Rania, but she looks down, trying to control her laughter. She nudges Eva lightly.

"Come on, Eva. Stop teasing your brother. Look at his face." Both the girls start laughing again.

"Girls? What's going on? Who is this professor you're talking about?" Mom speaks from behind Eva.

"Oh, Mom, please. I need an answer from Adam. Come on, Adam. Tell me, who would you protect?" Eva looks deeply into my eyes. *Is she fucking serious?*

I look at both of them, back and forth. This is news to me. My sister and the girl who I care about most, are charmed by the same man? And they both are taking it so lightly? My mood changes immediately and I get up from my seat. "Rania, can I talk to you in private?"

She looks at me, surprised, not expecting this. Eva laughs again, but Rania doesn't.

"Come on, Eva. Stop teasing him. He is serious." Rania looks at Eva and then at me. "Sit down." She grabs my hand and pulls me toward the couch again.

"Eva is just kidding. We are talking about a fictional character. Coincidentally, she and I have read the same book." She puts her hand on mine, gently. "You don't need to answer her."

"Oh, Rania. Your boyfriend is so dramatic. How do you deal with him?" Eva looks exasperated.

"So, there is no man?" I ask Rania fervently.

"No, Adam. There is no one. We are talking about a book." Rania is still trying to control her laughter.

"And you say this is only friendship?" Eva interrupts impishly.

"Okay, kids, no more talking. Dinner is ready," my mother breaks in. During dinner, Rania and Eva talk about books and discuss the male characters like high school girls. The rest of us enjoy their conversation and don't say much. I've never seen Rania talk so much to anyone. This makes me realize I have never asked her if she has any girlfriends, and she's never talked about any. Seeing her like this with Eva, sharing so much at their first meeting, makes me admire her more. Why haven't I ever talked to her about her book characters? She feels, she thinks, she fantasizes, just like any other woman, no matter how much she encapsulates her heart and hides her feelings. She talks about fictional men and their attractions; why, then, did she call herself dead meat?

I remember when Mom married Brian, he already had two sons. Neither of them are here, so I ask Brian about them. "Is it just us tonight? I was expecting your sons as well."

"Well . . . Scott has moved to Calgary and Nathan is in California for work. He'll be back by Christmas, though." We continue with general conversation, and after dinner we shift back to the sitting area for dessert. Rania and Eva are still busy talking and I just admire Rania, how pretty she looks tonight. Mom sits next to me, and she whispers in my ear.

"You remind me of your father. The way you look at her. It is completely Richard."

I look at her apprehensively, not sure why she's talking about him. "So, you still remember the poor man?"

She looks down at her lap, trying to find words. "He was the first man in my life, Adam. How could I forget him?" Our conversation catches other people's attention.

"Dad, why don't you come and help me with the dessert?" Eva stands up and takes Brian with her. Rania follows them, but I stop her when she passes in front of me, grabbing her wrist tightly.

"We're leaving, Rania. Let's go." I rise with her.

"No, we are not going." She pushes me down hard, so I'm kneeling in front of my mother, and commands, "You are going to listen to her, without speaking a word, and I will make sure you don't act like a jerk." Mom looks toward Rania, and then to me, and I stare at her in surprise.

"You can't be serious, Rania. I don't want to listen to her."

"Yes, you will. Enough of your nonsense, Adam. I will not let you hurt your mother and yourself like this for a lifetime. At least, listen to what she has to say, and then you can leave whenever you want." She is actually shouting at me. I'd never realized she possesses the power to control me, but I kneel here mutely, confused. She takes my hands and places them in my mother's lap, over her hands. Tears fall from my mother's eyes, and she looks toward Rania with hope. "Don't worry, Grace. I am here and I will make sure your boy listens to every word you say." Rania gives a flashing smile to Mom.

"All my life, Adam, I've wanted to tell you why I left you and your dad, but you never gave me a chance." Mom lifts my chin so I can look into her eyes. I pull away a bit and hold Rania's hands tightly. I never thought I would listen to my mother like this. *I'm still not ready.*

She takes a deep breath and starts. "We loved each other from high school on. Richard was very romantic, but he lacked practicality. I was young and didn't realize that romance isn't enough in life. When you have a family, you need to become professional and serious, putting your romantic fantasies aside. I got married at the age of twenty. Richard was only a year older than me, and not even graduated from University. We started out doing odd jobs, and then Richard got lucky and started a small business." She pauses for a moment. "When you were born, we were in a good financial situation. I didn't know that sometimes, easy money is also easily taken away. Your father developed a gambling habit. He used to lose, but he used to win too. Winning made him greedy and in a couple of years, we lost everything. I started working again, and Brian was my new boss. Brian became my friend and I used to share my personal problems with him." She looks toward Rania and then down at her hands. The whole time, she hasn't looked at me once.

"Richard became an alcoholic to avoid his frustrations, and used to come home angry every night after losing money in the casinos. He used to take money from me, whatever I tried to save for you. When you were five, I started expecting Eva and things got worse than ever. He was never there with me. I questioned myself many times—what happened to our love—but never found any answer. Richard was in search of quick money, but not getting it was making him more frustrated with life. Brian supported me emotionally more and more. I wouldn't have survived, if Brian hadn't helped me out. His wife had died giving birth to Nathan, and left him with two sons to raise on his own. I used to go during my pregnancy and babysit his two sons, and he gave me a good amount to run my house." A tear runs down her cheek.

"Richard wasn't even there when Eva was born. Brian was there for me instead, taking care of me during Eva's birth, and looking after you as well. You remember me leaving you, but you don't remember your father fighting with me, do you?"

She's wrong. I do remember their fights. "One night, Richard became angry and claimed that I was betraying him with Brian, and Eva was not his baby. I left that night, without saying anything to you, and took Eva with me." She pauses for a moment. "I know you must have wondered why I took Eva. Richard never accepted Eva as his daughter. You were his son. If I had taken you with me, he would have filed a complaint against me. I wanted Richard to be responsible with his life; that's why I left you with him." She covers her face with her hands, and then wipes her tears. "Brian gave me immense love, but never in my life have I spent a day without thinking of you.

"Richard came to me many times, after I married Brian, and begged me to accept his apology, but I wanted to be true to Brian. He helped me when I needed someone most. He was my best friend, my mentor." She holds my face in her hands. "I never wanted to leave Richard. I never wanted to leave you, Adam. I have ached for you my whole life. Please don't hate me." I shut my eyes; I can't believe what she just said to me. All those years, I have hated her for betraying my father, and never gave her a chance to tell her side of things. I never knew my father was such a coward that he didn't have the courage to come clean.

"I would have lived with Richard with no money, if he hadn't accused me of a sin. He didn't trust me, and when there is no trust in a relationship, everything else is destroyed. But I never wanted you to hate Richard. He loved you all his life. He lived for you, Adam."

Rania embraces Mom tightly, and she bursts into tears on Rania's shoulder. I see Brian and Eva looking at us from the kitchen, but they don't come in. I sit here silent and expressionless, looking at the two most important women in my life. I wouldn't have known about Mom, if Rania hadn't pushed me into coming. Mom said she owes her for a lifetime, but now I say I owe Rania for eternity. She has blessed me with a family. She has given me all my childhood memories back, although she wasn't even a part of it. Rania lifts me up from my knees to relax on the sofa. *How did she know my knees felt so weak I wouldn't be able to stand on my own?* Rania sits beside me and places her hand on my shoulder.

"Are you okay, Adam? Do you want to stay or do you want to leave?" I can't make eye contact with her, or with anyone. Brian comes into the room just at the right time.

"My love has cried enough for tonight. Let me cheer her up." He holds mother in his arms and she smiles in embarrassment. *This guy has truly loved my mother.* She's right; she wouldn't have survived without Brian's love and trust in her life. He takes Mom into another room, but before leaving, he looks at Rania. "Hey, beautiful, would you like some music?" Rania stands up and helps me rise as well. We head to the music room, where there's a grand piano, as well as a few saxophones and violins hanging on the wall.

Bryan sits down on the piano bench, and Mom joins him. He says to me, "This is your mother's favorite song. Though I'm a poor singer, she listens to me every time and applauds, as if this is actually my song." He looks back to my mother. "Happy Birthday, my love." He gives her a passionate kiss. "But tonight, I dedicate this song to this beautiful lady." He points to Rania, who stares at Brian with bemusement. "Who made this family dinner possible, who made my Grace happy tonight." He calls to Rania and she walks over, blushing hard. He takes her hand and kisses her knuckles. "Thank you very much for completing us." She looks down shyly, not saying anything, and then moves to the corner, leaning against the wall.

Brian starts singing "Since I Fell for You" beautifully with the piano, while looking at Mom with absolute romance. *This is love.* They don't care if there are others in the room. They just look into each other's eyes, as if the outside world doesn't exist for them. I remember hearing this song at the restaurant, back in February, before I encountered that enchantress. The song has brought back all my memories of her. I look toward Rania, who is completely engrossed in the song and the romance. *Is this her fantasy? To love, till the end?* She's the first one to clap when the song ends. Eva comes into the room with a tray of ice cream cups. I see Rania smiling at the ice cream, and then at me. I know she's thinking of our last ice cream experience. She picks up two bowls and hands one to me, and we all head toward the living room.

It has been a very emotional evening for all of us, and I guess ice cream is the best way to melt down moments of grief. Eva starts her conversation again with Rania.

"Can I call you someday and we could meet for lunch?" she says, while filling her mouth with ice cream.

"Yes, sure." Rania replies enthusiastically.

"How about going this Friday to a club? We will party and dance and—"

"Rania doesn't go to clubs," I interrupt. Everyone looks at me quizzically, including Rania, surprised at my response.

"That's all right. I can come with you, Eva." Rania looks at my sister, ignoring me.

"Cool. We won't tell your dramatic boyfriend where we're going." The girls give each other high fives.

"You know I can find you anywhere, don't you?" I ask Rania seriously. Her expression changes from cheerful to intense. She looks at Eva and then at me, confused. Eva is glowering at me.

"Do you stalk her?" Eva punches my arm. Rania smirks at us, which confirms it for Eva. "Oh my God! I cannot believe my brother is a stalker. How do you cope with him?"

"I am used to it now." Rania is talking to Eva, but she looks intensely into my eyes. "It's hard to change him."

Both the girls laugh at me, making fun of my habit. Mom and Brian watch us happily, entertained by our arguments. Eva is sitting on the glass table, facing us, so she turns her head around toward Mom. "Do you hear, Mom? You gave birth to a stalker. What did you watch during your pregnancy? A CSI series?"

Everyone laughs at Eva's question, except me. I glare at my annoying sister, but she doesn't get a clue. *She was never so talkative before.* Does Rania's company make her act like a kid? Eva fires questions at Rania and they both start gossiping about Hollywood actors and their hot sexy looks, comparing them with their fictitious book characters. Then Eva interrogates Rania about me, and she spills about the ice cream event in Edmonton. She makes it sound quite funny, about the gays watching me, and all of us laugh with her, including me. It is a joy to see, how one person can light up a whole room with her presence. Eva disappears for a while. The whole time, I haven't had a chance to talk to Rania, as Eva has kept her so busy.

"You seem to have fun talking about me." I look at her intently. She just smiles and ignores my statement. Eva comes back holding a board game.

"Since we are all here for the first time, let's play a game together. Mom, Dad, you both are in. And you too, Mr. Stalker. The game suits your personality." She puts the Clue game down on the table and opens the box. Rania giggles over her statement. We pick our characters, while Eva gives us a brief introduction about how to play the game. Rania plays very earnestly, but I keep staring at her, which she doesn't notice until Eva points it out.

"Stop staring at her, Adam. I'm not keeping your girlfriend. You can take her home with you." She snaps her fingers in front of my eyes, to break my concentration. "Concentrate on the game. You haven't found a single clue, Mr. Stalker." I see Mom and Brian smirking at me, and Rania blushes. *Why is my sister so irritating tonight?* She looks toward Rania and whispers, though everyone hears her. "Is he this intense in bed?" Rania locks her gaze on her cards and doesn't say anything.

"Shut up, Eva. You are being extremely annoying tonight." She is embarrassing Rania.

"And you are becoming too bizarre over your girlfriend, Mr. Stalker. Stop staring at her like that. You plan to eat her up tonight?" she asks seriously, but Rania breaks into a comic laugh. She is no longer embarrassed, and it seems like she's enjoying Eva's pestering. "You call me if he gets too hard on you. Okay?" Rania smirks and nods to her. We continue our game, though I still don't concentrate at all. I want to talk to Rania in private, but Eva has made it impossible. I have so much to say to her. Brian and I drink whiskey as we play, while the ladies have another round of ice cream. *What is it with females and ice cream?* It reminds me of what Rania told me at the ice cream shop and I smile in my head.

Since I was not concentrating at all earlier, I don't realize Rania has won and proved me to be the killer, holding all the cards of my character, weapon and room. Eva claps loudly at Rania's victory, like she has won. I don't know how much whiskey I have consumed but when I pour my next glass, Rania holds my hand and stops me with a look. I put my drink down without arguing. Eva looks at both of us, back and forth.

"Seriously? Mr. Stalker obeys?" She punches Rania lightly on her arm. "Good going, Rania. At least there's someone to control him." She winks at Rania, making her blush again. I check my watch, ignoring my sister. It's almost midnight. I hadn't realized that we've been here for five hours. It seemed impossible to come here without Rania, and her company made it so easy for all of us. Mom checks the time also.

"Oh my! It's midnight. Time passed so quickly." She looks toward Rania. "Now I know why my son feels so drawn to you, Rania. We all are." *Why is everyone embarrassing her tonight?*

I can't tell them that she's not comfortable with being praised. There's no doubt that she has charmed everyone. I will have to talk to mother and Eva in private, asking them not to bombard her with so much stuff next time. She'll run away. I also see she's getting tired, but she hasn't complained yet.

I stand up from the couch and face everyone. "It's very late. We should be going." Everyone gets up to see us to the door.

"Why don't you stay here tonight, Rania? Let him go. I can drop you home in the morning. We'll watch movies the whole night and read books together." Eva grabs Rania's arm gently. Rania looks at me, but remains silent. I know she doesn't trust anyone, not even herself, due to her nightmares. That's why she's never had a roommate in her apartment. It is her secret, to be kept between us.

"She has work tomorrow." I take her arm from Eva and lead her out of the room.

"You are so controlling, Adam," Eva says. "Just say you want her to yourself. What work would she have? Tomorrow is Sunday." I turn around and face her.

"Are you this annoying all the time, or is today a special occasion?" I give my sister a serious look. Rania giggles at my question, which makes everyone smile. We head to the main door and everyone hugs Rania tightly, as if they don't want her to go.

Mom kisses Rania on her forehead. "God bless you, child. I didn't know my son had the talent to find such a gem. Stay with him always." She holds Rania's hands tightly. "And thank you for bringing him here." Rania hugs Mom back without saying anything. They treat her like their own daughter, and I am an outsider, but it doesn't bother me. I'm delighted everyone loves her so much. We exchange good-byes and step out of the house.

It has gotten a bit cold since we came in. I rush toward the car, holding Rania's hand, and open the back door. We both slip into the back seat.

"Hello, Miss Ahmed. How are you?" Ali welcomes us from the driver's seat.

"Hey, Ali. When did you come?" Rania asks.

"Just a few minutes ago. Hello, Mr. Gibson." He looks at me and I smile back at him.

"It's Saturday night. Doesn't your boss give you time off?" she asks Ali innocently. Poor Ali looks at me, but doesn't say anything.

"It's not safe to drive after drinking, Rania," I explain to her.

"But he has a life too. You being the boss doesn't mean . . ." I put my fingers on her lips to silence her. She doesn't speak after that.

The car starts moving, and Ali asks Rania if she's interested in listening to music. She acknowledges him with a smile.

Ali turns on the local radio station and Rania asks him to increase the volume. She gazes out the window and immerses herself in the music. During one of the songs, she rests her head on my shoulder, closing her eyes. I can see she is hiding tears. My body shivers at her vulnerability.

After a while, the radio station plays "Iris." I look at her and concentrate on the words in the song. Right now, my emotions are exactly the same as those of the singer. I want to confess everything, and I don't want to go home tonight. There is something so strong between us and we are not able to find the connection. We don't speak during the whole ride. When we reach her building, I call her name, but she doesn't respond. She's fallen asleep.

ACCEPTANCE

♀

"Rania, wake up." I hear Adam's voice. I open my eyes and he looks straight at me. "Wake up, princess. You're home."

"Did I fall sleep?" I gape in surprise. He looks at me with a smile in his eyes. He takes me out of the car and we enter the building. I have no idea if he is coming upstairs with me or just dropping me at my door. I stay quiet and go with the flow. I know he is drunk, and it is better he should go home after dropping me. I enter my apartment and he follows me. I sense from his body movements that he doesn't intend to leave right away. When I go into my living area, he grabs my hand and pushes me down on the sofa. He sits on an ottoman, facing me, and looks deeply into my eyes.

I feel he wants to say something, but he is struggling with the words. He locks his gaze on me and takes both my hands in his, touching them to his lips. He doesn't kiss my hands, but his lips rest on my knuckles and he closes his eyes, not speaking at all. I stay still, not sure what to say. He opens his eyes for a moment and I see tears clouding them. *Oh my God! Is he crying?* I feel his tears on my skin. He sobs into my hands, and there is nothing for me to say. Finally, he kisses both my hands and places them on his eyes, as if he is holding a sacred and holy thing that will soothe them. He repeats the motion a couple of times, kissing my knuckles and rubbing them over his eyes. He has locked my hands so tightly in his that I cannot even free them to wipe his tears, but he manages to wipe them with my hands. When he has stopped crying, he looks at me with watery eyes.

"Thank you for everything, Rania." He kisses my knuckles one more time and rubs them over his eyes. "I didn't know I was blessed with the greatest gift from God. I believe in Him now. I know He exists and He has sent you to me, to guide me." He touches my hands with his warm lips and speaks through them. "I was living in the dark. The light you showed me today . . ." He kisses my hands again. "I would have spent the rest of my life hating her. I didn't know I was hurting her so much. Thank you for protecting me from the sin I have been committing since childhood." *Oh! He is talking about Grace.*

"You bring everything good into my life. I feel like you're living in me now, as a part of me. I am as much as you are, Rania. No more. No less. I begin with you and I end at you. Please don't ever leave me." He puts his head down on my lap, hiding his face, and whispers from there. "Thank you for taking out all the thorns from my life. Thank you for giving me what I missed all my life." He pauses for a moment. "You are an answer to all my silent prayers."

He is not declaring clearly that he loves me, but whatever he just said is more than I imagined in my life. My heart swells so painfully that I fear it will burst out in front of him. He still rests his head on my lap, pressed over my hands. I take out one hand and rake my fingers through his hair. He digs his head into my lap with physical force, as I run my fingers again and again through his hair. Right now, his body tells me he only wants warmth from me. He turns his head to the side, taking my other hand from under his head and entwining his fingers in mine. "I don't want to stay alone tonight." He sits up and looks at me pleadingly. "Can I sleep here?" His eyes are reddened with tears and dazed with alcohol, but right now he is too emotional to take out his alcoholic urges on me. He wants a friend, with whom he can share his heart and seek comfort. I can't say no to him, so I smile at him in agreement. "Thank you." He gets up and I look at him quizzically. "Let me get my night clothes from the car." He leaves the apartment immediately.

Did he plan to stay with me tonight? It is not the first time that he has spent the night with me, but somehow today it seems odd. Maybe because it was always me who had been emotional in the past. It is hard to accept him being as sensitive as he is tonight. I rush to my washroom to change my clothes. It has been a tiring evening. I am very happy Adam has met his family. They are all incredible, and extremely loving at heart. I wonder why he avoided them for so long. Perhaps he did not know what he was missing, and that is why meeting them tonight made him so emotional.

When I come back after changing into my nightclothes, I see Adam gazing at the shooting star picture hanging behind the dining table. He looks at me and then back to the picture.

"What is this *Arabian Nights*?" he asks, still gazing at it.

"It's a book with compilation of many stories for one thousand and one nights, based on old Arabic and Persian folk tales."

"Interesting. Have you read it?"

"I have been reading them since my childhood. Different authors have translated the stories in different ways. It is always interesting to read the different interpretations."

"What is it about?" *Why he is still lost in the picture?*

"It's about King Sheharyar. Having been betrayed by his wife, he promises himself to hate women for the rest of his life. He marries every night, a new virgin from his kingdom, and executes her at sunrise. He keeps on doing it until all the virgins in his kingdom are dead. His vizier has a wise daughter name Sheharzaad, who asks her father if she can marry King Sheharyar and stop him from doing this sin. Her father warns her that if she fails, the king will also hang her at sunrise. So they get married and when the King enters her bedroom, she starts with a story. The whole night, the king listens to the story intently and is captivated by his new wife, as she is a very good storyteller. When the sunrise comes, her story is incomplete, so the king has no choice but to delay her execution until the next night, when she will finish her story." I pause for a moment and Adam looks at me with keen interest. "So every night, Sheharzaad continues with a story, but doesn't finish it before sunrise, so Sheharyar keeps on delaying her death order. They are completely fictitious and magical stories within stories, blended together, and she doesn't stop for one thousand and one nights. That's all it is about." I smile at Adam, finishing my explanation.

"Can you read it to me tonight? I'd like to hear it." He looks at me pleadingly.

"It's too long, Adam. It doesn't end in one night."

"I will be King Sheharyar and listen to my Sheharzaad for one thousand and one nights. How about that?" He looks at me intensely.

"You can't be serious?"

"Yes, Rania. I'm damn serious. I want to hear the stories." He steps toward me, which makes me take a step back.

"I can give you a hard copy. You can read it yourself."

"I want to hear it from your beautiful mouth. The way you have started the story, I will only listen to it from you and no one else." He moves closer to me with his drunken eyes. I keep backing up until I reach the wall. He puts his one hand over my head, completely surrounding me with his presence. He lifts his other hand to touch my face and my body starts to shiver at his touch. His hand is under my ear, caressing my cheek with his thumb. *Where do I go? Where do I run?*

He is making me so nervous. Why does my body become so bloody weak, whenever he touches me? Why does my body betray my mind when he looks at me like that? It is as if this body has only longed for this forbidden fruit to sate its appetite. All these years I have avoided this feeling; yet, he comes into my life in a totally different way, and touches every part of my body without touching it. *How does he do that?*

"You make everything sound so magical. I want to experience the same magic with you in these stories. Will you read it to me?" I don't see any lust in his eyes. Just tenderness and sensitivity in his voice and gaze. I avert my eyes and look at the floor.

"I will get the book." I escape from the bondage created by his presence, and head to my bedroom to fetch the book. He follows and stands behind me to look at my bookshelf. "I have a hard copy, as well as one on my e-reader. Which one do you want me to read?"

"I think it might be better to read from your e-reader. I'll hold it for you, and we can switch off the lights and read it in darkness, right?" *Oh my! What does he intend to do besides listening?*

His sudden question makes me nervous as hell, but I pretend to stay calm. I should trust him. If he has promised to protect me, then there is no way he will harm me. I pick up my book reader and Adam excuses himself so he can go and change his clothes. I sit on the bed and he returns in a few minutes and sits next to me, after turning off all the lights and lamps. We are in complete darkness; just the light from my book reader is glowing. He tucks both of us under the comforter, puts his arm around me and snuggles me in his embrace. My body starts to warm up as soon as he wraps his arms around me. His musky masculine fragrance diffuses in my blood like a drug and engages all my senses. His back rests on the headboard, and my head and back rest on his chest. I can easily hear his heart beating against my back, but I hope he isn't listening to my heart, which is pounding like a drum from this closeness. At least, reading this way, he will not see my face and his intense gaze won't throw me off track.

He caresses my arms softly, and goose bumps rise all over my body. I feel a jolt of electricity, even though our skins are separated by fabric. The wobbly fabric is no protection against his stimulating heat. It is as helpless as me, as his touch takes me to the world of fantasy. A world where no past haunts me, where Adam and I are floating in a paradise of pleasure—a paradise which has this forbidden fruit. I imagine crossing to the other side of the line where he is waiting for me to savor it. I long to touch him, feel him, to engrave this fruit on every inch of my body. I imagine his teeth grazing my neck; his hands run down to the small of my back as he separates the poor fabric from my skin. He touches me everywhere, without touching me at all. I am on the cusp of losing control, when I hear his voice bursting my bubble.

"Rania?" *Shit. Shit. Shit. What was I thinking?*

"Huh?"

"You have something on your mind." It is not a question; it's a damn statement. *Why do I keep forgetting he is a powerful mind reader?*

"I really liked Eva. I am glad she is recovered from what happened to her." I divert the topic. *Where the fuck was I?*

"Hmm. She is more annoying now." Adam almost whispers in my ear. I don't realize his face was so close to me until he speaks. His voice burns my nape and burrows deep down to my nerves, splitting them apart. "If you get tired, let me know. I will stop," I inform him gently, opening the book in my book reader. *And I am losing control.*

"Hmm." His voice is sleepy. I don't know why he wants to listen to the story right now. I hear his heart pounding against me, but I ignore it and start to read.

"*In the name of God, the Compassionate, the Merciful! Praise be to God, the Lord of the two worlds, and blessing and peace upon the Prince of the Prophets, our lord and master Muhammad, whom God blesses and preserves with abiding and continuing peace and blessing until the Day of the Faith! Of a verity, the doings of the ancients become a lesson to those that follow after, so that men look upon the admonitory events that have happened to others and take warning, and come to the knowledge of what befell bygone peoples and are restrained thereby. So glory be to Him who hath appointed the things that have been done aforetime for an example to those that come after! And of these admonitory instances are the histories called the Thousand Nights and One Night, with all their store of illustrious fables and relations.*"

I tap my reader and begin the story.

"*It is recorded in the chronicles of the things that have been done of time past that there lived once, in the olden days and in bygone ages and times, a king of the kings of the sons of Sasan, who reigned over the Islands of India and China and was lord of armies and guards and servants and retainers. He had two sons, an elder and a younger, who were both valiant cavaliers, but the elder was a stouter horseman than the younger. When their father died, he left his empire to his elder son, whose name was Sheharyar, and he took the government and ruled his subjects justly, so that the people of the country and of the empire loved him well, whilst his brother Shahzeman became King of Samarcand of Tartary . . .*"

I continue reading my stories within stories, confirming with Adam from time to time whether he is listening to me. It is already past three, but Adam is completely engrossed in the story. I keep on reading, and don't remember when I finally fall into sleep.

* * *

I wake up; it is around ten in the morning, and Adam is gone. I assume he must have woken up and left, to take care of whatever business he usually does on Sundays. I feel too lazy to get out of bed, but I grab my phone from the nightstand where it is sitting with my book reader. I'm hoping Adam left me a message. In fact, he left two.

*You fell asleep and left me hanging, right at the beginning
of a story about an ensorcelled prince.*

I smile at that.

*You are an amazing reader. You bring out all the expression
of the author. What fool would read from the book, if he has
you?*

He makes me feel more and more blessed. I know Adam
expresses every thought that comes into his head. Sometimes, I'm
jealous that he can communicate so easily. I always want to make
him feel as good as he makes me feel, but words fail me. I know
that what he feels for me is more than just friendship, but the good
thing is that he has not admitted it. Or, more accurately, he knows
I am not ready to accept his feelings.

I step into the living room and find Adam busy in the kitchen.
He gives me his million-dollar smile.

"Good morning, beautiful. You slept well?"

"Yes, I did. Thanks to you. No nightmares."

He parks a kiss on my forehead. "Are you okay with scrambled
eggs? That's the only thing I know how to make."

"Are you making breakfast?" I look at him in surprise. He
glances at me with a nod and starts beating the eggs. "Adam
Gibson, cooking for me? It's a privilege."

"Stop saying my name like that. I feel like you're making fun of
me." He takes a deep breath. "It creates distance between us." He
doesn't look at me, but his words travel down to my heart. I watch
him making tea and toasting bread, and scrambling the eggs. He
watches me watching him. "The last time I made breakfast was
for my father. I never cooked anything after he died." He pretends
to be casual, but I see the pain in his eyes. He goes silent after
that and I don't speak a word until he serves everything on the
breakfast bar. I sit next to him on a bar stool and start the meal.

He says, "If you hadn't been there last night, I wouldn't have
gotten a chance to hear the truth. I guess my father felt too guilty
to tell me. Though he never said that Mom left him for Brian,
I assumed she did. I had no idea that my hatred and anger was
hurting my mother so much." He doesn't say anything else during
the meal. When he sees I'm finished, he swivels my bar stool and
scoots it toward him. "There is nothing left in my life that you
don't know. And you know things about me no one else knows.

You are my only friend, Rania." He looks intently at me and I can see from his eyes he is speaking the truth. I lift the corner of my mouth in a smile, to let him know I accept what he said. "I believe trust is a two-way street. I have traveled far on my side, but when I see you . . ." He seems to be reading my face deeply. "Your road is blocked." I look down into my lap, not sure how to react. I know where he is heading—he wants to know about my past. He thinks that me hiding things means that I don't trust him as much as he trusts me. I can see hurt in his eyes, but there is nothing I can do about it. *How can I tell him that I am bound not to speak the truth to anyone?*

He continues, "I want to remove all the stones from your road, but when I try to, you just add more." He's still reading my face, but I am unable to look at him.

"Didn't I tell you, the first time we met, that I can't offer you anything?" I speak in a low whisper. "I was clear about that, Adam, but you still accepted it. So why are you changing your mind now?"

"I'm not forcing you into anything." He closes his eyes for a moment, then looks at me again. "If at any time you want someone to remove those stones from your road, please call me. I will wait forever, if necessary." His words diffuse in my blood, making my heart swell so much that I am unable to find space to breathe within me. *It will always be you, Adam, and no one else.* I've never trusted anyone so much in my life. He watches me carefully, but I keep my face down. There is an awkward silence between us until he speaks again.

"Do you trust me, Rania?" I still look down, but I nod. "You know that no matter what happens, I will not harm you or go against your will?" I acknowledge him again. He takes a deep breath and continues. "If I ask you to . . ." He looks away, seeming to have difficulty speaking. ". . . to move in with me, would you accept?"

This time he doesn't take his eyes off me, but waits patiently for me to speak. I look away to avoid his true feelings, but don't say a word. *Does he know what he is asking?* I'm not his partner or his girlfriend. Why would he want me to move in with him?

"I don't know how you've been living alone for five years, relying on those pills. I realize you didn't get a roommate because you don't want to let anyone know about your nightmares. I can't leave you alone, Rania. It kills me." He tilts his head down to focus on my face properly, but I close my eyes to hide my pain. "I'm not asking you to give up this apartment. You can always come back, if you don't feel safe with me, but . . ."

"It's not right, Adam. I am committing a sin every day, letting you sleep next to me, but after all those years of living with nightmares, I'm too selfish to stop. I never ask you to leave, because I know you are the only one who can guard me against my nightmares." I shake my head in distress. "I don't know how you are doing it, but I can't let myself be even more selfish. I know you want me to move in for *me* and not for yourself, but I just can't do that to you." I inhale sharply and pause for a moment. "Every time you touch me, I feel clearly how you feel about me. I know it is not just friendship, Adam, and I cannot give you any more than this. I'm sorry." I look in his eyes. "There are no stones in my way. I am bound with ropes, and I'm the only one who can unwind them. But whenever I try to untangle them, it becomes more complicated than before." He still looks at me mutely, so I continue. "I want you to know that if I ever manage to separate all my ropes, I will travel on your road and no one else's. That is the only promise I can give you."

I stand up and walk toward the living room, while his gaze still follows me from the kitchen. I don't look back at him because I don't want to see the disappointment in his eyes. I feel so ashamed that I can't be like other girls. Adam has no shortage of girls in his life. I don't understand what makes him come after me. Why does he keep on saying that he sees a light in me, when I feel it is the other way around? I turn back to him and say, "Maybe if you give it some more time. We've only known each other a week."

"Sometimes it takes a lifetime to understand someone, but there are other times when all you need is a moment of trust. I am waiting for that moment, Rania." He looks deeply into my eyes. We stay here facing each other forever, until our silence is broken by a beep from Adam's phone.

He picks it up from the counter and checks the screen. "Sorry, I have an emergency. Can I use your room? I have to do a videoconference with a client."

"Sure." I smile at him, and he walks into my bedroom and closes the door behind him. Poor him; he works on Sundays too.

I look around my kitchen and smile at the mess Adam has created. *Why don't men clean, when they cook?* He reminds me of my father when he used to cook for me and Mom on the weekend, and then it would take us two hours to clean up the kitchen. He'd use every pot, pan and utensil to make a single meal. Though Adam just made scrambled eggs and toast, he's used nearly all the pans. I start cleaning my kitchen, waiting for Adam to finish his call. He left his phone on the counter; he must have brought his laptop in the bag with his nightclothes. He still isn't out by the time I finish, so I go on to clean the rest of the apartment.

It gets to be one in the afternoon, so I start making lunch. I decide to make chicken club sandwiches, with fresh orange juice. When that's done, I sneak quietly into my bedroom to offer my afternoon prayers. Adam is sleeping peacefully on my bed like a child, his laptop lid still open. I look at him for a few minutes and head to the washroom to take a shower.

When I come out he's still sleeping, totally unaware of anything around him. I know he went to sleep after I did and woke up before me, which means he probably got no more than five hours' sleep. I lay my prayer mat on the floor by the side of the bed and start my prayers.

CELESTIAL

♂

I open my eyes sometime around mid-afternoon, judging by the sun through the window. When I turn, I see Rania deeply immersed in her prayers. She is covered from head to toe, with only her face, hands, and feet showing, and such is her concentration that I feel like she is talking directly to God. I keep watching her, the way she looks down and then bows deeply, her lips moving constantly. She looks divine and sacred, purity and innocence shining from her. The light I see emanating from her is so strong that I would be afraid to stand in front of her—I would burn up from the intensity. It will surely burn me someday, but the truth is I want to burn myself in this light. I recall my confessions of last night. *Did I say too much?* She's my friend, so she would definitely have understood what I was feeling at that moment. She has restored chapters of my life, which were burned and destroyed so long ago. I can't ever repay what she has done for me, but I promise myself that no matter what happens, I will always stand by her side. *But how long will you be able to keep her in your life, Adam? You are only living in the present. What about the future? Is there a future? Her light may not be only for you. You may need to let her go someday.* My brain is bombarding my heart with bitter truths. I don't know how long this is going to last, but I don't want to let go of it.

I see her moving her head back and forth and raising her hands, as if seeking something from God. I wonder what she's asking of Him. If I were able to pray, I would pray for her, ask God to end her pain and set her soul free from her terrible past. Though I don't know the details, those scars were enough to give me an idea of what she's been through. She finishes her prayers and looks at me with a smile.

"You slept well?"

"You look beautiful in your prayer scarf. Very sacred and pure." She looks down shyly. I glance up at the art on the wall above her prayer spot. It is something written in Arabic, in a bronze frame. She follows my gaze to it, then looks back to me.

"What is that? What does it say?" I ask her, curious.

"Word of God, from the Holy Quran, an important part of prayer. It's called *Fateha*, meaning 'the Opening.'"

"Can you read it to me?"

She looks up at me in surprise. "You really want to know?"

"I want to know what you were saying to God, when you were praying," I say. She smiles and folds her prayer mat, then takes the frame from the wall and sits beside me. She moves her fingers over the Arabic inscription and translates for me.

"In The Name of Allah, Most Compassionate, Ever Merciful. All praises be to Allah alone, the Sustainer of all the worlds. Most Compassionate, Ever-Merciful. Master of the Day of Judgment. You alone do we worship and to You alone, we look for help. Show us the straight path. The path of those upon whom, You have bestowed Your favors. Not of those, who have been afflicted with wrath and nor of those, who have gone astray."

"You say this in every prayer?" I look at the frame and back to her.

"Yes, and much more like this." She stands up and hangs the frame back on the wall.

"It definitely looks like the word of God. A good approach to see the right path," I say, placing my feet on the floor. "But do you think He always listens to you?" My question catches her attention. She takes off her scarf and sits beside me again, facing the wall.

"He listens to everyone, Adam. If you pray on this mat or anywhere else, He always listens. About the answering—we humans are very impatient. Sometimes, we want our wishes to be answered on the spot, but what God has decided for us is much better than our imagination. We feel sometimes that He is not listening and not answering our prayers, but maybe, He has kept something for us far better than what our heart desires." She takes my hand in hers and looks at me. "So whenever you feel like making a wish, always wish that whatever He gives you, should be beneficial for you. In this way, all your good and genuine wishes would be answered."

"Sometimes, I envy that you have such a strong faith. How can someone possibly be—"

"That's what I am saying, Adam. Seek for the right path from Him and not the wishes. Your wishes will eventually be answered, once you are on the path." She looks into my eyes with sincerity. "When Grace was with your father, she might have wished for a happy life with him, but what God gave her was much more blessed. Now when you see Grace and Brian, don't you think they were meant for each other? God acknowledged Grace's goodness and He awarded her more than her heart desired. So when your wishes or prayers are not answered, don't think that they are not accepted. They are, but they will be heeded sooner or later, in a better form. More than you imagine."

We look at each other for a while. I agree with her, when it comes to Grace and Brian. I don't know what she wished for, but what she got meant her prayer was answered.

"Do you pray for yourself, Rania?" I keep looking at her, but she averts her eyes and stares blankly at the wall. "I mean just for yourself, asking Him to get rid of your nightmares?"

She stays quiet for a moment, then smiles. "I don't remember how I asked Him to end my nightmares, but when I see you, I feel that He has already answered my prayer." She walks out of the room without saying anything further, leaving me speechless. *Am I an answer to her prayers?*

How can she deliver those deep words so easily? Does she realize what she just said to me? If I am actually an answer to her silent prayer, then she has burdened me with a lot of responsibility. I will have to make sure that the reward she has got remains a blessing to her, and not a curse. If she is talking about how my presence keeps away her nightmares, then she may be right, but what about other prayers, regarding her past and her scars? *Am I an answer for that too?* There are so many unanswered questions piled up in my mind, but somehow, the boundary she's set won't let me ask them. I know if I try to cross it, I will burn myself. Should I take the risk, or should I wait for her to erase her boundaries and come out of her capsule?

I go look for her and find her busy in the kitchen, setting plates on the countertop.

"Lunch time, Mr. Gibson." She smiles at me innocently. I walk over and sit on the bar stool.

"You were making lunch, while I was sleeping?"

"Yeah, and cleaning my home also."

"It already looked clean to me."

"I like perfection, Mr. Gibson." She smirks at me. "I'm almost out of groceries, so I used whatever was available in my fridge." She serves me a plate with a sandwich and green salad. I take a sip of fresh orange juice, which tastes extremely good. I take a bite from the sandwich and look at her. She is waiting, probably for my feedback.

"Apart from the beauty and grace you carry in your body and heart, Miss Ahmed, you also possess culinary skills. You have impressed me," I say, with my mouth full. She giggles at me, and starts eating. "You always amuse me, Miss Ahmed. What other skills do you have? Is there any other surprise?"

She looks up from her glass and smiles. "Surprises." She emphasizes the word. "Jokes aside, I don't think I have any skills, so don't over-praise me."

"Oh yeah? You want me to count them?" I look around the room and then back to her. "Let's see. You are good in your field, I mean your graphic design thing, of course. And then you dance like an enchantress." I count her skills on my fingers and she smiles at me from her heart. "And you charm everyone around you."

"Really?" she interrupts with surprise.

"Oh, so you want me to count the victims. Let's see . . ." I hear her giggling at me. "Apart from the badly awestruck Adam Gibson, there were seventeen men at the party last week, who were deprived of the privilege of dancing with you. Then we have Mike, of course, and my family—Brian, Grace and Eva. There were also the Senator and his wife we met at the opera, and the other men who were literally drooling at you there, and the souvenir store girl, who was smitten, and then my special man Ali and . . ." She laughs heartily at my way of counting. "And I don't know how many more to come."

She shakes her head with her innocent laugh. "Ali? Where did he come from?"

"Oh yes, Miss Ahmed. You have charmed that poor guy too. He says *hi* to you before he even notices me, when he sees us together. As if I don't exist when you're around."

"He's only being nice to me."

"Oh, sure, whatever. So where were we . . ." I grin at her. "Your skills . . . as I see, you cook well, which makes me take a decision that I should come here every night for dinner. And there are many more, which are actually too personal to tell you right now, but best of all, you are an amazing storyteller." She looks down at her juice shyly, avoiding my smoldering gaze. "When you were reading the book to me, I actually felt myself back in time being King Sheharyar, and that you were my Sheharzaad, telling me all the magical stories."

"Then it is not my skill, Adam. It is the author's skill, which created an imaginary world for you."

"I agree a bit, but I don't think it would be the same if I read it myself. It wasn't me who created the imaginary world. I stepped into your world, the way you created the magic around us. It actually made me believe that I was part of those stories."

I take a deep breath. "In fact, you are a secret thief." I wink at her and she looks at me, perplexed. "You have stolen my capability of reading stories on my own. It could never be the same."

I think some more. "So, other than that, you know how to run and make a man chase and stalk you, even if that isn't his nature."

My statement makes her giggle. She goes into the kitchen to get something from the fridge. As she looks inside it, she says, "I am a good runner. It is truly hard to catch me."

"Oh yeah? I can catch you anytime, anywhere, Miss Ahmed. You have no idea how my intelligence service works."

She takes out the chilled water and pours some into a glass. "The catch doesn't require intelligence, Mr. Gibson. It requires stamina." With that, she grins at me mischievously, and I instantly read what is going on in her naughty mind. *So she wants to play games? She wants me to chase her?* I stand up from my seat, and she immediately puts the water down and runs toward the living room. I go after her and she screams with excitement.

"You don't know this, Miss Ahmed, but I work out for two hours every day. It has given me enough stamina." I keep chasing her. She runs behind one couch and I follow her. "You have provoked the wrong man this time." She runs crazily, like a child, still laughing, and I follow her like an idiot. She rushes into her bedroom and hops on the bed, rolling to the other side. I shut the door behind me and take a short cut to the other side, grabbing her arm and pushing her down on the bed. She screams again, still laughing, as I pin both her hands to the mattress, her wrists locked in my hands. But when she looks up into my eyes, she recognizes the intensity in them.

We both try to catch our breath, but I'm still pinning her wrists to the bed. I can feel her heart pounding under me. We look at each other, lost, saying no words. Our eyes say everything. *Is it the right time to kiss her?* As soon as I bring my mouth close to hers, she closes her eyes to avoid my heat. I am an inch away from her lips when she starts to breathe harder and opens her eyes, looking frightened. She glances toward the door, as if somebody is standing there, but I don't see anyone. I do feel the heaviness in the air that I've felt before.

"Let me go." She closes her eyes again. "Adam, please." I roll away, releasing my grip, wondering what happened to the laughing Rania who was here a few minutes ago. She sits up immediately, but her eyes are locked on the wall beside the door.

I don't know what happens to her every time I try to kiss her, but I can see there's something terribly wrong. I assume some asshole from her past has hurt her so much that her body is conditioned to reject intimate encounters. But it also seems like she feels someone's presence in our private moments. She's never frightened when we talk, or dance, or eat together. She is still panting, staring at the wall, and when I touch her on the shoulder, she shrinks back in fear and gives tiny scream.

"It's just me, Rania." She looks back to me. I see the same torture in her eyes that consumes her nightmares.

She walks out of the bedroom and I follow her. She fetches water for herself, but she is fighting hard for her breath, leaning against the counter. Her body language warns me not to try to get close to her, or even talk to her. I sit quietly on the couch, but my eyes still watch her every move. She busies herself with picking up our lunch plates and cleaning up the kitchen. She takes out the mop and starts mopping the floor. *Why is she cleaning an already clean floor? Is she one of those people who clean wildly to ward off panic attacks?* My phone chimes, breaking the silence.

"Yes, Ali. Yes . . . what? Are you serious? Who? That's . . . yes, I'm still here . . . okay, I'm coming down . . . you have security? I don't believe it . . ." I hang up the phone and Rania looks at me, bewildered. I go down to meet Ali in the lobby. He is waiting for me with the newspaper in his hand.

"Who do you think leaked the news?" Ali asks me. I look at the paper, which has a picture of Rania and me taken outside Moore's estate. There is another picture of us standing outside this building. The article says that many people saw me go upstairs with her last night, which to them confirms our relationship. *How is she going to face her father now?* I don't care what they write about me, but I don't want her reputation ruined.

I come back to her apartment and sit down on the couch without saying anything. She sits opposite me on the ottoman, but doesn't ask any questions. She's probably waiting for me to say something.

"Here," I hand her the newspaper. "Someone has leaked the news of our visit to my parents last night. It is also on the Internet." She just looks at me with shock. "And apparently, the media know that I stayed here with you last night. Some of the photographers are still downstairs, waiting to snap us together for their entertainment magazines."

Rania covers her mouth with her hands. I don't know what to say.

"Damn it!" I stand up, raking my fingers in my hair. "I should have backed up the security there, and outside this building."

She stands up to face me. "Adam? Are you afraid of being caught with me? If my company is spoiling your reputation, then . . ."

"It's not about my reputation, dammit. It's about you. I promised to protect your privacy. This news could easily reach your father, and then he would ask you to stay away from me, which I can't afford." I see her shocked face—her expression says she didn't see that coming. "I don't know for what bloody reason you're hiding your past from me, but I am damn sure that those vultures are going to dig out everything about you and I will have to read it in the papers." I move fiercely about the room. She sits down to regain her balance, as my response has definitely taken her off guard. "I can't protect you when I don't know what I'm protecting. I've tried to ask you so many times, but you kept pushing me away." I sit down on the couch and hold her hands. "They're not here for me, Rania. They're here for you. So please, if there's anything you haven't told me, tell me now." She just looks at me blankly and I realize she has no plans to spill the beans. Her phone chimes and she drops my hands to answer it.

"Hello . . . Baba? How are you?" There is a silence. "No, Baba . . . there is nothing like that . . . he is only a friend . . . just like Mike . . . I swear, Baba . . . I promise . . ." She ends her phone call and looks at me. It seems like her father hung up on her. She's trembling, and I wrap my arms around her. She bursts into tears. I see how hurt she is, but I don't know if it's the news or her father's attitude that hurt her. She wasn't this upset last week, when the first pictures were in the paper.

"This is the first time I've heard his voice in five years." She speaks into my chest, trying to catch her breath between sobs. "He didn't even ask me how I am . . . all he had to ask was . . ." She starts crying again. I tighten my hug to make her feel that I'll always be at her side. "I don't deserve any goodness, Adam. I am the worst daughter a man can ever have."

I pull her away to look into her eyes. She avoids any eye contact with me. I brush her hair away from her face and hold her face in my hands.

"Don't ever say that, Rania. You deserve everything good in life."

"No, Adam, I don't. Please, don't think so highly of me. My father hates me."

"Why do you say that, baby? No one can ever hate his child. And you are his only child. Why would he hate you?"

"Because I killed his wife, Adam," she screams at me. "I killed my mother. I took away the love of his life." She hides her face in her hands. I'm in shock. *How could she have killed her mother?* She can't even kill an insect. I move her hands away from her face so I can see her. She still doesn't look at me, but manages to speak. "He hasn't spoken to me since Mom's death. We lived like strangers under the same roof for three months. He didn't even say good-bye to me when I came to Toronto. And now . . . after so many years, I hear his voice . . . he never missed me, Adam. If Mom doesn't exist, then I don't exist. I am just a dark lost shadow now, living under a curse."

I have no idea what to say to all that. I don't really believe that she could kill her mother.

"I know you couldn't kill anyone, Rania. But I want to know what happened."

She inhales deeply and closes her eyes in pain. "Mom and I were in the car. I was driving. Baba was never happy with my habit of speeding. We had an accident with a truck, and . . ." Tears cloud her eyes. "I bloody killed her. Why didn't I die instead?" She hides her face in despair and starts crying again. *Why does she blame herself for an accident?* It could happen to anyone. Did her father make her believe that she actually killed her mother?

"I am very sorry to hear about this, but it was an accident. Why do you blame yourself?"

"Because I was driving. I was speeding." *So she can drive, but her confidence is shattered after her mother's death.* I wonder now, if the accident was so bad, if she was hurt too. She answers the question without my asking. "I was in a coma for three days. When I woke up, I heard from my aunt that my mom's funeral was over. I didn't even get a chance to say a prayer by her side. My dad never came to the hospital to see me." She takes a deep breath. I see how painful it is for her to tell me this. "I was in the hospital for ten more days. He didn't come once. I told myself he was in shock, because I knew how much he loved my mom. I deluded myself that he didn't want to inflict his pain on me, but that was not true. He didn't want to see *me*." She looks down at her fingers.

"One night after I came home, he got drunk and said everything that was burdening his soul. He blamed me for killing his wife, he told me how much he hates me, he told me he didn't want to see me ever again because I make him remember that his love is no more." She rests her head on the couch and closes her eyes. *How could her dad torture her like this?* And now, when she is finally able to move on, how can he try to stop her being close to me? Is this the reason why she pushes me away all the time? Because she thinks she killed her mother and doesn't deserve happiness? I hug her tightly to warm her from my embrace, but she is still trembling.

I have no idea how to comfort her, but I sit with her, trying to reassure her with my presence. She rests her head on my shoulder, but doesn't open her eyes. "I can't hurt him even more, Adam. I have taken everything from him. His job is all that's left. I don't want to ruin his reputation." She doesn't say she can't continue our friendship, but I know that's what she means. I promised to protect her privacy, but I failed. This problem seems to be a sign that I should leave her alone. *No, I can't leave her, when I know she is in so much pain.* I will never leave unless she asks me to. Right now, she looks exhausted. I hold her in my arms and start running my fingers gently through her hair.

"I haven't told anyone about this, Adam, what my dad said to me." She looks up at me. "Please, don't ever break my trust."

"Does Mike know?"

"I told you. No one knows. Mike knows about my mom's death, obviously, but not what my dad told me that night. It is too bitter to share."

I look into her eyes and say sincerely, "Thanks for trusting me." We go quiet again, trying to gauge each other's feelings, until she speaks again.

"Adam?"

"Hmm?"

"If one day I tell you some things about me, will you believe me?"

I look at her to reassure her. "I'd always believe you. I know you don't lie, Rania."

She looks down at my collar, trying to find words. "Even if . . . even if it sounds unreal . . . would you still believe it?" I check her face, trying to read every expression, work out what she's trying to tell me.

"I will wait for the day when you tell me everything. And trust me, I will believe you." I give her a kiss on her forehead and she closes her eyes instantly at my touch.

"If I tell you something someday that sounds unbelievable, will you believe me too?" I ask, brushing my fingers in her soft hair. "If I tell you . . . you remind me of someone I met but . . ." She looks at me quizzically, and nods. Her eyes tell me that she will believe me, if I ever tell her.

We sit here for I don't know how long. I feel like she needs me as much as I need her. We each lack something that can be found in the other, but neither of us knows exactly what. Finally, I ask her something I've wanted to ask since I visited Edmonton with her.

"If I ask you to give me two weeks of your life, would you do it?" She looks at me, her eyebrows furrowed. I know she doesn't understand what I mean. "I want to see this city with you. Would you show it to me?" She still looks puzzled. *Okay, I need to explain.* "Last night, when you were asleep, I saw the photo album you and Mike made. You guys have created so many memories together, it made me envious. You've visited so many places in and around the city. I don't have any memories with anyone. Would you make a memory with me?" She still doesn't say anything, so I continue, "I want to see museums, art galleries, tourist attractions, everything. I want to relive the life I missed. And I want to relive it with you."

"Adam, I don't know what to say. This is your city. You've always lived here."

"It's not that I haven't seen it. I went to the science center with my grade school class, and the museum during high school. But I never did things on my own, just for fun. I've never even walked down Niagara Falls Street." She opens her mouth in shock, totally disbelieving. "I've seen it from the top floors of hotels, when I attended meetings and conferences. But not close up. When we roamed around the streets of Edmonton, I realized how these little things create treasured moments. I want to build memories for myself." I take a deep breath. She listens to me intently. "I know it sounds totally strange to you, but can you take off from work for two weeks, until Christmas?"

She's still looking at me in shock. *Why isn't she getting this?*

"Adam Gibson wants me to be his guide?" She smirks mischievously. "I am honored."

"I'm serious, Rania. I want to see everything, the way *you* see it. You make everything magical. I'm tired of living an artificial life with meetings and conferences and public appearances all the time. I'm tired of being scrutinized: what I wear, what I do, what I eat, where I go. I just want to live a normal life. And I feel normal when I'm with you."

"So you don't think you'd be scrutinized when you're roaming around in public places with me?"

"I don't care, as long as it doesn't bother you."

"It doesn't bother me, Adam. You're my friend. It's okay if the paparazzi are chasing you and linking you with me. I have already told my dad that we are only friends. If he is not buying the idea, then I can't really help it. I know my heart is clear, so I really don't give a shit what people say about us."

SAMREEN AHSAN

"That's my girl." I smile at her sincerely. "So, will you give me these two weeks of your life?"

"Sure. Let me talk to Ben and tell him I'm taking off. I'm sure it won't be a problem. I haven't taken a vacation in years." She pauses for a moment. "But I have some conditions. If you agree, then I agree to give you my life for two weeks." I look at her quizzically, so she continues. "No spending money lavishly, no reserving places just for us. They are public places, so we visit them the way they are. Just like normal people. Okay?"

"Agreed. Anything else?"

"We will buy our own tickets and our own meals. And I expect you not to argue."

"You won't let me pay for the tickets? Why not?"

"Because we are not dating, Mr. Gibson. So be a gentleman and agree to my terms."

"Gentlemen don't let their ladies pay," I say blankly.

"Okay, then be a dirty friend. I want to be equal in this."

I roll my eyes at her. "Okay, agreed. Next?"

"We will travel the way I travel. You want to see the city through my eyes, then you will have to travel with me on public transport. No expensive cars and helicopter rides. Okay?"

"What? Are you crazy? You expect me to ride on subways and buses? Why would I do that? I have a car."

"Mr. Gibson, I know you have *cars* and not just one car. But like you said, you want to lead a normal life. If you think my life is normal, then no cars." She crosses her arms over her chest.

"You are impossible." I shake my head in disbelief.

"You can add that to my skill set you just mentioned." She winks at me with a flashing smile. I roll my eyes again at her.

"I agreed to your pay-your-own-way condition. You can't be serious on that. Come on."

"Okay, then split this condition. Anything within Toronto, we will use public transport. Anything outside the city, you can bring your grand cars, whatever." She is so hard to convince sometimes. Why do I always let her win? But I have asked such a huge favor from her, I have no choice other than to agree.

"All right."

She shifts a bit to face me directly. I see the excitement in her body language. "Okay, so where do you want to start?"

"Anywhere. I will just follow you."

250

"Will you be able to take off from your business for two weeks, Adam?"

"I have worked a lot, Rania. I'm tired of running. I need to rest."

"Cool. So be ready for surprises." She smiles at me.

"So tell me what amazes you, when you hang out?"

"The whole world amazes me. I haven't seen it all, but I'm pretty sure it is beautiful, because God has put perfection everywhere."

"So we will see the whole world one day, and amaze ourselves." I smile at her and she gives me a bewildered look. My phone chimes with a reminder. "Shit." I shake my head furiously. "I totally forgot. I have a dinner to attend at the mayor's house, tonight." I look at her, and she smiles. "What? Why are you smiling?"

"Nothing. I was imagining what the CEO of Gibson Enterprises will look like, traveling in a subway, hanging around in museums and other public places—the person who meets mayors and senators and endorses high-end brands. He will be encountering a totally different life."

"It's because you're making me do things I never imagined doing. You have the capability to tame anyone. So I better add that to your skill set." She giggles at my compliment to her. It is almost five in the evening and I have no choice but to go home and change for the party.

"How about you join me at the dinner? I will pick you up in an hour."

"No way. My Adam is not a CEO of an empire, so he would never expect me to accompany him to official meetings. The Adam I know is my friend, who still needs training on how to do justice to an ice cream," she says, adjusting the collar of my T-shirt. *My Adam! So very sexy.* "You go and transform yourself into a CEO now, and I will text you about the plan tomorrow."

"You are throwing me out of your house, huh?"

"Yes, certainly. Because this man right now is a CEO who is invited to some lavish party." She points to my chest. "And he needs to go there because he has already committed."

"All right. I'll call you when I'm done. I really wish you'd come, though. I'm going to be bored to death. All they talk about is politics." I wrinkle my nose in disgust and she giggles at me. I fetch my jacket from the closet, kiss her on the forehead, and leave for the boring dinner.

CONFRONTATION

♀

I don't believe I just agreed to roam around the city for two weeks with Adam. Photographers are crazily lined up outside my building to confirm if he stayed with me last night. So much is already out there, and now I've agreed to risk my privacy for him again. *What is wrong with me? Why do I agree to whatever he asks?* Never in my wildest dreams have I imagined that I would be spending days and nights with a person to whom I'm not married, who in fact is not even my boyfriend or my lover. What is in him that makes me trust him so much? I feel so different right now. So many emotions gush through my body and demand that I let myself go with his flow, that I should let him guide me, wherever he'll take me.

I walk down the memory lane of the last week. So much has changed in my life. I have met a person who makes me feel complete, who makes me feel that nothing matters to him besides my company. Who wants my companionship and nothing else. Who respects my boundaries, who admires me for who I am, and always makes me feel worthy of everything. Since the day we met, he has not let me feel alone. If he is not with me, he makes sure his thoughts surround me. I feel like I'm under some charismatic spell; that I'm incomplete if he's not around. *Will I ever be able to tell him that he completes me?*

I am lost in my thoughts, when my phone reminds me that there are other things in the world to focus on, too. Seeing Mike on my caller ID automatically brings smile to my face.

"Hey, how are you?"

"What's going on outside your building?"

"Oh! Where are you?"

"That's not the point. Are you in your apartment?" he asks with concern.

"Yes, why?"

"I'm coming up." He hangs up the phone.

Within a few minutes, I hear a knock at my door. I open it and Mike comes in, looking around as if he is searching for something. He looks so good in his casual clothes. I haven't seen him without a uniform in a long time.

"Where is that Richie rich?" *Why he is so derisive when he talks about Adam?*

I roll my eyes. "His name is Adam."

"Whatever! Where is he?" He finally manages to look at me. He seems agitated.

"He is not here, Mike. Why are you asking?"

"Things have gone so far with you two, and I have to read your life updates in the newspaper? Is this how you treat your best friend?" He comes close to me and grabs my arm. "What's wrong with you, Rania? What is he doing for you that I never did? Where did I fail?"

"It's not what you think, Mike." I shrug my shoulders to get him to release his grip. The anger in his eyes scares me.

"So . . . you like the royal treatment, huh? You should have told me that. I would have treated you like a queen, if you ever gave me a chance—"

"Stop it, Mike. Just stop it." I literally yell at him for the first time in my life. "How can you have such a low opinion of me? You think I am with him for his money? After all our years of friendship, you think I'm some gold digger?"

"No, baby, I'm not saying that. Please, I'm sorry. But with everything I'm seeing and hearing, tell me, what should I think?"

"You trust that gossip in the newspapers?" He closes his eyes in frustration and sits down on the couch.

"I have never loved anyone except you, Rania. The place you have in my heart, no one else can fill it. I know you'll never be mine, but Gibson isn't worthy of you. I've seen your life fall apart in the past. I just can't let your heart and soul crumble again." He looks up at me with sincerity. "He's only in this for the pleasure. He's not a man of hearts and flowers. Why can't you see it?"

I walk up to him and sit close enough so he can feel my presence. "I can't explain to you, Mike, and even if I try, I don't think you will be able to understand."

"Are you sleeping with him?" His question shocks me. I shake my head in disbelief that he could even ask me that. But should I blame him? A stranger, spending nights in my room, who the whole world says uses women only for sex. It's natural that Mike would think the same. But doesn't he know me?

"Tell me, Rania. Why are you so quiet?"

"I don't know what to say. But if it makes you feel better, he hasn't touched me once."

He looks into my eyes with high intensity, trying to read the truth in my face. "Then what do you guys do all the time? I'm sorry to be so personal, but I can't help being worried about you."

I place my hands on his. "You don't need to worry. We just talk. That's it!"

"He comes here to talk?" he asks sarcastically. "Since when have you started counseling?"

"Come on, Mike. What's the problem with being friends? Apparently, he doesn't have any friends."

"The whole city knows him, and you say he doesn't have any friends?" He twitches his eyebrow at me.

"That's his professional life. Just because the whole city knows him, doesn't mean he's surrounded by friends. But I told you before, there is nothing between us but friendship."

"How can you let a man stay with you the whole night? You don't even have a guest bedroom here. In all these years, you've never let me cross that boundary."

"Please, Mike." I am at a loss for words. "I don't know how to explain." He would never understand my nightmare problem.

"Are you falling for him?" he asks. His gaze gets deeper on me, shaking me inside and out. "Just say yes or no." I remain speechless, not sure what to say. If it is a no, then why am I taking so long to say it? And if it is a yes, then I know I am in trouble.

"Should I take this silence as a yes?"

"I don't know, Mike. Please, don't ask me."

"Your eyes say everything, Rania. I can see how you feel about him. I can only say he is the luckiest man alive, but if he ever does anything to hurt you or break your heart, I swear I will be the first one to kill him. You mark my words." Mike's sudden seriousness blows my mind. He goes on, "Just stay safe and don't give your heart to someone who doesn't know the meaning of love. I know he likes you, but I don't see anything beyond that."

I close my eyes and hide my face in my hands. "I can't help it, Mike. I am getting addicted to him." I don't believe I just said this to Mike. He pulls my hands away from my face and reads it keenly.

"Are you in love with Adam?"

"I don't know. Love is a very strong feeling to call it at this moment but . . . when he is not around . . . I feel incomplete. He brings life to me." After my declaration, a dam of tears opens and I let all my feelings out on my poor friend. He wraps his arms around me to comfort me. When all my tears are spent, he pulls me back and cups my face in his hands.

"That's what I was afraid of. I didn't want you to fall apart. Does he know?"

"No. I hadn't even admitted it to myself. I don't know how you got it out of me."

"It's because I'm your best friend. You should give me a little credit." He smiles at me generously, which makes me smile too. "What about him? Has he said anything about his feelings?"

"He has revealed a lot, more than I expected. He hasn't said he is in love, but whatever feelings he has are beyond my endurance. He keeps saying that there is something in me that is missing in him. I remind him of someone, but he doesn't tell me who. I know he is attracted to me and I am also attracted to him, but every time I try to take a step forward, my past pulls me back."

"Have you told him about—"

"No, I haven't. He has found out a lot about me already, but I'm afraid if I tell him, he will run away."

"But you need to tell him, before things get worse. You have no idea what you're getting yourself into. There are paparazzi standing outside your building, trying to find out if you are actually dating him. Don't you think they will dig out the details about you? What if Adam finds out about you from these newspapers? Isn't it better that you tell him yourself?" I know Mike is right. So far, Adam has shared everything from his past with me, but I haven't told him anything about mine, except for my mother's death. I am afraid if he hears about it from other sources, it will only bring shame to him. "I can't say if he's the right guy to trust that much," Mike says. "But if you think he's good enough for you, then I can only pray you get all the goodness you deserve. I can't stand to see you in pain." I smile at his sincerity. I know Mike cares about me a lot. "What about Uncle Bari? Dad told me he's not happy with all this. He is being questioned at his work."

I take a deep breath, not sure what to say. "I told Baba that Adam is just my friend, and since he is rich and famous, the press writes down everything associated with him." How can I tell him that I told my father that Adam is like Mike to me? If I place Adam in Mike's position, I am sure it will hurt Mike's feelings. And the truth is, they both stand in different compartments of my heart. With Mike, I can easily say that he is the person whom I know will never betray me or leave me in pain. Whereas with Adam, the feeling is nameless. I'm not sure in what part of my heart I shall put him, but he has touched every single place there.

"Uncle Bari spoke to you? For real?" Mike asks in surprise. I nod in silence. "There is nothing to worry about concerning your record. I've done a background check in the systems, and there's nothing. I'm sure Adam has done the same, but still, you never know how far the press might go. They know about your father and his position."

"Yes, I know. Adam showed me the paper."

"So where is he now? He left before the paparazzi showed up?" He smirks at me.

"No, he left a while before you came. He said he'd deal with the press himself. He had to go to some dinner at the mayor's house."

"Oooh, mayor's house. That sounds rich. So we two are back on track? Just you and me together?" His smile always melts my heart and makes me grin. "You know, girl, it has been almost four months since I've eaten anything cooked by you? The training lunches and dinners sucked big time. And you know how Dad cooks. So tonight, you're cooking for me, baby." He points at me and smiles devilishly. He relaxes on the couch, taking off his shoes, and puts his feet on the ottoman. "I'm going to relax and watch you cook for me tonight. Until your Richie rich stalker comes home, which I'm sure will be after dinner." I laugh at his comments about Adam. I don't know how these two men will ever get along.

"What do you want me to make?"

"Umm . . . how about lasagna? It's been a really really long time."

"Okay, let me check if I have the ingredients. Otherwise, you'll have to go down to the grocery store and get the things." I get up from the couch and head toward the kitchen. Mike has no plans to move; he seems to be in vacation mode right now. It is wonderful to see him like this; it makes me realize how much I've missed his company. His work requires a lot of time, but he still manages to make time for me because I know I hold a very special place in his heart. He browses the TV and comments about a new crime investigation series, and how it relates to what he actually does. Although he is engaged in TV, I know his mind is focused on me. I remember him once telling me, *One day, when you're my wife, I'll enjoy watching you cook for me and my kids.* I wonder if he is still thinking that.

Luckily, I have everything required for lasagna. When I put it to bake in the oven, my home phone rings. Mike gets up from the couch and answers the call.

"Yes?" He remains silent, listening. "Can you send the parcel upstairs?" He waits. "Okay, thank you." He hangs up the phone. "You have a delivery." *For me?* I haven't ordered anything lately.

After a few minutes, we hear a knock at the door. Mike answers and receives an orange envelope, addressed to me. He puts it on the counter. "Open it," I say. "I don't remember ordering anything." He picks up the scissors and cuts the envelope open. Inside is an entertainment magazine.

I open the magazine and am surprised to see Adam and me on the main page. Mike's jaw drops. Everything from the past week is there, like a rolling film on paper. Pictures from the opera, pictures of us walking on the streets of Edmonton, pictures in the hotel lobby, pictures at the entrance to the Moores' estate and then, Adam coming with me into my building. *What the hell is this?* I don't even dare to read what they have written, but the snippets tell me that it's complete gossip. Mike sees my expression and grabs the magazine from me. He looks at the pictures and I assume he is reading it.

"What the fuck is this? Is it true you stayed with him in a single suite?" *What?* I wasn't expecting Mike to ask me that. *Is it written in the magazine?* "You guys were staying together, Rania?" Mike still sounds shocked. I close my eyes furiously. I feel like running away and hiding in Adam's arms, to avoid all the questions bombarding me. *Baba! What will he think? Oh my God!*

"It seems like someone is stalking you. Watching your every move. Does Gibson know about all this?" I shake my head in negation. I'm still in shock.

My phone buzzes in the middle of our conversation.

> *I am so bored here. I told you, you should have come. What am I supposed to say about what's going on in the House of Commons? I'm hungry and don't feel like eating here. Miss your food. Can you cook for me? I'm coming home.*

Home? Did he call my apartment his home? *Oh shit!* I didn't expect he would be coming so early. He will definitely overreact, seeing Mike here. How can I ask Mike to leave without dinner? *Think, damn it!* I reply back instantly.

> *Dinner is already cooked. I have a guest. I hope you don't mind dining with other people.*

Within seconds, my phone starts to ring.

"You didn't tell me you were inviting people for dinner," Adam says, as soon as I pick up.

"It wasn't planned. You can come. Dinner is almost ready. I'm setting the table now."

"Who's there?" He gets very concerned.

"No strangers. Come over and see for yourself." *Please Adam, don't create any drama.*

"Hey, Rania, where do you want me to put this garlic bread?" Mike calls from the kitchen.

"Is Mike there?" Adam asks from the other end.

"Yes, he is. Come over. I've made lasagna." I try to be as composed as I can, but I'm pretty sure from Adam's huff that he is not comfortable with this at all.

"How long have you and Mike been alone?" He still sounds annoyed.

"Adam." I roll my eyes. "Bring some sodas and orange juice. I will see you in a while." I hang up the phone without listening to him further. I look toward the kitchen, where Mike is standing.

"Hey, we're out of sodas and no beers, either. Let me get something to drink. It's unfair to eat this heavenly lasagna without a pop."

"Adam is on his way. I've asked him to get drinks for us." I speak hesitantly. Mike looks at me, speechless and open-mouthed.

"You called Richie rich, to come here?" Mike asks, astonished. I nod in affirmation. "Is he going grocery shopping for you?" I sigh in front of him and take the lasagna from the oven, ignoring him. I know he is watching me speculatively, but I'm in no mood to answer him. I have one more drama coming over to my place, which I will have to deal with soon. "So Richie rich is finally getting domestic, huh?" Mike is enjoying this. I fold my arms over my chest and look at him with annoyance. There's too much going on at one time. Someone has been stalking me for a week. My life is printed in the papers. My dad is pissed at me. I have a best friend who keeps declaring his love. And I have a new man in my life, who is overly possessive and jealous of my best friend. *What next?*

I set everything on the table and ask Mike to join me. The lasagna is piping hot, so we both sit and wait for Adam to join us. I hear his knock at the door, and open it to find Adam holding a box of Coke cans in one arm and a bottle of orange juice in the other. He looks adorable doing domestic stuff.

"Hey, I missed you. The dinner was so boring. I had to escape." He looks at me from head to toe, as if meeting me after years. I grab the juice bottle from him. "Is this the one you drink?" he asks. "I thought I saw that brand in your fridge." He smiles and hangs his jacket in the closet. *He even remembers the juice I drink.*

I fix the collar of his shirt and smile at him. "Someone is looking really handsome in Armani." I wink at him and head to the kitchen. I try not to ogle him, as he looks extremely sexy and highly edible in his black tuxedo, much more edible than lasagna. *How can someone look so stunning?* It's so not fair to all the females. He follows me, and notices the magazine on the countertop.

"What the hell is this?" he says.

"I got this by mail, just a while ago," I say blankly, while taking out the glasses from the upper cabinet.

He turns around and sees Mike. Mike walks toward him and looks at him in anger. "Can you tell me what this is about, Gibson?" Adam remains speechless. I didn't see that coming, either. "Can you tell me why you are putting my friend's life in the limelight?" I can see how furious Mike is. He knows the backlash this could cause if Baba sees it. "Someone has been stalking her for a week. Her every movement is being captured and you don't see that coming? Are you blind or what?" He keeps firing questions at Adam.

"Mike, please."

"You stay out of this, Rania. Let me talk to him man to man." He ignores me and glares at Adam while Adam's eyes are locked on the magazine. I am sure he didn't know anything about it. *Stupid reporters!* "What is going on?"

"I'm sorry, I have to make a call." Adam leaves the counter area.

"You are not running away, Mister," Mike insists. I've never seen this side of Mike before.

"Listen, Mike, let me make a call. I will find out who's stalking her." Adam is not able to maintain eye contact with Mike.

"Better talk here. Put your phone on speaker. I wanna know what's going on." Mike crosses his arms over his chest. He is interrogating Adam like a typical cop. Now I see how he is at work.

Adam makes a call, and a guy picks up the phone. "Did you see *Entertainment Weekly* today?" Adam asks angrily.

"Yes, sir. I just found out that Ethan Murray had someone following your lady since she reached Edmonton." I see Adam's fist tightening with frustration. *Oh God! Of all people, that asshole is the one after me.* "He has hired a private photographer."

Adam tries his best to control his anger. "How sure are you?"

"I stole the photographer's laptop, sir. He had the pictures. And . . ." The guy stops.

"And . . . ?" Adam prompts.

My heart skips a beat. "And there were many pictures just of her. Close-ups."

"You have Murray's laptop right now?" Mike interrupts.

"Sir, I stole the photographer's laptop. But I am sure Ethan Murray has files too."

"I want to see those files," Adam says. "Send me copies immediately."

"Yes, sir. Right away."

Adam ends the call.

"This is bullshit," Mike shouts at him. Adam doesn't answer. "I'm going to find out how this happened, and don't you poke your nose in it." He points at Adam.

"Listen, Mike. I am as concerned as you are. But—"

"No buts, Gibson. If Ethan Murray—whoever that asshole is— finds out that you've hired an agent to go after him, do you think we'll ever be able to find out his true motive?"

I get in between the two distraught men. "Mike, I know you worry about me a lot, but trust me, no one can get to me against my will."

"Oh, cut out this crap about will, Rania. There's a man who is watching your every move. We have no bloody clue how he's planning to use the information. Are you getting what I'm trying to say here?" Mike's sudden look sends chills of alarm through me. I bite my lip in fear, and possibly Mike is able to read my expression, so he doesn't say any more because he knows I haven't told Adam all the details of my past. "I will try to find out what this guy wants. But this has to remain between us." Mike looks at Adam. "Just ask your agent to stay out of it for now. I'll dig out the details in my own way."

"He's dead. I'm gonna kill that bastard," Adam yells. "I don't care what happens to me after that, but I'm going to kill him with my own hands."

I try to soothe him. "Calm down, Adam. Please don't overreact. You—"

He interrupts me. "Overreact? Do you have any fucking clue what he's doing?" Adam looks at me with smoldering eyes. "And now your best friend blames me for everything."

"I'm not blaming you. But let me handle it, okay? I'm working with the law, so don't get involved." Mike looks at me. "Give me a day and I'll find out everything, but ask Adam to stay out of it."

Adam looks at Mike fiercely. "I can't leave her alone, Mike."

"I know that. I'm not asking you to leave her. All I'm saying is that stalking is considered a harassment crime." Mike faces me. "Rania, has Murray ever tried to harass you physically?" I shake my dead in denial. "Has he tried to approach you? I mean through excessive phone calls or emails? Or left something at your door? Anything like that?" I shake my head again. "So basically all he's doing is taking pictures of you secretly, and we can't prove it unless we either find that photographer and get him to testify, or get Ethan's laptop." Mike makes sense. "It's not a criminal harassment case yet. He was smart enough to only give the press the pictures with Adam in them. We can't do anything about that because Adam is a well-known personality. The media have gossiped about Adam's life, not yours."

Mike faces Adam and looks directly in his eyes. "I can see, Adam, that you care about her, but I want you to stay out of this. Your interference will only create more problems."

He looks back at me and continues, "Under the criminal code, we can only charge him if he trespasses on your property at night, assaults you, sends you threatening notices, or tries to intimidate you. So far, he hasn't done anything illegal that we can prove. So let me watch him and I will update you guys, okay?"

I am so confused right now that I want to run for the hills. I can't even breathe outside in the open air. I have no idea how far Ethan will go. Though I am trying to put Adam at ease, deep down inside I am scared, shit scared.

"Now everyone come to the table, please," Mike says. "Lasagna doesn't taste good if it's cold, and my beautiful friend has put lots of effort into making it for us." Luckily, I have a table for four, so we settle down with the men sitting on either side of me. Everyone is quiet. I see Adam controlling his frustration, but I have no idea what he is thinking right now. All I see in his eyes is too much worry for me. *Why can't he trust Mike?*

I'm sure Mike will handle the situation in the best way. Finally, my best friend breaks the heavy silence.

"Mmm . . ." Mike says, as he takes a bite of lasagna. "Where are your hands?"

"Huh?" I look at him quizzically. Mike takes my hand and kisses it gently.

"Never miss an opportunity to kiss a woman who cooks for you. You are the best cook on this planet. God! I love this dish." He takes another bite, like a famished beast. I giggle at him and look at Adam, who is looking daggers at him. Mike totally ignores Adam's gaze. "Will you pack this up for me—I mean, the leftovers? Then I can have it for lunch too."

Adam observes us, quietly. He looks as if he feels like a fish out of water—not part of the conversation. *What's eating him?*

"Don't you like it, Gibson?" Mike asks him innocently.

As I take a sip of my juice, Adam looks at me and speaks. "I know she's a wonderful cook. She made me lunch today, but I have other ways to thank and praise her. I will do it my way, once you leave." With that, the juice gets stuck in my throat and I start coughing hard. *I will do it my way. What the hell does that mean?* Adam rubs my back and tells me to look up at the ceiling. Does he have any idea what he just said in front of Mike? What is he going to think of me? Mike doesn't say anything, but I easily get the message from his eyes. I look down at my plate. Luckily, Mike changes the topic and shares a story about a woman who accused her man of having relationships with other women. His stories lighten up the atmosphere, making it easier for all of us to breathe.

With some of the jokes, I see Adam's lips curving at the corners, bringing his beautiful smile to his face. I see the tension leaving him. I have Mike to thank for that. If he weren't here, the situation could have gone out of control. How well he handled Adam, and me. He is definitely a true friend. We all finally start to talk about different topics, other than us.

"Have you ever thought of becoming a professional chef, Rania?" Adam asks me, out of nowhere. I scan Adam's expression, wondering if he's kidding. "I would like to finance something in the food business. How about I open up a fancy restaurant and you be the head chef. Hire your own staff, train the people the way you cook. What do you say?" I blink at Adam's unexpected question, not sure what to say.

"That sounds awesome. I'll be the first customer," Mike interrupts with excitement.

"I haven't thought about it, Adam." I look at both of them, back and forth. "I cook for pleasure. Never thought of it as a profession. I have no degree—"

"You have got flavor in your hands, baby. You know how to charge a taste bud and make someone crazy over your food." Mike compliments me in his own way and looks toward Adam. "I agree with you, Adam. She should pursue this as a career. She is wasting this talent feeding us." Mike winks at me. "Stop working with Dad. This is a *real* business. People won't stop eating till the world ends." I laugh at Mike's witticism. Adam watches me intently, and they both wait for my response.

"Are you guys serious?"

"I am always serious with you, Rania. What makes you think I was joking?" Adam's heated gaze penetrates through my eyes, down to my stomach, giving me hard knots. *There is no biological connection between eyes and stomach. How does he do it? Damn it!*

"I never thought about it. But thanks for appreciating my dinner to that level." I take a sip from my glass and smile at both the men for being so encouraging to me.

"Did you ask Ben about the holidays?" Adam changes the topic suddenly.

"No." I look at Mike, and then back to Adam. "I didn't get a chance after you left. I will ask him later."

"Any message for Dad?" Mike looks at me with concern.

"No, thanks. I will speak to him myself," I say in a low tone.

"Let him tell Ben. That's fine." Adam faces Mike. "Rania and I are taking off for two weeks. You just tell your father that she'll be back to work after Christmas." He takes a sip and continues. "Anyhow, she hasn't taken a vacation in years."

Mike looks at me quizzically, searching for the truth in my eyes. "Are you guys going somewhere?"

"Yes and no." Adam smiles, but looks at me. He takes my hand and continues. "Rania has promised to give me two weeks of her life. We're not going out of town, just spending time with each other, to get to know each other better. Right, babes?" *Babes? Is he doing this on purpose for Mike's benefit?* I see Mike's jaw dropping with shock. He wasn't expecting this. "So with all this trouble and tension, I guess this is the best time to escape and relax. What do you say, Rania?" Adam smiles at me with warm indulgence.

I have no other choice then to smile back at him hesitantly. I know Mike wants to talk to me in private, but I don't know how it is going to be possible. Adam doesn't plan to leave tonight, and I don't want him to go either. I'm as addicted to him as he is to me. I can't even name this feeling. After Mike takes his last bite, he looks at me.

"Do you have anything for dessert?" He questions me like a child. I shake my head.

"Then let's go for an ice cream." He flashes his smile at me. I smile at Mike and then look at Adam for his answer.

"You already had lots of ice cream last night with Eva." *So is that a yes or no?* I look back to Mike and he mouths silently, *control freak.* I purse my lips to stifle my laughter. I don't want Adam to feel we are talking about him, in front of him.

"It seems like some people have calorie issues here." Mike leans back in the chair. His phone rings, and he answers it. "Yes? Okay . . . hmm . . . all right . . . I'm on my way." He ends the call and looks at me. "Duty calls, my love." His look is annoyed. "I have to go, but you still owe me dessert. I'll stop by one evening and we'll go out." He ignores Adam and kisses my forehead.

"Wait. Let me pack the lasagna for you, Mike." I go into the kitchen with the dish, and Mike follows me.

"You didn't tell me you were going on vacation with him." Mike's voice is just above a whisper. "He is a total control freak. How can you stand him?"

I look back to him, while taking out a storage box from the cabinet. "He's a nice guy."

"Hell yeah! Maybe he is, but don't let him control you, Rania. He's acting like your master or something."

I laugh at Mike. "Oh God! You sound like it's a BDSM relationship."

"It looks like it to me, and I still don't believe that he hasn't touched you. He eats and drinks you, Rania." He passes his fingers through his hair. "If he ever hurts you, will you let me know?" He takes me by the shoulders to get my attention.

"I will never hurt her, Mike," Adam interrupts. He's standing at the corner of the kitchen with his arms are crossed, leaning against the wall. *Shit! How long has he been listening?* "And I will not control her against her will." Adam stands here calm and composed, watching both of us attentively. Mike moves away from me and picks up the storage box of leftovers.

"You better not. I have my eye on you, Gibson." He looks keenly at Adam and then proceeds to the door. I ignore Adam's gaze on me and follow Mike to say goodbye. He gives me a hug. It is always nice to hug him and feel the warmth and security of his arms.

I shut the door and head to the dining room to clear everything from the table. Adam still stands there, at the entrance to the kitchen, eyeing me speculatively. He finally moves, helping me clear the dishes. I load the dirty dishes into the dishwasher and clean up the mess. As I start to leave the kitchen, he blocks my way, looking at me in a very strange way. Mike is right; he is looking at me like he is drinking me. I avert my eyes from him, but his gaze still penetrates me as he moves closer. He cups my face with his hand, caressing my cheek with his thumb. Why do my knees always feel so weak when he touches me like that? Why doesn't my body obey my mind? *Damn me!*

His touch makes it hard to breathe. He looks at me keenly, his green eyes burning like fire, ripping my existence apart, peeling off my clothes, tearing through my flesh and bones directly to my soul. He touches my lips with his thumb, rubbing my lower lip gently, sending hot threads of desire along every nerve.

"You know, Rania, you are like a fire." He flicks his index finger gently on my face. My eyes close at his touch. "Open your eyes, Rania, I'm talking to you." His voice is like a whisper, but heavy on my ears, breaking down my barriers, revealing the real woman in me. *How can I open my eyes, if he keeps on touching me like this?* I manage to look at him. "You are a fire," he repeats. "I feel your warmth and compassion when I'm close to you, but when I touch you . . ." He pauses for a moment, touching my trembling lips with hunger, then continues, "When I touch you . . . I burn." *What kind of revelation is that?* I don't know what he is talking about. "You're making me change my beliefs on worship. I am worshipping a fire. I enjoy the comfort, take the warmth; I obey this fire, but I can't feel it because whenever I try to . . . I burn deeply and no one can see the scars. It's so strange, isn't it?" His lips move at the corners in a small smile. "You told me that only Jinn are made of fire. Though I truly don't know if they exist or not, I know you're not one of them. Who are you, then? Why do I burn, Rania?"

I look to the side, to avoid his consuming gaze. "I don't know what you're talking about, Adam."

"You know bloody well what I'm talking about." He rests his forehead on my shoulder. I am sure he can hear my heart, pumping so hard. He inhales. "A sweet intoxicating fragranced fire." He speaks into my neck, making my whole nervous system shut down. His eyes are heavy. I haven't seen this look before. I don't know what he intends, but I'm getting frightened. "I know you feel what I feel. Your body responds to my touch, but your soul . . ." He nuzzles my neck, passing currents through my body. "I know you feel it, Rania, but I also know that there is something else blocking us. Something I can't see. I feel the heaviness between us, every time I get close to you, as if some invisible force is pushing me away from you." He closes his eyes for a moment, then continues. "I have a feeling you know what it is. Why won't you trust me?"

Adam's words diffuse in my blood like a drug. I feel my body crumbling into millions of pieces.

"I do trust you, Adam." I look into his eyes with seriousness.

"No, you don't, Rania. Not completely, the way it should be." I realize Adam is miraculously turning all the hidden switches in my body. He has found the passage in my heart that I've never let anyone open. A passage that leads directly to my soul. Adam's way of declaring his feelings is a bit different, but I know he is talking about the concept of soulmates. *His soul is searching mine.* And my soul . . . I don't know where it is. I lost it a long time ago.

His eyes and his words tell me that he will find my soul someday, but it's impossible for me to believe that he can ever be my soulmate. I didn't think God created a soulmate for me.

"You should go home, Adam." I put my hand on his shoulder, pushing him away, but I don't have the courage to look into his eyes and say it.

"This is my home, Rania. My home is where you are. I find peace here." His voice is still full of warmth and passion. He speaks so low that I can hardly hear him.

"I mean your apartment. We need to get up early, if you want to see the museum. I have some work, too. Laundry and then prayers—"

"Are you kicking me out? You can do all that with me here. Do you really want me to leave?" I hide my face to avoid all the feelings crowding me. I know he will read everything from my face. I fall down on my knees, with my face hidden in my hands. The burden of his feelings is impossible for me to carry. He is holding my heart in his hand and there is nothing I can do about it. Nothing.

He embraces me tightly and gently rakes his fingers in my hair, soothing me with his tender touch. "I'm not going anywhere. Like it or not, accept it or not, but I'm going to be your shadow, Rania. A shadow that doesn't disappear at night." He kisses my hair softly. *How can I tell him that I love his touch so much? How can I tell him how I feel about him?* He understands everything, without me saying a single word. He picks me up in his arms and takes me to my room. I feel my head resting on my pillow. He tucks me under the warm comforter and moves my hands away from my face. I close my eyes, avoiding his questioning gaze. He wipes the tears from my face and kisses me softly on the forehead.

"At least, now I know you need me as much as I need you." His tender speech lets my eyes open. "You can tell me or not, but I sense there is a barrier between us. I know I almost push you over the edge when I try to find it—I'm never sure if you're going to fall down or fly up, but sooner or later you need to go off that cliff." He leans back on the other pillow and closes his eyes. "I don't know what this feeling is, Rania, but it's very strong."

He gets up from the bed and heads to the washroom, leaving me speechless and bewildered.

I hear him starting the shower. Maybe he's trying to relax. I feel that for every person, there comes a moment in life when he wants to break all the barriers and trust another person with everything, including his own life. I feel my moment has arrived, but I'm not sure if Adam is truly the right person to trust my life to and rely on completely.

What if I tell him and he doesn't believe me, throwing my faith down the drain? How can I trust that he is actually the right person? And even if he is, what's next? There can never be an *us*. We belong to different cultures and beliefs. Even if he believes my secrets, he cannot be my soulmate. It is impossible.

I see him coming out in his pajamas and T-shirt. He has marked his presence everywhere in my apartment. Anybody would think that he is living with me here, and he resides in my heart too. I want to give him my heart, body and soul, but I am too afraid of the side effects. I know his soul is searching for mine, but it is my soul that is wandering alone in the darkness.

He makes himself comfortable, relaxing on my bed, browsing his phone. He doesn't look at me or talk to me, which I really appreciate. I guess he is trying his best to give me some space. I get up from the bed and prepare myself for prayers, asking God to open the doors for me to guide my life down the right path. When I finish my prayers, I see Adam's eyes locked on me. He rolls over to face me.

"Can you ask your God to help me too?"

I smile at him. "He is your God, too. Why do you want me to ask, when you can ask yourself?"

"Because you are celestial, when you pray. I can see you talk to Him directly, and I am damn sure He is listening to you."

"You called me fire, a few moments ago, and now I am celestial?"

"Yes! You amaze me every time."

I ignore his comment and continue. "Why don't you ask Him yourself?" I watch him getting confused.

"Why would He listen to a sinner?"

"Do you know *the sin which makes you sad and repentant is more liked by God, than the good deed, which turns you arrogant?*"[7] He blinks at me. I take a deep breath. "Don't praise me so high, Adam. I am nothing like what you think." I get up and take off my scarf, and sit on the other side of the bed. He rolls over again to face me once more.

"Do you think it's a good idea to take public transport to the museum?" His sudden change of subject grabs my attention. "I mean, all the pictures and the news."

I sigh and look at him. "Yes, you're right. I will have to compromise on your luxury cars then." I wink at him, and that makes him smile back at me.

He pats my pillow. "Grab your book reader and lie down. I have one thousand nights left to share."

"You remember, huh?" I smirk at him and fetch my reader from my nightstand drawer.

"Of course, you've suspended your execution. I can't hang you till you finish your magical stories." Adam is back in his playful mood now. I feel so complete when he is cheery like this. "Can I take you to the doctor tomorrow? You stopped taking your prescription abruptly. That emergency doctor told me you would have to go back to your physician."

"That's all right, Adam. I am good without it." I put my hand over his. "As long as my shadow is with me, I have no worries." With my words, Adam pulls me toward him and settles me in the same position we were in last night. It is good I am not looking into his eyes. He tucks his head behind my shoulder and sniffs before he speaks.

"You are celestial, Rania. Your fragrance is divine. And it's not just a perfume. It's your fragrance. Every time I breathe you in, I travel to another world." He inhales again deeply. He rubs my arms with his warm hands, very gently, his raw voice sending encoded messages to my soul. It is truly a miracle that I am not melting here. "Thank you for Mom. Thank you for pushing me to forgive her. I was tired of living with a grudge. I don't know how you're doing this, lifting all the heavy weights from my soul. I feel so much lighter." He takes my hand, entwining his fingers with

---

[7]   *Ali ibn Abi Talib (607-661)*

mine, and touches them to his lips. "Thank you for completing me." He kisses my hand again. "And thank you for being . . . mine." My heart starts to skip once more, and I am dead sure it can easily be heard. He melts me with his words . . . every time. The air in the room seems to suck away, and my breath gets shallow. *Focus! Focus! Focus! Don't dwell in that world again, where his words take you.*

I combat our awkward moment by opening my book reader to continue from where I left off last night. *"Know then, O my lord, that whom my sire was King of this city . . ."*

I carry on with my stories within stories, not sure when I close my eyes and dive into deep sleep.

*   *   *

When I wake up it is six-thirty, and still dark outside due to the long winter nights. The first thing I notice is Adam sleeping on my shoulder, his arm wrapped around me possessively. *Oh no! This shouldn't have happened.* He seems to be in a deep, blissful sleep. How come I didn't wake up when he put his arm around me? Why was I so dead to the world that I didn't recognize his touch? *And the nightmares?* It feels like they were never a part of me. As if my demons can't come close to him, due to his powerful soul. I watch him sleeping, feeling the desire he has ignited in me—is he a dream that will fade away with time, or is he my reality?

I wish I could freeze this moment and live in my fantasy, where no past stabs me to death, where I can feel Adam's touch connecting to the real woman in me—a woman who was brutally murdered in the past. The angels on my shoulders writing my fate fail to communicate with me when it comes to Adam.

I slide from his arm gently, trying not to disrupt his sleep. I rush to the washroom and change my clothes, then start my prayers, asking forgiveness from God that I let Adam touch me. I let him get close to me even though it is not permissible in my religion, if he is not my husband. I don't promise to repent because I don't know if I can keep from letting him come close to me.

Oh God! Please help me. Only You can guide me. If he is the right man to trust my life to, then open all the doors for me. Untie all my

*ropes and clear all the barriers that are blocking me from trusting
him. If You have sent him to protect me, then show me the light which
can guide me to decide my own fate. If he is not the man to trust,
then why did You send him into my life? Why did You put so much
concern and care about me into his heart? Oh God! I seek forgiveness
for letting myself surrender to him. Please show me the path. Amen.*

When I open my eyes, I see Adam looking at me keenly. He
smiles as soon as our eyes meet. He looks adorably sexy with
his mussed morning hair. I close my eyes again and utter a silent
prayer.

*Oh God! If he is not the right guy then do not let my heart fall for
him. Please! Please!*

"A very good morning to you, my dear." I hear Adam's sleepy
voice.

"Good morning. You slept well?"

He passes his fingers through his hair. "Never slept so well in
my life. I am thinking of moving in with you. What do you say?"

"Mr. Gibson, moving in with me? In this small, one-bedroom
apartment?" I ask in surprise, smirking at him.

"This is a haven. It is home. And don't tease me with my
name. It sounds like mockery." He is actually laughing. "And if
I'm sleeping and eating here every day, I better bring my stuff."
I am not sure if he is joking or if he's really serious. I can't let
him move in with me. It is such a huge step. We are not even in a
relationship. He crawls into my mind conveniently and reads my
expressions. "So I'm not welcome in my haven?"

"Don't you want to go? The earlier we reach the museum, the
better it is." I change the subject, ignoring his desires.

He rolls back and rests his head back on the pillow. "Isn't it too
early? It's not even eight in the morning. I want to rest longer. Your
place is very comfortable, Rania. Though it is small, it gives me a
homely feeling every time I come here." I don't know what brings
him to my place. What do I have that isn't in his lavish home? He
rolls over again to face me. "You know, Rania, sometimes money
doesn't buy everything."

"But it is better to cry in a Ferrari, than on a bike." I wink at
him, cracking a joke. He laughs at my response.

"But, don't you think it's even better to cry in somebody's
arms, rather than a Ferrari or a bike?" His tone gets serious. I
know where he is leading me. "You know I have all the luxuries

at my place, all the amenities—you name it, and I have it. I have invested a lot of time and money to build that place, but somehow I don't feel complete when I go there, like the feeling I get when I come here. What do you think is missing?"

I look at him for a moment, and then smile. "I haven't seen your place, Adam, but I believe it is your heart that you forgot to put there. I guess you are placing your heart here. That's why you feel like it's home." He keeps looking at me in silence. I don't know if he actually got what I was trying to tell him. I get up from the floor, folding my prayer mat, and he takes my hand and makes me sit on the bed.

"My heart is where you are, Rania. Wherever you go, it will go with you." He takes my breath away with his declarations. How can he say such strong words, in such a simple way, without making it complex? Is this called a declaration of love? No, we can't fall in love with each other.

It is impossible.

If he is moving in that direction, I will have to stop him before it is too late for both of us. That path has no u-turn; it is a one-way road leading us to the darkness. I am already lost. I don't want this good soul to wander in the darkness with me.

"I'll go and prepare breakfast." I drop his hand and head to the kitchen.

THE CONFESSION

♂

Two weeks have passed—I didn't realize time actually flies. Rania fulfilled her promise and gave me the most treasured two weeks of my existence. For the first time in my life, I understood the true meaning of companionship. We visited all the tourist attractions, including fulfilling my desire of walking down the streets of Niagara Falls. From museums to art galleries, from Playdiums to theaters, from crazy malls to long walks under holiday décor, we did everything one could imagine. She has no idea what she has given me. A gift of memories I will keep in my heart forever.

We took an unlimited amount of pictures to create a memory book for me. She also forced me to keep my word about not spending money on her. We each bought our own tickets, just like a teenage couple with very little money. I like the feeling that she's with me just for me, and that money is the last thing on her mind. She already has my heart, what else could she take from me?

Mike was apparently able to get rid of the stalking photographer, or maybe Ethan was worried that we'd trace the pictures back to him. There were no more pictures of us in the magazines and newspapers. Also, I paid a good amount to the local papers not to print anything about her, even if they had found out. We visited a new place every day, and usually came home around six in the evening. Rania cooked for me daily. Sometimes, she also invited Mike to eat with us.

I was hardly ever going to my place. Rania never agreed to my request to move in with her, but she never asked me to leave, either. Every night after dinner, she read me *Arabian Nights*, which made me time travel with her into past centuries, until she finished the book the day before our vacation time was up. In those two weeks, I got a chance to visit her dance classes. When she danced, it was not her body that moved with joy, it was her heart that rejoiced.

Those were the best days of my life. She also taught me how to do justice to an ice cream cone. I had to book the entire ice cream parlor for her, as I couldn't let anyone see her licking the sweet flavor so seductively. She enjoyed teaching me as much as I enjoyed learning, though she didn't know I learned it when she taught me the first time. I was only pretending to be the fool, so that she could teach me again, and I could enjoy watching her lick it.

Our friendship flourished with each passing day, but in all those days of companionship, I couldn't find her heart. She was with me all the time physically, but whenever I tried to open myself up to her, she shied away. I was starting to develop a fairy tale fantasy that she was captured in some spell, and once I'd kissed her, the spell would be broken. I knew her body was feeling my touch, but whenever I tried to come close to her with the intention of kissing her, she would freeze, as if her soul had been pulled out of her body, making her a piece of dead meat.

Was she telling the truth, when she told me on our first meeting that she had nothing to offer me? Why did I always feel that she wanted to take that path with me, but something was blocking her? She's different from all the other women I've known. She doesn't plan for the future. She only lives in the present, or perhaps, her past is not letting her step into the future.

For the whole two weeks, I tried every possible way to dig her past out of her, but I failed. She has enclosed her heart in a hard shell and thrown it away in some deep dark well.

There were also more strange incidents in the middle of the night. Several times I woke up to find her in the dark closet or washroom. From the other side of the door, it sounded like she was speaking to someone in a strange language, but when I came in, she was staring blankly as she had in the hotel room. Every time that happened, I asked her about it in the morning, but all she would say was that I was either dreaming or hallucinating.

I tried leaving evidence to let her know I wasn't dreaming. One night, when I saw her standing in the closet alone, talking to someone, I took out one of her scarves and placed it on the bed, so that the next morning when she woke up, I could tell her that I took that scarf out because I found her in the closet. But strangely, that evidence also disappeared in the middle of the night. I started to worry that she might suffer from a sleep disorder. That could be the reason the doctor had provided the pills. But most people who sleepwalk don't talk as well. I wanted to take her to the doctor, but if she wouldn't believe there was a problem, then he wouldn't be able to treat it.

But the thing I most wanted to know about was the scars that marred her skin and wounded her soul. She had made me promise never to bring them up, as she didn't want to walk down that horrible path.

I also had lots of arguments with Rania about her attending the summit in New York. I needed to attend a conference in Toronto on the same dates, and I was worried about her going without me, so I kept asking her if she could drop the plan. She insisted that she needed these kinds of summits to boost her career. Imagining her in a different city, alone with Ethan Murray, was scaring me to death. She kept telling me that I should trust her and there was no man in this world who could seduce her, but I also know how shrewd Ethan is, and Rania is very innocent in these matters.

During our vacation, my mother called us and invited us to a Christmas Eve party that she's organized in a grand party hall of the Ritz Carlton Hotel. Mom has been looking forward to this party, and she expects all her kids to be there. She invited Rania before she even invited me, making me feel that Rania is very important to her. Eva called the next day to take her out shopping, to get a dress for the party. I tried to convince Rania that I would buy her party clothes, but she wouldn't let me buy anything for her. Those crazy girls dragged me into every store, but they didn't find anything they liked. I never knew shopping with females could be so tedious. When they liked something, it would be too expensive, and when they found something with a good price, they didn't like the fit. Are all females the same, or are the ones I have just terrible at shopping?

Finally, I managed to get them to Holt Renfrew, and convinced them that they could buy anything their hearts desired without looking at the price tag, as a Christmas present from me. Eva went crazy with her brother's generosity, and picked up some useful stuff. Rania was still reluctant to buy anything with my money. She'd pick up a dress, check the price tag and put it down without even trying it on. I know how gorgeous she looks in those designer dresses; she blew me away the night of the opera. I asked Eva to convince Rania to buy something, but she didn't listen to either of us. Finally, she shut me out, saying that she would wear the same dress I got her for the opera. Since she had only worn it once, and no one had seen it other than me, she considered it to be a new dress. She also said that, as expensive as it was, she couldn't justify wearing it only once. I had no other option than to let her win, like always. I tried to convince her many times that whatever was mine was hers, but I guess money was the last thing she would ever consider.

I really love the feeling that I have one sincere friend who sees beyond my riches, but sometimes she is so needlessly difficult that it's impossible to deal with her. Every girl wants her man to spend money on her, but she never let me spend a single penny. I decided that after the Christmas party I'd give her the necklace I wanted to give her on our first date, and tell her my feelings.

I don't know where my life is taking me, but imagining it without Rania is inconceivable. My eyes search for her when she's not around. My body craves her when she's not there. Since the day I met her, not a moment has passed that I haven't thought about her. Every time I see her, I want to kiss her passionately to let her know how I feel. I know she has feelings for me too, but they are always defeated by her awful past. She said she trusted me, but she doesn't trust me enough to share her haunted memories. I know Mike is aware of her past, but I would never dare to ask him, as it would hurt her. The darkness that she holds in her eyes draws me to her, maddening and amusing me at the same time.

Today is the evening of the 23rd of December, the day before the party, and I'm stuck in a press conference in Halifax. I wanted Rania to come with me, but she prefers not to get involved in my business obligations. This conference will go on for a few more hours, but I should be back in Toronto by morning so that we can go to the party together. This night seems endless without her—I don't know if I will be able to sleep. I wonder if she will be able to sleep without me, or if her nightmares will scare her. Right now, I'm with people from all over North America, discussing green homes and their advantages on saving energy. I try hard to concentrate, but my heart is stuck back in that one-bedroom apartment. They ask me a couple of questions, but once Ali notices I'm not paying attention, he answers on my behalf. *My mind is completely fucked up.*

If I don't tell Rania how I feel about her, my life will never move forward. But I've also been eager to tell her that she looks like the same woman who cast a spell on me with her dancing, back in February. I decide to tell her about it after declaring my feelings. I'll tell her that I feel she is the same woman who captured my heart at first glance. I will tell her that the darkness in her eyes reminds me of the woman, dancing under enormous lights. I don't know if she will actually believe my story, as that place never existed, but this way, at least, she will get the message that she is the one who has captured my heart. I promise myself that I'll tell her everything that I have been holding in for so long.

Adam Gibson! You are in love.

Ali's cell rings, and he excuses himself and leaves the press conference, which forces me to pay attention to the questions coming from the media. Ali reappears after a few minutes, but instead of sitting, he whispers in my ear.

"Come out, Adam, there is an emergency." I excuse myself and step out of the conference hall, looking at him quizzically. "There is a fire on the sixteenth floor of Archeries condominiums, building number two."

I feel like someone has bombarded me with a drone. I say, "That's Rania's floor. It's not her apartment, is it?"

"The one next door," Ali says. "The fire department is already there, but . . ."

"But what?" My heart skips, making it difficult to breathe.

"We have news of two casualties." He pauses and gulps for a second. "Both are dead at the scene. I'm trying to call Rania, but her phone is off."

She's dead?

I fall on my knees, as if someone has pulled the rug from under my feet. Ali supports me and helps me sit on a nearby couch.

"I'm pretty sure, Adam, there's nothing to worry about. Let's just pray she is safe. I have asked Frank to update me every few minutes. I have sent him Rania's picture, in case he's able to locate her. They have evacuated the entire building; there's no one left inside. I am here to get the news, so you can go inside and carry on—"

"I want to go back, Ali," I interrupt.

"The conference is almost over."

"I said I want to go back now!" I yell. He makes a few calls to hire a private aircraft so I can leave immediately. He goes back into the conference hall, probably making excuses for my absence. I close my eyes and cover my face with my hands, resting my elbows on my knees.

Oh God. Please don't take Rania away from me. Because of her, I started to believe in Your existence, and You can't do this to me now. Please, make sure she is safe. I take a deep breath. *Oh Rania, call me, please. Tell me you're okay. I'm dying a thousand deaths every second here. I will take you back from God, if you ever plan to leave me. But you know best how to talk to Him. Tell Him I need you. Tell Him I haven't loved anyone so deeply in my life. Tell Him if He plans to take you away from me, then take my life as well. We'll meet in Heaven.* I feel Ali's hand on my shoulder for comfort. I have never cried in public like this, but my existence is crumbling around me.

People notice me falling apart, but I don't care. All my memories of her roll through my mind like a movie. I still feel her innocent face in my hands. I still smell her fragrance on me. I still hear her laughter at my jokes. I still feel her holding me tight during her nightmare. I still feel her fingers passing through my hair, to calm me down.

No, Rania. You just can't leave me.

Ali hugs me like a brother and lets me cry. "She can't go away like this, Ali. She can't leave me."

"Don't worry, Adam. I have a strong feeling that she's all right."

"Then why isn't she picking up the phone? Call her friend Mike. Ask him to find out."

"I did. He and Ben are not in the city. But I informed them because Ben owns the apartment." Ali has tried everything.

He takes me to board the aircraft. During the whole two-hour flight, I keep trying to call her, hoping she will pick up, even though I know her phone may have been burned in the fire. There is still no news from Frank. The two bodies that have been recovered were unrecognizable without DNA testing. The journey seems endless. My money, my power, my riches, they all failed to keep her safe.

By the time I reach Toronto, it is past midnight. I rush immediately to Rania's building, where the fire has consumed my life. It's crowded with media people, fire trucks and police cars, but in all those people, I can't see my Rania anywhere. I keep yelling her name, but there's such a stampede that no one hears me. Freezing rain is falling, but the fire has such a hold that the rain isn't affecting it. Everyone is soaked, running around like crazy searching for their loved ones. My life seems to come to an end, like the Day of Resurrection has already arrived, and there's no escape.

I get surrounded by reporters and photographers.

"Mr. Gibson, when did you get this news?"

"Mr. Gibson, we heard your girlfriend is in the building?"

"Mr. Gibson, have you been able to find your girlfriend?"

"Mr. Gibson, have you identified the burned victims?"

"Hey, please, back off." Ali pushes everyone away from me. "Mr. Gibson is not in a state to be talking to anyone right now. Please let us find her and pray that she is all right." After thirty minutes of searching the crowd, Ali asks me if I will go to the hospital to identify the burned bodies, to see if one of them is Rania. *No, I can never do that.* I have a firm belief that God has saved her for me. I'll never admit that she is no more. But Ali convinces me that they have looked for her everywhere.

When I reach my car, I see someone standing under a barren tree. My heart skips. It's Rania wrapped in her bed sheet— which I slept on last night—water dripping down her body. She's trembling with cold, in the freezing rain with no coat. I rush to her and pull her into my arms, kissing every inch of her face, not caring how she will react.

"Rania . . ." I hug her tightly. "Thank God, you're okay. You have no idea what I've been through. I almost died." I keep kissing her, savoring her physical presence. "I was so frightened. I can't imagine my life without you." She stands mute and unresponsive, wrapped in her cold sheet. "I promise I will never leave you alone again. Oh, Rania, you have no idea how much I love you." I realize that in my happiness and excitement, I forgot to ask how she is. *How can I be so selfish?* I hold her face in my hands and ask if she's okay, and she starts crying, shaking helplessly.

"I lost everything, Adam. I have nothing left. My home, my possessions, my memories, everything is burned into ashes." She trembles with pain.

"No, baby, you will get everything back. I promise to give you everything back. I can't thank God enough that He saved you."

"I am homeless, Adam. I have no shelter now." She sounds agonized. I hear Ali calling for medical help. "My picture of my parents has been burned too. That was the only memento I had of them together." She collapses on my chest and lets out all her fears.

I hadn't thought about it like that. All I cared about was that she was alive. I hadn't considered what she had lost. The paramedics come immediately and the medical assistant says Rania is severely chilled and is in danger of developing a high fever, if she is not taken care of properly. They take her into the warm ambulance, and she's trembling so much that she's not even able to respond to them.

"We need to get her wet clothes and this sheet off," the medical officer advises me. As soon as he touches Rania to take away her sheet, she pulls away, and looks to me with blank eyes. She is not so out of it that she doesn't know that someone is revealing her body. I know she'll never let a man take off her clothes in front of so many people, but she isn't realizing that the wet cold clothes could worsen her condition. I see her holding her handbag tightly under her arm. I have no clue how she managed to save her bag.

"Mr. Gibson, we need to take her wet clothes off. Please ask her to cooperate with us."

"Can't you see she's traumatized? She won't take her clothes off with all these people around."

The medical assistant sighs and says, "Okay, we'll leave and close the door. Just get those clothes off her." He gives me a couple of blankets, and they leave us alone in the ambulance.

"Rania, you need to listen to the doctor and get out of those soaking clothes. I'll turn my back and you can undress and wrap yourself in the blanket. Here." I take off my jacket and give it to her. She is shivering too hard to hold anything. "You can wear this under the blanket, if you feel uncomfortable." She's shaking so much that her body won't do what she wants. She can't even lift her hand to take off her sheet. "I want to help you," I say. "I will only look into your eyes and nowhere else, but please, let me do it." She still looks at me with blank eyes. I start helping her, lifting her arms and taking off her sheet.

She's wearing her nightclothes. I know how modest she is, but she's so worn out that she doesn't even have enough energy to speak. I lock my eyes with hers so she doesn't get the slightest idea that I'm looking at her body. I pull off her T-shirt, then draw her closer and snake my arms behind her to unhook her bra. I keep my gaze locked on hers. I pull down her pajama trousers, and she steps out of the wet clothing, holding my hand firmly. I cover her nude body with my warm jacket, buttoned up to her neck, and wrap her in the blanket. She's wearing her bedroom slippers, which are also dripping with cold water. I take off her slippers and put my socks on her feet.

I lay her down on the paramedic's stretcher and call the medical officer. He checks her in detail and writes a prescription for her to take home. He informs us that she has already been given a combination of ibuprofen and diphenhydramine citrate, along with a heavy dose of sedative to calm down her fever and pain, but she has been advised to sleep well for tonight. Since she is too weak to even walk, I pick her up to carry her to my car. The photographers attack me again, taking pictures of our misery.

"Mr. Gibson, do you know the reason for the fire?"

"Mr. Gibson, is this the daughter of UN secretariat you have been dating, these past weeks?"

"Mr. Gibson, can you tell us how your girlfriend is feeling right now?"

"Mr. Gibson, we heard your girlfriend's apartment is completely burned down. Is this true?"

I ignore the people and make my way out of the crowd. Ali keeps pushing the reporters and photographers away from us. Rania rests in my lap all the way home.

It takes almost twenty minutes to reach my apartment. She seems to be warming up, not shivering so hard. In the elevator, she's very quiet, looking down at her feet covered with my socks. I have no idea what she's feeling right now. It's very traumatic for her to lose everything, but I vow to give it back to her. After all, her home was my haven too. When I open the door of my apartment, she smiles.

"Is this your place, Adam?"

"Yes. Since you're here, you may call it home now."

"It's beautiful . . . it's . . . out of this world . . ." She gawks around her. "I thought homes like these only existed in magazines and commercials." Her mood seems to be lifting, now that she's somewhere safe. "Oh my . . ." She kneels down on the floor and touches the white flooring. "Holy shit, who puts marble on floors in Canada? And it's heated . . ." She looks up at me with shock, still touching the floor.

"Oh yeah! I have a thing for marbles and granites. I know most Canadians don't use it because it's so cold in winter, but I always used to admire marble floors in warm countries. So I installed radiant heat. Now get up, you need to rest." I give her my hand and help her stand. She looks around the whole foyer area, admiring everything as if she's in some magical kingdom.

We step into the large living area and I see her eyes sparkling with the lights and colors of the living room.

"Who designed all this?" She looks at me in astonishment.

"If you're asking from an architectural point of view, I designed this building, including the floor plan of this place, but I got some interior designers to decorate it."

"It's beautiful, Adam. It seems like one of those places on HGTV million-dollar listings."

"Well . . ." I rub the back of my neck and face her. "It actually is. They were after me to film it." She wanders around until she finds her most favorite place, the kitchen.

"Holy crap! What a kitchen." She covers her mouth with surprise. "Oh my . . . the countertop is amazing." She spreads her arms over the granite countertop, to feel it on her fingers. I see the excitement in her eyes. I assume she hasn't seen anything like this. "Look at the gas grill. Eight burners on one baby? Wow!" She keeps amusing herself over the appliances. "This is perfect, Adam. It is like a dream kitchen. I could spend a whole day here."

"Really?" Her remark surprises me. "It's yours, anyhow." As soon as I say the words, her expression changes.

"I have nothing left, Adam. This is your house, not mine. I am homeless." Tears start coming from her eyes again, and she hides her face with her hands.

"No, baby. Please don't cry. I promise I will bring your home back."

"I don't know if the insurance . . . ah . . . none of my stuff was insured." She speaks behind her hands.

"Don't worry about the insurance, Rania. I will bring back everything you had in your home. I remember every single thing. I promise everything will be okay. You are here, alive, and I don't think we should ask for anything more than that. I still don't know how to thank God for listening to me." I pull her hands away from her face and wipe her tears. "I'm here, Rania, and I will never leave you. I'll give your home back to you, just the way it was. I promise." I take her out of the kitchen and lead her to the bedroom.

She stops looking around the apartment; her excitement over my place is gone. Her loss has hit her again. I settle her on my bed and take some clothes from the chest of drawers.

"Here," I put a thick T-shirt and pajamas next to her. "You can't sleep in this jacket. Please, change. Make yourself comfortable and try to feel at home. I'll be out here, okay?" I kiss her on her forehead and leave the room.

I give her plenty of time to relax on her own. My phone starts ringing as soon as I come out of the washroom. *Who's calling me so late?*

"Yes?" I pick up the unknown number.

"Where's Rania?" I hear a familiar voice.

"Mike, is that you?"

"Yes, Adam. I just heard. Where is she? I've been calling her for two hours." I hear Mike's voice breaking from worry.

"She's all right, Mike. Just a bit shaky. She's lost everything. I guess her phone was in her apartment. I don't know how she managed to escape out of that death trap."

"Can I talk to her?" he asks instantly.

"I don't think she's in a state to talk to anyone at the moment. When I found her, she was soaked and freezing. She has a bit of a fever, but the medics treated it." I pause for a moment and take a deep breath. "She's in a very vulnerable state, Mike. Even I can't talk to her."

"Where were you, when it happened?"

"I was in Halifax. It took me two hours to get there." I sigh again. "I don't want to imagine what she was doing alone under a tree, all soaked with the rain for two hours. I'm thankful to God that she's alive."

"Yes, for sure. I feel bad I wasn't there for her. When you talk to her, please tell her I called. Tell her I tried my best to come down tonight, but because of Christmas, all the flights are booked. I'll be back by the 25th in the afternoon."

"Sure, I'll tell her. Right now, I just hope she sleeps peacefully for tonight. It's very important for her health." I look over at the closed door and shut my eyes.

"Adam, do you suspect anyone is behind the fire?" Mike asks, concerned.

"What do you mean?"

"I just learned that the fire started in Tammy's apartment, Rania's next-door neighbor. She hasn't been home for two weeks, and they say someone left the portable heater turned on in the kids' room. I spoke to Tammy a couple of minutes ago, and she says she doesn't have a portable heater." My heart sinks at Mike's words. Is Rania's life in danger? "I know it sounds strange, Adam, but tell me, do you have any enemies?" Mike's question shocks me.

"But why would anyone want to harm her?"

"They don't necessarily want to harm her. Everyone knows about you two. Maybe someone is trying to harm you through her. It's a passive way to torture someone." He takes a deep breath. "I suspected Ethan Murray, but he hasn't been in Toronto. Is there anyone else that you think might be after you?"

"No, Mike." I start to shiver. The thought of someone burning Rania because of me is killing me.

"I'm going to investigate it personally. I have asked for CCTV tapes for the whole building, for the past two days. Somehow, I have a feeling this was deliberate." I'm having trouble breathing, thinking about the implications. "Please take care of her and let me know if you find anything. I'll call in the morning, once she's awake."

Mike hangs up the phone, leaving me worried. I run to the bedroom and open the door without knocking. Rania is sleeping peacefully. She looks wan and pale. If someone wants to harm me, then why not go after me? Why would anyone hurt such an innocent soul? This is all because of me. If I hadn't followed her that very first day, none of this would have happened. What will I do if something happens to her? I hold her hand tightly, but she doesn't move or respond to my touch.

I won't let anything happen to you, Rania. I promise. I will protect you till my last breath. I love you.

AN ENCHANTED KINGDOM

♀

I open my eyes and see Adam sitting at my side, holding my hand tightly in his. He kisses me on the forehead as soon as I blink at him.

"Good morning. How are you feeling?" He looks at me lovingly, brushing hair off my face. I look around to see where I am. I remember Adam bringing me to his place, but I don't remember sleeping in this bed. I clearly remember Adam taking my clothes off inside the ambulance and wrapping me in the blanket, never taking his eyes off of mine. I still see how much pain he has gone through since the fire, thinking I might have been killed. My pain seems to wither in the face of his agony. It looks like he hasn't slept for a single minute.

"I feel heavy. My head is spinning."

"Do you want to sleep some more?" he asks me tenderly.

"No. What's the time?" I look around again.

"It's noon. Would you like something to eat?"

"No, I . . ." I look down at myself, realizing I am wearing his clothes. I pull up my blanket to hide my upper body.

"I'll wait outside so you can change. I've got a few clothes for you to wear. They're in the closet, there." He points me toward a white double door. "You may find a few things in the drawers, too. Make yourself comfortable, okay?"

He leaves and I get up, my head still feeling heavy, and find the door to the washroom. The bedroom is huge, with a custom white bed, larger than any king-size bed I have seen in my life. I notice that everything in the room is white. It looks like a cozy, serene place to relax. I can't understand why he would leave such a nice room to sleep with me on that queen-size bed. The thought that the place where Adam liked to stay doesn't exist anymore brings the pain rushing back.

I step into the large washroom, with its exquisite white French vanity, cultured marble sink, and high-end faucets. I look up at the vanity light, wondering where this kind of stuff is available. I haven't seen it in any hardware store. The jetted bathtub is enormously huge, able fit four people easily, with their legs stretched out. The glass shower column is colossal, with a rain shower. This is kind of a washroom I've only seen on TV.

I notice that there are personal products on the counter, including a new toothbrush. All of them are brands that I use, so they must be for me. He seems to have remembered everything, as if he has memorized me. I wash my face and brush my teeth, then step outside the washroom to search for the closet. I'm amazed at the size of the walk-in closet. The right side is filled with Adam's expensive clothes and accessories. On the other side of the closet, I see feminine clothes hanging neatly. *I have got a few clothes for you to wear.* Does he call this a *few*? There are four times as many clothes as I had in my tiny closet. I touch the fabrics of the clothes, admiring the taste of whoever brought them. I can't believe they're actually for me, but as I pick up one shirt, I see the Holt Renfrew tag attached to it. All the clothes are new. I open the custom drawer at the side of the closet and find a number of silk and woolen scarves. In the next drawer, I see all colors of very expensive undergarments. I pick up one bra and check the size. *Shit! How does he know my size?* I want to hide in embarrassment. I notice none of the tags have any prices, as though they've been deliberately removed. A knock at the door interrupts my thoughts.

"Are you in there, Rania?" Adam calls.

"Umm . . . yes."

"Is everything okay? Can I come in?" He slowly peeks his head inside. "You haven't changed yet? You didn't like any of the clothes?"

"Adam, this is . . ." I look around the closet. "Is this—"

"This is all for you. I managed to get them this morning, when store opened. They delivered before you woke up. If anything doesn't fit, put it aside, and I'll get it exchanged." He smiles affectionately at me.

"I can't take all this, Adam. I mean, this is too much . . ."

He comes closer to me and rests his hand on my shoulder. "None of that is important now. The only thing that matters is that you're safe. This is nothing. Please accept it. Don't even think of it as a favor. Please." I see the sincerity in his eyes and arguing with him means I'll break his heart. He hugs me tightly, and I feel my body dissolving. He still looks shaky and broken from last night.

"You didn't sleep, Adam?" I speak with my face in his shirt.

He pulls me away and holds my face in his hands. "I couldn't. When I thought I lost you, I almost died, so after I found you, I couldn't close my eyes for a single minute. I still can't believe God actually heard my prayer. I didn't even know how to pray, but He still listened to me." I see the appreciation for my life in his eyes. "He does care about me, Rania. I never knew I was so important to Him, that He would listen to my silent prayer. But how did you escape the fire?"

"I don't know how I escaped from there, Adam. I woke up to hear the fire alarm. First I thought I was having a dream, but when I saw the fire outside my bedroom, I couldn't believe it. My mind was a blank. All I could do was wrap myself in the sheet. I still don't remember how I got out of the building." As I speak, I see him closing his eyes to hide his pain. His hands start to tremble on my face. "When I was trapped by the fire, I thought I'd lost everything, and this was the end. I never valued my life, until I saw death in front of my eyes. I thought I would never be able to . . ." *I thought I would never be able to tell you how much I love you, Adam. I realized it last night, when I saw my life being taken away from me and believed I'd die with no love in my life.* "I thought I would never see you again." I change my words; I don't have the courage to confront my feelings for him.

He hugs me tightly again. "Please don't say anything more. I won't let anything happen to you. I promise." I feel he is experiencing everything with me, as if he was there at the time of the fire. "I want you to relax now. Everything is going to be fine. Take anything you like to wear. It's all yours. I'll see you outside." He kisses my forehead with quivering lips and escapes from the closet. I remember him kissing me passionately last night, all over my face, when he found me under the tree. I also remember him telling me he loves me, but he hasn't said that again. Did I imagine it, in my traumatized state, or was it something he actually said? And even if he did, am I ready to hear it?

I flush my mind of all these wild thoughts, realizing Adam must be waiting for me at the breakfast table. I am pretty sure he hasn't eaten anything today. I search for normal clothes, but all I see is expensive apparel. I finally pick up a pair of jeans and an ivory-colored DKNY blouse. The Chantelle undergarments fit me so well, it's like I shopped for them myself. The ivory blouse looks awesome, when I check myself in the mirror. I look expensive and worthy. He is making me feel worthy. I step out of the closet to brush my hair at the dresser. It is a beautiful white French antique dresser, with a very few items on the top. What surprises me is I see my perfume and basic makeup on it. He even knows the shade and brand of the lipstick that I use every day. I see the exact same brush that I had. Everything is the same, like a replica of my own dresser, but in another room.

I don't know how long has he been noticing these details and memorizing them. It makes me feel really special. I step out of the room, barefoot, to look for Adam. There is a large wide passage, with multiple white doors on each side. I imagine myself wandering in an enchanted castle from *Beauty and the Beast,* where Belle is lost and completely captivated. I walk slowly, ignoring all the closed doors, till I find stairs at the corner of the passage. *He has a double-story apartment*? Is it really an apartment, or is it a house? I clearly remember entering through an elevator. I go down the very wide heated marble stairs, and see Adam talking on the phone in his living room, walking back and forth on a thick deep blue-and-white-striped rug.

"She's doing okay, Mom . . . no, I can't ask her . . . I don't think she's in a state to attend a party. I'll stay with her . . . okay, I'll let you know." He looks at me and hangs up the phone. "You look . . . beautiful." He observes me from head to toe. I look down at my feet shyly, but manage to smile at his appraisal.

"Thanks to you. Anyone would look nice in this blouse." I pass my hands over my waist to feel the soft fabric. He smiles back at me and shakes his head.

"Come. Let's have something to eat." He takes my hand and leads me to the kitchen, where I see an Asian lady working. She turns around when she hears our footsteps.

"Hello, Miss Rania. How are you doing this morning?" *Do I know you*? I look at her quizzically, and then at Adam.

"She's my housekeeper, Julianne," Adam whispers in my ear.

"I am good. Thank you, Julianne." I sit down on the bar stool next to Adam. Julianne is in her early forties. *So she is the one who keeps this place so organized and tidy*? Everything is so neat and clean in this apartment that I feel like I shouldn't touch anything, in case I get it dirty.

"Mr. Gibson mentioned this morning that you like pumpkin bread. I have baked some for you. Would you like to try it?" She places the warm bread in front of me. I smile back to Julianne and pick up the bread. She places tea in front of me and offers Spanish omelet and buttered toast to Adam with his coffee. She exits the kitchen, leaving the two of us in privacy.

"Thank you for everything, Adam. I didn't know you knew so much about me. You even know . . ." I try to find the right words. ". . . very personal details." He smiles from the corner of his lips, still looking at his plate. He looks up at me and brushes my hair off my shoulders.

"You should acknowledge your presence in my life. You are precious to me." His words are filled with passion, melting me deep inside.

"I know. Thank you." I avert my eyes and look down at my lap.

"And you should give me some credit for spending time in your closet. I got to know a lot about you from there." He winks at me mischievously. "I never mentioned it, but I have memorized everything about you. How you eat, what you eat, what you wear, everything. If you want to call it obsession, then yes, I admit I am obsessed with you, but I call it passion." He takes a deep breath and closes his eyes for a moment. "The only thing I couldn't find is your heart. But someday, I will." Why do I feel so uncomfortable every time he declares his feelings? Why do I feel like hiding, or burying myself somewhere? Why do I feel his feelings will fade someday, just like my fantasies? I ignore his passion and turn to face my plate.

"You were talking to Grace, when I came down?" I change the subject. He frowns at me for avoiding his declaration. "Yes, she wanted to know how you are." He takes a bite of his toast.

"That's very sweet of her. I will thank her, when I see her tonight."

"We're going?" Adam looks at me, surprised.

"We're not going?" I fire the negative question at him.

"No, I mean . . . I thought . . . you might not feel like—"

"Adam, I'm fine. What happened, perhaps it was written in my fate. Those things were never mine, I guess. And Grace has planned this evening for quite a long time. She wants all her kids to be there. I know if I don't go, you won't either, so we will go together."

I see utter contentment on Adam's face. "Thank you so much. I'll let her know." We continue our breakfast, until he breaks the silence again. "Oh, by the way, Mike called. He wanted to know how you are. He will be flying back on Christmas morning."

"Why is he coming back? I thought they decided to stay with Uncle Joe, till New Year's."

"That's what people do when they care. Also, the apartment was under Ben's name, so he has to come back to make his insurance claim."

"How did you get to know about the fire?"

"My company built it. I have to make sure that the fire didn't have anything to do with the construction."

"You built that building?" I am surprised to know that. He smiles shyly at me, as if it is not a building, but just a piece of paper. "I didn't know that."

"That's because you don't take any interest in what I do." He smirks at me in a teasing way.

"I have no interest in your money, Adam. You know that very well."

"Yes, I know. But you should know what I do for a living, so that you stop complaining and arguing with me when I get you something." His tone is very serious.

"I am not interested, Adam, and I don't need anything from you. I didn't accept your friendship for your money, so—"

"I know that very well, Rania. I don't think you're greedy, but all I want to ask is that you stop arguing with me, if I want to give you something of my own free will. So please, get used to it. Try to accept the fact that whatever's mine is yours." *What kind of confession is that?* Why would I take his money?

"Adam, you have earned your money with hard work. If all of a sudden I come into your life and consider your money as mine, that's not fair to you."

"You're not taking it. I *want* to give it to you. Why don't you understand the difference?"

"But why do you want to give it to me? I don't need it," I argue again.

"You don't know how important you are in my life? Do you want me to go through it again?" I see his expression. "You've been taking care of me since we met. You helped me confront my own demons, pulled out all the thorns from my life. Buying you clothes is nothing. And if it bothers you, consider it as a very minor way of showing I care. Okay?" There is no point in arguing with Adam. He is always in the winning position. He has different ways of showing he cares, and I'll have to accept him the way he is. After finishing our breakfast, Adam gives me a tour of his apartment— or, I should say, his magical kingdom.

On the main level, I see the living room again. Everything, from the art, to the décor, to the furniture, is perfect. The room is tastefully furnished with pastel blue suede couches that complement the deep blue-and-white-striped rug I noticed before. There is a huge silvery white mirror, just above the antique console table, and the walls are very light blue.

I am actually awestruck by his kingdom. The entire room gives me a cozy and warm feeling, very serene, as if I am in some country cottage by the lakeside. I always expected Adam's place to be decorated in dark colors, but it turns out to be totally the opposite. He opens a large sliding door, which takes us to a grand dining area. The dining table is dark mahogany, with room for twelve people, holding a beautiful centerpiece that catches my attention as soon as I step inside. The walls are honey-colored, giving it a very warm and inviting feeling. After the dining area, he takes me to the terrace or patio or garden, whatever it is. It is a huge space, with beautiful patio furniture and a fire pit, not to mention a state-of-the-art barbeque grill and a huge swimming pool, which is enclosed in a glass wall. I am cold outside in this temperature, but this sight and Adam's enthusiasm is making me warm. The view from his terrace is awesome. I can see the whole Toronto skyline from here.

"It's beautiful, Adam. And I can't believe you have a pool on your terrace." He is actually enjoying showing his work to me.

"I haven't shown my place to anyone. You are the first one to come here, Rania."

"Really? I am honored, then. So how high are we?"

"The building has thirty-five floors. You can see we are on top." He looks at the view proudly.

"Are there others living here too, in this building?"

"Oh yes, each floor has ten apartments. It's a residential building."

"And you own the whole building?" I ask, surprised. He nods in silence. "And you are occupying the space of ten apartments, on one floor?" He smiles again at me, in affirmation. *Holy Shit!* If all the apartments are rented, how much money is he receiving every month—from this building alone? He smiles shyly at my weird look. Then he grabs my hand in excitement and takes me up a spiral staircase.

"Come on, let me show you something."

When I reach the rooftop, after five minutes of spiral steps, I am astonished to see a helipad. Adam is excited to show me everything he has designed. I totally believe him when he says I'm the first person he is showing it to. The excitement in his eyes makes it clear. In the face of his elation and charm, I don't feel cold, even barefooted.

"This is my baby." He shows me his helicopter with pride. "I will take you for a ride. I hope you're not scared of heights."

"No, I am not. I would love to ride in your baby." I start to rub my arms, to warm myself.

"Shit! I didn't notice you're not wearing anything warm. You will catch cold." He takes my hand, but rather than traveling back down the spiral steps, he takes another door, which leads us to an indoor passage. We both stop to catch our breath, after running in the cold weather. He takes me to an elevator and we head down two levels, back to his apartment.

"Oh my God, Adam. It's breathtaking. Everything is so amazing. You have your own private castle, up in the clouds, just like in Jack and the Beanstalk." He laughs at my remarks. We enter his apartment once again and he shows me the rest of the lower level.

Besides the gigantic living room, warm dining room and ultra-modern kitchen, there is a huge private study. He opens the door and announces, "This is my favorite room, where I spend most of my time." I feel pride in his voice. The ambience of the study is completely different from the rest of the apartment. I feel like I'm stepping back in time. The décor is much darker, with wood paneling and dark wooden furniture, just like a typical study from the eighteenth or nineteenth century.

"Wow! I feel like I'm stepping back centuries." I look around his library. "I never knew you read." I gently touch his lavish collection of books.

"They are mostly architecture and designing books. Not the kind you read. But let me know if you want any books, and I'll get them." He looks at me tenderly, rubbing his lower lip with his finger. There is a huge, solid wood study table, with his papers and designs scattered over it. Behind his chair are floor-to-ceiling windows that open onto the terrace, and the marvelous view of the Toronto skyline. I turn around and notice a large framed copy of the picture of our first dance together. I blink at him with surprise. I wasn't expecting to see this picture in his house. It's placed where he's facing it every time he sits in his chair.

"I told you, this is my favorite room. Now you know why." He smirks at me innocently. "When you're not around, I look at this picture and talk to you." I see fire and passion in his eyes. At this very moment, I truly feel he is drinking me in.

"And when are you not around me, Adam?" I roll my eyes, with a smile. "Since we have met, you are always with me." I move to the other side of the room and open a sliding door, where I find a huge game room with a pool table in the center. "You play pool?" I look at him, astonished.

"Not really. I told you, no one comes here. It was just part of the design. I know how to play, but I think you need to have a good partner. I have played with Ali, a couple of times, when I used to work late on my designs."

"Are there more surprises in this castle?" I grin at him with amusement.

"Castle?" He laughs and shakes his head. "Come on, I'll show you the rest."

He slides open a glass door from the study, which leads to the pool that I saw earlier from the terrace. I marvel at the number of marble stones inlaid around it. It has a separate hot tub, to blissfully enjoy in any weather. He presses a button and in a blink, the glass ceiling opens to the sky. I gawk at the perfection of the work that has been done in this pool area.

"It's always good to swim under the warm sun. We only have a few months to enjoy that weather." He smiles innocently and I try my best to capture this moment, the twinkle in his eyes as he proudly shows me his home. I walk to the other side of the pool and notice a huge canvas resting on a large easel, but the canvas is covered with a sheet. I look toward Adam, who comes up behind me and removes the sheet. I gape at it, completely astounded to see an oil painting of my face.

"You are etched in my memory, Rania. I can sketch you whenever I want." His raw voice sends my body to the crest of desire. I turn around, seeing his heated gaze bore into me, as if he actually is memorizing my features. "But someday, I'd like you to pose for me, so that I can make sure I'm not missing any fragment of the beauty that God has blessed you with." I blink at his words several times, not sure what to say in return, though I'm pretty sure he is not expecting anything back from me. He knows what he has said has left me dumfounded and speechless.

We return to the living room and he opens another door. It is a theater, with a huge collection of movies and an immense projection screen with multiple black leather recliners in front of it. The walls are painted deep purple. *It's a real theater.*

"You never told me you have a cinema in your home," I say. "Why'd you choose to go out, when you have this?"

"If I had asked you to come here and watch a movie in this room, would you have agreed?" he asks innocently. *Oh, he knows me so bloody well.* I purse my lips to hide my smile.

After that, he takes me upstairs. The walls along the passage are decorated with beautiful artwork; whoever designed his place must have very good taste. The first room on the right is the state-of-the-art gym.

"So that's the secret of your perfect physique." I wink at Adam.

"You think so?" he asks, while closing the distance between us. "Do you ever get attracted to me, Rania?" His eyes are so intense; it's a miracle I'm not melting. I try to look anywhere other than at him, but it's hard to avoid his burning gaze. *Where do I go? Where do I run?*

"How about the other rooms, Adam?" I change the topic to avoid the awkwardness here. I know I always spoil the moment. I just don't want to give him false hopes. If I tell him everything about me, I know he will run away and I'll never see him again. I am too scared to imagine my life without him. He closes his eyes and rakes his fingers through his hair.

"Let's go. I'll show you." On the other side of the gym is the guest bedroom, beautifully decorated in beiges and browns. Another door, next to the guest bedroom, is a guest washroom, done all in gray and black. I have never seen a washroom like this. *Who puts a Jacuzzi in the extra washroom?* The opposite door is an amazing laundry room. I smile when I see the extra-costly washer and dryer, with custom-designed cabinetry.

"Your laundry rocks."

"Are all women like you, Rania?" he asks me, surprised.

"What do you mean?" I look at him, passing my hands over the deep gray laundry machines.

"I mean, do all women crave the latest appliances? I thought women would go for designer handbags and shoes and diamonds. You're different." I giggle at Adam's remarks about me.

"Good to know that you finally know me. I told you I'm not like other women." I grin at him, and exit the laundry room.

"No doubt about that." He follows me out of the room. The last room is, of course, his bedroom. I open the door myself.

"Oh well! I have seen this. I must say, your castle is enchanting, Your Majesty. Is that it? Aren't you going to amuse me more?" I tease him naughtily and sit at the corner of his bed, spreading my hands on the soft white sheet and crossing my legs. "Aren't there any more surprises, King Adam?" He walks toward the bed, looking at me seductively.

"The king has unlimited ways to surprise his queen in his own chamber. Never tantalize him." He sits closer to me. *So Adam Gibson is in a playful mood.*

After what he has done for me, he deserves a little boost. I know he has been in pain since last night and I want to ease his mind.

"Oh, really?" I flick my index finger over his chest, which is covered by a T-shirt. "I can't wait, then." I lick my lips in a sexy manner and laugh at him, rolling over to the other side toward the headboard. He closes his eyes for a moment and when he opens them, he crawls after me like a beast, not taking his eyes off me.

"The king has wild intentions for his queen. And if the queen doesn't obey her king in his chamber, she might get locked in a dungeon." He creeps slowly toward me. I pull away, getting closer to the headboard. "And the king has extreme punishments in the dungeon. Is my queen ready to accept the king's commands, or does she want to be locked up in the dungeon forever?" He smiles, his intense green eyes alluring. I laugh at his seriousness.

"So I can expect his highness's generosity in his chamber?"

"Oh yes, my queen. The king will shower you with his bounties. All my queen has to do is trust her king, and surrender." He is an inch away from me. He gently pulls away my scarf and throws it on the other side of the bed. "Is my queen ready to surrender now?" He flicks his index finger over my lips. My body starts to burn at his touch. *Shit!* I shouldn't have provoked him. *Is he serious?*

"Does his highness promise to be gentle with his queen?" I look into his eyes, trying my best to drag out the conversation. He wants to play games. He takes my hand and kisses the back of it.

"The king will be as gentle as a dove." He comes closer to me and nestles his face into my neck. "But if the queen defies her king and violates the rules, then the dungeon is not far away." *Stop it, Adam. It's not a game anymore.*

He is seducing me, and I must say he is successful enough to inflame a burning desire in me. My body starts to vibrate at his touch. "And if the queen obeys her king, then a time will come when the king will surrender his throne to the queen." He plants a soft kiss on my collarbone. "Then the queen can rule over the king and his kingdom . . . forever." He kisses me again on my neck. *What is going on with you, Rania? Why are you letting him rule your body? Why can't you push him away, like you always did before?* I don't know what is happening to me, but I don't want this moment to go away. My back is resting on the pillow and I am trapped completely under Adam's body. His eyes and his body silently scream at me that he is extremely aroused, but I still see the sincerity in his eyes. Somehow, with this entire alluring act, I don't see lust in his eyes. It looks more like love to me. But if he loves me, then why doesn't he say so?

"The king has waited for this moment for so long." He caresses my neck with his lips, transferring a thousand watts of current in my spine. Our breathing and heartbeats start to increase at the same pace. "The king's chamber was barren without his queen." He takes my hands and locks his fingers with mine. "I want you to feel me, Rania." He whispers in my neck and gently kisses under my ear. "I know your body wants me, as much as I want you, but just for a moment, unlock yourself from all the barriers, and feel the passion between us." His lips travel slowly to the other side of my neck. My body is getting so weak and so bloody aroused with his touch. I'm losing my senses. He moves his head up and looks directly into my eyes. I see his eyes burning with desire. "I want to open all those bindings of yours. Just for a moment, let your soul meet mine. I promise to take care of you, forever." He brings his lips back to my neck and I close my eyes to let myself go with his flow.

He keeps kissing me passionately on my neck, and I feel like the air in the room has been sucked up and we are floating in a vacuum state. I feel his burning lips and my breath gets shallower with each kiss. I try to savor the blissful moment that he is creating with his ecstatic desire, and at this moment, I really wish to escape with him to his world of fantasies, where there is no pain or scars, where no memories of a haunted past reside, where the fear of losing Adam doesn't exist. My body desires to make love with him passionately. I have never felt anything like this before. As soon as he puts his lips on mine, his phone chimes loudly in his front pocket, breaking the steamy moment between us. He pulls away and takes the call.

"Yes?" He frowns, but never takes his eyes off of me. "Yes, this is Adam Gibson . . . yes . . . Hello, Mr. Bari . . ." *Shit! It's my dad?* "Your daughter is in safe hands, Mr. Bari. You don't need to worry about . . . yes, she is fine . . . no burns . . . yeah, we should all thank God, nothing happened to her . . . yeah, the whole floor caught fire . . . almost ten people are burned and two of them are dead . . . it is indeed very tragic." He takes a deep breath. "She is my guest, Mr. Bari . . . no, I will take care of her." I hide my face and pull my knees up to my chest. Why did Adam tell my father I am staying with him? *Oh God! What will he think of me?* "I have taken a vow to protect your daughter. I cannot think of harming her at all . . . I don't think she is in a state . . . thank you . . . good day."

He hangs up the phone, annoyed. Though my face is hidden, I know he is looking at me; I can feel his gaze. The moment we were in before is gone. I shouldn't have instigated it in the first place. Why did I even start this game of seduction with him, when I know how he feels about me? It is not fair to play with his feelings and mine.

I feel his body shifting and leaving the bed. I lift my head to see where he is going. He comes back into the room with a box in his hand, and sits next to me.

"I guess you lost your phone in the fire. Keep this. It's the same number." He places the new iPhone box in my hand.

"Adam. I . . ." I keep looking at the box, shaking my head.

"No arguments, Rania." He gets up from the bed and heads toward the closet. "All your contacts are retrieved, in case you were wondering. You can turn the phone on now." He enters his walk-in closet.

I open the box and turn on the phone. There are many text messages from Mike, wanting to know how I am doing, if I'm okay, how did I manage to escape from the fire. I don't feel like talking to anyone right now. I can't believe Baba called Adam to ask about me. *Does that mean he cares?* But why didn't he talk to me? I don't want to ask Adam about it. I hear him talking to me from the closet.

"Have you decided what to wear this evening?" I never thought about it. I had planned to wear the dress he'd bought me for the opera, but since I don't have that any more, I will have to think about it.

It is already two in the afternoon, and since it is Christmas Eve, the stores will probably be closing within a couple of hours. I follow his voice and enter the closet. He looks at me, smiling.

"You know what are you going to wear tonight?" How does he manage to be so gentle with me, even when I ruin the moment? He glances at my clothes and pulls out one dress. "What do you think about this?" It's a beautiful black lace shimmery gown.

I've noticed he likes lace on women's clothes. I don't know if he has chosen this or not, as he was with me all the time. On my weird look, he answers my question without my even asking.

"Natalia was capable enough to arrange for a few evening dresses. You have more. Try them on and let me know if you find anything suitable to wear, otherwise, we will go to the mall right away, before it closes." *Suitable?* This closet is worth more than a hundred thousand dollars, and he is asking me if I'll be able to find anything *suitable* to wear? I feel like he has put the whole damn store in here. I don't deserve all these riches.

"This is beyond my expectations, Adam. You didn't have to spend—"

"Sshhh . . ." He places his finger on my lips. "You are still in the king's chamber, and this is a part of the king's generosity." He smirks at me seductively. *So the moment is not lost at all.* "I like to see you wearing all these beautiful gowns. Now try some on and let me know which one you plan to wear." He starts to gently rub my lower lip with his fingers. "You are very beautiful, Rania, but tonight I want you to look the way I see you. Would you dress up tonight, only for me?" I keep looking into his eyes, which are filled with a burning desire and perpetual passion. I have not dressed up for anyone before. "You might not know it, but there are almost three hundred people coming to the party, very famous people. I'm bringing a lady with me for the very first time. It will be our first public appearance as a couple." I nod my head, agreeing with him. He smiles again at my acceptance and takes a few steps back. "I have called someone to pamper you, before you get ready. They will be coming shortly. We have to get to the party around six." *People to pamper me? What does that mean?* "In the meantime, decide what you want to wear. I just want you to imagine me tonight, when you get ready. That's it."

He leaves me alone in the closet. *Is this some kind of test for me?* He wants me to look good, only for him. *How do I do that?* I have to come back here to his *chamber,* after the party, and I have a gut feeling that things will steam up again in this room, once we are alone.

I wander in his closet, wondering where to start. Of course, he wouldn't do anything against my will, I know that, but what if I want it too? What if I melt in his arms and let myself flow with him? I cannot imagine touching the forbidden fruit. *No way!*

I put all the wild thoughts aside and decide on the black dress he just picked for me. I try the dress on inside the closet, but decide not to show it to Adam until tonight. I don't want to ruin the surprise. The black Valentino lace dress fits perfectly. I take it off before Adam returns, and pick up a Chantelle black lace bra with matching panties.

Natalia certainly has a good taste. I open the rest of the drawers, under the lingerie section, and am surprised to find out that he has even got me matching sandals, boots and bags. From Jimmy Choo to Christian Louboutin, I have everything in this closet, from pumps to wedges, from handbags to clutches, from Burberry to Fendi, from YSL to Gucci. When he said he wants to place the world at my feet, only if I will trust him, was he talking about this generosity? I pick up shimmery Christian Louboutin high-heeled sandals to match the shimmers in the dress, and select the black Fendi clutch to go with them. It is like a freaking shopping mall inside the closet, with no price tags. There are some high-end European brands that I've never even heard of, or rather, it was beyond my reach to even think about them.

I open the corner-most drawer, just beside the mirror, and am amazed to find the accessories to go with the clothes. There are boxes of Hermès, Chanel, and other high-end brands for scarves, hair accessories, watches and jewelry. I open each and every box, admiring the selection, and wondering about how costly they are. It is good that none of them have price tags, otherwise, I wouldn't have accepted them, but I know this is all damn pricy. I was never a designer freak, but when I look at these precious things, I can relate to the feeling that money does buy happiness. These riches are making me happy. But I always wanted to earn these things on my own. What did I do in the past, to deserve Adam as my gift? I feel like I am using him, which takes the excitement from me. I never wanted things like this from someone else's pocket.

I hear a knock at the door. "Can I come in, Rania?" he asks me gently.

"Yes, please." I gather everything, while he steps inside the closet. "Is there anything wrong?" He looks at my worried face.

"No, umm . . . I . . ." I have no words to say it. "Adam, this is too much—I'm sorry, but I can't accept all this. You need to return these—"

"Sshhh . . ." He puts his fingers on my lips again to cut me off. "I told you this is my way of showing I care. Please, let me do it. Don't take this feeling away from me." He pauses for a moment. "When I look at you now, alive, in front of my eyes, I don't desire anything else, Rania. You are all I want, no more, no less." He looks down at my arms, holding the dress and undergarments, and smiles at me. "I can't wait to see you wearing all this for me."

And I can't wait to tell how much I love you, Adam. Yes, I will tell you tonight after the party that I do love you. I will tell you everything about me tonight. It will be up to you to love me back or leave me. I will accept whatever you choose for my fate.

"What?" He smiles at me with tenderness. "What are you thinking?"

"Umm . . . nothing." I look down with confusion, hoping he didn't read my eyes. I have to open my heart to him, myself, not through my eyes.

"Some ladies are here waiting for you. Please, come down." He takes my hand and exits the closet, taking away my things and placing them on bed. We reach the living room, where two ladies are waiting for us. I still don't understand why they are here.

"Hello, Miss Rania. It's an honor meeting you. I am Cynthia, your makeup and hair artist, and this is Emma, your masseuse and aesthetician." I shake hands with them in astonishment. I look toward Adam, who is smiling at me. "We were requested by Mr. Gibson to pamper you and help you get ready for the party tonight." She looks toward Adam. "Mr. Gibson, we would appreciate if you could let us know where to set up?"

"Oh yes, please, follow me." Adam starts walking, taking my hand in his. The two ladies give each other strange looks. He leads them to his bedroom. "You can start your work in our bedroom. All Miss Rania's belongings are here." *Our bedroom?* He looks at me. "I know I owe you a foot massage from Winnipeg airport." He winks at me. *He still remembers that?* "I will get ready in the other room. You carry on and enjoy your treat." He kisses my forehead, leaving me with these two girls.

My royal treatment starts with waxing, scrubbing and a relaxing massage. Surprisingly, they have brought the whole spa with them. Within a couple of hours, I am massaged, scrubbed, polished, waxed, even manicured and pedicured. One of the ladies shapes my eyebrows, and after all the basic treatments, they ask me to put on the dress that I intend to wear tonight. I put on my black dress and sit in front of Adam's grand dresser. The ladies treat me as if I am a princess, getting ready for a royal ball. The makeup and hair have done wonders for me. I can't believe how gorgeous I look after this treatment. Adam knocks at the door around six in the evening, to check if I am ready.

THE ROYAL BALL

♂

I sneak into the bedroom, where I find my princess getting ready for me. I'm stunned to see the beauty in front of me. *Holy fuck! She looks so damn hot.* Emma and Cynthia wait for my response, as I walk toward Rania. She has always looked wonderful to me, no matter how she's dressed, but tonight she looks like an enchantress who has been mistakenly dropped from Heaven, where only perfection resides. She looks so pure and divine that I can't even dare to give her a sexy look, or even touch her. Although, I want so much to rip off her dress right at this moment and make love to her passionately, to take her to the level where only ecstatic fantasies flow.

This is the first time I've seen her in a black dress. The color matches her eyes and hair. Cynthia has tastefully styled her hair, giving her the look of a seventeenth-century queen. My flashing smile to Rania informs both the ladies that I am more than satisfied. They probably have read the intensity in my gaze, and they take no time to pack up their belongings and exit the room. Rania thanks them for their marvelous effort, but I'm so awestruck I don't even look at them. They close the door behind them, leaving us in complete privacy. *Did she truly imagine me, while she was getting dressed? Does she love me the way I love her?*

Rania is still sitting in front of the dresser, but I'm sure she can see the wildness in my gaze. I stand behind her, looking at her beautiful reflection in the mirror. She smiles at me kindly, her eyes sparkling like onyx. I kneel down behind her to come down to her level, but don't take my eyes off her in the mirror. I place my hands on her shoulders and whisper the poetic words of William Wordsworth in her ear.

> *And now I see with eye serene*
> *The very pulse of the machine;*
> *A Being breathing thoughtful breath,*
> *A Traveler between life and death;*
> *The reason firm, the temperate will,*
> *Endurance, foresight, strength, and skill;*
> *A perfect Woman, nobly planned,*
> *To warn, to comfort, and command;*
> *And yet a Spirit still, and bright*
> *With something of angelic light.*

She smiles shyly and looks down, avoiding my eyes.

"I have no words to express how beautiful you look right now. I guess there aren't enough words in the dictionary to express it. I wonder, when God made you, what was the angels' reaction? I'm sure they must have argued with Him to keep you in Heaven." Her cheeks burn in a blush, and oh how I love this shade of her skin. My fingers pass from her shoulders to her arms. She starts to feel my touch now, as I feel her delicate skin vibrating under my fingertips. The fire last night has shaken both of us, and without saying anything about it, we have become close, very close.

"Cynthia and Emma have done a wonderful job. You didn't even thank them. They gave their time and worked on me, on Christmas Eve. That's a huge favor." She looks at me through the mirror.

"I don't take favors. But yes, they have done a beautiful job. I like how your hair is done. And the smoky eyes are . . ."

"Thanks for treating me like Cinderella." She smiles through the mirror. "I feel like I'm in a fairy tale, an ordinary girl, getting dressed for the royal ball by a fairy godmother. But this time, the fairy godmother is none other than her actual prince charming."

"So you think in this story, Cinderella found her prince before the royal ball?"

"Cinderella found her prince a long time ago. It took her a really long time to recognize him." She speaks passionately, looking into my eyes. I see desire flaming in them, as much as I have in mine.

"Now that Cinderella knows that her fairy godmother is actually her prince, this fairy godmother wants to add one more thing in this preparation." I take a box from my jacket pocket and look at her. She watches me quizzically. "Cinderella is not supposed to refuse her godmother or prince, whatever. It will break the spell."

She remains quiet as I take the thick diamond-beaded chain out of the box, the one I wanted to give her the first time we met. Her eyes are full of surprise and the look of *I-don't-need-it*. I ignore her expression and place the necklace around her beautiful neckline. She closes her eyes and lets me lock the chain behind her neck, shifting her hair over one shoulder. *Oh fucking hell! She smells so intoxicating.*

I move closer to her shoulders, to inhale her fragrance more deeply. It diffuses through my nerves like an addiction, always, since I've met her. I hear her heart pumping faster at my touch. I kiss her softly at the back of her neck, where the necklace is clasped, and her body starts resonating. I drop a few kisses on her shoulder; she turns her face to the side, giving me space to go wild. If I don't control myself, we'll never get to the party. I slide my fingers over her collarbone and she starts to hum with pleasure.

"I'm never going to let you go, Rania. Ever." Her body signals me that she heard every word I just said. "Do you trust me, when I say that?" I see her through the mirror. Her eyes are closed, but she opens them instantly when I say the word *trust*. She turns around and looks at me face to face. Her eyes are wet, as if she is about to burst into tears.

"I trust you more than I trust myself, Adam. But there are a few things that you need to know. You don't have to say how you feel about me. I can see it in your eyes, in your words. But . . ." She closes her eyes for a moment, takes a deep breath, and looks at me once again. "But before anything, I want to tell you about myself. I haven't told you before because I was afraid you would never want to see me again and . . ." She places her hand on my face. "I don't want to lose you, Adam."

Is this her way of confessing her love? Does she really feel the same as I feel for her?

"There is nothing that can take you away from me, Rania. No matter what you tell me, my feelings for you won't change." I kiss her forehead, and a single teardrop falls from her eye.

"It's not what you think, Adam. I am not what you see." She inhales sharply. "It's very complex."

"I will wait for you to open your heart to me tonight, after the party. Tell me everything, and I'll listen. We'll have the whole night to talk and share ourselves. But right now, I think you should not spoil Cynthia's efforts." I smile and wipe the tear from her cheek. She giggles innocently and turns to face the mirror, to see if her makeup is getting spoiled. We both stand up and she looks at me from head to toe.

"You look very handsome, Mr. Gibson. I am sure lots of ladies are going to have cardiac arrest at the sight." She watches me with tender loving eyes and adjusts my jacket with her delicate fingers.

"I'm sure the men will die too." I smirk at her and she laughs heartily. "You look tall tonight." I look at her feet to see what she is wearing.

"That's because Cinderella is wearing her glass slippers." She holds up one foot and proudly shows me her sparkling sandals. I see how happy she looks, wearing all these gorgeous things. At least, this has helped her forget last night's incident for a while. I hold her hands tightly and touch them to my lips.

"I don't know what I would have done, if anything had happened to you last night. You need to tell me how to thank God. I have no words."

"You don't need any protocol to thank Him, Adam. He knows how grateful you are. He lives in your heart, and He listened to you when you needed Him, because you have truly acknowledged His existence."

She pauses for a moment and reads my face. "This has brought us closer. Hasn't it?" I agree in silence. Our feelings have changed from a close companionship to the long-desired lovers. She checks the time and tells me that we're going to be late for the party.

"Do you have your phone?" I ask her, while taking out socks from the drawer.

"Yes, why?" she asks, fixing her necklace.

"Because Eva is supposed to come to the party too," I tell her. "And you know how she is. She'll drag you somewhere, and in such a huge gathering, it will be hard for me to find you." She laughs at Eva's name and puts her phone in her clutch. I hand her a few pre-signed checks, which makes her look at me quizzically. "Keep them. Lots of people ask for donations. I'm sure they'll ask you too, once they see you with me. I don't want you to be embarrassed."

"I cannot donate from my own pocket?" She sounds offended. *Not again.*

"You can, but the donations are normally in the thousands, and—"

"And I can't afford them?" She sounds broken, this time.

"That's not what I meant, Rania. I mean it's a grand ball. Lots of rich people are expected to come. They donate heavily, just to get in the news. They compete with each other. The more you donate, the more acknowledgement you get."

"Then what's the point? You don't donate to show off. You donate to help people. And if you want to help, you don't need to tell the world about it. It's like throwing your own good deed down the drain." She has a point too.

"I know what you're saying, but if you donate from your own pocket, the media may say bad things about you, and I don't want that. Now please, don't argue, and keep those checks with you. Trust me, you'll need them." I come closer to her and take her hands. "I'll be there with you all the time, but just in case, if you're alone, this will help you."

She gives me a look saying she is not buying it at all, but she doesn't say anything. Within a few minutes, we drive off with Ali to the party. On our way, she thanks me for the beautiful necklace and all the pampering treatment she had the entire day. She looks happy and relaxed. A complete makeover since last night, when I found her shaking and soaked under the tree. I wonder what she has to tell me after the party. I expect she may tell me that she had a man in her past, the same asshole who burned her and made her afraid of falling in love with anyone. If she's going to tell me that story, then it won't bother me. I want her to forget her cruel past and I'll help her do it. She has no idea how much I'm in love with her, but I'll convince her.

During our ride, she talks to Ali about books. I've known him for ten years, and I didn't know he's a reader like Rania. They talk about some books and authors I don't know, but when they start on *Arabian Nights*, I join the conversation. The three of us talk about our favorite magical story, and enjoy the discussion for the whole ride.

We reach the hotel in twenty minutes, as it's not really far from my place. At the entrance to the party hall, I see Eva yelling at us in excitement.

"Oh my God, Rania! You look so gorgeous tonight." She speaks so loudly that the people nearby look at us speculatively. "I wonder that Adam is not dead by now." Eva nudges Rania's arm and she giggles.

"Trust me, Eva, I'm already having cardiac arrest." My response makes Rania blush like a rose. *Oh my! She will kill me tonight.*

"Come on, let's go see Mom and Dad." She grabs Rania's arm and pulls her into the crowd, completely ignoring me. Brian and Mom are delighted to see her. They both hug Rania tightly before they even look at me. *Okay! I don't exist, or what?*

"You look very beautiful, Rania. I wonder how all the men here will be able to stand it." Brian looks at Rania and then at me. "You keep an eye on your girl. Don't blame me if any of my guests hit on her. Look around, all the men were already swept away when she walked across the room." He winks at me, and my mother laughs. I pull Rania close to me, my arm snaking around her waist.

"Don't worry, Brian. I don't plan to let her out of my sight. I know how many men are eyeing her, but trust me, no one would dare to ask even for a dance." Rania is blushing again. Mom pulls Rania away from my embrace and suggests introducing us to her extended family. For the first time, I'll finally get a chance to meet everyone in Moore's family.

It's a big hall, accommodating almost three hundred people. There's a huge bar at one corner and buffet tables set on the other side for the holiday dinner. Across the room is a dance floor, where people are having fun choosing their own music. I didn't know Mom also invited her own brothers and sisters, from all across the globe. I'm also surprised to see my dad's extended family. I didn't know Mom had invited anyone from my dad's side. I meet all my long-lost cousins and all they keep saying is how lucky I am, having Rania with me.

Everyone seems to be smitten by her. Not just the men, but the women are admiring her too. I meet Scott and his wife Tina for the first time. I have seen Scott in pictures in the news with Brian, as his son who will one day take over his business. I still don't see Nathan, their other son. Rania gets excited when she sees thirteen-month-old Scott Junior. Even the baby seems to adore her, coming to her instantly when she spreads her arms. It's getting hard for me not to notice all the attention she's getting.

We meet and greet people from different circles of life. The media take dozens of pictures, but Rania doesn't seem to be bothered by it. I'm getting the feeling that she's accepted the fact that she's officially my girlfriend now. I keep her hand in mine, not letting it go for a single moment. We also meet Brian's parents, who flew all the way from England to attend the party. Edward Moore, Brian's father, is in his eighties, but even at his age he doesn't neglect to praise Rania's beauty.

"My eighty-five years of experience says that it is very hard to cope with a beautiful lady like her," Edward Moore says to me, while holding Rania's hands. "Especially at gatherings like this." He looks at Rania through his thick-rimmed glasses. "And don't make the mistake of losing her. You won't find anyone else like her." Rania smiles shyly, looking down at her feet. Edward's compliments are getting beyond what she can accept. She looks at me to rescue her.

"I intend to cherish her forever, Mr. Edward." I shake the old man's hand firmly.

"Then, if I last until next Christmas, I hope to see Adam Junior with you two." Luckily, Mrs. Edward interrupts him.

"Oh, Edward, stop teasing the poor girl. You're embarrassing her. They are very young; they have plenty of time before having babies." She takes Rania's hands and places them in mine. "Edward will drive you crazy. You two carry on. I am sure you have more people to meet." With that, she grabs the old man's arm and pulls him away.

I watch Rania admiringly. The thought of marriage, and imagining her having my babies, is very gratifying. I never thought I'd love anyone so much that I'd want to spend the rest of my life with her. What the old man said was true. She is to be cherished forever, and without taking vows, I can't have that privilege. She looks at me once and then shifts her gaze around the room to overcome the awkward situation. Her habit of twisting the ring on her index finger tells me that she's uncomfortable.

She engages herself with baby Scott, to ease her mind, until suddenly Eva comes from nowhere and yells out.

"Guess what! Aunt Marie is here, all the way from Scotland."

"Who's Aunt Marie?" I ask Eva.

"She's Mom's second cousin. You don't remember, Adam?" She looks at me, and then continues. "Oh yeah, how would you know? She's a very famous fortuneteller in Scotland. A professional. I've heard she communicates with spirits—you know, dead people and all."

Rania laughs and shakes her head in disbelief. "She must be lying, then. She can't be seeing dead people, Eva. It is not possible."

"No, but that's what she says. She talks to the spirits and then she tells the future." Eva's tone gets serious.

"Then they would be the other spirits. Not the dead ones." Everyone looks at Rania as she speaks. "Those who are dead, their souls are up in the seventh sky. If she says she talks to the spirits, then they could be the other ones. I mean the Jinn. They can't be dead people."

"Are you serious?" Eva asks Rania, her mouth wide open in astonishment. Even I wasn't expecting Rania to be talking about spirits and dead people so confidently.

"Think of yourself, Eva. If those dead people had no power when they were alive, how would they predict your future now when they're dead?"

"Why don't we meet her and find out?" Eva takes Rania's hand to go meet Aunt Marie. Rania pulls her hand away and freezes.

"No, Eva. You carry on. I don't want to meet her. I don't believe in fortunetellers." Rania looks at my sister with a very serious expression.

"Why is that?" I ask Rania. I'm interested in this conversation too.

"I can't show her my hand and ask her about my future. Not if she might be contacting the Jinn."

"So you mean to say she tells the wrong future?" Eva asks.

"I am not saying she is wrong. If she is working professionally, I am sure she is right. But . . ."

"That's fine. Don't show her your hand, but let's meet her. I want to know if she sees dead people or not. Come on."

Eva grabs Rania's arm and takes her to a large separate room. I follow them. I have a strong feeling that there's something wrong. When we enter the room, there are lots of people surrounding a fifty-year-old woman sitting in the corner, and she is reading palms one by one.

As soon as Eva and Rania approach her, she opens her eyes and looks at Rania dubiously, in a way I don't like. I get a strange feeling, as if Rania is in danger, and I pull her toward me. I feel the same heavy air that I've felt so many times when I was alone with her, trying to get close. But now we're surrounded by people.

"Please, everyone leave. I will continue after a thirty-minute break." Marie's words are directed to the whole room, but her eyes are on Rania. What surprises me is that Rania is looking at her in the same way, as if they share something unspoken. We start to leave with the others, but Marie commands, "Not you, Rania." We all freeze in our tracks. How did she know Rania's name? Rania leaves my embrace and walks toward Marie, her arms crossed over her chest, looking suddenly confident. Eva and I exchange looks, trying to work out what's going on, but our feet are frozen and we are unable to take a step. I feel like a line has been drawn and we are standing on the other side of it. Rania is walking toward danger, but I can't follow her. She looks intently into Marie's eyes, until the old lady smiles at her.

"Finally, I have a chance to meet you personally," Marie says in her sharp voice. "I have heard a lot about you. He has told me everything." Rania's gaze gets more intense as Marie speaks; she looks at the blank wall as if someone is standing there. Eva and I exchange another silent look, but we don't dare to speak in the middle of this weird conversation.

"I am glad he has one friend, Marie, whom he can talk to." Rania looks at the old lady, and then to the wall. *What the hell is going on? Who is she talking about?* "What else do you know about me?"

"Don't ask me, Rania, how much I know. I don't think you would want to hear, especially when we have intruders here." Marie glares at me and my sister. Rania averts her eyes from the old lady and turns to leave, but Marie calls her back.

"Don't let the shadow chase you, Kiya." At that word, Rania freezes and turns back to the old lady. *Who is Kiya?* "You have already found your soulmate. He is the only one who can pull you out of the darkness. Don't lose him this time." The old lady looks at Rania sharply. Rania's mouth is open in shock, and her body starts to shake. "You don't know who I am talking about?" The old lady steps closer. "The one who sneaks into your darkness and guards your nightmares. Why can't you see him?" Rania's face pales at the old lady's words. She looks at me with a blank face for a moment, and then escapes from the room in an instant. Eva and I stand here, still frozen. I don't know why I can't move. I want to follow Rania, but I feel like someone has chained me.

Marie puts her hand on my chest and says, "Go and guard her." When she pulls away her hand, I'm able to move my feet. *Shit! What was that? This is so bloody creepy.*

I run after Rania, but she seems to have disappeared into the crowd. After a few minutes of searching, I see her running toward the exit. I chase her at full speed and grab her by the waist.

"Hey, Rania. Where are you going?" She hides her face from me, digging her head into my chest. Her body is shaking, but I don't know why. "What's wrong, baby? How do you know that woman?"

"Please take me home, Adam. I can't stay here."

"But what happened? Who is that woman? And who is Kiya?"

She pulls away. "I am not answerable to you, Adam." She looks around. "You carry on with the party. I will go home with Ali."

"No, Rania. I'll take you home, but please tell me what just happened." I pull her back into my embrace, but she resists. "All right, we'll go home, but let's just say goodbye to Mom and Brian. We can't leave without that." She nods in silence and follows me to where my mom is busy entertaining her guests. As soon as we reach her, a male voice sounds behind us.

"Rania Ahmed?" Rania turns back, and looks at the guy with shock. She puts her hands to her mouth with excitement.

"Nathan?" She steps toward him and he offers her a tight, warm embrace.

"I can't believe you're here. I thought I would never see you again." He hugs Rania tightly, lifting her feet from the ground. They're meeting like long-lost friends.

"I can't believe it either. Three years, huh?" She smiles and pulls away from Nathan's embrace. I clear my throat to distract her attention and she looks at me. "Oh yes, Nathan. This is—"

"Adam Gibson. Who doesn't know him?" Nathan offers his hand for a firm handshake. I accept his gesture instantly.

"Pleasure meeting you, Nathan. How's everything?" I try to be courteous, as much as I can.

"Do you guys know each other?" Rania looks toward both of us, back and forth.

"This is my parents' party." Nathan says. "How about you?" He looks at Rania quizzically.

"It's my mother's party too," I interrupt. "And she's with me." I pull Rania toward me and wrap my arm around her waist. Nathan glares at us, as if he's not buying the idea of us together. *What's his damn problem?* He looks at Rania with a question, and she smiles shyly and looks down.

"I can't believe you're dating someone, Rania." He looks at her as if he plans to eat her. *Doesn't he follow news?*

"Why? Is that a problem, Nathan?" I ask, frowning.

He keeps staring at her. "You're involved with *him*?" He shakes his head and passes his fingers through his hair.

"All these years, I kept thinking it was our cultural differences that came between us. I just can't believe I never mattered to you."

"It's not what you think, Nathan. I was in the middle of my University studies. I wasn't ready for marriage." Rania speaks in a low tone, to avoid anyone listening to our conversation. *Marriage? What? He proposed to her in the past?*

"You guys dated?" I look at Rania in surprise.

"Dated? Ha! I wish . . ." Nathan responds sarcastically. "I thought no man existed on this planet who could charm her." He pats my arm. "You are one lucky man." He smirks at both of us.

Just in time, Mom shows up. "Nathan, darling. How is my son doing?" Mom hugs Nathan tightly and kisses him on his forehead. "Did you meet this pretty girl, Rania? She's Adam's girlfriend." She looks at us proudly.

Nathan puts his arm around Mom's shoulders. "You remember I told you about a girl, during my degree program?"

"The one you wanted to marry and we got the ring for?" Mom asks in surprise.

"That's right. She's the one." He cocks his head toward Rania.

Mom gapes in astonishment. "I can't believe it." Rania looks extremely uncomfortable at this moment. "But you told me she refused you because . . ."

"That's right. I don't know how Adam got so lucky." Nathan looks at me with furious eyes.

"You never told me he proposed to you." My gaze gets intense on her.

"There was nothing to say." She averts her eyes from me and looks toward Nathan.

"If you don't mind, Mr. Gibson, can I steal your *girlfriend* for a few minutes?" He looks at me and then at Rania. "Some dudes from the university are here. You wanna see them?"

"Hang on, Nathan." Mom stops him from moving further. "Tell your friends that dinner is served. Rania, Adam, please, join us for dinner."

We all sit at the large family table. Rania sits next to me. When Scott Junior starts to cry in his mother's lap, waving toward Rania, she takes the baby and cuddles him, letting him play with her necklace.

"Tina, can I give him mashed potato?" Rania asks Scott's wife.

"Oh, he's a fussy baby. He doesn't eat anything. I try to give him vegetables and mashed fruits but God, he's a terrible eater."

"Just like his father," Mr. Moore says, and everyone laughs. Rania mashes green peas and potato and adds some butter. Everyone watches as she starts singing the nursery rhyme *row-row-row-the-boat,* to which the baby responds excitedly and opens his mouth. She keeps doing it, till the baby has had around twenty mini-spoonfuls of mashed vegetables.

"I think you'll have to move in with me, Rania. He likes you to feed him." Tina winks at her, and thanks Rania for feeding the baby. "You should eat now." She offers to hold the child, but he refuses to leave Rania's embrace.

"Do you want me to feed you?" I whisper in her ear, but accidentally my moron sister hears it.

"Oh my God! Look at the romance." Eva puts her hands over her mouth. Annoyed, I glare at my sister, but she doesn't stop.

"What happened?" Nathan asks, sitting at her other side.

"Adam offered to feed his pretty lady . . . with his own hands . . . ooo." *Why is my sister so irritating?* I roll my eyes and frown at her over Rania's shoulder.

"I'm fine. I will manage," Rania says, almost in a whisper. The baby is sleeping peacefully, resting his head on her soft breasts, holding her chain in his small fingers. She tucks the baby more closely over her body.

"I thought you were a magnet to men only, but damn . . . babies too?" Nathan pops his head toward her in amazement. "Well, I guess he's a man as well. Who wouldn't want to sleep like that?" Nathan's remark makes me choke on my wine.

"Eva and Nathan, stop teasing," Mr. Moore commands his spoilt kids. "Tina, take the baby from Rania, so she can eat." Tina gets up from her seat and Rania hands the sleeping baby to his mother. No one dares to speak for the rest of the meal. Finally, when we're finished eating, Nathan asks again if he can take her to meet their old friends.

Rania's eyes sparkle at the idea. She looks at me and I pull my arm away from her waist to let her go. A moment ago, she wanted to go home, and now, after seeing Nathan, she seems to forget everything. The way Nathan is looking at her, I am damn sure they had a past. He can't have been proposing to her out of the blue. *Why didn't she ever tell me?* But if I think about it, she's never told me anything about her past. I've shared everything of my life with her, but she's still a mystery to me. I'm always finding new secrets *about* her, but never *from* her. First the old creepy lady, and then Nathan, my mother's stepson. Nathan takes Rania's hand and leads her into the crowd, where a few people of their age are standing. They're all surprised to see her. She seems to forget her worries for a moment, and I let her enjoy the time on her own. After all, we have a whole night waiting for us. She told me she would like to share her past with me tonight. I just can't wait to know. I go over to the bar and settle myself with another glass of wine. She is quite far from me, but my eyes are guarding her across the distance. In the background, they are playing "Amazed." I keep looking toward her, focusing on the song and how it fits my current feelings. She truly amazes me. She glances at me a couple of times during her conversation. She knows I'm watching her. Nathan says something to his old friends, and they all look in my direction. I assume he's telling them Rania is going out with me. I'm in the middle of my drink when Mom joins me.

"How is she doing, after last night?" Mom asks with concern.

"Better than she was." I shake my head. "I thought I lost her."

"She's here with you now, darling." Mom places a comforting hand on my shoulder.

"You know what, Mom? In all these years, I have built so many houses and residential properties. I have donated so much to provide shelter to the poor. But the woman I care about most is feeling homeless right now. And there's nothing I can do about it. It's so strange and unfair. Isn't it?"

Mom takes a deep breath and says, "God has different ways of doing things. You should be thankful that she's safe."

"I am. I have no words to express how much." We both look toward Rania and Nathan, busy talking.

"The world is very small. I didn't know she was the same girl who captured Nathan's heart." She faces the crowd, taking a sip of her wine. I cock my head toward her, to grasp what she is trying to say. "Nathan told me he was in love with an Arab girl. He even asked me to help him buy the engagement ring for her. He wanted to propose, before graduation, so that they could get married right afterward. She refused . . . telling him that because of their cultural differences, her father would not allow it. I don't know how that goes with you."

"Her father is still not buying the idea of us together. And to tell you the truth, Mom, she considers me only a friend." I keep looking out at the crowd, but I know my mother is watching me keenly.

"Are you serious? Can't you see, Adam, that she is in love with you?"

"Did she tell you that?"

"Did you tell me you love her?" she asks me instead. I blink at her in astonishment. *How does she know?* "No, Adam, you didn't, but you're my son and I can see it in your eyes. And I see the same spark in her eyes." She puts her hand on my shoulder. "You have lived your life all alone. I'm glad you found someone who is true to you. I know she sees beyond your riches, and that's what makes her special. But just remember one thing. Don't lose the trust you have in her. She is beautiful, wise, and intelligent, and you will come across many men who will want to take your place. You need to trust that she has chosen you, and not the others. Don't ever let skepticism come between you. If there is doubt in a relationship, then it doesn't stand a chance."

She takes a sip of her wine. "I know you're looking at her right now, with Nathan, and it makes you unhappy. But don't make the mistake your father did, and spoil your relationship with distrust." I listen to my mother's advice intently. My father spent the rest of his life trying to make up for that single mistake, but he couldn't. I can't let myself do that, if I claim I love her. Love requires faith and patience.

She spends a long time with her friends, and it's getting hard for me to breathe and control my feelings. To compensate, I consume as much alcohol as I can. She looks even more seductive to me when I'm drunk. I walk over to her, ignoring the crowd, which is looking at me. When I get close enough to tell her, in front of everyone, that I *do* love her, Nathan grabs her hand.

"You have got to dance with me to this song. Let's relive the memory." And without giving us any chance to look at each other, he rushes her onto the dance floor and starts dancing with her crazily to "She Bangs." Rania is laughing heartily, swirling in his arms, not caring if I'm watching or not.

"I can't believe they remember all the moves, even after three years." One of the guys in their circle of friends speaks out.

"They practiced that one for almost six months," another guy says. "That's why they won the competition. It was a breathtaking performance. I always thought they were a couple. Look how they move together when they dance."

My blood boils with envy. I see Rania and Nathan dancing seductively, like a perfectly blended couple. The way he is touching her everywhere, during the dance, and the way she swooshes around in his arms, it seems like he's claiming her whole body. All the people around them are watching and clapping at their extraordinary performance. *So this is a blast from their past?*

They performed in some competition, and even after all these years, both of them still remember all the moves? The sight of Rania getting so physically close to someone is spiking adrenaline in my body. The insecurity, fear and anxiety overwhelm me, and I head for the dance floor, drink still in my hand. She is laughing with that man, avoiding and ignoring my eyes on her, as if she's escaped to some other world where I don't exist. When I reach the dance floor, that's when Nathan touches her neckline with his fingers, as a part of the dance move, and she closes her eyes in pleasure. My jealousy overflows and I smash the glass on the floor.

The music stops and everyone turns to look at me with shock. I pull Rania out of Nathan's filthy hands, grab her neck, and kiss her wildly on the lips, without even looking at her expression. After a few seconds I push her away and glare at her with my burning drunken eyes.

"You are mine," I yell. "Do you hear that? Don't you dare dance with anyone. You are fucking mine." She looks at me with utter shock. I didn't realize my ferocious kiss had bruised her soft lips, and her lower lip is bleeding. She flicks her finger on her wounded lip and a single tear runs down her cheek as she looks at the drop of blood on her fingertip. She looks around, and runs toward the exit.

"Asshole," Nathan shouts at me, and runs after Rania.

Suddenly, everything around me is frozen. I feel like time has halted. I fall down on my knees and start rubbing my hands over the shattered glass. The photographers start clicking my painful moment, until Brian pushes everyone away. My mother rushes toward me.

"Adam, what are you doing? You have injured your hand." She picks up my hand, which is soaked in blood and pierced with fine shards of glass.

"I lost her, Mom. I lost her." I look at my bloodied hands fiercely, taking deep, agonized breaths. Mom looks at me with tears in her eyes. She doesn't say anything to comfort me. She knows what I've done.

"My pride, my envy, destroyed everything. I lost everything with my own jealousy." I shake my head in disbelief. "You warned me, Mom, but I . . ." Tears start clouding my eyes, until I can't see anything around me. Suddenly, something crosses my mind and I look to my mother for help. "Where did she go? Where *would* she go? She has no home. Everything was burned last night. Mom, find her. Where did she go?"

SAMREEN AHSAN

Author's Note:

I hope you've enjoyed *A Silent Prayer*. Adam and Rania's story continues as Rania's mystery unfolds in the sequel, *A Prayer Heeded*.